THE CONVERSION OF
IGNATIUS MORIARTY

To darling Grace;
a fantastic Volunteer,

Seamus McNinch

April 15, 2017,
Ban Muang Klang
Chomthong, Chiang Mai

THE CONVERSION OF IGNATIUS MORIARTY

Seamus McNinch

Library of Congress Control Number: 2016914223
ISBN: Hardcover   978-1-5245-1702-1
                 Softcover   978-1-5245-1701-4
                 eBook   978-1-5245-1700-7

Print information available on the last page.

Rev. date: 09/23/2016

To order additional copies of this book, contact:
Xlibris
1-800-455-039
www.Xlibris.com.au
Orders@Xlibris.com.au
743947

FOREWORD

I have been asked by to write a *Foreword* to this novel for three reasons:

First, I have close personal knowledge about the life and thought of the author.

Second, I have been a Professor of Literature, specializing in the history and form of the novel, for more than forty-five years.

A third reason is that while the book seems simple on the surface, on closer reading it turns out to be much deeper and more complex than one might at first have imagined.

This needs some explaining:

I have known the author since 1992, when I met him in Bangkok, Thailand, where he had first served as an Intelligence Officer at the British Embassy, and, having resigned from government service, was working as a security and ethnic minority development consultant. At this time I was teaching courses on the History of the Novel in the English Department of the prestigious, Chulalongkorn University.

I knew him as a part of my expat circle of friends and drinking companions.

Seamus, as I and his close friends know him, had been born in Northern Ireland, a clever son of a well-respected schoolmaster, a good boy who grew up to become the recipient of a scholarship to attend Oxford University and read Modern Languages. What this means, in short, was that Seamus developed into a well-educated linguist and scholar - to the point where eventually he had read almost all of the great books of world literature, and most of them in their original languages. Impressive indeed!

After finishing his studies, he pursued a career as a military officer in the British Army, and after training he was sent -- in the prime of his life – back home to the placc of his birth and childhood, to become an intelligence officer in that terrible period of modern history in Ulster, known as The Troubles. The situation between Catholic and Protestant, between Republicans and Loyalists, between the authorities and the common people at that time was of a mind-boggling complexity to any outsider - just as the situations narrated in his book are of considerable complexity! Despite all of this, by the time you finish reading his tale, you will almost feel you have been there in the Troubles too.

As Seamus was at the centre of the action, and – importantly – had been born and bred there, he knew what was truly happening on all sides and so, as a writer and an intelligence officer, he knows exactly what he is talking about, on all sides and levels.

This is an inside story which nobody knows better than him, and it is related to us in the way it was unfolding, as the plot was incrementally and unexpectedly thickening – progressing on its way - and then swiftly building towards ultimate release in a momentous climax!

Even though the novel pivots around a single character, it is really more of an inside account of the Zeitgeist of the period and the people surrounding the protagonist - in an epoch of history which may never have been recorded quite so carefully and clearly, and in such minute, objective detail before.

The scatalogical language used in the presentation is necessary to make the language realistic – to give local colour to the characters – to make their manner of speech culturally believable, and it is for the same reason that the text contains a lot of erotic imagery to introduce an underlying sense of sensual reality into what on the surface would appear to be just a prudish puritanical, republican or Loyalist or authoritarian slice of society.

As with Shakespeare or Faulkner, this is "a tale of sound and fury" which documents the incompetence, idiocy and tragedy evidenced in the actions of all involved. Often down into the tiniest fragments of local speech, in Tristram Shandy like accumulation of detail.

There is, perhaps, more density of detail than one might expect, but in the end, we find that no word has ever been wasted, and that everything meticulously mentioned eventually ties all together into a well-balanced organic whole, with coherence and unity.

The story sometimes seems to have a cast of thousands, all carefully divided into groups and sub-sets. I am convinced that it would make an excellent action-packed film, seen from the air, for which the director of cinematography would need to have a field officer's inherent sense of planning, organization and discipline just to be able to keep track of all the groups of combatants and of where they were at any given moment in the plot's movement. I can imagine that Seamus might have planned-out the plot and its development by visualizing the groups much as in a war-game, using toy soldiers spread out over a complex table-top battlefield, complete with topography and buildings, hills, trees, shrubbery, roads, vehicles and all.

Above, I have explained how Seamus, from his Oxford days, came to be at home with the form and development of the novel, and, thus, it comes as no surprise that his central character appears in the form of a traditional picaresque protagonist, who is an anti-hero, and who serves as a tool for stitching the events of the tale together in series. He does not grow or develop or become more mentally aware by the end of the story.

He is not like the figure in a Bildungs-roman or a Kunstler-roman or in Goethe's *Faust,* who learns as he struggles his way through life and becomes wiser, based on experience. He is not a character who evolves a new philosophical view. This novel is rather a tale in which the main character remains no more intelligent or becomes in any way superior to the other ignorant, obnoxious and ridiculous characters who surround him – regardless of whatever their level of privilege or ignominy may be.

I shall not give away the story by hinting how the narrative unfolds. My purpose, here, is simply to help the reader get started with reading the book. If one sets off on the wrong foot - looking for a hero to admire or imagining the picaresque protagonist to embody some thinly-disguised autobiographical character with whom to identify – one will surely get lost and become confused.

As an aside, before I go on, if I may be allowed to make some personal comments, I would add that I first read the manuscript of this novel, some time ago, when I was in a Thai hospital after having had heart-complications. When I was well enough to sit up in bed and read, after getting a few pages into the story, and getting a proper feel for things, I got to laughing so hard that my nurses were afraid I would break open my stitches, and they took my copy of the manuscript away from me.

Another thing I should also mention, is that Seamus often repeated to me that every character in the story had actually existed in real-life, and the book, rather than being an imaginative creation of fiction, was based on a factual reality, all the way through, in full comprehensive detail, which was even stranger than fiction. Read it and see!

The book often reads like a satire based on over-exaggeration, as in Heller's *Catch-22*, but in this case, the exaggeration was hardly necessary. The actual facts and the actions of the characters are so utterly bizarre and so fully absurd that the reader finds himself in a world where everything that is happening seems beyond belief!

I ought to note here, however, that the author's purpose is not to ridicule or punish people for their faults and ignorance but rather to improve the world by humorously letting us see for ourselves where and how it could be better.

Thus far, I have avoided dropping too many author's names -because I do not wish to sound like a stodgy Professor - but some academic comments are, perhaps, now in order – to suggest where Seamus's novel has lots of parallels in World Literature. He, as a writer, is drawing on traditions that run throughout the history of the novel as a literary form.

Those in the know will tell you that the use of a picaresque central figure to tie a multi-event tale loosely together was a common device in early Spanish Literature and is best known as used in Cervantes' *Don Quixote*. In French, Voltaire's *Candide* was written following this genre. Both landmark works paint a gloomy picture of human nature based on a lack of morality and corruption of mankind which we see wherever we look into human society. The innocent traveler wants the world to be good but, unfortunately, it turns out to be a lot worse than he could ever have imagined.

In the development of the English Novel, Fielding's *Tom Jones* is the classic picaresque adventure, while Defoe's *Moll Flanders* follows the same genre, using a female figure. Richardson's *Pamela* is another example and there are many more. What is important for the reader to understand is that, in each case, the author is giving a critique of a morally corrupt society at large, through the eyes of a relatively innocent victim of circumstance, who is sometimes sexually vulnerable; from the uneducated-classes; who usually cannot do much to protect him/herself; and who helps him/herself survive by using his/her wits alone as best he/she can.

We as readers make judgments about the settings, characters and social situations presented, and we are able to develop a much wider world view than that of the poor protagonist – given his limitations. Moreover, the world view shown through the skill of the author can sometimes even become epic in proportion – making us widen our horizons – as we find, for example, in Joyce's narratives about Dublin or in Swift's *Gulliver's Travels*; or to stretch the point across the Atlantic, in Melville's *Moby Dick*, or Mark Twain's *Huckleberry Finn*, or Salinger's *Catcher in the Rye*. In each case, the writer seems to be asking, "Just how ignorant, cruel and stupid can people be? Whether in religion, in government, the military or in other aspects of society?"

It is an author's job to describe the human drama, to tell it as it is, and a great artist should be able to do it with epic reach. As readers of World Literature, we can see the world as tragedy or as comedy, or as both, and we ask ourselves, " How low and how high can humanity reach?" Many of us in our lives have known the lowest of the low, and some of us have reached for the highest of the high and reached surcease from sorrow.

An author in his art can express his pain and find relief in describing the ignorance of the people and the cruel things he sees in his society, and by telling his story he may even grow and somehow find release.

James Joyce once visited Carl Jung in Zurich, and after they had finished talking, Jung's advice to Joyce was that he should "keep on writing" – in other words, he should keep on doing what he had been doing as an artist because he felt it brought him mental relief and release. He was working it out on his own, Jung felt Joyce's art was helping to ease his sense of spiritual pain, thereby also triggering positive energy – in the arising of a creative sense of release.

There is certainly a lot that I will never know about Seamus McNinch, but one time I jokingly asked him why he had no hair, and he said, "It all fell out in Northern Ireland because of the tension in the air."

His novel tells about a catastrophic series of events which he experienced personally, up-front, in the mid-70s in Northern Ireland, at the time of Harold Wilson's failing government. Seamus struggled through this period as best he could, and he survived to tell the tale.

Writing this novel was a kind of catharsis for him. It was good for him, and reading it might be good for you too, if it helps to give you some sense of understanding, relief, and release. Smile.

Professor David Holmes

PROLOGUE

———•● 🔆 ●•———

"In war, truth is the first casualty."
Aeschylus 535 – 456 BCE

"Great is the truth, and mighty above all things."
1st Esdras 4.35

Seamus McNinch is, of course, a pseudonym. Shakespeare, Le Carre, McNab, Ryan, and many others are all pseudonyms. Why? Because the authors chose not to reveal the truth in a non-fictional manner through either fear for their personal security or social status, or because they were bound by strict legal oaths to "higher authority" never to reveal the truth. McNinch, like the others mentioned above, was left with only one way in which to get the truth across to the public at large, and that was by fiction.

The events in this fictional tale are all based on truth. The protagonists on all sides, Republican, Loyalist, military, intelligence organisations, are based on actual personalities well known to the author during the Northern Ireland Troubles of the seventies. Let us never forget that "person" and personality" is derived from the old Greek root "persona" – "mask". That the events told here and the personalities you meet here are exaggerated, is because by such exaggeration more of the "truth" may be revealed to you.

The general public thinks that the Troubles were caused by Protestant majority oppression of a Catholic minority in Northern Ireland, with the Catholics at last standing up and fighting for their Rights. To the ordinary Republican in Ulster that may have seemed the case. But that was just "fact" and "reality", two things very, very different from the "truth". The truth was that those two old comrades-in-arms, "power" and "money", were what was inspiring the leadership on both sides of the religious/political divide. And very soon those two old comrades would begin to find willing counterparts in the military hierarchy and in the corridors of power of Stormont and Whitehall.

Since I cannot tell you the truth in a non-fictional manner, by reason of solemn and binding oaths given (and the undoubted repercussions should I break those oaths), I have chosen the method of a black fictional comedy of errors. I hope you will bear with me and find out the horrifying truths herein contained. If you do, then please look around you at the "facts" and the "reality" of the greater world around you today, and try to seek out the truth – for your own sake and the sake of generations to come. Those two old comrades-in-arms are out there – and everywhere, and you, dear readers, are being played as pawns! I wish you well in this frightening – but *true* - Game of Thrones.

CHAPTER ONE

It wasn't that Ignatius Aloysius Moriarty was incompetent or a fool, although most people would, with justification, have concurred with such a view. Rather, Moriarty was a professional walking disaster area, an ever-recurring thermo-nuclear nightmare in the happening, and a right pain in the arse to boot (and there were those who had booted him with great satisfaction to themselves and some not-inconsiderable pain to Moriarty's posterior.).

But it wasn't all Moriarty's fault, for what hope could you expect for an Ulster Presbyterian with such an archetypal Catholic string of names as 'Ignatius Aloysius Moriarty'. These names had justifiably engendered a certain blood-lust among his fellow Protestants at Carnaughts Academy for the Sons and Daughters of Not-So-Gentlefolk, as his Primary School had once been termed by the local General Practitioner, or as the just as unfortunately local RUC sergeant in the neighbouring village more aptly and accurately put it, 'a festering dunghill of fucking little perverts who think failing the 11 Plus is matriculation into bloody Sodom and Gomorrah Open University.'

And Sergeant Simpson, whose tenure at Kells and Connor RUC Station, or the 'Barracks', as it was lovingly known to one and all, had been brought about by the mass execution of the bestial passengers of a pig lorry, while acting on not-so-accurate intelligence from a not-so-sober PIRA source along the border with the Free State, had every reason imaginable - and some, indeed, abominable - to regard the alumni of

Carnaughts Academy as the offspring of the Devil's worst transvestite shag. For Sergeant Simpson, once upon a time an able man, with an illustrious career of maintaining Protestant hegemony and the status quo ante Troubles no longer before him, was a Cullybackey man, and therefore ought to have won the gold medal in the great Olympics of sectarianism. He had a deep sense of what a good Protestant should look like and act like, and an equally good sense of what a bloody papist looked like and should die like. It offended Sergeant Simpson to the quick to have to accept that the inhabitants of his security bailiwick, where not a living Catholic could be found, were not the good Citizens of the Free Presbyterian Paradise ordained by the Reverend Dr. Ian Paisley, but were mentally handicapped, sexually abnormal, morally degenerate descendants of a one night stand between the Devil's daughter and Finn MacCoul's prize boar.

But if anything offended Sergeant Simpson more than the fact that his superiors failed to accept that the ambushed pigs on the border - albeit not the Finnerty Gang on a rocketing raid to massacre the military at Cullyhanna, had, after all, been of Catholic ownership and from the Free State and, therefore, fair game in a free-fire zone, was that the biggest albatross around his red Cullybackey neck was Ignatius Aloysius Moriarty, the insufferable, snivelling little excuse for a git. As the good Sergeant thought, anyone living in the environs of Kells and Connor with a name like that was either someone's idea of a sick joke or - more likely - a fucking Fenian fifth columnist masquerading as a sick joke. And even though he had beaten the shite out of the little bastard on every occasion he could catch him alone and in the dark, and pissed enough not to answer in kind, Moriarty refused either to give up the ghost or emigrate to Australia where his family name and undoubted lack of intellect would have ensured him a meteoric rise to prominence in politics, or - more likely - exile to Tasmania for buggering disenfranchised koala bears.

Ignatius, after several years of having the nocturnal shit kicked out of him while wending his way homeward from any one of a number of pubs, had begun to suspect that somebody had it in for him - in a rather major way. The trouble was, as he had such an incredible gift for getting anything wrong, he had managed to offend everyone within a fifty-mile radius since nine months before birth, and thus he had no criteria on which to isolate his main source of late night/early morning assault and battery. So popular was Ignatius that a local farmer, Bobby Graham, had spent six months in the Waveney Hospital in Ballymena after an abortive attempt to run Moriarty down in a Fordson tractor ended up with Moriarty somersaulting fifty feet through the air to a safe landing in a steaming midden, and Farmer Graham arse-over-tit down a twenty foot gradient, into which he was swiftly and painfully pursued by one ton of best 1955 vintage agricultural technology.

And once, while vomiting his way merrily home from a still he had perchance found in Jock Allen's peat bog, Moriarty had meandered in front of a bus full of not-too-sober Broughshane Masons, who were returning home from an over-convivial banquet in Belfast. The result of this particular encounter was a hand brake turn both Paddy Hopkirk and the SAS bodyguard teams would have been justly proud of, a one hundred foot skid, a sonic bang into the parapet of Kellswater Bridge, a spectacular slow-motion flight by a noble blue Leyland Viking (which ended in the total obliteration of Farmer Graham's cow-shed), and an impressive funeral in full Masonic regalia two days later. (At this funeral His Grace the Bishop of Galway, sole Mason and, indeed, sole Protestant in that far county, had given an impressive eulogy - before disgracing himself two hours later by singing the 'Sash' in Paddy McCallion's pub in Ballymena with his pants and gaiters round his ankles, his apron round his bum, and a pint of Bass balanced on his wife's beatitude. All would have been well for His Grace the Bishop - despite the fact that Paddy McCallion, Purveyor of Liquor to the Protestant Community, was the local IRA Commandant and the biggest bum-bandit in Ballymena - if the local Worshipful Master had not boked up his Guinness all over the marble-topped table, thus causing the good Bishop to lose his footing, fall forward from grace on to the counter, and circumcise - without the aid of anaesthetic - his elegant staff of office. The sight of the Bishop's bare bum under his apron flap was too much for McCallion, who shouted "up the IRA", and was paradoxically trying to get up a Protestant Bishop, when the Lodge's Junior Warden, who fortuitously happened to be the local RUC Detective Inspector, stepped in and arrested him under the Prevention of Terrorism Act).

So even when not physically present (and there was, as sure as hell, no way he was ever mentally present anywhere) at the scene of any disaster within the fifty mile radius of his ramblings, a close examination of every such disastrous event invariably revealed that Moriarty himself had initiated the train of events that led to the ultimate catastrophe.

Brave men had from time to time attempted to rid society of the threat posed by Ignatius Moriarty. The result was always the same. Somehow or other Moriarty was saved through his own brilliant incompetence, while the well-intentioned assassins seemed always to meet with a terrible retribution. For example, there was Sammy Coulter, who had lain in wait for days in the hedgerow of a sunken road near McCrory's pub in Slaght, after burying a blockbuster of a fertiliser and diesel mix bomb at the bottom of a boortry bush, where Ignatius - under autopilot - was wont to have a good slash after a night out. True to form Moriarty at last staggered down the lane, stopped, slashed, farted with that soul-searching liquidity which always has the perpetrator saying mournfully "Oh Shit!", and staggered on.

Sammy, who had been frantically pressing the two bare wires of his command detonated mine on to his battery terminals, and was cursing Eveready, the Pope, and any other bastard he could think of in his frustration, finally broke down in tears and walked disconsolately down to the boortry bush to retrieve his dud device for another day. Unbeknownst to Sammy, a pregnant sheep. wandering aimlessly across the hillside. chose the site of his flat battery and two connected command wires to urinate, thus creating an effective and perfect circuit and sending Sammy Coulter in a fine red mist over at least two and a half townlands. Two hundred yards down the lane the blast wave hit Ignatius, causing him to fart again in empathy, fill his trousers, and thank God that he had tied bailer twine round both legs above the knee, just in case of such eventualities occurring as a rat running up or fourteen pints of Heinz baked beans and Bass-driven bowel movement running down.

The local UVF company, under the leadership of 'Fingers' Davidson (so called because his left hand had no fingers on it, due to having been in the process of opening the door of a getaway car after a bank job on behalf of the future of Protestantism, just as the car accelerated unsympathetically off without him), had spent months in planning the demise of Moriarty. As Fingers told his band of brainless volunteers, "Moriarty is the nearest thing to a fucking Fenian we've got around here, so he'll bloody well have to do!" As Fingers and three of his feckless band drove down the Antrim line in a souped-up Morris Minor, disguised as a non-getaway vehicle by a bale of hay and an occupied pig-creel sticking out of the boot, Moriarty was trying to stay on the footpath and walk the opposite way. As Morris and Moriarty neared, Moriarty tripped over an undone bootlace, fell prone to the ground and was unscathed by the hail of bullets.

Not so unscathed were Fingers and the Boys, who had the unfortunate experience of running out of ammunition just as a Bedford four tonner full of Paras came the opposite way. The Paras had been beaten in a 'friendly' football match at the Royal Irish Ranger's Depot in Ballymena and had been prevented by their accompanying officer from kicking the living daylights out of the Rangers after their defeat became obvious (they certainly teach the young Ruperts all about man management at Sandhurst). Neither had they been permitted to rape and pillage the streets of the little market town because it was Protestant and was, therefore - supposedly, but totally erroneously - 'on our side.' To twelve steely-eyed, hyper fit, totally dedicated mass murderers in red berets the appearance of a Morris Minor full of guns and Fingers, going like the clappers at sixty miles an hour, belching blue smoke, and scattering a hay bale and a pig creel containing a two hundred weight sow (experiencing some understandable stress) all over the road, was just too unbelievably good to be true. Twelve full SLR magazines, six PVC rounds, and a stale cellophane-wrapped NAAFI sandwich later, Fingers and his merry men became the subject of an enquiry by a Special Tribunal in Whitehall, martyrs for the Cause, and the reason for street parties all over Catholic West Belfast. For the next week Paras on patrol in the Ardoyne found that the sniper's bullet had been exchanged by an ecstatically grateful Republican community for as much tea as they could drink and as much nooky as they could stand to attention for up against the walls of Flax Street Mill. And Moriarty? Well, he woke from a concussion in the act of embracing an occupied pig creel, which only confirmed his increasingly widespread reputation for having a predilection for forbidden flesh.

In the end things got so bad that mothers locked up their children and farmers their livestock, if Moriarty was seen or even rumoured to be in the area. Indeed, as the seventies passed with a succession of bangs into the eighties, the only remaining social intercourse that Ignatius enjoyed was his frequent encounters in dark alleyways and deserted country roads with his nemesis, the masked and avenging Sergeant Simpson, Cullybackey's answer to Attilla the Hun. As the townlands centred on Kells and Connor appeared to Ignatius to empty more and more of their human and animal population, he made a painfully slow and semi-conscious decision that it was time to assert himself as a Presbyterian and as an upstanding member of the community. He made, in fact, a decision which was to be as significant in Irish history as St. Patrick slinging out the snakes; as Cromwell's decision to solve the Catholic problem by barbecuing the good citizens of Dundalk and Drogheda; as Michael Collins believing - right up until the hail of bullets smacked him in the gob - that common-sense, compromise and moderation would prevail; as the H-Block inmates thinking that Maggie Thatcher really could give a fuck if they wandered round bollock-naked in mid-February spreading shite on walls - Ignatius Aloysius Moriarty decided to join the Orange Order!

Ignatius, of course, could be excused for not fully understanding the extent of the danger he was about to cause to the very fabric of Protestant society in mid-Antrim. But still, in his rare moments of sobriety he realised that it might be rather imprudent just to walk up to the door of an Orange Hall and say, "My name's Moriarty and I've come to join." Although bedwetting, bestiality. and chronic insanity, could be traced by the Mormon Church through several millennia of generations of Moriartys, none of his ancestors had ever willingly committed suicide - unless drinking yourself to death can be looked upon as taking your own life, in which case the Clan Moriarty surpassed even the very enviable success story of the Japanese secondary school system. Ignatius had enough experience of being filled in by total strangers, let alone by people he knew - including members of his own family - not to make the mistake of taking a direct approach with the Archangel of Doom and his hellions, namely Big Bertie Mulholland and the Boys. He would have to think up a more subtle approach to entering society.

For several weeks Moriarty pondered over his pints. At last, one evening in Molloy's public bar, he shot to his feet, overturning a table full of other people's drink, and shouted out "I've got it!" Whereupon the pub emptied, and those who had been present scratched themselves psychosomatically for days afterwards. Moriarty, a look close to orgasm on his face, cornered the frantic owner of Molloy's at the end of the snug, grasped him in a tight embrace and said again, in a rather effeminate high-pitched falsetto voice, "I've got it!"', with the immediate and unintentional result that one of the finest Protestants in Kells and Connor, Billy Stevenson, whose only crimes in life had been to own a pub called Molloy's and to water the whiskey, succumbed to a premature death through massive heart failure. Ignoring the body Moriarty staggered to the door and exited into the night.

Halfway up a dark entry the masked avenger, Sergeant Simpson, waited impatiently for his prey. He had been somewhat alarmed by the earlier exodus of crotch-scratching locals from both doors and some of the windows (glass and all) of Molloy's, but had since settled back into his normal routine mood for nocturnal violence. With a look which - surprisingly - mirrored that on Moriarty's face, he watched the attempts of the hapless Ignatius to negotiate the widest village Main Street in all Ireland, by rubbing shoulders with the walls on both sides. Bouncing off parked cars and ricocheting off the village pump and occasionally spinning round to walk back the way he had just come, Moriarty was in exactly the right state of matter over mind that Sergeant Simpson was partial to, that is, too fucking blootered to fight back.

Like the last frame of the Rake's Progress, Moriarty passed the entrance to the alley, whereupon the masked avenger leapt out behind him, brandishing aloft his weapon of the evening, a blackthorn stick, symbol of Protestant hegemony over the Catholic oppressed and bloody sore on the pate and shins. But just as the blackthorn stick descended in a two-handed belt, Moriarty, tripping once again over his own feet, as was his wont, spun round with a look of pure ecstasy on his face. Looking directly into the masked avenger's eyes, Ignatius shouted out with demonic glee, "I've got it!" Sergeant Simpson, who had never before seen the Devil, even under drink, suddenly met him for the first time. Dropping the blackthorn stick, he took off up the street screaming at the top of his lungs, "He's fucking got it! He's fucking got it! The little bastard's fucking got it!" and words to that general effect. Meanwhile, as lights came on in upstairs windows and double barrelled shotguns poked menacingly out, Moriarty, belching and farting rhythmically in contentment, passed on his way to glory by way of two gardens, a privet hedge and an unfortunate collection of rather fragile ceramic leprechauns (Made in Taiwan), which appeared in the dim moonlight to have been intent on protecting a dog turd by a goldfish pond prior to their sad obliteration.

Now the workings of the mid-Ulster Protestant mind, aided by drink and abetted by centuries of inbreeding and cultural deprivation, are a marvel to behold. It is for this very reason that the cream of mid-Ulster's manhood has so frequently found fame and fortune abroad. In the case of Moriarty, whose ancestors' devotion to the propagation of *homo sapiens* within the family unit was the subject of many learned medical and psychiatric treatises, six hundred years of incest had produced a brain that could only be described as capable of elevating incompetence to the genius level. For Moriarty was no fool. Yes, various doctors had certified him as lunatic - or as they put it so much better in the medical profession in County Antrim, a 'fucking eejit' - but even the cream of the specialists had been awed at the sheer brilliance of his frequent acts of lunacy. As Judge Evans had once phrased it in his summing up in the County Court, "I find you Not Guilty as charged, for not even a lunatic could successfully copulate with a five hundred pound White Race boar." But, fucked it, Moriarty most certainly had!

When it comes to true genius, the dividing line between brilliance and madness is very fine. For Moriarty, who had failed on every occasion to walk the chalked line in Kells and Connor Barracks, this line was not only fine; it was a virtually invisible tightrope. Moriarty, if he had tried, could have counted up each of his original thoughts without having recourse to removing his socks; but few though they may have been, their effect on public morale and safety, let alone the survival of the gold standard, had been truly devastating. For when Ignatius' excuse for a brain surged with the electrical charge that in other more normal people means mental activity, the axis of the Earth shifted by degrees, the sun's magnetic field weakened, and the black holes at the far end of the galaxy yawned wide in eager anticipation. If Nostradamus, being a Fenian, had not been banned in mid-Ulster, experts there would have made more accurate interpretations of that seer's obscure projections by a close observation of the Moriarty family brain waves down through the ages than by trying to make sense out of a load of foreign gobbledegook. Intelligence, of course, is relative; and in Moriarty's family background a lot of relatives had been inter-involved in the evolution that brought Ignatius Aloysius to his seventh original thought in thirty-five years of blissfully blattering his way through humanity.

Moriarty's stroke of genius was to prove to be like many strokes – potentially fatal to the patient. The true stroke of genius is simplicity. There is nothing of genius in Einstein's Theory of Relativity, as no one except Einstein has ever understood it. And as sure as hell's a hot place full of Frenchmen, there are few in mid-Antrim who would understand the relationship between E and MC; though there are many who would like to use the 50 kiloton result over Ballymurphy any night of the week, and bugger the fall-out if it drifts over to Liverpool! To most upright Orangemen in the Ballymena area, Enola Gay could have been a fucking Catholic catamite for all they cared about other people's misfortunes.

But back to the electrical discharge which was causing the orgasmic look on the visage of one, Ignatius Aloysius Moriarty. What, we ponder, could such a brilliant incompetence have created in its infertile and unused upper regions while under the influence of the Charrington brewery? What could be so magnificently simple? What could possibly ease Moriarty's entrance into the bosom of the Orange Order in the early 1980's and, thereby, bring down the Soviet Union, cause Arab to shake hands – murderously - with Jew, see a bloody Geordie (and the brother of a Knight of the Realm, to boot!) take the Republic of Ireland to the World Cup (twice), have the Vietnamese leave Cambodia voluntarily and Princess Diana equally voluntarily leave the heir to the Throne? What caused these and other upheavals yet to come? Simple! Moriarty would learn to play the Lambeg Drum!

CHAPTER TWO

S laght Orange Hall stood on the edge of a minor country road a few miles from Ballymena and a million miles from the twentieth century. From its position on a hill overlooking rolling fields of Protestant privilege, the Orange Hall, an ugly off-grey painted breezeblock structure put up over a weekend and two cases of whiskey, was the veritable hub of the local community. The inhabitants of the townland were Protestants of the most committed kind. Nobody in the community would have dreamed of buying a green car, and any stranger lost or inadvertently driving through in a vehicle of such a colour was invariably stoned - or worse! Even the Army refused to drive though except in desert-camouflaged armoured cars. The fact that the trees and fields around the townland were green for most of the year was a source of constant irritation to the local Free Presbyterian Minister and full-time demagogue, the Reverend Bertie Mulholland, whose brand of Protestantism left no room for any namby-pamby Christianity. Children grew up in Slaght with the oddest ideas on sexuality, stemming from the knowledge imbued in them from birth that the Pope was the 'Whore of Rome' and, furthermore, that they should take every possible opportunity to 'Fuck Him'.

'Big' Bertie, as he was called behind his back (and indeed by many of the local widows while on theirs), was in favour of the death penalty for Catholics, Anglicans, foreigners (i.e. anyone outside of Mid Antrim), indeed anybody who was not a member of his own exclusive sect. When he had heard that the GOC Northern Ireland was a Catholic,

Big Bertie had ordered barricades put up on all the roads leading to the townland and had declared UDI and loyalty to the Queen. Now this had really confused the hell out of the simpering chinless wonders from Whitehall, who inhabited the cobwebbed corridors of the Northern Ireland Office, that is, after they had spent two hours searching for Slaght on their extensive maps at Stormont. The barricades were only taken down after the tenth person in the community had committed suicide by starvation after three months without any outside supplies reaching the beleaguered enclave.

The Malone Bakery man had pleaded in vain at the main barricade on the Ahoghill Road, telling Big Bertie's man that the Bakery hadn't employed a Catholic in its eighty years of existence. Even twelve hours of upside down suspension by his toes from a chestnut tree could not make the deliveryman confess to being a warlock of the Antichrist and a cavorter with the hags of hell. If it had not been for the timely arrival of a Company of UDR, in which the bread man was a proud and savoured member, he would have hung there until the next chestnut season, and his shrivelled nuts would have been playing conkers with the best of them.

Now the UDR is a wonderful organisation and renowned for looking after its own and taking no prisoners, but its performance on that day left a teensy wee bit to be desired, for so excited were the soldiery at their first and last ever close encounter with the prospect of fellow Protestants and themselves in open confrontation, that they immediately cut the bread man down. Well, what's wrong in such a good Christian act as that, you might well ask? You see, it would have been okay if the bread man had not been suspended by his toes twenty feet above the concrete driveway leading up to the Orange Hall. Nonetheless, the bread man's death from a broken skull and neck was total proof to Big Bertie, an ardent aficionado of the criminological assiduity of the Witchhunter Pursuivant, that the bread man had been lying all along and that the Malone Bakery was peddling buns and loaves contaminated by Fenian faeces after all. The subsequent trial and conviction for manslaughter of the UDR Sergeant who had wielded the cutting instrument was further proof to Big Bertie of the extent to which the Pope and his pestilential spawn had infiltrated the judiciary.

Now some of you, who have had the fortunate experience of being incarcerated, in solitary confinement, in a Bombay gaol since the mid-Sixties, may be wondering, "What is an Orange Hall?" This is a good question! Unfortunately, as few of the great minds of British or Irish history have ever shown much desire to research this particularly significant phenomenon, you will be forced to accept my word for what follows. Indeed, while an explanation of what Orangeism purports to stand for and what its relevance is to coffee prices in Brazil may be a subject worthy of funding the establishment of a new branch of Behavioural Science at one of the better Uzbeki universities, to go into too much detail would probably only bore the casual reader and confuse the issue. Nonetheless, in the next few paragraphs essential information pertinent to a fuller comprehension of the chaos to follow will be imparted to you. It is important, however, that you take this information at face value and do not attempt to seek a deeper understanding of its relevance to your own community, as such a course would endanger your ability ever to fulfil a useful social function (for example, giving the wife one, of a Sunday afternoon).

In the panoply of Ulster Protestant Gods two names are of paramount, albeit paradoxical, importance. Firstly, Oliver Cromwell, Lord Protector of Orangeism, mass murderer and detester of everything Irish, is famous in European history for his beheading of King Charles I of England and a little bit of Scotland. This explains why all Ulster Protestants are rabid monarchists. (The descendants of these same Protestants transplanted by Cromwell in the mid sixteen hundreds from Scotland, where they were being a right pain in the rectum, were to rebel against Whitehall in the early twentieth century and sign a Covenant in blood that they would fight England to stay British. Now this caused a lot of problems for young Winston Churchill, who shared Cromwell's hatred of the Irish, but, being a more modern man, he made absolutely no distinction in his hatred between Catholic and Protestant. Resourceful man that he was, Churchill solved this intractable problem by persuading a rather reluctant Austrian monarchist to get himself assassinated in Sarajevo, thereby starting the First World War. Churchill didn't call it the First World War until he started the Second one in order to stop a short German erstwhile monarchist right-wing socialist from killing large numbers of non-Catholics and non-Protestants without prior written permission from the League of Nations. In a brilliant '*coup de main*' (or more accurately a '*coup de grace*') Churchill then persuaded the bloody Covenanters to form themselves into an untrained "Ulster Division" and die to a man in the trenches at the hands of a German Protestant King's Lutheran armies within a year of their arrival by scheduled cattle boat from good old Blighty to protect King Billy's sworn enemies in a Catholic and Republican France.)

Secondly, there is King William of Orange, a short red-faced Dutchman who spoke no known language and who had been invited to kick a pro-Catholic King of England out of Ireland for internal English political reasons that we need not go into at this time. Actually, while a monarchist, William was not really of royal blood - well, no more so than any of the Windsors, but at least his mother was not called Victoria and wasn't a bastard - he was in reality only a Duke. But the English have never been too fussy about such niceties. King Billy, as the good people of Ulster call him, had two saving graces - he was Protestant and he didn't like Frenchmen. To increase his physical stature, he was hoisted every day on to a fat cushion on the back of a big white stallion and dressed in a red coat with padded shoulders and a black wig. It is this strangely historically accurate larger-than-life image of King Billy that now adorns artistically the gable ends of buildings throughout Protestant Ulster. At a series of minor skirmishes against the unfortunate King James and his French troops, King Billy grew in folkloric stature to pop star dimensions. Indeed, songs about his exploits are known, word and tune perfect, by every Presbyterian in Ulster and Glasgow to this day, and if the British Royal family had copyrighted these at the time, the rest of the European Union could now be passing some "value time" by shoving their bloody ECUs up their derrieres!

It was from this near-dwarf Duke of Orange that the cult of Orangeism came, but unfortunately, unlike what happened with similar cults at Jonestown and Waco, the practice of self-immolation did not catch on. But there is hope yet! Now, being of Scottish Presbyterian stock, the Protestant community in Ulster, while having (purely for self-protection) sensibly given up wearing plaid skirts, was singularly lacking in culture or tradition of any form. The Church did not allow it. It was, therefore, necessary to find a suitable organisation to emulate and to copy that body's ritualistic idiosyncrasies. The early eighteenth century gave the followers of King Billy - long after his death - a brilliant example to emulate, that is, Freemasonry. Now Freemasonry was established and has rigorously stuck throughout its history to promoting the principles of universal freedom and equality, and teaches to this day that a man's religion is his personal belief and none can impose their views on God upon him. (Try telling that one to the Ayatollah!)

Well, that was a bit of a problem at first, but easily solved through contemporary universal Ulster Protestant illiteracy. What the good moral descendants of King Billy chose to emulate was the Freemasons' love of dressing up in colourful aprons, sashes, collarettes, gauntlets, with swords and batons and banners and mysterious symbols all over the place, and secret signs and words to keep out the non-initiated, and lots and lots of clandestine goat-shagging. And thus came into being the Orange Order. And just as Freemasonry formed for itself other degrees and Masonic bodies, so too did the Orange Order spawn organisations like the Black Presbytery and the Apprentice Boys etc., etc., ad nauseam. As the Masons met in their Temples or Masonic Halls, so did the Orangemen meet in Orange Halls, but while the former used their venues to proselytise universal love and beneficence (and, for some, the chance of earning a few bob, or getting off a drunken driving charge), the latter had more important and immediate matters to consider - after all, they lived in the real world, and God was on their side, and there was but one God, and he didn't like Fenians one little bit!

The Reverend Bertie Mulholland was the Master of his Parish and the Master of his Orange Lodge. Big Bertie, like all men of the cloth, led through example and through fear. Even the Reverend Dr. Ian Paisley, self-styled Chief Protestant of All Ulster and one-time purveyor of T-shirts to the Papacy, was known to hold Big Bertie in some awe. After upchucking his dinner on reading the Reverend Mulholland's famous treatise on *'Transubstantiation and Its Deleterious Effects on Pig Marketing in the Braid Valley'*, Dr. Paisley had considered emigration to Sicily as a wiser course of action than attempting to confront Big Bertie on any issue of politics, religion, or animal husbandry. A later much-publicised pamphlet entitled, somewhat musically and dramatically, *'Come Back Torquemada to Ballyjamesduff'*, and subtitled, *'The Use of*

Non-Anaesthetised Sterilisation in Religiously Sub- Human Communities in Northern Ireland', revealed to Dr. Paisley that his first assessment of Bertie Mulholland, as 'a raving lunatic', was all too accurate, and that any attempt to rationalise with the weirdo would be akin to himself walking up the Falls Road alone on the Twelfth of July in full Orange regalia clutching an olive branch and a dead pigeon.

Like all Free Presbyterian Ministers, the Reverend Mulholland knew sin. It was all around him. Everywhere he went in his Parish he felt its insidious presence. He knew that he alone was without sin, and that those around him had to be dragged kicking and screaming to the true path of righteousness. He was not just an erudite writer of socio-agro-economic religious treatises, however, as he took a very "hands-on" approach to his work, and did not feel it beneath his calling to beat the shit out of transgressors or personally to prepare the curriculum of weapons training classes held at the Orange Hall on every Tuesday and Thursday night except in September, when he went into what his parishioners were told was "retreat" at his caravan at Portrush, but in reality was something more like an annual sexual version of "Custer's Last Stand" with Big Bertie playing Sitting Bull. For, like all great men, or, at least, like all men who think themselves great, Big Bertie had his Achilles Heel, and his had the same problem that the Greek athletes had first experienced - if you are not careful, your foot-rot will become a significant and much publicised part of the public domain. For Bertie Mulholland was possessed of a libido the size of Antrim Round Tower, and his (already most impressive) libidinous peccadillo was increased in proportion to the availability of women's clothing, worn not by women but by none other than himself. Add to this a predilection for leather cutaway underwear, Japanese balls, Indian camel whips, and an overwhelming urge for auto-eroticism when in the paroxysms of religious fervour, and Big Bertie was a latter-day version of the Manhattan Project's 'Big Boy' on a very shortened fuse.

There was nothing that could bring out the religious fanaticism and demagogic oratory more in Big Bertie, that is, other than, say, the BBC announcing that St. Peter's in Rome had succumbed in its satanic entirety to a cataclysmic earthquake, or that the Pope had been invited (and had with pontifical graciousness accepted the invitation) to visit

Bulgaria on his tod for a walking holiday, than the funeral of one of his parishioners. His eulogies for the poor departed were famous for miles around, and the aisles of his modest church veritably flowed with brine, as he and the assembled congregation wept at the loss experienced by the poor widow - except Big Bertie was crying for joy, not in condolence. Other Ministers of Religion marvelled at these passionate pulpit outbursts from their comrade in crime and spoke among themselves about the obvious benefits of such cathartic tear-stained ceremonies, as all had either noted themselves, or had had it reported reliably to them, that the poor widows of Slaght Parish were so emotionally drained after the funeral services that they made truly astonishingly rapid returns to light from the slough of new widowhood's despond. The deceased was no sooner in the ground than Big Bertie began his series of follow-up home visits to the widow, where, by a skilful combination of prayer and 'hands-on' personal counsel, he brought red blushes to the cheeks - and with a particularly pliant candidate, red blushes to his own through use of various sado-masochistic flagellations of his posterior, which he had learned while researching the confessional and motivational methodology of the Jesuits for his famous tract, 'Ignatius Loyola and Slash and Burn Agricultural Methods of the Karen Hilltribes of Thailand and Burma'. Indeed, many women in mid-Antrim, realising that their older husbands were not long for God's Earth, moved house to the Parish of Slaght prior to the unfortunate's (sometimes precipitated) demise, in order to partake of the consolation that only someone of Big Bertie's understanding of the normal Ulster Protestant male's 'once a month-for the first five years if your lucky- on your back and don't enjoy it-I'm on top-shut your gob-thank God that's over-I'm off for a pint-do the milking or I'll gie you a clout' sexual mores could have an insight into - and not get arrested.

But the thing about Achilles heels is that now and again someone gives you a tap on them with the steel toe of a hobnailed boot, and this had happened to Bertie Mulholland in the case of the good Widow McKelvey. Now Mary McKelvey, nee - it was said - Thompson, while a regular attender at Church, where she occupied a pew all to herself and glared un-Presbyterianly at the pulpit throughout the whole, two hours twice a Sunday, excruciatingly boring service, was the closest Slaght had ever had to an enigma, or even a variation on one. Of her husband's 100 per cent Protestant antecedents there could be no doubt whatsoever. Mike McKelvey had been a powerhouse of a man, whose massive frame and equally massive taciturnity had led to him being classified as the most effective - and most feared - centre forward who had ever played for the Blues, that disastrous excuse for a football team that was the embarrassment, over succeeding decades, of the not-so-good people of Ballymena.

Ballymena United, as the club was properly called in the Ulster League, had seen its heyday in the immediate pre-war years, when mammoth men like Jock McNinch had been famed for being bad losers, even in the opening minutes of the first half, and had gone on to win successive international caps across pitches strewn with broken femurs and swollen balls. Even referees had not come out unscathed! But the war years, mysterious diseases contracted in so-called exotic, smelly, foreign ports, such as filthy postcard Cairo and licentious Cairnryan, and an aptitude for prodigious quantities of drink, had wiped out the vicious aggression that made up for lack of talent, and the fifties and sixties had seen the demise of United as a viable sporting entity. The seventies surpassed the two preceding decades by such internal upheavals within the club that the name 'United' was best described as a 'misnomer', and the unity within the team could be more aptly described as equivalent to that between Thatcherite and Heathian Toryism.

Mike McKelvey had been a throwback to the pre-war era, a scythe across the field of sportsmanship, a man, who, when he did score a goal, usually hospitalised the goalie at the same time - and never with less an injury that temporary elephantiasis of the gonadic regions. And as he slaughtered and slew his way to footballing infamy, Mike McKelvey succeeded also in failing to conceal his verbal dyslexia. His sole understandable vocabulary, other than guttural simian grunts, were words such as 'Fuckem', 'Kickafuckinshitoutoem', 'Takethatyoulittlefuckinshite' etc. Nonetheless, Mike had been the sole person to pass the Eleven Plus in Slaght Primary School and had gone on to an interesting education (for the teachers, that was) at Ballymena Academy, where, having been banned for life in the Under Thirteens from playing Rugby Union, and having been immediately thereafter approached by the Karelius Brothers to play Rugby League for St. Helens, he made inter-provincial level in cricket, as a bowler who never had to knock out the stumps, because the other team invariably retired early and voluntarily through period pains or chronic diarrhoea brought about by abject fear and an overwhelmingly urgent desire to see Mummy rather rapidly.

Mike McKelvey had gone to Liverpool in early August of the previous year for a so-called pre-season 'friendly' game against Everton, which the latter had won convincingly by twenty-seven goals to one - but had a very poor showing during the ensuing League and Cup season due to the number of broken limbs and broken marriages among its team and both first and second reserve benches, caused by a marauding McKelvey who had been told by Big Bertie that all Everton players were Catholic, and that he should, therefore, 'fuck them over good and proper.' It was later that evening that a grateful Liverpool Manager at last found Mike in an insalubrious establishment near the docks, where he had just had a rather successful altercation with several members of the local constabulary, who were at that minute trying to call - through broken teeth and jaws - for re-inforcements from the interior of the ladies' toilet.

Mike found himself in possession of an envelope - a very large and thick envelope - full of fifty pound notes, the equivalent of several hundred successful Saturdays' wheeling and cheating at the Fair Hill in Ballymena. And all just for having himself some fun! When asked what he was going to do with the money, Mike - not customarily known for being able to put one word logically or comprehensibly behind another - whispered into the Liverpool Manager's face, "I think I'll get married." "Do you have anyone in mind?" replied the Manager, whereupon Mike's face dropped to the spit and boke strewn floor. "No good wi' wimmin, me" he replied. "Well, now", said the Manager, with a demonic glow entering his blood-shot eyes, "I think I can help you out there, son. Youse and me are goin' to do usselves a wee favour."

And so it was that Mike McKelvey - that same night - was introduced to a woman calling herself Mary Thompson, of no fixed abode at that particular time, being, as it were, on the run from the Women's Royal Army Corps Barracks in Guildford for the heinously understandable crime of "dyke-bashing". Mary had the beauty of Ursula Andress and, in some ways Ursula's figure too, if you can imagine Sean Connery in his wig cavorting on Caribbean beaches, with a six foot eight inch 220 pound amazon! For Mike McKelvey, it was love at first sight, he having looked forward for years to the pleasure of a woman dominating him in the same way that his beloved mother had not stinted herself to do until her unfortunate accident with the muck spreader one sultry September night.

And as for Mary, well, she had been looking for years for a man who would let her wear the trousers and could take a good hammering without having to visit the Intensive Care Unit every time. The Manager of Liverpool, who knew more about Mary than he or she were letting on, was a man of infinite compassion and considerable cunning, and managed (for after all that was what he was paid for) to procure (which is a word used totally advisedly) a defrocked Catholic priest, by the name of Seamus Heany, to perform a quasi-illegal nuptial ceremony at four o'clock in the morning on the steps of the Protestant Cathedral with a clerical collar made out of a folded and not so clean handkerchief purloined from a nearby drunken tramp, who, unbeknownst to himself, acted unpaid as the best man. Mike was so intrigued by the size of Mary's biceps and how they appeared in some mysterious way to be linked by a set of pulleys to her enormous breasts, as well as being by now four sheets to the wind, that he didn't even notice that Seamus Heany, not the only priest to have left the Catholic Church for over-indulging his private little fantasies once too often, conducted the abbreviated wedding ceremony in pig Latin, not a language normally used in the Free Presbyterian Church - at least not in Bertie Mulholland's.

That evening, after being secreted during daylight hours by the Liverpool Manager in an abandoned tannery, while armed police and part-timers from the TA roamed the streets, looking for the Ballymena United team in general and Mike McKelvey very much in particular, bride and groom were smuggled on to the Belfast ferry in the back of an empty cattle lorry on its way back to Ireland after transporting another generation of hapless, mad cow diseased calves to the Continent for the *nouvelle cuisine* industry. The Liverpool Manager stood on the dockside with tears in his eyes, as well he might, since it's rare that you fuck up Everton's season before it's even begun, and at the same get rid of an embarrassing problem threatening to cause your own team's relegation to the Tierra Del Fuegan Fourth Division. You see, it would definitely not be accepted by the fans in Liverpool, were it ever to come out that the team's pre-season training had consisted solely of harbouring a wanted and AWOL criminal, who had serviced everyone from the Captain down to the old man who cleans the toilets - and all recorded for posterity on the new non-erasable video installed for security purposes - particularly when everyone in Liverpool knew fine well that Mary was not nee Thompson but was the fruit of the loins of a tinker's daughter called Moira O'Flaherty and the robust, former Cardinal O'Shea, not one of the best kept secret scandals in the annals of Anglo-Catholicism No! There was good reason for tears, what with Everton screwed and Mary not nee Thompson on her way to purgatory.

It did not take long for the new Mrs. McKelvey to settle down into her unexpected Protestant existence. Her husband, she found, was a well-to-do farmer in his own right, due to his industriousness in the fields and his ability to strike a good bargain in the Fair Hill (or strike the other bugger if he didn't), as well as his earnings from football, which had miraculously boomed by his single handed slaughter of Everton's pride and glory. Her husband, she also found, was a man of many hidden talents, one of which sent her immediately into the greatest heights of ecstasy she had ever experienced - and again, and again, and again. Coming home early one afternoon from wrestling a seemingly homosexual bull on to the back of a heifer, and showing it in no uncertain way (with the additional help of a couple of good blows right between the eyes with a two-pound hammer) what it was expected to do from now on, Mary found Mike in the bedroom, dressed in a crotchless and bumless suit of sequinned PVC, and having a wank. A terrified Mike, now used to and enjoying his good hammerings, immediately fell to the floor and licked Mary's dung-caked feet, muttering in between his slobbers, "Mummy, don't hit little Mikey for being a naughty boy!"

Mary, remembering first the hidings she used to get from Moira O'Flaherty, and then the nocturnal visits of her stepfather, Tinker Tom, who had been determined to get some of his own back on Cardinal O'Shea (and as often as possible), for the first time in her life experienced truly maternal and paternal emotions, and after beating the living daylights out of poor little Mikey, to his considerable but rather painful contentment, subjected both of them to an orgy of sexual dimensions, the like of which has not been seen since the Friday afternoon that the barbarians invaded Rome at Happy Hour.

From that day forth all was sequins and plastic, at least four times a day. But excess takes its toll and soon little Mikey was but an inanely grinning wraith. He gave up football, to the relief of the others in the Ulster League (including his own team). He would have let the farm run to ruin and passed his latter days as a polythene-clad twinkling satyr, if Mary had not been man enough to do the work of two, as well as finding time to give private bull and boar consultations. Outside a good pre-coital thumping and more orgasms per day than a buck rabbit with horse liniment on its balls, Mike retained one sole interest - his playing of the Lambeg drum. And it was the drum - not sex - which was his eventual downfall, some few months before this tale began; and it was the drum that caused the widow McKelvey to glare with violence in her eyes at the pulpit in Slaght Free Presbyterian Church twice every Sunday for two excruciatingly boring hours while all other widows present looked enraptured at the magnificent angel who had been sent by a beneficent heaven to succour them in their hour of need. For Mary McKelvey held Big Bertie Mulholland responsible for the sudden demise of her wee Mikey and her lack of anything more exciting to get het up about, other than strangling bullocks and mowing down fornicating cornfield picnickers, in season, with her combine harvester.

Lambeg drumming had been in the McKelvey family for three hundred years and, from father to son down the generations, a deep pride in actually making music out of this bizarre instrument had been instilled. Mike was no ordinary drummer. Ginger Baker would have sat down with his mouth open and cried, if he had ever heard Mike blattering the massed Orangemen into a rabid froth of murderous desire to walk bare-footed to Rome and kick the fucking infallibility out of the dago bastards before breakfast. When Mike played, the hills reverberated with the power and the passion of his music, and croppy boys for miles around were forewarned that the 'hunting season' had begun, and that a little trip to live off social security in Southern England, or a visit to old Aunt Aggie in Dublin (which was about the same thing), was definitely called for until the wet nights of Autumn and 'Match of the

Day' on the TV got the Protestant bastards under some semblance of emotional lock and key again.

The loudest reverberation that Mary nee perhaps not Thompson could remember hearing, that is, until her first spell-bound evening listening to her husband wake the dead with his drum, was the night that her stepfather, Tinker Tom, had returned home to the caravan after a successful day's dealing in Bradford, where (he wholeheartedly believed) he had taken the Pakis for a good ride playing the 'old three card trick' in a poofter's pub called 'The Brown Hole of Calcutta' (much-frequented in the late seventies and early eighties by strapping Welsh Guardsmen, seedy senior members of MI6, and the usual assortment of aspiring Conservative Party politicians). Tinker Tom, of course, had never studied his Kipling, and thus did not know that it was a little dangerous to attempt 'to hustle the East'.

The assembled Patels, Dixits (pronounced, I am reliably informed, 'Dickshit', which may explain why it was a poofter's pub), and Bumwallahs had quite early on realised that they were being ripped off, but - good natives that they were - delayed ripping Tinker Tom's head off until they could fathom out his trick, and then make money out of it themselves on visits back home to the sunny sub-continent. It took five hours, and the consumption by Tinker Tom free, gratis, and for nothing, of twenty pints of Guinness and six plates of increasingly hot 'curry du jour' before they eventually twigged how he was doing it, through a - by then - slightly understandable alcoholic lethargy in Tom's old legerdemain. What then ensued was a fast and frantic midnight chase - Tom followed by thirty screaming abdabs, waving scimitars and worse things in their hands - through the blighted streets of benighted Bradford and uphill into the Yorkshire Dales, where the tinkers had hidden their encampment behind the Duke of Bloodlock's home farm dunghill.

Arriving at the campsite and finding the whirling dervishes still uncomfortably close on his heels (they were under the leadership of one Doctor (struck off) Mahitme Buckshee, former over-worked chief abortionist to the randy Raja of Wogga Wogga, and now doing "rather well, thank you, old chap" in the human organ transplant spare parts business), Tinker Tom tried - unsuccessfully as it turned out - to vault over the steaming midden. The good Doctor Buckshee, who had already priced in his head what extortionate amount he could get for such a phenomenally strong liver and good set of kidney's as those of Tom on the Bombay Stock Exchange, reluctantly had to hold back his troops and counsel a rapid retreat, explaining that the dunghill contained certain matters, which his acute olfactory observations indicated to be of an all too obvious porcine faecal nature and "the bloody British weren't going to catch a Buckshee with that old pork-grease bullet-biting trick again."

When the coast was clear Tinker Tom clawed his way out of the mess he had got himself into, and, after cursing himself for forgetting to put the top back on the half bottle he always carried in his pocket, banged and battered his way into his humble caravan. Whence he abruptly exited some seconds afterwards, having sobered up dramatically quickly at the sight of his good lady, Moira O'Flaherty, in bed with the pony and obviously well on her way to the finishing post in the Bladon Races. This caused him suddenly to remember that you shouldn't run five miles uphill in Yorkshire at midnight with twenty pints of stout and six plates of vindaloo inside you, unless, of course, you are in training for the Asian Games! Making it to the Elsan at the edge of the field just in time, and not forgetting to drop his pig-shit covered corduroys, Tom sat down and, with a deep sigh of relief, relaxed his sphincter.

Rather too abruptly! Because when he recognised the mushy peas he had eaten for supper ten days earlier rushing in a brown-green-brown spectral mist across the field, trying futilely to escape what appeared to be their fratricidal pursuit by a supersonic miasma of mushroom covered hornets, he realised that he had died. Light travels faster than sound, however, and when the initial thunderclap and its successive ricochets followed a micro-second later, Tom had reason to wish he had indeed died, rather than have to wander the hills and dales of England, forever wearing a horse's tampax and a set of heavy-duty incontinence pants, to make up for the original hole in his arse which was no longer there.

And so it was, with the emotion of peristaltically re-experiencing the happiest day of her childhood, that Mary now listened to the drum.

And Mike, seeing the look of crazed joy on his wife's face, began to bang the drum with a fury and passion he had never had before in all his musical career. The drum had become a multi-sensual foreplay, a bearer of good tidings and hidings to come. And all had gone well and would have continued to go well, if the coitally interrupted Bertie Mulholland had not risen in a foul temper from a poor grieving widow's bed to find out what all the bloody racket was, and thus play his first part in the climactic chain of events that were ultimately to follow. If! Oh! Only if, the Reverend Mulholland had not that day arrived in the back field of McKelvey's farm to see a naked Mike parading up and down in the long grass with his drum strapped to his chest and his erectile tissue beating time on the bottom in rhythm with the drumsticks; and Mary, naked as the day she was born, gambolling after him, for ever like a baby elephant trying to grasp a hold of its mother's trunk, the poison that is jealousy would not have become the elixir of good Bertie's life; and the scalpel that is vengeance would not be now in the hands of poor Mary.

CHAPTER THREE

s the blackthorn stick is to beat Fenians over the head, so is the Lambeg Drum to beat into Protestant skulls the desire to use the blackthorn stick to beat Fenians over the head. To those of you who have never seen a Lambeg Drum, let it be said that it is big. No! It would be more accurate to say that a Lambeg Drum is fucking massive. More than three feet in diameter and some fifty odd pounds in weight, carried on the chest by a leather strap suspended round the neck by your average five foot six Orange drummer, it is a sight to behold. In order to know where he is going, as the average mid-Antrim practitioner of the Lambeg is unable to see over the top of the monstrosity, another dwarf Protestant, specially bred for the purpose in the townland of Rasharkin (a hamlet where they literally keep everything in the family), marches in front, playing on a fife. Now this system of drummer and fifer, developed after centuries of tragic accidents to Lambeg drummers, works fifty per cent of the time, which some of you might think is not bad for an Irish invention. This fifty per cent efficiency normally occurs on the early morning of the great Protestant festival of the 'Twelfth of July', while marching to a muddy tract of morass called, traditionally, the 'Field'.

The 'Twelfth' celebrates the victory of the afore-mentioned, somewhat physically disenfranchised, obscure Dutchman over some equally obscure, plainly mentally diminutive Frenchman at a piss-trickle of a river crossing in Southern Ireland. (And well might you ask what a Dutchman and a Frenchman were doing slaughtering themselves all over the pleasant Irish countryside? But look on the bright side; this was one of those rare occasions, when the Irish were able to be spectators at someone else's demise in respectably large numbers.)

Anyway, enough of history for the moment. On the way to the Field most drummers and fifers are fighting fit and fit for anything, as opposed to later, when they become fighting drunk and fit for fuck all. The downfall of the drumming community stems from an aspect of this annual ceremony celebrating the death of never enough French Catholics. This consists of the drinking of an inordinately large number of toasts to the 'Fucking of the Pope' and the 'Deflowering of the Whore of Rome'. While the good leaders of the Orange Order rant and rave at the masses through the sheets of rain coming in from Catholic County Donegal to the West, dressed in their Orange sashes and their clerical collars, the rank and file whip themselves into a murderous frenzy with the help of their more ancient and much more responsive non-Protestant Celtic Gods, 'Cream of the Barley', 'Old Bushmills', or a wee drop of the 'cratur' from the still in Jock Allen's bog. Then, the rain persisting and the mud underfoot now a skating rink, the parade of Orange Lodges exits the Field to head for the nearest village or town, to continue fucking the Papacy indoors under the glad eyes of the local Catholic publicans. It is this return journey from the Twelfth Field to the mid-Antrim version of civilisation that has proven so dangerous to the survival of Orangeism.

Can you imagine the potential for mayhem that is caused by a totally drunken Lambeg drummer, whose fifer is so pissed he cannot walk, let alone toot, and who has - to aid his return to the pub, and unbeknownst to his drummer in the rear - been strapped to the front of the drum by his braces? With nothing to direct him pubward except his bouncing off the hedges and walls on either side of the road, and burdened down by too much whiskey and beer, and with a passed-out, pissed fifer dangling at the front, the Lambeg drummer is no longer carrying an instrument of music. He is wielding a veritable machine of war! Most fatal drumming accidents occur at intersections on hills, when the parade turns right or left but the blind pissed and blind sighted drummer goes straight on. First to die, when the drummer loses his footing going downhill like the clappers, is the unfortunate fifer who undergoes a rapid transformation from dead drunk to plain squashed dead. The drummer himself is usually next, and after that any poor unfortunate Protestant bastard finding himself in the path of the runaway war machine. It is a strange paradox that this mighty symbol of Protestant power has never killed a single Fenian over the last three centuries, although considerable property damage has been done by trying to get both drum and drummer, with or without fore-attached fifer, through the front door of many a Catholic pub.

This, then, is the juggernaut of Protestant domination over an intellectually and culturally superior, Catholic minority of fellow Irish whiskey drinkers that Ignatius Aloysius Moriarty proposes to mount, with the same dedication and zeal that the male members of his family have shown to the myriad mammal species through the centuries.

Now you just can't go into Curry's and buy a Lambeg drum off the shelf! Each one is custom made by craftsmen, whose forefathers have passed down the secrets of their making over the generations. Moriarty, pissed though he was, realised that this could be an obstacle to his ambitious plan. Brave eejit he might be, but even he could see only the prospect of death by attempting to contract a Lambeg drum maker to produce a masterpiece of Protestant humiliation of Fenian perfidy for a man called Moriarty. He could, of course, use a false name, but Moriarty remembered with agonising clarity the last time he had used a false name to prove his Protestant-ness. He had walked into a pub in the centre of Larne one bright Summer's Saturday, having got on the wrong bus, by being pointed in the wrong direction to Ballymena, yet again, by a slight over-indulgence the night before. Burly dockers, all of whom looked as if they had fucked several popes already, if their tattoos were anything to go by, had immediately surrounded him. "Who's you? What'syername? Who the fuck do ye think yer lookin' at ye fucking wee git?" were the greetings extended to Moriarty by one of the largest papal buggerers, who would have well deserved the name 'Onan The Barbarian', if Moriarty had had the word 'barbarian' in his lexicon (although he had, indeed, been a worthy practitioner of Onan's ambidextrous art form since the precocious age of six). Sobering with a dramatic rapidity, Moriarty at once realised that he was in a major disaster area. He'd better use a false name, and he'd bloody well better pick a good Protestant one. "Adams", he blurted out. "What's yer first name, ye snivelling, wee, snot-nosed cunt?" was Onan's reply. Quick as a flash, indeed the sort of flash that occurs when a detonator goes off, Moriarty replied, "Gerry" and, in the last micro-second before detonation, Ignatius came to the brilliantly blinding realisation that, this time, he had truly mega-fucked-up.

And fucked up fair enough he had! It required a team of four surgeons and the consultant proctologist at the Royal Victoria Hospital to remove the flagpole and Union Jack from his bum. It wouldn't have been so bad, if this could have been done in the privacy of an operating theatre and under general anaesthetic, but in the town square of Larne, twenty feet up, in front of a crowd of thousands (and more arriving by the bus-load every minute from the neighbouring villages), on five different TV channels (including CNN live), and the medical team perched on an extendible Fire Brigade ladder, was something else. (But at least his rather pungently expressed views on the role of the US as 'world policeman' had wiped the supercilious smile off the face of that 'suspendered' old fart, Larry King. If Ignatius had not been otherwise somewhat physically pre-occupied in trying to supervise the extraction of flags of all nations and assorted bunting from his backside, the cheesy-grinned fucker would have been wearing 'braces' - and not to keep his pants up, but his fucking teeth attached to his jaws!) The gentlemen of the Royal Ulster Constabulary had, of course, been their usual less than sympathetic selves and had called him a "fucking pervert", as if it had been his own idea to impale his posterior on a flagpole for the predilection of viewers world-wide!

The only good thing to come out of the whole incident was the report that surfaced in the 'Irish News' several days later, that the Provisional Army Council had met urgently and had unanimously (well, all except one) agreed that the real Mr. Gerry Adams might just possibly be some kind of weird MI5 Protestant fifth columnist trick and, therefore, would have a more significant role in future in the political arena, where levitating twenty feet over a town square with a flagpole up your bum would no doubt convince the Conservative Party to withdraw its troops forthwith from Ulster and sell the place to the Turks, who, as Lawrence of Arabia and many other public school-educated English were well aware, are known to be more into that sort of thing.

"No!" said Moriarty, "I'd better think of some other way to get hold of a big drum."

Several weeks passed peacefully by in mid-Antrim while Moriarty's full mental powers were channelled into solving complex drum procurement problems, a socially useful change from his normal pursuit of unconsciously working on his private agenda of bringing Armageddon to Ulster, before the Almighty had got Paradise ready for the reception of any Christians who might - just on the off-chance - be found to be temporarily visiting the Province when the "big day" came.

Things, indeed, were so quiet that Sergeant Simpson, just released from an involuntary spell in Purdysburn Mental Hospital at a reluctant government's expense, began to consider a new approach to his superiors for re-instatement to Special Branch and a good posting to somewhere more conducive to his genocidal talents. Personally he fancied a go at a couple of years in Portglenone, where a Catholic monastery had somehow survived the recent troubles relatively unscathed. Now! *There* was a target for the new theories on euthanasia for Fenians that Simpson had learned from a fellow-inmate at Purdysburn, the defrocked Bishop of Clogher! This former prelate was famed throughout Christendom for his startlingly refreshing research into recreating the virgin birth through a painstaking thrice-weekly regimen of nocturnal visits to nunneries and girls' school dormitories, dressed as a slightly overweight reincarnation of Elvis Costello. But Simpson, if mad, was nonetheless methodical. He never left the dry closet at the back of the Barracks with unfinished business undone, even if it took two readings of the 'Belfast Telegraph' and most of his shift before overtime clocked in.

And he certainly had some unfinished business to clear up before he could be sure of convincing his superiors at Castlereagh of his sanity and of gaining their logistical support for 'Plan B', as he called it. 'Plan B' was to be a wide-ranging RUC-controlled para-military operation, aimed at finishing off the work so sadly left incomplete by Simpson's personal historical hero, Oliver Cromwell, namely, the ethnic cleansing of the Catholic population and the removal of all its religious edifices, by a co-ordinated campaign of arson on a scale never before considered in the history of the world since the Big Bang Theory of Bomber Harris. Of course, 'Plan B' would not be simple to put into effect, since most of the lazy Fenian bastards never went to Mass! But Simpson had thought that one out too. A carefully worked out programme, well advertised and orchestrated in advance by Saatchi & Saatchi, of bingo, free booze, free fish and chips, and compulsory bomb-making lessons, should be enough incentive to get a viable majority of the bastards into a selection of the right places at the right time. The other buggers could be mopped up later in tit for tat and twat for twit operations (the former for men and the latter for women) by roving bands of Gauleiter Bertie Mulholland's half-trained zombies.

But the unfinished business must be completed first. Sergeant Simpson was going to "fucking do that wee pseudo-Fenian git Moriarty, if it was the last thing I do". And, as we will see, what a prophetic statement this was to prove to be. But more of that later. A lot of polluted water was to pass under Kellswater Bridge before Sergeant Simpson was to learn - the hard way - that God didn't give a tinker's curse for Cullybackey, Protestant hegemony, Lord Carson's bloody Covenant, the good name of the RUC, or the price of whiskey for that matter. What Sergeant Simpson had never been taught in his Free Presbyterian youth in Sunday School, was that God was a Judaeo-Christian concept, who was on the side of children and the innocent, and since there were very few Jews, fewer Christians and almost no innocents in Ulster (except in prisons for the criminally insane), he only visited once a year to bring the Christmas presents, and even then there was no need to harness more than one reindeer to the sleigh. And something else the good Sergeant's Protestant upbringing had in no way readied his brain or bottom to comprehend was that Satan, in all his goodness, had prepared some very special treats that were designed to be enjoyed in perpetuity; treats that were to make the thought of a flagpole up your arse a reason for rejoicing at Hell's beneficence. Yes, Sergeant Simpson was shortly about to find that, whereas bad Catholics go to Purgatory for a bit of a poking with a red-hot trident, bad Protestants are Hell-bound for the duration - and with bells on it!

While the 'Beast of Beleek', as Simpson had been known during his better Special Branch days, was contemplating suitably slow and bloodcurdling revenge on Moriarty, the latter's fetid imagination was rather constipatedly - but totally bloody miraculously - excreting the germ of an idea. Now germs are infectious little buggers and can mature into contagion. But Moriarty's germ was to the Black Plague what Sinead O'Connor is to Dana - no contest! In the history of medical science the words 'kill or cure' have been all too frequently apposite. Moriarty's germ was a killer; of that there can be no doubt. It was going to have a greater effect on mid-Antrim Protestantism than measles on the North American Indians, and replace the names of Ghengis Khan, Oliver Cromwell, Adolf Hitler and Pol Pot in the Guinness Book of Euthanasia Records. In one fell swoop Moriarty was unintentionally going to rewrite the Book of Revelations and single-handedly put the Four Horsemen of the Apocalypse on the dole queue.

"Yes, I've got it!" cried Moriarty, this time fortunately not in a public place. He knew fine well where there was a Lambeg drum going spare and unused - at the Widow McKelvey's house, of course! He all too vividly remembered the dreadful occasion of the drumming contest at Slaght on the night of the third Saturday in May, just four weeks past; the night that Mike McKelvey had become a brief living legend in his own time, before succumbing to his horrific injuries fifteen minutes afterwards. Moriarty had been there, blootered as usual, but still sane enough to remain as incognito as an anaconda down St. Patrick's Y-fronts, the object of the evening being drink and entertainment, and definitely not the arousal of the murderous passions of Big Bertie's goon squads. It had been the night of the annual drumming contest, where, after weeks of sheep and cattle aborting all over the Antrim countryside to the 'Blam, Blam, Blam-a-dee-Blam' of a hundred individually-located Lambegs, wielded by perspiring aspirants to fame under pre-season intensive training, tractors had arrived from every conceivable mid-Ulster hamlet and hovel, bearing their trailer loads of ruddy-faced Protestant mums and dads and their frightful offspring, to hear Ireland's finest give it rooty-toot.

The contest took place in accordance with time-honoured tradition, with all the drummers and their fifers lined around the sides of a natural rural amphitheatre (big word for what was actually a wee valley), and overlooked by the not-so-inspiring breeze block Orange Hall, standing proudly on the top of the tallest hill, and trying desperately not to look like an extra-terrestrial version of a Chinese dry toilet. The object of the whole exercise, which had in actual fact all the musicality of playing the Jews harp to the accompaniment of the massed guns of the Soviet Guards Armoured Artillery Front Army, firing on the move over the quaint cobbled streets of Bonn on a wet Saturday night, was to see who could drum loudest and longest without bursting any essential blood vessels, like the pulmonary artery, or the other one which takes blood to your willy at embarrassing moments when you're a teenager. The last man to keep his footing and his rhythm was the winner, which was quite a feat at the best of times, what with the drummers all bursting for a piss after the compulsory pre-competition thirst slaking, and the fact that after a couple of hours most of them were suffering from severe concussion, due to the cacophonous din swelling round them, enhanced by the amphitheatre's natural acoustics.

The evening had gone well, with the kids running around gorging themselves on dulse and yellow man, greasy chips and sausages of indeterminate origin, stuffing ice-creams and bottles of Cantrell & Cochrane's fizzy lemonade into their stomachs, as if the word was out in Primary School that that night was going to be the Last Supper. And of course, just when it was getting good, the little bastards were boking all over the place, or shitting their pants, and screaming to go home to Granny. But a good clout round the ear was usually enough to stun the little fuckers into a satisfyingly sullen silence. Dads were at that stage just after mellowness and just before belligerence, that is, they had reached the point where they realised they were too drunk to drive home and not yet at the point where they couldn't give a damn if all the peelers in Ireland were lined up with torches across the road in front of them - they were a-comin' through. A planned break in the drumming then took place, both to enable drumskins to be tightened and new rattan drumsticks to be strapped by leather thongs to the participants wrists, for the fifers to have time to dig the accumulated snot out of their silver tubes, and, naturally, for more stout and whiskey to be downed in prodigious quantities by all and sundry, except, of course, the vomiting youth.

And it was then that one of the most heinous crimes ever perpetrated in Ulster (and, By God, there have been some good ones) was hastily conceived, and shortly afterwards hatched. You see, Big Bertie Mulholland had not been the same since the afternoon he stormed round the side of the hedge at the corner of McKelvey's back field and saw Mike and Mary doing the unexpurgated version of the baby elephant waltz. So traumatising had been the sight that, instead of marching right up to the fornicators in the full height of his Free Presbyterian fury, and remonstrating with them about noise abatement, and the need to wear clothes even on private property in his Parish, and telling them in no uncertain terms what he thought about their disgusting behaviour, and what an effect it could have on public morale and old Mr. Cunningham's heart (if the old bugger had managed to get his telescope focused in time from his cottage on the far hillside), he had leapt sideways into the brambles and passed the next twenty minutes in an apoplexy of voyeurism.

Two things had struck Big Bertie during those twenty long minutes. Firstly, he was not only lying in brambles, but also in a pleasant bed of nettles lovingly entwined with the best of that year's poison ivy. Secondly, while Mike's playing of the drum was of a fervour and rhythm he had never before heard, and while he had been for a short time transfixed, indeed, mesmerised, by the syncopation of Mike's rather splendid example of masculine hole-stopper, he had never seen a finer set of buoyancy tanks than those jiggling round within fifteen feet of his very eyes. "God'" he said to himself in silent and sincere prayer, "Wud you look at that! She must have been put together in Harland and Wolff." (God, however, was unfortunately not there that day to share the wonders of his bounteous creation - albeit with the assistance of the shipbuilding yard that made the Titanic. God was otherwise engaged in his usual pursuit of trying to swap Ireland with his old friend Nick for a second chance at bringing peace in our time to Palestine, but the Devil was having too much fun in the Gaza Strip seriously to consider the offer, and, anyway, what did he need with the Irish? They were totally capable of fucking anything up without his advice or intervention.)

The Reverend Mulholland, by the end of fifteen minutes, was not only in abject agony, through his inability in his little hideout to scratch the welts that were beginning to cover his body from bald head to sweaty feet, but had the added problem of trying to remain prone when part of his body was very evidently determined to pole vault him into the midst of the McKelvey's pastoral frolics, and, thereby, immediate exposure. Then something happened that took the pressure off Big Bertie's problems. (No! It's not what you were thinking, you dirty-minded little reader, you!)

Mary, having at last been able to get a strangle hold on Mike's quivering baton, began to draw her blam-blamming little drummer boy in the direction of the hayshed, where she was going to show him a few tricks that none of his previous dwarf fifers from Rasharkin had ever grasped, and turned, by chance, to face good Bertie full frontal and not five feet away from his self-imposed Purgatory. "Jasus," he intoned inwardly, "You could drive a bloody double deck Ulsterbus through that!" And as his eyes were transmogrified by the sight of the most delicious looking sugar plum that he had ever seen, and a buzzing like a chain saw began to thrum in his ears, a sudden flash of Spring lightning tore across the sky. In the eerie, micro-second flare of light Big Bertie saw something his lust had not permitted his eyes to focus on before. Across Mary's close shaven mons veneris (a study of Latin was still compulsory for Presbyterian Ministers, even if only to be able to curse the Pope in his own language) were tattooed the words '**Mea Culpa: Lourdes 1978**'. "Well, fuck me!" said Bertie aloud, the McKelveys by now proceeding obliviously through the hayshed door in double-quick time, "I'm sure I've seen that before." But try as he could, he was unable to recall exactly where, or in what context, he had.

Anyway, for the time being he had more urgent matters to attend to, such as getting a lift to the Waveney Hospital to get his cuts, scratches and swellings attended to before putrefaction set in. And so, with some considerable difficulty he extracted himself from the bramble thicket and slouched off down the hillside with his hands trailing on the ground, to all intents and purposes a shaken and changed man. For, despite the increasing pain of his injuries, his mammoth erection would not go down (partly the cause of the excellence of that year's poison ivy), and for the first time in his life he coveted another man's wife - while the husband was still living.

As half an hour later he flagged down the truck that carries the animal guts from the Ballymena slaughterhouse to some infernal glue or sausage factory, Big Bertie came to the terrible realisation that there was only one thing to do. Mary McKelvey would have to become a widow, and as soon as bloody possible, for he couldn't carry on loping around like some bloody latter-day Quasimodo all the time, just to hide the monstrosity trying to dig its way out of the front of his trousers and attack the populace at large.

Now, when evil begins in Ireland, it usually begins with a bang, and the driver of the guts lorry, old Stinky Fullerton, had two shocks too many at the one time. First of all, no one ever in his right mind had tried to hitch-hike on his truck, the smell of which made the pervasive odour on the battlefield at Culloden, the morning after the big party, seem like the scent of a field of carnations after an early morning rain. And secondly, he had never expected to meet the good Reverend Mulholland hunched over at the side of the Antrim Line, all covered in blood and big bumps, and apparently trying unsuccessfully to wrestle a couple of ferrets that had entered his trouser pocket in search of the contents of a paper bag of black balls to suck on. So clutching his heart instead of the steering wheel, and with both feet firmly jammed - mistakenly - on the accelerator pedal, Stinky passed straight and painlessly to hell in a second, while the gut lorry mounted the bank at the side of the road and couped over, spreading the innards of fifty best Friesian bullocks and associated animal matter all over the road for at least fifty yards in a North-South direction. Next to arrive on the scene was a bus load of Ballymena United supporters, which ended up the other bank, after a futile attempt by the driver to brake on a newly-laid road surface of large intestines and cow cud.

When the emergency services arrived, they were convinced that they had come upon the site of the most catastrophic road accident in Irish history, with hundreds dead and dying, but two hours with the Fire Brigade hosing down the scene found only a lot of shocked football supporters, a dead and fast decomposing Stinky, and the Reverend Bertie Mulholland, who appeared to have been wrestling with Satan himself for the souls of all Mankind - and had apparently lost. Bertie, however, was not dead, because while swimming gamely in the sea of blood and guts, trying to make for dry land or Kellswater - whichever was nearest - he had suddenly remembered where he had seen the tattooed words before, and while this recollection caused him, foolishly, to open his mouth to shout "the fucking Fenian bitch," and thereby ingest something absolutely disgusting, it did nothing whatsoever to lessen his enormous problem. "There is only one thing for it", Big Bertie thought to himself, "McKelvey will have to go, and at last I'm going to get my own back on John the Twenty-Third!"

And so it came to pass that, on the night of the Lambeg drum competition, the Reverend Bertie Mulholland was putting the final touches to his plan to murder Mike McKelvey by presenting him with the winner's cup, filled to the brim with triple-distilled poteen, coloured with tea to make it look like cheap beer and with an artificial froth on top, achieved, after a bit of trial and error, by the addition of half a bottle of Enos and a dab of Instant Whip. It was the tradition of the competition that the winner downed the contents of the silver cup in one go, that is, four pints of Bass, in a single gulp and without removing his lips from the said vessel. And as a matter of honour before one's defeated peers, this tradition had never been broken. The effect on the brain, let alone the heart, liver, kidneys and other more or less essential organs, of four pints of neat poteen was an unknown factor, as nobody in his right mind had ever attempted the feat, but most of those lesser mortals, who had attempted to consume a second bottle of Jock Allen's best triple still, had died with gills to spare.

All that was needed now to ensure success was for McKelvey to win the bloody cup, and Bertie had little doubt of that, for two reasons. Firstly, he, as the closest thing in Slaght to a 'man of God', and thus the only one who could be considered honest and neutral, always chose the winner. And secondly, the soon to be widowed Mary nee never on your life Thompson had made sure that Mike was in better blattering form than ever before, even if other parts of him were undeniably and totally fucked.

The sun was beginning to set over Catholic County Donegal in a vengeful splendour of orange haze to the West (a fitting omen with the Twelfth coming up), when the drumming competition drew to its finale, with Mike McKelvey blamming on as if the night were still young, blood pouring from his wrists, where the leather thongs attaching his drumsticks to his big hands had cut mercilessly into his flesh. But Mike was oblivious to pain or fatigue, because he was playing for his Mary, who had promised him that she would strap on a set of drumsticks herself, all for him, if he came out the winner. As the last contestants staggered and fell to the beer and boke soaked ground, Mike gave a final triumphant Blam-a-dee-Blam Blam Blam, and stood there with a look of infinite bliss, to the rapturous applause of all around - and no one was happier, or clapping harder, than the good Reverend Mulholland.

"I'll be getting on home now, Mike," said Mary as she gave him a chaste public peck on the cheek. "I'll not be long, love", he replied. "I'll get me cup and maybe catch you up on the way." (Oh! What prophetic words were these!) And as Mary tripped gaily off down the hill towards the farm, Mike strode proudly to the door of the Orange Hall where an ecstatic Mulholland stood waiting with the silver cup and its frothing contents outstretched in his hands. Willing hands helped Mike off with his drum and sticks, and he presented himself erect in front of his murderer. "It is a proud man you should be tonight, Mike McKelvey", said Big Bertie. "You have gladdened the hearts of the good people of Slaght this day, and no one is a happier man than meself. Now take this well-deserved cup and a good big breath, for you wouldn't want to be shaming yourself and spoiling this great occasion by spilling a single drop of our traditional champion's quaff. Get it down ye, boy, get it down ye in one!" And as a chorus of drunken voices began the chant, "Down! Down! Down!" Mike McKelvey raised the cup to his lips and swallowed as he had never in his life done before. With a finishing flourish he held the cup aloft and, wiping his nose on the back of his shirt sleeve to remove the final traces of Enos and Instant Whip, he shouted to one and all, "Boys, I sure needed that! It's terrible thirsty work blattering that big drum. Well, thank you all. I'm off home for me tay."

Big Bertie's look of happiness changed rapidly to one of frantic confusion. "Are you sure you're feeling all right, Mike?" said he. "Never better, Reverend. Never better." "Will you not stay a wee minute and have another one?" said Bertie. "No thanks, Reverend. I'd better be on me way", replied Mike, and, with a wave to the crowd, lifted his drum with one hand and fitted the straps on his shoulders, grabbed his sticks from behind his braces, and shouted, "I'll give youse a wee tune as I go." With which the crowd parted and Mike began the steep downhill march from the door of the Orange Hall to the road. He was just getting into his second 'Blam-a-dee-Blam' when, wrong-sighted by being fifer-less, he stepped into a puddle of fish and chippy spew, slipped backwards, over-corrected and went forwards, to the point where Newton's Law of Gravity took over, due to the weight of the Lambeg Drum, and he began a slow motion roll forward to the gate.

All would have been well if the usual useless helping hand (or in this case a foot) had not tried to intervene and stop Mike and his drum. But all the kick did was to cause the combination drum and bum team to veer to the right on to the road and thereupon commence the half-mile downward spin in the direction of the main Ahoghill Road. Mike and the Lambeg had got up to about forty miles an hour when they shot past Mary, by now within seconds of having become the Widow McKelvey, just as she was about to enter the lane up to her house. Mary, initially thinking that she had just narrowly escaped being run down by a speeding Lambeg Drum, fast came to the conclusion that she was wrong, and that it had been an almost hit-and-run by a bum and a drum, as she could see both, in rotating succession, accelerating away from her and into the growing dusk. She was still standing at the gate scratching her head and trying to figure it all out, when the crowd from the Orange Hall came round the corner and down the hill towards her in hot pursuit.

"What the hell's going on?" she shouted, as the massed tractors and trailers sped past. "Oh Jasus, Mary, it's Mike. He's on his way to Ahoghill wie the drum", was the panicky response she got. And with that Mary shot off on foot after the convoy and overtook them before they got past the next bend. At last they began the ascent of the big hill that rises up to meet the Ahoghill road, but only to be confronted by the bum drum machine coming back down, having obviously failed to achieve sufficient momentum to coast to the top. Thirty tractors and trailers piled high with pissed Protestants, and faced with a new musical version of the Grim Reaper's scythe, veered right and left, ploughed through hedges and fences, crashed into each other, overturned and many other things, leaving bodies of deceased and deceasing in a mangled heap of tissue and machinery, that hissed and moaned for twenty slow motion seconds, before bursting into a cheery flame that soon became a roaring conflagration.

The only people unscathed were Mary and the good Reverend Mulholland, just arrived in his Ford Cortina. But what of Mike? Well, he was rather dead. In fact he had succumbed while the drum was getting into second gear some thirty yards from the Orange Hall, and had, therefore, missed all the subsequent action. But apart from being a bit flatter and longer than usual, he was unscathed by the fire, as his (and the drum's) first impact with the leading tractor of the convoy had shot them into the air, to a landing ten feet up a telegraph pole, where they were now swaying lightly in the night breeze with a good view of the bonfire.

This, then, was the scene that a very drunken Moriarty came upon as he staggered down the road, having delayed his exit from the Orange Hall in order to finish off whatever booze had been left behind by the now deceased pursuers. It was too dangerous to approach the fire and see if there was anyone not too well done that could be saved, as there were still occasional explosions occurring, when the fire found concealed bottles of poteen and other tasty liquid comestibles that had been hidden away on tractors and trailers to assist their owners to find their way home. Big Bertie and Mary were standing under the telegraph pole, trying to figure out how they could get drum and Mike down without adding themselves to the body count, when the first Fire Brigade tender arrived from Ballymena and relieved them of the problem.

Moriarty was still there, hidden in the bushes in a field overlooking the holocaust, when Mary turned round to Big Bertie and said, "It's all your fault. This was all your doing." Now this scared the good Reverend somewhat, because he had begun, quite rightly, to consider himself technically innocent of Mike's death, as it wasn't the poteen that had done him in, but a combination of barf, drum, and a well-placed kick at the right moment. So he began to panic, wondering how in earth

Mary could have found out about the Mickey Finn in the cup, as she had already left when Mike had downed his poison. Immediately he decided that he'd better use his trump card in order to defend himself by a quick attack. "You're a Fenian, Mary, and you can't fool me. I know all about you and your kind and what you were up to in Lourdes in seventy-eight. So you keep your wee secret and be the good Protestant Widow McKelvey, and I'll keep mine."

Now, despite the urge to toast Big Bertie over the dying embers of the fire, Mary could see that there was no sense in endangering the new found life and wealth she had found, even if the love had been a bit short-lived and was now hanging up a roadside pole in a last embrace with a Lambeg drum. And so she agreed immediately, although she was to wonder afterwards why the good Reverend had looked so relieved at the time. "Did he really have something to do with Mike's death, after all?" she thought to herself, as she and the drum were being driven disconsolately home in a police car in the growing dawn, while Mike went the other way to be presented to an overworked coroner in Ballymena. And like all good women, without the use of the slightest iota of logic, she smelled a rat, and began from that day forward to plan her retribution on Bertie Mulholland, and any other bastard that got in her way. Big Bertie went back to the manse to commence drafting his sermons for what was going to be a major series of funeral services, maybe even a record for the Church in mid-Antrim, and also to plan the "hands on" visits to welfare the new widows that had been added to his list of onerous tasks. But how was he going to get into Mary McKelvey's skirts and get her out of hers? That was going to prove to be a bit of a problem, but prayer, and a lustful mind, should eventually come up with a solution before Mike McKelvey was too long in his grave.

CHAPTER FOUR

T he General Officer Commanding Northern Ireland, Lieutenant-General Sir Hector MacTavish, KBE, DSO, MC, Croix de Guerre, was a distinguished practitioner of the military art, and had served with dignity, and some considerable success, in most of the brush wars that had occurred during his thirty-two year career as an officer and a gentleman. With aplomb and insouciance he had slaughtered natives across the width and breadth of the Empire, and when the latter organisation could no longer produce enough cannon fodder, through territorial bankruptcy, he made an example of subduing revolting people in the Commonwealth, by eliminating them - with or without the prior sanction of that excuse for an organisation's newly independent and delightfully genocidal governments. A stickler for discipline, and a man who expected no soldier to do what he himself had not done at some time or other in the past (within the broad limits of acceptability as laid down in the Army Act 1955 and the Manual of Military Law, naturally), he was loved or feared by all who served under him, and by none more so than his ADC, Captain The Honourable Peregrine Smythe-Gargle, a scion of a noble and down at heel, white collar criminal Yorkshire family now living in hard times on social security and tax haven on the Costa del Sol. Perry adored the 'Old Man', as he referred to Sir Hector when surrounded by his own peers and a fast expanding clique of fawning subordinates, and basked in the glory reflected by the General on all those who served him unquestioningly.

When Sir Hector had been appointed GOC NI in the middle of the previous year, he had approached his old Regiment, the Blue Jackets, and requested (obviously from Sir Hector the equivalent of a demand) that they send him, as ADC, a suitably bright, brave, and able young officer, one of the calibre fitted to follow in the glorious footsteps of the most decorated officer the Regiment had ever known. The Regimental Adjutant of the Blue Jackets at the time was a certain passed-over Major Pinkerton Jolly, who himself had had the unfortunate experience of serving under Sir Hector, while he had been a flush-faced and very briefly enthusiastic Second Lieutenant, straight out of the Rupert mill at the Royal Military Academy Sandhurst, and 'Sir Hector' was plain old 'Hector', a Company Commander, and a right promotion seeking, arse-licking sadist, and part-time mass murderer of exotic and endangered species of the human race.

'Pinky', as his 'chums' at New College had most unfortunately permanently dubbed him, had been the product of a much further Left than Bessie Braddock working class father, who had made his millions the hard way, by a lucky draw of Littlewood's Pools, and who thenceforth saw to it that his only son received the education denied the father by poverty and social injustice. For Jolly Senior had been an Acting Lance-Corporal in the Tenth Battalion The Blue Jackets throughout the North African and Italian campaigns, where he had learned a healthy respect for his officers, all of whom seemed to share an equal ability in making wrong decisions and getting away with them - usually at the cost of a Company and a half of simple yeoman soldiers' lives. So Jolly Senior was determined that 'good old Pinky' would become an officer in his old Regiment and right the wrongs that he and his fellow Socialist 'muckers' had suffered, by effecting the mass destruction of the 'old school tie' officer corps.

And so, by the time-honoured methodology of a suitably large donation to the Blue Jackets Regimental Benevolent Fund (and a further equally time-honoured donation - slightly more private but of a similar generosity - to the pocket of the Regimental Colonel), he succeeded in his intention of getting his prat of a Lower Third Degree, red-brick university educated, tripe-eating, quasi-socialist son not only into Sandhurst, but also into one of England's premier regiments and longest established status symbols.

After one week under plain Major Hector MacTavish, Pinky had come totally to share his father's views on the necessity of bringing a total and early halt to the propagation of the officer species, and the following two years of being permanent Duty Officer, because he had accidentally shot Major MacTavish's horse clean dead from under him (while actually aiming at his rider's head), had done precious little to change his opinion. For years afterwards Pinky remained uncertain whether MacTavish had been rather understandably annoyed at him for killing his favourite mount, or whether his own subsequent trials and tribulations had been because Hector, professional as he was to the very quick and core, had been mortified (unfortunately not fatally) at Pinky's 'damn poor musketry skills', since he had failed to hit the miserable bugger as planned.

Pinky was determined to fulfil Sir Hector's wishes to the letter and already had a candidate in mind, none other than Lieutenant The Honourable Peregrine Osbert Smythe-Gargle, a supposed Yorkshire mini-Lord Fauntleroy, who seemed totally incapable of putting two words of English together without inserting the third word "Rather!" and having the aid of a mouthful of sticky gobstoppers. Pinky's pet hate, for obvious good reason, was when the 'chinless wonder' insisted on interjecting "Jolly good show! Sir. What?" at every not-so-veiled suggestion or downright blatant order to "Fuck off, Smythe-Gargle" that Pinky uttered. Apart from being sure that the twerp was trying to patronise or demean him by constantly insisting on saying "Jolly" every five seconds, his annoyance at this one-man public school freak show was bitterly enhanced by his total failure at breaking the bastard, at best, or cowing him into submitting his resignation from the Army, at least. The only satisfaction that Pinky had ever had out of his dealings with Smythe-Gargle, was his submission to Infantry Manning and Records Office of an addendum to the blighter's Annual Confidential Report, which read, "I would not recommend breeding from this Officer, particularly as I have observed that his men follow him closely, out of mere curiosity", and then forging the Regimental Colonel's signature beneath it.

The English upper classes, in Pinky's opinion, seemed to have a deep desire to be publicly humiliated and bull-whipped, as if this was "All part of life's great game, eh what? Jolly good show, Sir, if I may say so.

What?" So Pinky had been delighted to send a letter by motor-cycle courier to Sir Hector, extolling the "100% true Blue Jacket, minor (but just the right class) English Public School, Sandhurst," simpering, sycophantic, pandering, toffee-nosed virtues of the little prick, and even more delighted to receive a telephone call shortly afterwards from God Himself, who said, "Good choice, Pinky, what? Well done man! Knew you'd come out all right in the end with a bit of discipline. Sorry about the old non-promotion, old boy. Keep up the good work. Jolly good! Send young Smythe-Gargle across as soon as possible. Make sure the blighter knows the old Ps and Qs, eh what!"

But instead of suffering dismemberment at the hands of Sir Hector, Perry Smythe-Gargle quickly became the Old Man's closest and most trusted confidant, and it was obvious to all at Headquarters Northern Ireland in Lisburn, County Antrim, that the General regarded the pimpled youth, who had been immediately and prematurely promoted Captain on appointment as ADC, as the son that Lady MacTavish had never borne him - at least not before running off with Seamus Moriarty (no known relationship with our friend, Ignatius Aloysius), a former Parachute Regiment Sergeant, and at that time water bed manufacturer from Slough, on the night before Sir Hector's return to Blighty after another excursion into the ulu to pacify the already peaceful population in the hinterland of nowhere important, by the application of modern, scientific, non-lethal, anti-riot techniques and lashings of good old-style torture, the sort that even the French Deuxieme Bureau would have been proud to emulate.

While exasperated at yet another sign of the upper class English military ability to conceal total incompetence under the tight wraps of 'fwightfully-fwightfully' self-styled comradeship, Pinky was at least left with the hope that the IRA might not appreciate the little bastard's in-bred superiority, and would take the first opportunity to blow him and Sir Hector from Lisburn to Kingdom come. As the months wore on, however, Pinky's faith in the deviousness and skill of the Irish terrorist began to diminish, as the IRA seemed to concentrate solely on hard targets, like Margaret Thatcher or the First Battalion The Parachute Regiment, and to leave the easy ones regrettably and confusingly alone. Still, thought Pinky, there is another year to go, and anything might still happen. And Pinky, passed-over, and pissed-off with the lot of them as he was, had for the first time in his less than distinguished career made a brilliant military appreciation, which - if there had been any justice in the system - should have been used as a text-book example at Staff College in Camberley for generations to come. But such things only happen in wartime. In peacetime the full might of anal-fixated military incompetence is allowed to be practised to a degree that, one would think, ought to ensure the early surrender of both opposing forces in the very early days of any normal major conflict.

And so it had happened that one night, while sitting in a not so splendid isolation at the bar after dinner in the Officers Mess of RHQ, Pinky, semi-ostracised from social intercourse with his peers and juniors through being Regimental Adjutant, and therefore capable of posting anyone to Hades on a one-way ticket across the River Styx; fully ostracised as a passed-over, scholastically *infra dig,* chappie by his superiors, most of whom were ten years junior to him in age; and completely and utterly ignored by the mess staff, through that typical British Army inverted snobbery of the non-commissioned ranks, because he did not speak "like an Ossifer, nor even one of them Gentlemen, what like you sees on the BBC"; and with only the Padre to talk to, and he hadn't had a sensible thing to say since he had been caught drunkenly trying to stick a broom handle up the bum of an otherwise sympathetic, blond haired, pimply-faced, Army Catering Corps private, Jones 231, in the Royal Corps of Jamstealers' Officers Mess in Berlin the previous year; found himself, half-pissed and quietly fuming, going into his sixth double pink gin. Not that he liked the bloody stuff, but it at least was almost pure alcohol, and the jokes about his customary drink's colour and similarity to his own nickname were about the only times that he had a half-decent conversation with a fellow officer these days, or a chance to send some fucking smart-aleck joker on a sixth months compulsory Projectionist's course at the Services Kinema Corporation, where the nearest thing they had to a blue movie was the flag blowing in the wind outside the neighbouring Royal Air Force base HQ building.

The bar gradually emptied without a single person saying "Goodnight, Sir" or even "See ya, Pinky, old boy, what!" and Pinky found himself alone with the keys to the cellar (his due, as President of the Mess) and a fucking bad temper. Even the bloody poofter Padre had drifted off to fill in his subscription form to the 'Paedophiles Monthly' or some other scintillatingly erudite Hershey bar publication, focusing on pubescent Filipino garbage collectors dressed up in hand-me-downs, given a good scrub with carbolic, and all answering to the name of Bang-Bang. "God! Isn't this just fun?" muttered Pinky, thereby summing up his illustrious career to date. As the gin bottle went down, now with the absence of Angostura Bitters, not needed any longer due to the absence of the audience of future Chiefs of the Defence Staff, Pinky began to reminisce on the only good days that he had had in his long and lousy career as Regimental spittoon.

Pinky had served a total of nine 'roulement' tours in Northern Ireland, all of them as Intelligence Officer of one or other of the three regular battalions of the Blue Jackets. Most of his contemporaries had served no more than two such tours, and almost all had walked away with an MC or, at least, a Mention in Despatches - but not a single fucking honour for our Pinky, no sirree!

When he had once asked - in a moment of embarrassingly regrettable stupidity - why he had done nine tours and no other single Blue Jacket officer had done more than three, the haughty reply had been, "Well, Pinky, you must understand that the other chaps are all career wallahs and can't be wasting too much time on side issues like bloody Ireland, except to collect the odd gong, now can they? And apart from that, Pinky, you understand these Irish chappies, coming from the same sort of background as you do. Set a thief to catch one, Eh what!" Ask a silly question, and get the bloody truth! But nonetheless Pinky had greatly enjoyed his tours as Intelligence Officer, because even though he was not over-endowed himself with innate intelligence, and knew even less about the collection of other people's secrets, it had given him the repeated God-given opportunity to turn round to fucking Colonels and Majors - in large numbers, too, frequently - and say, in answer to their puerile and decoration-seeking operational intelligence questions, the magic and infuriatingly unassailable words, "**Need to know, *OLD CHAP*, need to know, WHAT**!" Now, that had really pissed the self-glorifying, backslapping buggers off!

As the gin bottle neared its ultimate conclusion and Pinky was mischievously contemplating going to the fridge in the Mess kitchen and wanking off (as he had several times done before) into the clotted cream which the Regimental Colonel kept as his own personal preserve for mixing, disgustingly, with his bloody muesli every morning at breakfast, an idea, a rather malicious one, indeed, a totally court-martial-producing-if-ever-caught-which-would-be-bloody-unlikely-to-say-the-least of an idea, squirmed out from the subterranean regions beneath the years of imposed tarnished pride and prejudice within the now evilly grinning skull of one unloved and unappreciated Pinky Jolly.

"'Jolly fucking Roger' is the fucking name from now on," said Pinky ecstatically to the mirror behind the bar, before grabbing another bottle of gin and signing it to the mess bill of the silly old fart of a retired Colonel who passed out as Curator of the Regimental Museum of Horrors frequently, and staggered off to his room for one of those all night planning and drinking sessions that had been the norm back then, when he knew fuck-all as an Intelligence Officer in Ireland, and the massed bums and bugles of the Blue Jackets knew considerably fucking less.

As he lurched down the corridor, kicking at the doors of anyone below his rank and not beneath his contempt, Pinky paused - and, after pausing, he smiled in a way only ever seen in the Mess once before, on that historic day when Captain Willoughby-Thing, or whatever his name was, caught sight of the visiting WRAC Colonel Commandant bending over to tie an errant bootlace at the door to the Ladies bog. "O'Shaughnessy, Liam O'Shaughnessy! I wonder where you are tonight, my little darling? Now, you owe me one or three, don't you, you little shit? You're my man, Liam, old son. You're my very man!" And with that Pinky unlocked his door and entered his room. Planning had begun!

Meanwhile, back at HQNI, Sir Hector MacTavish, swagger stick in hand, was marching briskly back to his office from the rather poorly attended weekly TOP SECRET intelligence briefing for all officers of the rank of Brigadier and above who could be trusted with a secret. Accompanying Sir Hector, one pace behind and to his left (to keep out of the way, through prior painful experience, of the expansively brandished swagger stick), followed the good Perry Smythe-Gargle, for all intents and purposes like a lap-dog about to come on heat, and who, being the Old Man's ADC, had also sat in on the meeting.

Surrounding these two latter-day heroes was a phalanx of Royal Military Police bodyguards, all pretending to be members of the SAS, and brandishing a most lethal collection of weaponry, which very fortunately - at least up until to several weeks after that very day - had only come close to killing the Range Warden at Pirbright outside Aldershot, the 'Arsehole of the British Army', as it is correctly described by any and all who had served there. The nearest living Republican was suspected to be about twenty miles away, a 90 year-old, retired Little Sister of Mercy, who had devoted her adult life to succouring the heathen in Ouaga Dougu instead of bearing a succession of insufferable, fatherless little bastards as her seven older 'blood' sisters had done; but still the RMPs were on the alert, as the General was their ticket to a cushy life and a lot of bragging in front of the wife's relatives, and apart from that, Sir Hector could be unexpected at any moment to veer off tangentially to the normal path, thereby necessitating the bodyguard team to leap canals, climb fences, garrotte the odd innocent passer-by, leopard crawl down drains, and do all the other pseudo-macho things that they had been trained to do by a despairing SAS troop at Pontrilas on the English-Welsh border, during their indoctrination into the totally pointless mystic art of saving seemingly worthless senior officers' lives from the excesses of marauding, drug-crazed Pan-Arab Colombian Catholic mercenaries, hell-bent on the destruction of the Last Night of the Proms, and under the pay of Pope Ayatollah The Turd of Beirut.

As the twelve baby Audie Murphys marched in step, just like the Toytown woodentops on parade, on either side of the General and young Perry, old Paddy, Chief Gardener at HQNI since 1938, and therefore considered not worthwhile putting through any form of positive or even negative vetting, watched with interest, noting yet again that an attack on Sir Hector and his little prize prick would be a dawdle, if effected from the front or rear, where the right and left flanking automatons of the RMP obviously considered the blank files would do the bodyguarding bit.

"Afternoon, Paddy. Make sure the old wicket is well rolled for Saturday, old chap, there's a good man," shouted Sir Hector as he passed by in quick time. "Fuckin' eejit!" said Paddy, respectfully, under his breath, while doffing his cap with the one hand and pulling his now wispy white forelock with the other, in the way that the bloody absentee landlords liked it, and just as he had seen Victor McLaglan do in *'The Quiet Man'*, seconds before he hit John Wayne a right haymaker of a dig in the gub. "More like a bloody funeral cortege, that lot. Or at least they would be, if I could get sumthin useful for the boys," he added to himself.

Paddy McGonigle, lover of flowerbeds and loather of wickets, while green-fingered, was no member of Greenpeace, although his politics could certainly be described, in the Irish context, as being of the 'Forty Shades'. Paddy was a long-standing agent of the Chief Intelligence Officer of the Belfast Brigade, Provisional IRA, one Phelim O'Malley, also known by the nickname of 'Phelim the Ferret', and feared by Protestant UDA and UVF, Catholic OIRA, PIRA and INLA, the non-sectarian NIO and SF, and all the other bloody abbreviated organisations, who kept bouncing into each other with the same indiscriminate regularity as a drunken rugby team on a wet Saturday night, owing to his long track record as a man who would be prepared to cut off his own balls, if the Cause required a eunuch with a five pound Semtex bomb in a Marks and Spencers plastic bag to infiltrate No. 10 Downing Street - although most men entering there under the new Prime Minister, Margaret Thatcher, were already morally and emotionally castrated. And so, in order to fill his weekly quota of titbits from the top at HQNI, Paddy shafted himself into his wheelbarrow and padded after the General, Perry, and the woodentops, doing his best to keep in step, which was difficult, what with the left leg being somewhat shorter than the right, and remain innocently unobserved.

"Spanking weather today, eh what, Perry, me boy?" said Sir Hector, "I think we'll take the long way round this time, what?" "Jolly good idea, Sir," replied Smythe-Gargle, who was calming himself down from the unwelcome frisson he had experienced at the mention of the introductory word "spanking", which still retained unpleasant connotations of the fearful Nanny Allbright and her rather unsympathetic attitude to Perry's little bed-wetting foibles. "Perry, I'm a bit concerned about what that Special Branch wallah, what'sisname, said today at the old Int briefing." "You mean Chief Inspector McCambridge, Sir", said Perry. "Yes. That's the chappie, McCambridge, very able for a native, what? You know, Perry, he's not often wrong in his assessments of what 'Paddy's' up to (which almost caused McGonigle the Gardener to side-swipe an oncoming platoon of "Aieeyes Raaight", vacant-eyed, drool-slobbering, left and right handed saluting, educationally sub-normal 'chunkies' from the Pioneer Corps and blow his cover), and I think we ought to take seriously what he said about something going down in mid-Antrim, what?"

"You mean that place called Slaght, Sir?" asked Perry. "Very place, me boy, very place. Bloody hard to find on the map, wasn't it, eh? You know, Perry, we mustn't let people like McCambridge get ahead of the old game, even if the Secretary of State is happy that he's a white man and on our side, what?" "Absolutely not, General", said Perry, not having a clue what the Old Man was talking about. And with that sixth sense that is imbued into successful senior military officers when they are talking to their juniors, and, therefore, most assuredly intellectual inferiors, Sir Hector explained. "Mustn't ever let the local Int bods get the upper hand, Perry. If they do, Ops get fucked up, and the politicos begin to forget who carries the big guns round here. Can't have the old tail wagging the bloody dog, can we now, what?" "Yes Sir," was all that Smythe-Gargle could think of replying, now completely confused by what should obviously have been a brilliant, high-level insight into the inter-relationship of the intelligence community, the army and the chappies from Whitehall, which, if he could only understand it, he could share with his little clique of admirers that evening over the after dinner port in the Mess.

"Bit of a rum do, that! All those Prots burned to death and that fellow run over by his own drum and then strung up a telegraph pole. Have to agree with old McCambridge though, eighty dead farmers in mid-Antrim at the one time is a bit above the old law of averages, eh what?" "Most certainly is, General", said Smythe-Gargle, "Do you think it was the IRA, Sir?" "Stands to reason my good fellow", replied Sir Hector, trying his superior best not to sound too painfully condescending. "Hardly likely the blighters did it to themselves, what?" "No, Sir, but how did the IRA lure them all together at the same time and place. Proddy's not all that clever, but he's surely not *that* daft either, is he, Sir?" Sir Hector thought over his ADC's last remark for a long minute and then said, "Quite right, me boy, quite right", which brought a smile of childlike joy across young Perry's acne. "Well spotted, Perry! PIRA must have had someone on the inside. Yes, smells like one of Phelim the Ferret's jobbies!"

Old Paddy, beginning now to sway from side to side as the hill took its toll on his rickety undercarriage (and the wheel on the front end of the barrow wasn't doing too well either, into the bargain), was nonetheless "compost mentis" enough to be intrigued by Sir Hector's last remark, as his forty and more years of spending half the bloody time spreading manure on cricket pitches, to "bring them on for the season, what, old boy", had led him to a deeper understanding of the British Army's abbreviated lexicon than most anyone else in Ireland, and one word he had thought no Englishman knew the meaning of was 'jobbie'. "Phelim had better watch his arse", thought McGonigle to himself unthinkingly aloud, and thus immediately drawing the unwanted attention of Sir Hector and his cohort to his not-so-hot pursuit. "What's that, Paddy?" asked the General. "Feeling I'd better water the grass, Sir Hector", gasped McGonigle, with the quickness of mind that had kept him alive all those years in the British Lion's den. "Jolly good show, old boy", was Sir Hector's response, and, in a *sotto voce* aside to his ADC, bellowed another useful lesson that only the British had seemed ever to appreciate. "Nothing like a loyal old retainer to keep things shipshape and Bristol fashion, as the old rum, bum, and baccy blue jobs say, eh what, Perry?" "No, Sir. I mean. yes Sir", was Perry's confused reply.

"We'll cut across here, chaps" shouted Sir Hector to the surrounding monkeys, and turned left to ascend the steep hill through the pine trees towards his palatial official residence. Behind lurched McGonigle, already breathless with exhaustion from pushing his un-oiled barrow up what felt like the steep side of Slieve Donard, and with its full load of horse manure, originally intended for the rose beds, but now more likely partially to accompany the gardener in the ambulance to the nearest hospital, at least the way his heart was thumping with excitement and exertion. As the military echelon swung immaculately left across the kerbstones and leaped two by two in unison over the knee-high red brick wall surrounding the residence grounds, McGonigle's enthusiasm for the intelligence collection game spluttered and conked out. "Ah! Fuck it!" he groaned, and sagged forward and uncaring, headfirst into his barrow load of dung.

But before he passed out among the voracious accompanying bluebottles, he heard Sir Hector say, "Better get old Mooney from the SAS to have a look at this Slaght business, what with the Twelfth of July coming up. Can't have the Protestants and Republicans massacring themselves without permission, now can we, boy, what?" "No, Sir. I mean yes, Sir! Which one should I say, Sir?" enquired a now fully tongue-tied and brain-twisted ADC. "Got you that time, didn't I? Actually, you would be quite right either way, Perry, me boy. Doesn't really matter who's killing whom, as long as we're the old scorekeeper, eh what", said Sir Hector, as he strode manfully forward up the hill, chortling fondly to himself at what he believed was a rattling good original joke at the expense of poor Perry Smythe-Gargle. "Mooney will soon be on to the bastard, who ever it is. Excellent fellow! Once murdered a Commonwealth Prime Minister, you know. Not one of the darkie ones either! All a bit hush-hush still, of course. Excellent job. Bloody Foreign Office still thinks it was the Commies, but then they would, wouldn't they, Perry, me boy? Devious load of self-servers your normal diplomats. Ask the buggers who's right and who's wrong and the blighters answer with a 'Yes'. No bloody multiple choice answers for those chappies, that's for sure. What do you think, Perry?" "You are absolutely right, Sir", said Perry, it having dawned on him at long last that 'Yes' and 'No' answers were both highly complex monosyllables and thus full of hidden pitfalls, and that the English public school system hadn't substituted words like 'absolutely', 'jolly good', 'rather' or 'spiffing' just to improve the upper classes' vocabulary. No way! Where the English are involved, you can be sure that white means white and black means black, and that, apart from these two racially colourful descriptive words, extensively used during the days of Empire, but now considered 'rather non-you' and apt to piss off the do-gooding lefties, the remaining one hundred thousand words in the Oxford Dictionary are not meant to be taken at face value, otherwise the unemployable buggers in the Foreign and Commonwealth Office would be seeking social security to a man.

And, without further ado, Sir Hector and Perry entered the French windows of the residence, leaving the bodyguard team to patrol the grounds and terrify the hell out of the postman and the milkman, and anyone else who had a justifiable reason for being in the vicinity. One hundred yards down the hill, Paddy McGonigle was coming slowly to his senses in a buzz of houseflies, horseflies, bluebottles, dung beetles, late afternoon butterflies, midges and early evening moths.

"Oh Shit!" said Paddy, "I'd better get the hell out of here and see our Phelim before it's too late." For Paddy, quite reasonably, considered that he had just overheard that the 'authorities' were on to one of the Ferret's more outrageous exploits, and that any minute now the assassins in the sand coloured berets would be hoorin' down the Antrim Line in bloody souped-up Range Rovers in search of fame and Phelim. And so, abandoning the wheelbarrow with little sense of loss, Paddy raced bow-legged, and in a port-starboard-port rather nautical way, back to his gardener's shed, hosed himself down, changed into a spare set of dungarees and set off on his circuitous and secure route to the Falls Road headquarters of the Belfast Brigade, by means of the shuttle service Ulsterbus that plied its way to and fro from Catholic West Belfast to HQNI four times a day, carrying the Army's locally-engaged civilian cleaning ladies and bottle washers, none of whom had received any more serious security vetting than had our precious Paddy.

It was dark by the time Paddy was ushered into the presence of the most feared man in Ireland, having been man-handled blind-folded round the corner from the Brigade Headquarters to the 'safe' house at Mrs. Mullen's two doors down and up the stairs. "Come in Paddy", was the answer to his minder's knock on the door. "You've got sumthin for me, have you, boyo?" asked Phelim O'Malley, with a glint in his eye.

It was dark in Lisburn, too, when the man they knew as the 'Rat' squirmed through a sewer pipe and into the dry closet in the servants' quarters at the back of the scullery to the GOC's residence, on time and smelling ripe for his appointment with Sir Hector and Fate, and all arranged on the open phone that late afternoon by Peregrine Smythe-Gargle. "Come in Colonel Mooney", was the answer to the Rat's scratching at the library door, where Sir Hector and Perry were toasting each other, with half full snifters of Hennessey XO, to the fully expected on the dot punctuality of the GOC's insalubrious guest. "You've got something for me, I believe, General?" asked Lieutenant-Colonel Mooney, masked, and yet not Gazetted, highly accomplished, murdering marauder.

It was dark too, when the burly figure of Liam O'Shaughnessy, Belfast Brigade Commander of the Provisional IRA, in the disguise of a leading terrorist, knocked softly on the door of Room 666 of the Europa Hotel. "Come in, Liam, me old darling", was the reply from within, and, as soon as he had entered, Major Passed-over Pinky grabbed the most hated man in Whitehall and most other parts of the United Kingdom of Great Britain, and disputed parts of Northern Ireland, in a manly embrace and whispered huskily, "I've got something for you, Liam, my old friend, something nice!" which Liam could only take one way under the strangeness of the physical circumstances, but then, as you and I know, Liam was dead wrong.

It wasn't so dark in Mary McKelvey's kitchen in Slaght where she was tearfully and desultorily cooking herself a rather over-squashed road-kill rabbit stew (run the poor little dazzled bugger down herself, she had, in the main beams of the Austin Cambridge, and enjoyed it), and plotting the demise of Bertie Mulholland, when there was a knock on the door and a timid voice said, "Mrs. McKelvey, I think you've maybe got something that could help me. Can I borrow yer Lambeg Drum?"

It was bright as day in the Reverend Mulholland's bedroom, where he was trying out a varied selection of fish-net stockings and matching suspender belts and cursing the day that bloody, ball-hair catching tights had ever been invented. The brightness was caused by the arc-lights strategically positioned to present the good Reverend's few better points in the best light, in order that Canon's most expensive and up to date automatic could prove that the camera can lie after all. And while Bertie was flashing and the Canon was flashing, the Tormentor of Sinn Fein and Fenian Sinners turned full frontal to the wardrobe mirror and, arching archly backwards, said, "I've got something for you, Mary nee O'Flaherty. *Tua culpa*, ye Fenian bitch!"

It was dark and dank and gloomy in the dog-turd bestrewn hedgerow near McCrory's pub, where Sergeant Simpson lay awaiting the return of Moriarty from whatever foul and bestial perversion he was in the process of nocturnally practising, licence-less, in the Parish of Slaght, to which the Avenging Angel had followed him in the last flickerings of dusk, not two hours before. "Where could the bastard have fucked off to this time?" he wondered, as McCrory's Pub had already turfed out its greatest profligates and biggest reprobates at least an hour ago? And, to make matters worse, it was beginning to piss down with rain, and the good Sergeant (him without his waterproof cape or a condom to protect the fuse on the stick of sweating Frangex he had intended to stick up the right passage, put a match to, and thereby thwart any potential dreams that Ignatius might have of siring a banshee) began to shiver with ague and with anger.

And it was even darker six feet into the McKelvey farm's front yard, where Ignatius lay in a steadily deepening puddle of red-hued rainwater, brought by the lowering storm skittering in from Catholic Donegal in the West, where he had unconsciously found himself after a bloody good blattering around the bake by an underseasoned, lukewarm, hit grab and run, rabbit stew, rather more robustly assisted by the cast iron receptacle in which it had been cooking, wielded by an apoplectic Widow McKelvey in her suit of armoured underwear. As death through drowning competed with the otherwise resuscitative cold rain in a battle over whether Ignatius would recover what little senses he had remaining before he became deceased, sozzled and sodden chicken feed, once the rooster got his act and his broody hens together for reveille at four o'clock in the morning's dawn's early light, the half door opened and a muscular un-masculine grip hoisted Moriarty over a C-Plus-Plus bra-ed back and took him inside, where he was very gently placed in the coma position on a horse hair settee before the Aga cooker, and spoon fed the now salt, pepper, sage, rosemary and thyme improved stew, that had only an hour and a half ago aided and abetted in an attempt to shrug him off this mortal coil.

As he began, reluctantly, to take in his surroundings, Ignatius's first sight was of a blood-stained Lambeg Drum staring at him from the other side of the room, while a voluptuous voice wheedlingly coaxed at his left ear with the sugary words, "So, you want me Drum, Moriarty?" Now Moriarty, convinced temporarily that he was either in Hell or very definitely in the wrong ward at Purdysburn, came to an immediate decision that being a Protestant was a dangerous thing in the wrong place, and that he should have shot himself with his Mother's twelve-bore before even contemplating trying to prove his credentials as a bloody Protestant, and even worse - asking the all-too-recently bereaved Mary nee a bastard but now a fucking amazon McKelvey to part with her late lamented's big blatterer.

But two hours later, after half a murdering cast-iron pot full of good stew and one hundred and twenty minutes of Mary McKelvey plying him with Stewart's 'Cream of the Barley' and sweet words about how Mike McKelvey would want him to carry on the tradition of musically marshalling the Protestant ardour to deeds of superhuman valour, and, thereby, enabling himself to be accepted in society, Moriarty was a new man - albeit with the addition of some considerable seeping scar tissue that had not been there when he had set out on foot to Slaght at six o'clock the previous evening. It was with a glow on his cheeks and a throbbing in his cicatrices that Ignatius exited the half-door at three in the morning, with a half bottle of the 'cratur' for the road home, and the extracted promise that he would be back at nine o'clock sharp on the dot and stone cold sober, every morning until the Twelfth, at the hayshed in back of the farm, for six hours a day daily tuition in Lambeg drumming a la Mike McKelvey, but without the unmentioned perks of the job, nor the necessity of wearing a crotchless and bumless sequinned diver's suit.

And it was dark as bloody pitch, that darkness that you can only get in Ireland just before the dawn comes up like bloody Kiplingesque thunder, to remind you of the excesses of the night before, when Ignatius sauntered past McCrory's Pub and stopped a hundred yards later for a slug of his half bottle and a good slash in the dike, before continuing on his way home. Unbeknownst to Moriarty he had unzipped in front of a semi-comatose Sergeant Simpson, now in the advanced stages of hypothermia and, therefore, unable to say a bloody word to help himself, though he did open his mouth rather unfortunately, initially to attempt a croak of "Help!" and, remarkably quickly afterwards for a man in his physically parlous condition, to try and enunciate a non-medicinal and inaudible deep-throated gargling "Fuck off!". Zipping up with unseeing and genuinely non-affected nonchalance, Moriarty strode off, bruised but exhilarated into the gloom, leaving the good Sergeant to drift into double pneumonia and to become the target of considerable interest for a score of bladder-bursting, early dawn-patrolling Slaght farm dogs, before the milkman found him and, reluctantly, and under some pressure from the Reverend Mulholland, drove him - an hour later and after he had finished his deliveries, and scoffed a bully beef and mustard sandwich, and had two good cups of tea from his Thermos flask - among the empties on the back of his battery-powered colossus at well below its twenty miles an hour maximum speed to the Waveney Hospital, and all the time hoping the bastard would die, on account of a pending court case concerning Sergeant Simpson having caught him with several hundred corpus delicti brown trout of varying illegal weights, and an equally and rather more legally weighty problem of two pounds of diesel and fertiliser mix explosive, which had been intended to stun to death the next pond full of wee dappled darlings.

Later the same morning, while Ignatius was definitely not enjoying his first drumming lesson, and was dutifully learning, for the first time in his life, how painful it was to be a good Protestant, the Waveney Hospital Matron, with a sigh of relief, transferred a raving and delirious, schizophrenic Simpson by padded paddy wagon to Purdysburn, whence he had only so recently come. The only mistake that the medical services in Ballymena had - with the benefit of hindsight - unfortunately made, in their acceptably obscene humanitarian rush to get rid of the lunatic, was to inform RUC Headquarters at Castlereagh, where after a great deal of humming and hahhing and denying that the poor bastard had ever been born, let alone been a member of the Constabulary, at last the Waveney Hospital Matron had got through to a Chief Inspector Bob McCambridge, who had put her somewhat aback by saying, "Thank you, Ma'am. How very, very interesting. Don't you concern yourself now. I'll handle matters from here on. Thank you for your kind consideration. Have a nice day!"

The stage was set! The denouement was approaching! All that was needed now was the catalyst, or a bloody good electric detonator. But that will come. Have no fear!

CHAPTER FIVE

In the back bar of the Republican Club in the Ardoyne the following afternoon, a significant meeting took place between Liam O'Shaughnessy and Phelim O'Malley. "I've got something very important to tell you, Phelim," said Liam. "And I've got something very interesting to tell you, Liam," answered the Ferret. "But before we start, give the barman a shout and get a round in, and then you can begin with your story, because I'm still not right in me head about whether I heard mine correctly or even if I was where I was when I heard it," said Liam. "Begod, Liam, you've got me confused already. But I'll get the beers in and you collect your thoughts," replied Phelim, thinking that maybe O'Shaughnessy was just getting over a bad bottle of stout from the night before, and hoping that it wasn't the first sign of the plague of nervous breakdowns that had removed more than a few Belfast Brigade Commanders over the last ten years of the Troubles. Phelim had had to shoot the last one himself, and blame it on the Stickies, after the bastard had informed him that he was now a born-again Christian and was going to reveal all, for a sizeable fee, to the Sunday Times Insight Team, and use his new wealth to establish a religious retreat at Carrick-a-Rede for alcoholic, unmarried, non-denominational, under legal age, Gaelic speaking mothers.

But while one part of Phelim's mind was already working out which outfit would take the blame this time for the sudden demise of Ulster's leading IRA commander, the other and larger part was involved in the much simpler task of ordering two pints of Guinness and a couple of wee chasers, as well as two bags of smoky bacon potato crisps. As soon as the order arrived and the first mouthfuls of stout were on their way to heaven, Phelim began to relate what Paddy McGonigle had told him. When he had finished his tale Liam said, "Well, they can't pin that Slaght business on us, now can they." "No way, Liam," replied O'Malley, "No bloody way. But since we know it wasn't us, then who the hell was it? The buggers would hardly torch themselves, would they? I know the Red Hand boys are capable of almost anything, but surely not even that bunch of spacers would do a trick like that? What do you think, Liam?" said Phelim.

Liam pondered for a moment, and the moment dragged out into a minute, and the minute continued well over its limit, until Phelim thought that his Commander had either had a quiet stroke or had been through a couple of pipes of happy baccy before the meeting - another good reason to keep a close eye on him from now on! "What I think, Phelim, is that since they're not going to change their bloody minds, no matter how much we deny it, we might as well come out of the closet and take the full credit. Use the secret code and telephone the Belfast Telegraph. Make it sound good, now, plenty of blood and guts and no regrets. Say it was carried out by the Padraic Pearse ASU - that'll have the Army chasing their arses for a couple of weeks looking for something that doesn't exist, as usual. Tell them that they were acting on information from an 'inside source'", who had provided us with cast iron evidence that the Prods were on their way to rape and massacre the poor Sisters of the Immaculate Conception in the nunnery at Toomebridge. Make sure you mention that it was all plotted and planned out of the nearest Orange Hall. That'll give them something to think about before the Twelfth, and by the time they're on the way back from the Field, pissed as newts, they'll be ready to beat the shite out of every innocent Catholic still living in mid-Antrim, and that'll be no bad thing, for the majority of them are a load of gutless, unhelpful bastards anyway. All bloody middle-class doctors and school teachers and proud of their bloody circles of toffee-nosed Protestant friends. Serve the snotty bastards right!

"For you see, Phelim, this could be the break we've been waiting for. Nothing like a good tit-for-tat massacre on the Twelfth and in front of the TV cameras to stir things up a bit. Things have been too quiet lately. We've been losing a lot of support since the Paras shot them Prods on the Antrim Line. We need to get back to grass roots and bury a lot of dead as soon as possible, otherwise youse and me'll be out of a fucking job!" Phelim, who had been at first astonished, then surprised and now intrigued by what Liam had to say, erased any immediate plans for his Commander's execution from his mind, at least for the time being. He was about to interject, when Liam held out his hand for silence and continued. "But we need to be sure that the buggers will go for it, Phelim. Mustn't leave anything to chance. We better get the local boys to do a bit of stirring themselves, to create the right atmosphere, just in case the bloody Prods are too thick to think it out for themselves. What do you think?" "Fucking brilliant! That's what I think," replied the Ferret.

"Who've we got in charge in Ballymena these days, Phelim?" asked Liam. "We've got a wee bit of a problem there, Liam. There's nobody with the right leadership clout at the moment. Don't you remember? McCallion, the OC, got arrested under the Prevention of Terrorism Act. As far as I know he's still in Ballymena RUC Barracks, pending one of their bloody kangaroo courts" said Phelim. "McCallion? That fuckin' faggot. If it wasn't that he kept his fucking pooftering to Apprentice Boys, I'd have had the bastard knee-capped years ago!" said Liam. "Aye! He's an odd ball, right enough, but don't be too hard on the fucker, Liam. He has got his potential uses. Do you remember that hoor wi' the terrible dose that we sent to Aldershot on the game. She did all right, didn't she? Fucked all three battalions of the Parachute Regiment in three weeks, gave them all the clap, and caused the Royal Army Medical Corps to run out of first, second and third line war reserve supplies of Riffidin. And she made herself and us twelve thousand quid into the bargain. If she hadn't fallen for that big RSM, Nobby Johnson, or whatever his bloody name was, and moved in permanently to his quarter half an hour before his wife moved out, she'd have screwed her way through all three Services within six months. Maybe McCallion will have similar success," said Phelim hopefully.

"More likely that some big-dicked Grenadier Guardsman would tear his arse asunder just before ripping his head of his fucking shoulders, that's what I think. But, maybe you have something there, Phelim. Though I can't stand queers meself. Anyway, what bloody good has McCallion's arse-banditry ever done the cause? It's been as quiet as an eighty-year old toothless hoor's crotch in Ballymena for years. You tell me, Phelim," said Liam. "As regards the operational side, not a lot. Bit of a yellow streak there, maybe." "More likely a fucking brown one, if you ask me," interjected Liam. "Good one, Liam. 'Fucking brown streak.' I just don't know where you get them, honest I don't. But, seriously, on the intelligence side he does get us a lot of good inside info from the crack he hears in his pub for starters. Seems that half the fucking UDR use the place to get pissed and write their reports. McCallion even put in a photocopier for them, free of charge!

"You should see the stuff he gets. Some of its unbelievable! You'd be amazed at the number of Prods who seem to think that we're a serious threat to the security of places I've never even bloody well heard of, and certainly wouldn't want to go through on a dark night, according to what I've read from the UDR Intsums. One of their bloody reports even quoted a 'high-level PIRA source' telling them that Buckna, that pokey, wee, one-pig village up the Braid Valley, was about to be invaded by the Cork Flying Brigade! Jasus! The fucking Flying Brigade disbanded after the Civil War, nigh on sixty years ago, if I'm not mistaken. And apart from that Liam, some of McCallion's boyfriends are quite high up, you know. It's amazing what you can get for a good blowjob in Ballymena, McCallion says. He might talk a lot of cock, but I still think he's got his uses, or at least he would have, if he wasn't festering away on his backside on three greasy meals a day in the bloody Police Barracks" said Phelim.

"Hmm!" said Liam. "That gives me an idea. What if we sprung McCallion out of Ballymena Barracks before the Twelfth and got him to stir up a bit of trouble in and around the town? That would be no bad publicity, now would it?" "Bloody good idea, Liam," said Phelim, "because this year's Twelfth Field in mid-Antrim is scheduled to be in Slaght itself, just right across from the Orange Hall." "Fucking roll on!" said Liam. "Couldn't be better. If McCallion lives to see the thirteenth of July he can carry on creaming out the rest of Antrim for all I care. And if he doesn't make it, they'll be singing ballads about him from here to Timbuktu for years to come. Nothing like a good high-profile martyr from an oppressed minority to keep the old war coffers full. Might even get some of those bloody arty-farty queers in Dublin to put their hands in their pockets for a change. And think of all them poofters in California? Fucking hundreds of thousands of the bastards! A lot of them must surely be Irish-American by the law of averages. We'll get the boys in NORAID on to it, if all goes well. But for the minute you get on with planning his escape, Phelim, and at the same time see what you can do to organise a suitably gruesome and public death for that bugger McCallion. On the Twelfth, if possible. Anything you need, just let me know.

"Now, what about this Mooney fellow, Phelim? What can you tell me about him?" "Well, he's got an awful fierce reputation, Liam. He's bloody bad news. They nicknamed him the 'Rat' when he was in the Paras years and years ago. Always slinking round back alleys, playing wi' guns and bombs, and sticky-fingering other people's wimmin, or so the story goes. Appears he may have got rid of some embarrassing little problem for our Maggie's wee bastard, some time back, and since then she thinks the sun shines out of his hairy arse. He's been over here for about a month now, pretending to do be doing something about computerising licence plate numbers. Load of balls! The bugger's obviously here on some sort of special operations." "Is he SAS, then, Phelim?" asked Liam. "He's been off and on, but even the boys at Hereford can't keep up with the bugger. He's a fucking lunatic. I'll tell you what I think, Liam. Our Maggie's sent Mooney over here as a one-man, once-and-for-all solution to the Brit's Irish problem. We'd better watch our backs or we'll be up against the wall without a blindfold or a last fag, and five seconds from being fitted out with wings and getting our first lesson on tuning a couple of bloody harps!"

"Hmm!" said Liam again; causing Phelim to wonder what devious plot his Commander was in the process of hatching this time. Surely big Liam wasn't going to come up with two good ideas in the one week? "You know what, Phelim?" said Liam. "No, I don't, Liam. I was hoping you did," said Phelim. "Wouldn't it be just great if we could lure this mad bugger Mooney into being the one to get rid of McCallion? Can you think of the bloody publicity? 'Unarmed Catholic homosexual buggered to death by sex-crazed SAS Colonel and tea and crumpet mate of Maggie!' The Brit papers would have a field day. They'd be paying the coroner a fortune in backhanders just to look up the poor deceased's hole to see if he was hiding any last minute words. The 'News of the World' and the 'People' would have every queer from John o' Groats to bloody Land's End on the warpath through the streets of London. Jasus, McCallion wouldn't be a martyr. The man would be a fucking saint! And if we could manage to kill Mooney shortly afterwards in justifiable retribution for tampering with the consenting adult legal pastimes of an Ulster bender, just because he was a Catholic and a freedom-fighter, think of the embarrassment for that oul' bitch Thatcher and her fucking toadies in Stormont!"

"I think you might be asking for a bit of a tall order, Liam," said Phelim, "For one thing, there's sure as hell nothing queer about Mooney, at least in the sexual sense. And from what I hear there's thousands of dead bastards all over the world what's tried to blooter Mooney and not lived to tell the tale. He's rumoured to have single-handedly, in fifteen years, doubled the score of dead nig-nogs that it's taken that bloodthirsty old basket-case MacTavish damn near thirty years, and the full-time co-operation of as many divisions of dumb squaddies, to reach. The man's a bloody menace. I think we might be biting off a wee bit more than we could chew." "Aye! It could be so, it could be so," replied Liam, "but keep it in the back of yer mind anyway. You never know what might come up between now and the Twelfth. In the meantime, what do you think Mooney'll do about this Slaght thing, Phelim?" "I'd bet a pound to a pinch of shit that at this very moment our Maggie's pet rodent is briefing some of his SAS boys to put OPs on the place. You see, they'll need to collect the intelligence before they could do anything worthwhile." "Good," said Liam, "and you'll do yer best to make sure the bloody OPs have plenty to report about, won't you, Phelim?" "I sure will, Liam. Just you leave it to me!"

"Now, Phelim, that wee thing I was going to tell you. It's bloody unbelievable! You remember that wee fucker, Pinky Jolly, the permanent IO of the Blue Jackets. You know, the one we persuaded that I was his agent, and fed all that shite to for years?" "God, Liam. Who could ever forget him? Christ, he was the best thing since sliced bread that we ever had. He'd fall for anything, that eejit. What about him? He's surely not over here again as bloody IO, is he? He must be pushing on for being pensioned off by now?" "Well," said Liam, "our Pinky the Prize Prick is over from across the water, "*on holiday*", he says, but the truth is he's still galloping round on his old hobby horse, blethering on about finding ways to slow-murder that old bugger MacTavish. Must have a fearsome grudge against the oul' fart, but why he has is one thing I've never been able to get out of the bastard." "You certainly managed to get every fucking intelligence document that ever passed through his hands out of him, Liam," laughed Phelim.

"Aye. It's a pity most of it was a load of bloody shite. But it did show us what they didn't know, which was a hell of a lot. But our Pinky, see, calls me up out of the blue on the old contact number, plays the silly bugger, putting pressure on me, saying he'll tell all to the 'Irish News' if I don't see him immediately. And so, to play his silly bloody game, I goes round to the bloody Europa, to where the cunt's booked himself a fucking suite!" "The Europa, Liam!" exclaimed Phelim loud enough to let Dermot, the barman, who worked part time as a snoop for Special Branch, come to the rapid (and totally correct conclusion) that he was on to the next Brigade bombing target, and would earn himself a couple of bob out of this one. "Jasus, Liam, you could have got yourself blown up, man!" "My old arse was twitching, that's for sure, Phelim, because I couldn't remember what day the boys in the New Lodge had got the next go planned for. Sweated me ring off, I can tell you." "Did the bugger have anything new to tell you, Liam, him having come all the way over here. Must have been more important than the last time?"

"Oh aye! I think this time our Pinky might have got something, all right. It just depends how we can put it to good use. It's like this you see. According to Pinky it appears that good old Sir Hector MacTavish has got one of them 'Achilles tendons', after all." "Ye mean 'Achilles heel', Liam?" asked Phelim. "Aye! That's the bit. I knew it was something Greek. Anyway, Pinky says the ranting old fart in Lisburn used to be married, did you know? Well, it seems that the good Mrs. McTee, who must have been blind drunk, or loopy-bloody-loo and gaga, or pretty cheesed off at the unfortunate size, either way, of her hubby Hector's dick, for one day she upped stakes and ran off wi' a bloke in the Paras, a sergeant by the good Catholic name of Moriarty. Apparently you only have to mention the bloody name and Hector, me boy, goes off his fucking rocker and into bloody lunar orbit. Pinky says that if you can catch him at the right time and drop the name Moriarty into his lug hole, he'll either have a heart attack or go totally ape-shit and fuck up anything he's up to at the time, just to get a chance to strangle the wife-stealing bastard.'"

"Bejasus, Liam, that gives some food for thought, now, doesn't it?" "It sure does, boyo," said Liam, and I'm sure that a man of your devious bloody mind can come up with a wee trick or two to play on our favourite general. I'll give you a wee while to think on it. In the meantime you've enough to do, what with getting McCallion out of clink and figuring a way to martyr him, and - if we're lucky - crucify that bastard Mooney on the front door of Slaght Orange Hall at the same time. "And what about our Pinky, then?" asked Phelim. "We'll leave him to stew in the Europa for the time being. If he survives the next bomb, then we'll maybe have a further use for the bastard. You never know what might happen, do you? But whatever happens, Phelim, I think we're in for a bit of fun for the next couple of weeks. Make it happen, Phelim. Give them a good hiding and give us a good laugh!" "You can count on me for both" replied the Ferret, with what O'Shaughnessy at first took to be a smile spreading slowly across his face. But, after a cold chill had run down his spine, Liam shivered, for it was the sort of smile that a blind man would have been hard pushed to see, as they say in Belfast. It all had the warmth and humour of an alligator chewing a fat Texan's leg, and that, any Texan will tell you, is not a load of laughs.

Later that evening Dermot the barman met, on emergency arrangement, with his Special Branch handler and informed him of what he had overheard, that is, that the boyos next target for a bomb was the Europa Hotel, and stuck his hand out for his customary fiver. The Branch officer grabbed his hand, pulled him in a flash towards him, kneed him three times in quick succession in the balls, and finally nutted him with his forehead right between the eyes and across the bridge of his snotty nose. "The fucking Europa Hotel, you say? The bastards try to blow the fucker up every month, you twat, and who gives a stuff, 'cause it's always full of fucking journalists, waiting to get their rocks off as they emulate shredded wheat flying forty feet into the bloody air. Get out of here, you little shit, before I bloody tar and feather you myself and string you by your dick from that bloody lamp post!"

And as a disillusioned Dermot crawled his painful way homeward, the blood in his eyes, together with a slight preoccupation with the drill-hammer throbbing in his loins, caused him to take a route that no normal man from the Ardoyne, either drunk or sober, would have dared to contemplate. At last, an agonised hour later, he seemed to see a hazy white light ahead, which surprised him, as the Paras had shot out all the street lights in the Ardoyne years ago. He stopped and huddled beside a wall, wiped the gore from his eyes, and as his vision began to clear he looked up to see a full moon, and illuminated below it - with sudden and abject horror - a painting of a big, black haired man in a red coat, mounted on a rearing white horse and brandishing a silver sword, charging left to right over a gable end wall. And underneath the portrait of King Billy was a scroll of gothic script, which, his brain frantically tried, eventually with some success, to tell him, spelled out the ominous words, 'Shankill Boot Boys Kick Shit'.

The barman's last words, as the midnight patrol of Boot Boys' steel-toed 'taig-tacklers' began to rain down upon him, were, "Hail Mary, Mother of God! Please don't hurt us. I work for the Branch", but that only quite electrically increased the fervour of the good and fatal kicking he was in the first throes of experiencing. As he passed into unconsciousness on the way to meet 'Old Supergrass' below, he heard the sound of a mammoth explosion not far away to the North, as the Europa Hotel resident's bar and a fairly average night's complement of sensation-seeking pissed journalists commenced their scenic flight over the city's roof tops, in a race to make their deadlines in Hell before the Shankill Boot Boys could finish their unexpected late night *piece de* no fucking *resistance*, with a rat-a-tat-tat to the spacer's head. Dermot, the now ex-Ardoyne barman, was thus assured a rather more advanced place in the queue for job interviews at the furnace, although the former Special Branch agent still found himself behind a whingeing arsehole from the 'Guardian', who was complaining about the terms and conditions of his new employment, and was attracting unfavourable attention from a big bloke in black who seemed to be somewhat right of centre politically, at least from the look on his fangs when the prat from the press started going on about fair play.

But look on the good side! At least the bloody journalists ensconced on inflated and falsified expense accounts in the main bar of the Europa Hotel that *'fateful'* evening had got the first *'true'* scoop of a lifetime, the one that they had been so ardently and so *'professionally'* looking for - and which most of them so well deserved. After so many sickening years of paying under the table and down back alleys for manufactured untruths, and manipulating reality to sensationalise and sell, the self-appointed purveyors of public bloody morals had at last got their well-merited place in fiction - one hundred feet in the air over Belfast and looking out for Santa Claus and his reindeer, or ET on a women's bicycle, to escort them to where the 'stuff' of Pulitzer Prizes is really made, the hard way, up the fucking blunt end!

Sometimes in Ireland - not often, we must accept - all's well that ends well! And those still around at the closing page of their personal history may well find a pot of gold at the end of a rainbow - if they don't mind getting wet and believing in fairies!

CHAPTER SIX

——•• ⚜ ••——

Phelim O'Malley had been quite right. At the very moment that he and the Belfast Brigade Commander had been plotting in the back bar of the Ardoyne Republican Club, Colonel Mooney was briefing two hand-picked patrols of the Mountain Troop of D Squadron, 22 SAS, in a Nissen hut in the TOP SECRET compound at Palace Barracks outside Hollywood. The compound was TOP SECRET because the SAS were not in Northern Ireland, according to Margaret Thatcher in Parliamentary Question Time. At least Harold Wilson had had the decency to tell the truth to the Press when he had sent them to Ulster in the seventies, although there had been some ungenerous and anonymous critics at the time, mainly murky figures in MI5 and MI6, who thought that Harold, by publicising what would normally have been a highly classified military and State secret, was either hoping the IRA would run away to the South in panic, or had lost his code book and was trying to get some bizarre frantic emergency signal to BOSS.

In order to conceal the fact that the 'top secret' compound existed at all, it was hidden behind two electrified chain link fences, between which patrolled ten positively-vetted Doberman Pinschers who were rarely fed, and a further fence constructed by the Royal Engineers out of triple coils of razor-sharp German S-wire. At each of the four corners armour-plated watchtowers were located, all of which were manned by a minimum of two guards armed with enough sophisticated weaponry to topple the Government of Mexico on a wet Saturday afternoon. Strategically placed in full view around the perimeter was every conceivable type of state-of-the art electronic eavesdropping device, intruder alarm system, low-light level CCTV, electro-optic image intensification equipment, thermal imager, and other esoteric items I daren't mention, because they are even too secret to come under the Official Secrets Act. To top it all off, between the electrified chain-link fence and the triple coiled wall of German S-wire, there was a twenty foot wide minefield strip with plastic undetectable anti-personnel mines, buried one every square foot. And in accordance with the normal practice of NATO armies in such matters, the humanitarian code of the Geneva Convention had been rigorously followed and the area was dotted with warning signs saying 'Danger! Minefield!'

Just lately, as a finishing touch, anti-aircraft searchlights had been installed to sweep at random intervals up and down the Belfast-Hollywood Road, in order to give added defence against any attempt at attack by rocket or mortar teams from passing vehicles, or bombing raids from hijacked helicopters or low-flying Libyan Airlines Boeing 747s. This latest line of defence had already proven successful. On the first night of searchlight operation the watchtowers' double-twin Oerlikon machine guns had opened up on a darkened helicopter coming in low over the sea towards the compound, and had shot it down in a spectacular ball of flame. The Royal Air Force, whose Puma it had been, and who, at the direct order of the Cabinet Secretary himself, were clandestinely delivering, without navigation lights, the new secure communications equipment ordered by the recently arrived Colonel Mooney, were understandably, and to say the least, not too well pleased! Two nights later the watchtowers repeated their earlier success by blinding, with sixty thousand candlepower, the driver of an articulated lorry loaded with twenty tons of eggs on its way to the Larne ferry, and due in London to feed the good citizens of the capital by late afternoon the following day. The result of this particular incident was a brief shortage of traditional English breakfasts in the East End and a bloody great uncooked omelette scattered over some one and a half acres of County Down. Nobody would ever be in the position of accusing our Colonel Mooney of leaving anything to chance!

Secure in the knowledge that no one could possibly suspect or, even if they did, ever be likely to accurately detect where his Special Operations

HQ was located, Colonel Mooney stood at the front of the hut and briefed his boys. Squared-off in front of him was a 'table, six-foot, folding', covered to floor level with the obligatory 'blanket, lightweight, wool, OG', which the Army Methods of Instruction course at Beaconsfield insisted was to prevent bored soldiers from being distracted by looking up the kilts of Scottish briefing officers while the latter were seated in front of them. The full gamut of audio-visual equipment required to ensure effective briefing by good British Army tick-tock automatons was on hand for Mooney's convenience and the others' distraction, even including the compulsory slides of nude women with big tits that Beaconsfield said were to be interspersed with the real subject matter in order to keep the simple soldiers and less sexually experienced junior officers alert. Mooney had this day used some of his own personal collection of exotic erotica, as his experienced men were old hands and unlikely to perk up at the usual old Royal Army Education Corps Victoriana. Mooney had, wisely, vetted his naughty nudes slides prior to the briefing, to ensure that he did not capture one of the lads' attention too much, by portraying his wife open-crotched in front of his peers. Mooney was a very good example of the best in British Army officers. He knew each of his men personally, and most of their wives intimately, and called their children, many of whom shared a certain physical resemblance, by their first names, and never forgot their birthdays.

That same morning Mooney had flown over Slaght in an Alouette helicopter to recce the area and had identified two good OP sites. He had also, with the assistance of the Cabinet Secretary, whom he had called directly, secured an overflight by a Phantom F 4 photo-recce flight using IRLS, in order to detect any command wires for bombs which might be in the area. An AEW Nimrod of the Royal Air Force from Lossiemouth was also on 24 hour station, as of midday and for the duration, circling in a such a tight figure of eight over the area immediately due South of Ballymena that the crew were already all airsick to a man. Mooney also expected, as long as the special relationship between Maggie and the Americans continued, that the Cabinet Secretary would shortly be able to persuade the Yanks to swing one of their big spy satellites over the target area every three hours. Then he would have on-line video, and, within four hours of each pass, computer-enhanced and PR interpreted blow-up photographs in black and white and full colour by day, and infra-red by night, would be rushed in by F-16 from the USAF base at Mildenhall to the former RAF base at nearby Sydenham. Once that was in place, Mooney would be ready to go to war. But the first thing was obviously to do as Phelim the Ferret had correctly assumed. The OP teams must be briefed and infiltrated into their hide positions before dawn at four o'clock the following morning.

The first team, call-sign Delta 1, was commanded by Sergeant 'Lofty Clark', a twenty-five year veteran with a gruff sense of humour and the strength of an Aberdeen Angus bull. He was correctly nicknamed 'Lofty' as he was five foot six inches in his free-fall boots. The British Army, which has traditionally sent newly trained recruits, who were cooks and truck drivers in civilian life, to the Royal Corps of Transport and the Army Catering Corps respectively, sees no need to flaunt such long-standing and well-tried tradition when it comes to the matter of nicknames. The second call-sign, Delta 2, was led by Corporal Bryan 'Sticky' Dick, a former convicted poacher from the West Country, who had joined the Parachute Regiment from its well-proven recruiting ground, the County Court. He had thence, after three years of devastating the wildlife of Surrey and Hampshire, while based in dismal Aldershot, passed selection for the SAS at Hereford with the highest marks achieved by anyone in the history of the Regiment, mainly through his incredible ability to live off the land, unheard and unseen, except for numerous piles of feathers, fur and bones. Sticky was a man of great taciturnity and famed in the Regiment for his apt one-liners. When asked to give his appreciation on how a band of terrorists camped high on the djebel in Oman should be most effectively attacked by a full SAS squadron, complete with air cover and naval gunfire support on call, Sticky, who had commanded the close recce team to gather intelligence on the target, had replied, "Bit late for that now, Boss. Gutted 'em myself last night." The other members of the two OP teams were just as professional and as cold-blooded as Lofty and Sticky. Colonel Mooney had chosen well.

"Well, lads, now you know as much as I do," lied the Rat, "So to summarise, here's what I want you to do. Two OPs, one in that gorse clump on the hill top overlooking the Orange Hall and the big field where the Twelfth celebrations are to be held, and the other in the thick hedgerow on that hill overlooking the McKelvey place. Both OPs can cover all the entry-exit routes to the area and they are sited to be able to provide mutual protection in the event of any emergency. Not that there's any chance of that, is there lads?" And they all laughed good-humouredly in that special way that men, who have mutual respect for one another's total professionalism, are accustomed to do, especially if someone hints that anything could go possibly wrong.

"Now. You've got everything you need. I want Lofty and Sticky to go away and work out their Orders and come back and run them past me in two hours. You others can get all your kit together and get some test firing done. I've booked the range, but on the off chance of some other bloody unit being there, tell them to fuck off, or they'll answer to me and Maggie Thatcher! You will be on the choppers by midnight and at the drop off point near Cromkill at 0030 hours. One hour infiltration to target, two hours digging of the hides and, Bob's your uncle, all ready and in position for stand-to thirty minutes before dawn at four o'clock. Textbook! Any last minute questions?"

"Yes, Boss," said Lofty. "In the event of something happening, are we to follow the Yellow Card?" (The Yellow Card was a set of rules of engagement for the use of soldiers in Northern Ireland, whereby you were supposed to shout "Halt or I fire!" three times, in warning to the terrorist who had just shot at you, in order to make the game fairer and keep the body count on the IRA side down as far as possible.) "No bloody way, Lofty. Anybody takes a pot shot at you, you slot the fucker into the next county. Okay?" "No problem," Boss, said Lofty with a grin like a Cheshire cat. "Boss, if we see anything going down from the OPs, and we can get a good target in our sights, what do you want us to do?" asked Sticky. "Take no action other than to immediately report to me. I'll be standing by with the Quick Reaction Force and we'll move in on whatever you designate for us. Don't want to be caught in the crossfire, because you lads are too fucking accurate! Mustn't make my girlfriends grieve the rest of their lives away, must we, Sticky?" said the Rat, at which the Nissen hut was filled with raucous laughter, such was the reputation of Mooney's sexual exploits across six continents. And with that the briefing split up and all departed to perform their various preparatory tasks, leaving a confident but pensive Mooney to pore over his maps and photographs once again.

For what the others did not know, and indeed even the GOC NI himself was unaware, was that Colonel Mooney *did* have a secret agenda, given to him in a very private verbal briefing from his hero and increasingly close friend, the PM herself. He had been ordered to carry out the clandestine execution of terrorist leaders, where their identities and guilt were, through intelligence confirmation by the SAS themselves, beyond any shadow of doubt. No Yellow Card for our Maggie's beautiful boys. Oh no! Her only caveats to Mooney had been to make any surgical assassinations of such terrorist godfathers look as if their religious and ideological opponents did the dirty on them, and to do his best to keep the score relatively equal on both sides of the political fence, so that no one organisation would get the upper hand. As Maggie had said to the Rat, "Colonel, it is my opinion, and one well shared by my advisors, that Ulster can only have a limited number of actual or potential terrorist leaders. In fact, when I consider the calibre of my Unionist Party colleagues, I confess to being surprised that there are any leaders there at all. Cut these petty thugs down one by one and they will soon run out of replacements. Then the rest will calm down and do as they are told. Just don't get caught, Colonel, that is all I ask. This is a deniable operation." By that, Mooney knew full well, the PM meant that she would deny ever having issued the orders to him. But that was all right to the gallant Colonel. He had never been caught before in any deniable operation, although he had made it a point of always leaving his calling card, namely, a trail of blood that circled the globe!

On that same day Chief Inspector Bob McCambridge was sitting in his office pondering over the future of Slaght. McCambridge had spent all but the first three years of his long RUC career in Special Branch, and, with only three years to go to retirement, he was determined to put an end to the Troubles once and for all. He knew more about the seamier side of Ireland than anyone else on the divided island, and for that reason his superiors had given him the task of setting up and leading a highly secret operation to gather intelligence that could be used to clandestinely assassinate any and all terrorists who had the temerity of defying the law of the land. The fact that such an operation was in itself

illegal was of little significance to the hierarchy of the RUC. If Maggie
Thatcher hadn't the balls to give the order herself, then the job would
still have to be done.

McCambridge's problem, however, was that he knew bugger all about
Slaght or its environs. Since the mid-Antrim area contained few Catholic
enclaves, there had been virtually no indigenous terrorist activity over
the past decade. Of course, there had been the one attempt to blow
up the Barracks in Ballymena, but that had been an 'imported' job,
the work of a van load of the boyos from Belfast, having a wee bit of
a lark while on their way to a week's well-earned R & R by the sea at
Cushendun. McCambridge had been confused by the 'Slaght Slaughter',
as the newspapers put it, with unaccustomed under-statement. What
with the only local IRA leader of any note, McCallion, in the nick,
the last thing anybody could have expected was the incineration of
eighty pissed Protestant farmers on a lonely country road. And apart
from that, McCallion kept well away from any acts of violence, other
than blowing up the odd transformer from time to time, just to keep
the Belfast boys off his back. It wasn't that McCallion didn't have the
brains for it, mused McCambridge; it was because the Ballymena IRA
Commander was as yellow as a daffodil, and as bent as a fir tree on the
Faeroe Islands. So, who the hell could have conceived the plan that
damn near widowed half of mid-Antrim? If the boyo who did this one
was only just beginning, Jasus, he'd wipe out the Protestant majority
before the end of the year! "Yes!" said McCambridge to the filing
cabinet in front of him, "This is certainly a job for the 'laundrymen',
as McCambridge had code-named his group of specialist intelligence
gatherers and 'hit-teams', for the simple reason that they swanned round
their target areas in a series of under-cover laundry vans.

McCambridge pressed the intercom button on his desk and was
connected to his outer office. "Yes Sir," was the prompt response. "Mary,
get me the laundrymen, double quick. I don't care where they are or
whatever they're doing, they drop it and report here now." "Yes Sir,"
replied Mary, smiling to herself at the picture of the boys leaving their
scrubbing boards and mangles, tearing off their pinafores and leaping
into their armoured, souped up, 'Scrubbers Incorporated' vans and
breaking all the speed limits, as they raced to HQ at Castlereagh.

"Another good cover blown." she thought to herself. "Wonder what they'll get up as next week? Probably 'The See-through Window Cleaners', or maybe 'The Suck-up Septic Tankers'. God! It's getting like a bloody circus round here these days. Circus? Yes, that's what they should become. A bloody circus!" Just then the intercom buzzed again.

"Mary, have the boys got back from Purdysburn yet with Sergeant Simpson? No, Sir. There was a bit of a problem," said Mary. "What is it this time, Mary? Did they get lost without a map and couldn't find where fucking Belfast is again?" sighed the Chief Inspector. "No, Sir. There was a bit of an accident. Apparently Sergeant Simpson had to go to the bathroom on the way back, and by the time they had found a filling station with a loo, and figured out how to get him out of the straitjacket so that one of them wouldn't have to wipe his bum, it was too late. Anyway, they say they'll be here in about half an hour, as soon as they hose the van and the Sergeant down, and get him a clean pair of trousers."

"They'll be in even bigger shit when I get hold of them, useless bastards." grunted McCambridge. "Honestly, Mary. I just don't know where they recruit them from these days. Do you? Most of them wouldn't know their arse from their elbow unless you labelled both for them - and not in joined-up writing either. God's strewth! What did I ever do wrong to deserve this? Sometimes I think I'd have been better off joining the IRA. At least, if you're a Fenian, you can get a drink on a Sunday, and you don't have to go to Church and be told you're a sinner and doomed to hell for eternity by some pasty-faced Presbyterian pervert who thinks he's Adolf bloody Shickelgrueber, and with a subversive record as long as an African bull elephant's dick!" "Yes Sir." said Mary, understandingly, for although she had heard her boss make the same defamatory statements a thousand times before, she too despaired at the future of Protestant Ulster when she observed the mental dwarfism of the new generation of Special Branch officers.

Forty minutes later four burly plain-clothes officers manhandled a hooded, cuffed, leg-ironed and straitjacketed and hog-tied Sergeant Simpson into Chief Inspector McCambridge's office. "Get those fucking things off him!" screamed McCambridge. "What the hell do you think he is - Jack the fucking Ripper? Jasus Christ, boys, he's one of us after all. You, McFetridge!" said McCambridge, pointing at one of the slightly less unintelligent of the four officers. "Go and get him a cup of tea. And the rest of you, fuck off out of my sight before I think of something nice for you to do, like sweeping out the sewers at the Crumlin Road Gaol with your fucking toothbrushes. Get out of here! Now!" And as soon as the room had cleared of potential night-soil shifters, McCambridge turned to Sergeant Simpson, led him to a chair and pushed him gently into it.

"Jimmy, how are you feeling?" asked McCambridge, who had known Simpson since their schooldays in Cullybackey. Indeed, they had joined the RUC on the same day and their careers had paralleled each other until McCambridge's better brain and greater luck at not getting caught had caused them to drift further and further apart in rank and social status. "What did they put you in for this time, old friend?" "Pneumonia, Bob. Honest to God! Fucking pneumonia!" said an obviously exhausted Jimmy. "Hells bells, Jimmy! They don't lock you up in fucking Purdysburn for a cough and a bit of a nose drip! What the hell did you say or do to them in the Waveney in Ballymena?" said McCambridge. "Well, as you can imagine, Bob, I wasn't in me right head when they brought me round. All the penicillin or whatever shite they had pumped into me didn't help either. So as they were setting me up for another jab of something up the bum, I just sort of lost me rag, and told them what I was going to do to that wee cunt, Moriarty, as soon as I catch the little bastard. Anyway, the doctors and nurses were a bit overcome by the scope of my imagination, though I don't think I used too many medical terms. They thought I had gone off my rocker, and they weren't too bloody far wrong, because I'm not just going to exterminate that fucking little shit. First I'm going to pull the hairs off his balls one by one; then I'm going to castrate him with a blunt pair of pinky scissors and dip his syphilitic dick in caustic soda; and after that I'm going to make him into the biggest pin-fucking-cushion in the whole wide world by hammering six inch nails into every square centimetre of what's left of his skinny carcass; and I'll finish him off by tapping out the *Last* bloody *Post* on his skull with me Black and Decker drill on hammer action; and before the last light of fucking Fenian incomprehension fades from his beady little eyes, I'm going to rip off his lower jaw and piss down his throat and asphyxiate the little fucker! I'll teach the bastard to pee on me when I'm otherwise indisposed!

"Jasus, Jimmy. No wonder they sent you back up the road to the loony bin. If I didn't know you for so long, I'd take you there meself, right now. Calm down, lad! Who's this bugger, Moriarty, who's got you so all het up?" asked a curious McCambridge, who knew his old school friend as a staunch Loyalist but not as any more of a blood curdling extremist than anyone else from Cullybackey with a gun. "Ignatius Aloysius Moriarty is the biggest, walking, fucking disaster area I've ever come across, and as you know fine well, I've seen a few bad ones in my time! Everywhere he goes there is fucking mayhem. Jasus, Bob! I'm convinced he was behind that awful mess at Slaght. He was definitely seen in the vicinity that night, for sure. The trouble is I can't pin a bloody thing on the bastard. He's a slippery as the slime on a Bann eel's bum. What's worse is that the little shit struts around like a nancy boy on heat, pretending to be a Protestant, but how the hell could he be with a Fenian name like that. He's a fifth columnist, I'm certain of it. He's sure as hell not on the side of God and the Reverend Ian Paisley! He's just using a Catholic name to help make us believe that he's a Protestant because nobody would be daft enough to pretend to be a Protestant and use a Catholic name unless they really were Protestant. Now would they, Bob?"

"Hold on a minute, Jimmy. I need to think that one through for a wee bit, replied McCambridge. And having pondered over Simpson's last remark for five minutes, and counted out possibilities on the fingers of his left hand, the Chief Inspector's face cleared and he smiled knowingly. "You know, Jimmy, you're right. It's called reverse logic. You make out something to be the opposite of what it's not, in order to make people believe that you are the reverse of what you think they think you are. See?" "Well, I'm sure you're right, Bob. You always were the one with the brains at school. But what are we going to do about it?" answered and asked Sergeant Simpson.

"First of all, Jimmy, you are going to tell me every last thing that you know about Moriarty and about Slaght. Then you are going to have a good rest and tomorrow you are on your way to Ballymena to do a wee bit of ferreting for me. But this time you're going back on the streets as an Inspector. Congratulations, Jimmy! You're re-instated in the Branch. You and I are going to sort a few twisted problems out in mid-Antrim and then we're coming back here to Belfast to arrange a wake for that bastard Liam O'Shaughnessy."

"O'Shaughnessy? He's not dead is he?" asked Simpson, with a look of both joy and disappointment (presumably at not have been the instrument of death) on his red face. "Not yet, Jimmy. But he fucking well soon will be. We've got the old *carte blanche*, Jimmy. We can go ahead and murder the bastards now, as long as we put in a report, in triplicate, for destruction." Simpson, who didn't understand what a *'carte blanche'* meant, nonetheless got the drift. "Jasus, Bob! Did I ever tell you about Plan B?" "Not now, Jimmy. Concentrate on Moriarty and Slaght for the minute. There'll be plenty of time for planning your retirement later," said McCambridge. And for the next two hours the two of them huddled over successive cups of tea, while Simpson briefed the Chief Inspector on everything he knew, and a lot that he had made up just for the hell of it, just as any good Special Branch man in his position would naturally do.

At four o'clock that afternoon Chief Inspector McCambridge entered the main briefing room and stood behind the rostrum on a low dais at the front. Before him stood the forty men of "Scrubbers Incorporated", most of them with painful looking, chapped, red hands and dark rims round their eyes. This latest undercover scheme had been one of the toughest assignments to date, and now that the cover had been blown and half of Catholic West Belfast was short of clean sheets and underwear, the boys of the Branch were delighted. It really was time for a change, in their opinion. Anything would be better than scraping skid marks of Fenian bloomers!

"Be seated, men! Now, I'm sorry to have to scrub the laundry job at short notice. I know you were getting right into it and on the point of making a clean sweep of the bastards. But there was no choice. Something big's come up. You are all going for a wee excursion in the countryside for a few days. Now, there's someone I want you to meet." The door to the briefing room opened and in walked a freshened-up

Simpson, who strode to the dais and took his place slightly to the side and rear of the Chief Inspector. There was an audible murmur in the room as the officers looked at one another and muttered under their breath, such things as, "Holy God! Would you look at what's just crawled in! It's that loony, Simpson" or "Shit a brick! Who let that bastard out?" or "Bring out your dead! The black plague's back" and "I'm putting in a transfer to the other fucking side!" For, you see, Simpson was as loved and admired throughout his chosen profession as all such self-seeking psychos usually are. But then, isn't it true that an artist is rarely recognised in his own time? So why the hell should it be different for raving eejits like Simpson? His genius was of a type common to the RUC, namely, the IQ level was in inverse proportion to the innate potential for mayhem.

"Now, men! For those of you who don't know him, this is Inspector Jimmy Simpson, who will be running this operation for the next few weeks," said McCambridge, thereby initiating a lot more murmurings, such as "I'd rather be bollock-naked on point duty on the Fall's Road" or "Fuck me! What stupid cunt made that bastard an Inspector?" or "I hope they've ordered forty more beds for the Royal Victoria Hospital, because we're bloody well going to need them, if that fucker's in charge!" and "It's not bloody beds they'll be needing, but extra shift workers at the crematorium!"

"Quiet, now, lads. You can all congratulate the Inspector later. Listen carefully now while I explain the background to this operation and how we are going to carry it out," said McCambridge. And for the next hour he had their undivided attention, as, to a man, they listened to the tale of horror that had been taking place in mid-Antrim behind their backs and without their knowledge. What was unfolded to them was unbelievable! How could one man, this mad Moriarty, until today a total unknown, have achieved so much, while the rest of the Republicans were fighting a last ditch stand from behind their barricades and pints of Guinness. They'd need to watch this one, that was for sure! The percentage survivability figures had just taken a big dip downwards for prematurely retired Belfast laundrymen!

After the briefing was over McCambridge returned to his office to continue with the mountain of paper work that threatened to avalanche down upon him every working day of his life. At six-thirty he opened the middle drawer of a filing cabinet and took out a bottle of Black Bush and a glass, poured himself a good snorter, and thought for a moment. He then picked up the telephone and dialled the private number of Captain The Honourable Peregrine Osbert Smythe-Gargle at HQNI. The phone rang for several seconds and then a voice said crisply, "ADC to the GOC speaking." "Captain Smythe-Gargle, I'm glad I caught you. It's Chief Inspector McCambridge here. I've found out some interesting info on that terrible Slaght business. Have you got a pencil and paper handy?" And when Perry answered, "Affirmative, Chief Inspector!" McCambridge began to explain the details about the suspected IRA undercover mastermind, I. A. Moriarty. When he had finished, McCambridge added, "See what you have on your records, if anything. And see if MI5 or MI6 know anything. This bugger must have received high-level training from somebody. He's too bloody high calibre to have learned his art throwing petrol bombs over backyard walls." Perry immediately agreed and thanked the Chief Inspector for his good offices, promising to pass the information to the 'Old Man' at their *tete a tete* dinner one hour later that night. Cordial farewells were exchanged and McCambridge returned to his whiskey.

"That should cover my arse," said McCambridge to his filing cabinet. He knew exactly what was going on, for he hadn't got to his rank by just spying on the enemy. He spent at least 50 per cent of his effort in spying on his so-called 'own side'. It was the only way to ensure that you had all angles covered and didn't get your own profile in the firing line. All too often he had seen brilliantly conceived operations transforming into Whitehall farce through his 'own side' inadvertently intervening in something they knew nothing about and, thereby, totally screwing everything up. A little leak here and there - even to the opposition - usually helped to reduce the odds of all the participants not being present for all the wrong reasons at the right time and place for the shoot out. "Mustn't let that mad fucker Mooney miss out in the fun and attack the wrong fucking place, must we now?" he continued to muse aloud as he poured another good dram into his glass. "If I can get enough of the murdering bastards all together at the same time and place, we'll make sure that the law of averages is okay and that chance is taken out of the old equation."

And with that he picked up the phone again and dialled an even more secure number than that of the ADC to the GOC, namely, the number of a newspaper reporter on the staff of the Belfast Telegraph, who believed that he was 'privileged' in being the recipient of private 'off-the-record' briefings from Chief Inspector McCambridge, and who did not know that the good Chief Inspector fully realised that five seconds after he had put the phone down, the reporter would be arranging an urgent assignation in some suitably dark alleyway to pass on the confidential information to none other than Phelim the Ferret himself. Machiavelli was a fucking Eyetie amateur in comparison to our Bob from the Branch!

At nine-fifteen that evening General Sir Hector MacTavish sat down before the unlit hearth in the be-chandeliered library of his magnificent residence, replete after his (larger) share of a nice little Gewurztraminer and a bottle of Bordeaux with a lot of body in it, and four glasses of port, - as well as, naturally, the chewier comestibles which had gone with the excellent selection of wines. Perry went to the immense mahogany sideboard and poured two glasses of Hennessey XO, a large generous balloon for a much more mature General, and a slightly more modest ADC's portion for himself. "Well, Perry. What was it that old McCambridge passed on to you?" asked Sir Hector. "Rum sort of a story, Sir" replied Perry, all about some terrorist mastermind surfacing in connection with that dreadful Slaght affair. Seems to be a totally new name. MI5 and MI6 know nothing about him. Most intriguing. Maybe an alias of some sort. Got a strange ring to it though!" "Well, me boy, what is the bloody name then. Get on with it!" "Yes, Sir. Sorry Sir. I mean, absolutely, Sir. The name, according to McCambridge, is 'Moriarty'."

"Morifucking what?" bellowed the General, unfortunately forgetting that he had been swallowing a mouthful of brandy at the time, and thus immediately beginning a severe coughing, choking, spluttering and snorting fit that turned his face a most hideous bilious reddish-purple colour and caused him to spray the (fortunately) unlit fireplace with best brandy. When he had at last calmed down enough to be able to sip a refreshened and even larger balloon of cognac without the assistance of the Heimlich manoeuvre, Sir Hector, to Perry, looked angrier than he had ever seen him, even angrier than the day that one of the chunkies at the main entrance to HQNI had dropped his rifle while saluting the General's passing staff car - but then the General's views about chunkies were well known, especially in the corridors of power in MOD. They had certainly been made well known to the poor unfortunate Royal Pioneer Corps ex-Corporal that day! Perry looked on nervously as the full gamut of murderous emotions flitted back and forward across his patron's face. He hoped that Sir Hector was not building up to a heart attack, or worse, an attack on his ADC!

"Get me Mooney on the phone, immediately!" gasped the General. And after a long minute Perry handed the receiver to his boss and retired quickly to the comparative safety of the far side of the room, ready to make a break for it through the French windows and - most probably - get shot by the Keystone Cops patrol, still dashing hyper-tactically from bush to bush in the garden outside. "Mooney, MacTavish here! Got some bloody bad news, old boy. That Slaght affair. Got the name of the mastermind behind it. Moriarty. Yes! It could be just a coincidence, couldn't it, but damned unlikely, what? I'm sure it's the blighter. Has to be! After all he was a weapons and explosives expert in the Paras, wasn't he? Yes, of course I know you trained him, otherwise I wouldn't be bloody well talking to you about it now, would I? Now you see here, Mooney. You get that bastard, if you have to burn down every hovel in the whole of blasted mid-Antrim to root him out. And I want him to die slowly, Mooney, very slowly. Do what you did to that Prime Minister wally, but don't rush it this time, all right. You need anything, short of a tactical nuclear strike, you've got it. Wait one! I think I could even wangle the nuke! This is war, Mooney, out and out war. What? Yes of course you can have it in writing. First thing in the morning. Now get on with it, man. Do what your famous for, kill the bastard and all that's his. Yes! Bloody Lady MacTavish too, if you can find the bitch!" And with that Sir Hector slammed down the receiver and flung his glass at a terrified Smythe-Gargle. "What are you cowering for there, you pimply, pusillanimous, little prick? Go and get me my pistol, now! We keep our weapons on us at all times from now on. We're at war, boy, or is that too much for your toadying, little, fogged-up brain to understand?"

And as poor young Perry Smythe-Gargle experienced the nearest he had come to falling in action, the scene changes to the back bar of the Ardoyne Republican Club, where a new barman, also working part time for the Branch, had just brought the fresh glasses of stout, with two wee chasers, to the table where Liam O'Shaughnessy and Phelim O'Malley were ensconced in an appraisal of the latest information from their well-informed source inside the 'Belfast Telegraph'. The new barman was in the motions of slinking respectfully away, when he heard the Ferret say, "Moriarty. Ignatius Aloysius Moriarty. He's not one of ours. He's certainly not one of the Stickies, and the INLA haven't got anyone with brains enough to open a wet paper bag! So who the fuck is he, Liam?" I don't know, Phelim. But you had better find out before somebody else gets him. This sounds just like the sort of boy we've been looking for. Hell! If he can get eighty Prods in one go, and in the one night, on a lonely country road, the fella will have a field day in the Shankill on a Saturday afternoon. Find him for me, Phelim. Find him before those fuckers Mooney, McCambridge and MacTavish do!"

And later that night the new barman (who was not called Dermot) passed on to his Special Branch handler what he had overheard in the Republican Club, for which he received kind words and a fiver. Lucky for him he hadn't overheard anything about the rapid expansion of the hotel industry in North Belfast, wasn't it? But that's life, isn't it?

In a TOP SECRET Nissen hut near Hollywood Colonel Mooney stared fixedly at the wall, lost in thought. At last he shrugged himself and stood up to stretch. "Well, well, well!" he said to no one in particular, he being alone at the time. "Isn't this world just a wonderful place? *Carte blanche* in writing from Sir Hector to do just what I was going to do undeniably anyway. But no matter, a little more backing is always useful. But Moriarty? He was good, but I didn't think he was that good, even if it was me that trained him. Too many brains and too little dick to be a real leader. Couldn't believe it when he ran off with that ugly, toffee-nosed bitch that Sir Hector called a wife. God! She had a face like a Clydesdale, only hairier. Wonder where she and Moriarty are now? Last I heard they were beachcombing in Bali or somewhere daft like that. Can't be Moriarty! Can it?" And with that the rat picked up the receiver of his secure telephone and dialled a number that rang in a gloomy office in an even gloomier building situated two spits and a fart South of Waterloo Station in London.

But we leave Colonel Mooney to have his secure telephone conversation and, thereafter, prepare his final words to his brave men. Enough confusion has been caused for one day, even for Ulster. We will now swing into the action phase of this work. Those readers who tend to vomit uncontrollably at lurid descriptions of unfortunate reality may continue to read for several further chapters with a modicum of somewhat relative safety. The interesting naughty bits, for the more perverted among you, are also still some way ahead. For the next few pages we will carry out an in-depth appreciation of the military mind, of the intelligence game (as practised by non-intelligent practitioners), and of the quaint social mores of the mid-Antrim country folk, albeit with an initial visit for all of you to that wonderful place, Ballymena, where the people are of such a most miserly bent, that Isaac of York would have admired greatly, as long as he wasn't short of a bob and looking for help. As the old adage goes, "If you are Ballymena with your Ballymoney, you'll never have a Ballycastle for your Ballyhome." Droll people the North Irish - or not, as your viewpoint may be! Enough idle prattle. Let's go to war!

CHAPTER SEVEN

---※---

A t 2359 hours, exactly seven days and one minute before the entrance of that fateful Twelfth of July into the history books, one Alouette and two Scout helicopters of the Army Air Corps took off into a star-filled sky from somewhere near a TOP SECRET compound in Palace Barracks, Hollywood. The nervous pilots, who knew all about the fiery and 'highly classified' conclusion to the Puma that had failed to achieve the clandestine communications equipment delivery, had asked Colonel Mooney, just once too often, if the searchlights were out - and would stay out, and were even more nervous now in the knowledge that he was later that morning going to ensure that they would spend the next two years very delicately burning leeches off each other's balls with soggy cigarette butts, while on foot patrol in festering Belize. (The removal of gonadically positioned leeches is a well-tried British Army method of finding out who your real friends are. When it works, it's referred to as the 'buddy-buddy system.' When it doesn't, it's called 'Ouch! You fucking bastard! Just you wait until *you* need help!' The helicopters, nonetheless, showed the lack of confidence of their pilots in the Rat's assurances and angled sharply Northwards at dangerously low level after take-off, and disappeared, engines straining to their danger limit, into the night.

In a sheltered field, lying in a dip in the landscape and, thus, hidden from the neighbouring roads, far from any farmhouses or other habitation, and almost half-way between Slaght and Cromkill, a training exercise of the Slaght Protestant Young Farmers Union was taking place, under the keen eye to technical detail of none other than the Reverend Bertie Mulholland. The theme of that night's exercise was the 'Pre-dawn self-propagation of the common button mushroom in naturally fertilised cow pasture', or at least that would be what the participants would tell any RUC or UDR patrol in the most unlikely event that any gentlemen from those two wonderful organisations were not yet in their beds and breathing whiskey fumes into the faces of whichever wives had foolishly forgotten to have a headache, or who could no longer give a damn about what happened to them anymore, as long as the drunken bastard didn't take all night moaning and groaning and trying to get the bloody thing to stop slipping out, just like the last time he had come back pissed as a newt.

This nocturnal agri-educational excursion, as you may have correctly twigged, was only a fiendishly clever cover for the culmination of another graduation class of Slaght eighteen year olds, now sufficiently comfortable with the double and single barrel shotgun, the 1915 Webley 45 revolver, the .22 Bird Gun and a variety of fertiliser-based explosives to be a danger not only to themselves but to society in general, for at least the length of time it took them to wipe themselves out while putting their training to such useful effect, as removing stubborn boulders from soon-to-be ploughed fields or fishing for trout without a licence. By star and moonlight Big Bertie and his closest aides looked proudly down the line of eight young farmers, the future of the quasi-human Free Presbyterian race.

"Boys!" said Big Bertie, "I am well pleased with all of you. Now, as you know the Field is going to be at Slaght in seven days time. After the dreadful thing that has happened to us, I'm sure that you will be the first to appreciate that we are at war here. You must be prepared to die for Slaght, boys. There may very well be trouble on the Twelfth, so I want youse to be ready. If anything at all happens that day, you are to head directly to the Orange Hall, get your weapons, and take to the battlefield under your commanders, and blow them Fenian bastards back in bits to Rome! Have you got me now, lads?" And with the innocence of youth the Young Farmers of Slaght swelled their chests and shouted, "Yes, Reverend Mulholland!" and Big Bertie felt like Lord Cardigan on the night before the Charge of the Light Brigade. For to

Big Bertie, these young men were the first, and thus truly expendable, line of defence against an invasion of looting and plundering, sex - and unfortunately not drink - starved Republican rapists who would not wait until the next millennium before marauding Northwards from heathen Belfast to ravish his lovely townland. "Just like those 'Assyrians who came down like the wolf on the fold'," thought Bertie, "except the shower of ruffians from parts South who would descend on Slaght would not be coming with 'cohorts all gleaming in silver and gold' - that's for bloody sure! They'd be a raggedy-arsed bunch of sub-humans, straight out of the Stone Age exhibits at the Natural History Museum!"

"Right lads, you've got one final wee exercise to do. You're to give me and the old blokes with me thirty minutes, and then you are to try and sneak your way, in your two patrols, back to Slaght and up to the Orange Hall before dawn at four. Any of you who can make it without getting caught, can march behind me to the Field and back!" Now, there was an honour worth dying for - to a man! And so Bertie and the older men slunk off to lay in wait for the young farmers and to have a bit of a crack at the poor wee lads' expense. For the older men had been through this exercise so many times that they knew exactly where, when and how the lads would make their way back. A bit of innocent fun dousing the boys with pre-positioned buckets of pigshite had never hurt anyone, and was a good lesson to the new lads, not to be over-confident. It was all good clean fun - or it would be when they got to the Orange Hall and washed the pigshite off themselves, and had a good, big, greasy, fried breakfast put down in front of them.

Half a mile away a dark blue Ford Cortina drew into a lay-by and sat with its engine idling while four black-clothed men got out, crossed the road, climbed the hill and disappeared out of sight. This was one of Phelim the Ferret's best intelligence gathering teams, acting under orders to get into position before daylight and observe the activity in and around Slaght Orange Hall. They were to make no approach to the target until just after three-thirty, when Phelim's knowledge of British military tactics told him that the SAS would already have their OPs in position and would be concentrating on the road network and buildings in front of them, as the latter became visible in the growing dawn. A prior daytime reconnaissance had come across a derelict hay barn on an old tumbled down, abandoned farm on a hill two hundred metres to the South of the high ground, where Phelim, quite accurately again, expected Mooney's men to dig in, in order to have the best view of the roads and the Orange Hall. The loft of the barn should give adequate coverage of the area, although the intelligence team would not be close enough to make positive identifications of any of the 'players' in the unfolding tragi-comedy.

Phelim had made only one small miscalculation. None of the able operatives he had hand-picked had ever - willingly - been outside of the ghettos of Belfast before, and especially at night, and alone, in a dark and eerie and undeniably alien Protestant countryside; neither had they been Boy Scouts or the like, for the closest these particular four 'hard men' knew about the 'Call of Nature' was having a good shit after a night on the pop. From the closing of the Cortina's doors and the sound of it mournfully accelerating into the distance, all four felt like hitch-hiking virgins who had just thumbed down a bus full of rugby players coming back pissed from the game and well into the bottom half of the third barrel of Newcastle Brown. For just as the aforesaid virgins would realise, once the door of the bus shut closed behind them, the dawn was going to see them with a totally different - and not necessarily pleasanter - outlook on life, and a few aches and pains in areas previously unaccustomed to vigorous exercise. As they waited for their pre-planned time to move forward and into position, they involuntarily shivered, although the night itself was of a gentle and balmy warmth.

At exactly 0035 the two Scouts, which had contoured the land for the last ten minutes, in order to remain unseen and to allow the geographical features to muffle the distinctive sound of their engines, dropped swiftly to the ground in an open field some seven hundred yards Northwest of the cross-roads at Cromkill on the main Antrim Line. Like spectres, four heavily armed figures carrying rucksacks and a variety of sophisticated modern technology rushed from each helicopter and moved off some thirty metres before turning round and giving the thumbs up to the pilots, who were observing them in the dark with the benefit of their night vision goggles. A split second after getting the signal, both helicopters rose fifty feet into the air and sped off at a sharp, nose-down angle to contour back by a different route to some ten minutes from the LP, whence they would rise to one thousand feet and speed back to a hot shower, an egg banjo, and a pint of beer at their base at RAF Aldergrove, prior to commencing packing their tropical kit and awaiting their posting orders to Belize, with the unpleasant prospect of all the concomitant insect life of that zoological cesspool to look forward to with dread.

And at some 1,500 feet and approximately 500 metres to the North of the LP the Alouette of Colonel Mooney circled at the minimum safe speed while the Rat surveyed the scene to his South through a starlight scope. "Must be getting tired," he said to himself. "I'm sure I can see six or seven four man patrols down there! Nonsense. It's a trick of the light, or maybe the batteries in this thing are on the bloody blink." And, after one last look at the darkening countryside, and seeing no addition or deletion to the original number of patrols, he shook his head and turned to the pilot, and said into his microphone, "Okay! Off to the Ranger's HQ in Ballymena and a few hours sleep before dawn." The Alouette banked sharply to its right and headed due North towards the increasingly bright lights of not so beautiful (but a damned sight more attractive in the dark) Ballymena, to join up with the remaining men of D Squadron, who had arrived earlier that evening, some by Puma helicopters which would stay with them for the duration of the operation, and others by specially high performance-engined, cut down, long wheel-base Land Rovers. "Everything," thought the Rat, as the Alouette circled down to a textbook landing on the heli-pad on the parade ground, "is going exactly according to plan." But, as you and I know, fuck all was going anywhere near according to plan out there in no-man's land. And so it was that, as the Rat slipped into a fitful three hours sleep, troubled by phantom patrols popping out of everywhere his customary erotic dreams could take him, the true events of the night were beginning to unfold.

Big Bertie had got himself comfortably into position, bucket of pre-positioned pig-piss (with a fair proportion of liquefied solids, just to give it some 'Oomph') to his side, and was sucking his way through the first layer of a brandy ball, when he heard the sound of someone approaching. "Fucking little shites," he thought to himself. "Didn't wait anywhere near like thirty minutes. Bastards! Well, they'll fucking get what they deserve." And so Big Bertie waited with increasing impatience the arrival of the first patrol of Slaght Young Farmers Unionists, Class of 1980, to appear in the gloom. Slowly, very slowly, he raised his bucket to shoulder height, being careful not to let it slop noisily or smellily over his good self. And sure enough, around the edge of the hedgerow came the first darkened figure. The bucket swung and hit the bugger with full contents right on his open mouth, as he gaped in total astonishment. "But what's this?" said Bertie to himself, as he took off like a rocket along the other side of the hedgerow to his next pre-positioned bucket. "What the hell was that? Looked like a bloody Martian. Good God! All this servicing widows is draining the guts out of me. I'd better start taking it a bit easier. I'm beginning to imagine bogeymen in the dark." And it must have looked like a bogeyman in the dark, to Bertie, but it was only a highly effective trained SAS killer, wearing night vision goggles at the time, and now wearing night vision goggles and a bucket of diluted pig shit, and most incredibly fucking pissed off.

There was a lengthy pause before Big Bertie heard the sound of a twig break some five feet to his front. "Got another of the bastards," he thought to himself with a grin, and raised his bucket, just as Corporal Sticky Dick came silently out of the murk behind him and gave him a karate chop that would have severed his head from his neck, if he hadn't been wearing his best starched Minister's collar, which cushioned the blow. Big Bertie slipped slowly to the ground, but only because Sticky had no intention of letting him, or the bucket, fall noisily and alert any other crazy fuckers who were wandering around in the pitch black with buckets of shit, as part of some incomprehensible and disgustingly weird sort of Celtic initiation rite. And within five minutes Sticky had located another of Bertie's henchmen, complete with associated bucket, and disposed of him in a similar fashion to the good Reverend.

Motioning his own patrol into an ambush position, Sticky waited patiently for any approaching sound. Sure enough, four yokels pretending to be Arnie Schwarzenegger and brandishing a motley collection of shotguns and .22s came tripping up the tree line. Two bucket of pigshite went airborne in a stream all over them, and four rifle butts followed a microsecond afterwards on to the backs of their skulls.

"What the almighty fuck's going on here?" whispered one of the SAS troopers to Sticky. "Beats me. Let's get the fuck out. It's getting late," said Sticky, and Delta 2 made its way tactically - and now even more so - in the direction of their OP position.

Six hundred metres away to the Southwest, and almost in a parallel line to Sticky's Delta 2, moved Lofty's Delta 1. Their first excitement of the night had been to come across four men armed with a strange collection of weapons that must have come out of a Peruvian museum. After quietly removing the said weapons from their owners, and removing the said owners from their senses, they had strung the second patrol of Slaght Young Farmers Club naked by their toes from a convenient oak tree, and moved on. The next excitement was when Lofty walked into the contents of a bucket of pig-piss coming the other way, and was too stunned to avoid it. A brief chase and a couple of grunts later, and a senior member of Big Bertie's flock was strung by barbed wire to a gate and swinging gently to and fro in the night breeze. It was at this point that Lofty held a brief O-Group with his men. "What's going on here lads? I'm fucked if I know!" said a slightly steaming Lofty. "Jeez, Lofty, you don't half fucking honk!" said one of the others. "Looks like Mooney's intelligence is a bit off this time, Lofty," said one of the others. "I agree," said Lofty. "From now on we had better be better than good, otherwise we'll be right in the shit." "You already seem to be, Lofty!" whispered one of the others, who only managed to duck out of the way in time as a haymaker sped straight from the right shoulder towards his nose. "Come on, lads. Let's get to that fucking OP, before it gets light and the whole fucking parish turns out with buckets!"

Two more of Big Bertie's men were walking shoulder to shoulder, and buckets in hand, back down a sunken lane, heading in the direction of the distant Orange Hall, and most disconsolate at not having been able to "get" any of the young lads. "Bit of a waste of time that, eh Arthur?" said one to the other. "Aye, Phil! Must have trained the young buggers too well. Anyway, what the hell are we doing dandering along here like a couple of eejits at two o'clock in the morning wi' buckets of pigshite in our bloody hands. Catch yerself on there, man! We'll chuck them in the bloody dyke." And they did just that, and then strolled on back to a good cup of tea and a cooked breakfast - at which the numbers present would be considerably below expectation - totally oblivious to the fact that they had passed within feet of death at the hands of four armed and highly wanted IRA terrorists, who were now lying apoplectic and covered in pig piss and worse on the other side of the afore-mentioned dyke. These latter four were shortly afterwards seen struggling limpingly up a hill side, and cursing loudly to themselves, by the members of Delta 2, who were beginning to compare Slaght at two o'clock on a summer's morning to Piccadilly Circus at rush hour on any day of the week before Christmas.

But things gradually swung back into a semblance of order, at least on the trained military side, for by three-thirty on the dot both Delta 1 and Delta 2 were dug in four feet underground in excellent OP positions overlooking their respective targets, the McKelvey farm and the Orange Hall, and the routes in and out. The smell of pig-shit on the clothes and bodies of some of their band did not really affect them, other than to cause some comradely banter, for they were all going to begin to smell ripe in the days to come. It was time now for stand-to and to await the arrival of the new day over Slaght. There was a lot of work to be done, that was for sure, to figure out what made this place tick, and, most urgently, to try and come up with something sensible to report to the Rat about last night's bizarre events. None of them had ever experienced anything similar. What the hell was it all about?

As dawn filtered its uncaring pale beams across the townland of Slaght, four filth-covered and exhausted IRA senior intelligence cadres arrived at last at their destination, the dilapidated hay barn overlooking, at a distance of 200 metres, the nearest hill, and, further away, Slaght Orange Hall and where the Twelfth Field was to be. After they had successfully avoided, through none of their own doing and two buckets of shit, their first ever encounter with the SAS, they had suffered further trials and tribulations. And none more so than the unfortunate leader of the gang, one soon-to-be-demised Cathal Fahey, an ex-mill worker and long-time recipient of the beneficence of the state he wished to overthrow.

Our poor Cathal had fallen temporarily foul of a barbed wire fence, which he had subsequently found to be electrified, as the pulse shot through it, just as he was entangling a particularly stubborn barb from the scrotal skin containing his left testicle. Shortly afterwards the unfortunate Cathal had stumbled upon, and slap bang with the right foot into, a gin trap that would have been sufficient to entrap a grizzly bear. It took some considerable pain and deliberation before his associates could figure out how the damn thing worked, and tramp it open to remove his foot. So pleased was Cathal to have the right foot and remains of his smelly hush puppy free and grasped agonisingly (yet astonishingly still attached to his leg) in his two hands, that he began - as is the wont of all good Irishmen on occasions such as these, to dance a celebratory jig. Whereupon his remaining uninjured foot (the left one), complete with a second smelly hush puppy, sprung the bloody gin for a second time. We need not go into the opinions of Cathal and the other three about nettle beds or bramble clumps, and other rural pleasures to which the denizens of city back streets are usually gloriously unaware. Let us just say that all four somehow or other reached the barn, albeit less than unscathed, although they did have a certain pastoral aroma by that time about them.

On entering the barn, just as the first true rays of sunlight were slanting horizontally from the eastern horizon, our four intrepid heroes found themselves in a corrugated iron vault, at the far end of which was a loft which could be reached by a rather dangerous looking and wood-wormed ladder. On the floor of the loft they could make out a bed of mildewed hay, which to them looked like the interior sprung mattress of true Paradise. They staggered - and none more than Cathal - across the derelict building towards the ladder, raising eddies of fine dust in their wake. "There's been no-one here in years, by the looks of it," said one of the gang. "Well, we're only here for fucking twenty-four hours, thank God!" said Cathal. "Shut your fucking gub and get me up that bloody ladder before I die." he added with some feeling in his voice.

With the help of the other three Cathal was gradually aided to the top rung of the ladder, and was about to be hoisted by six willing hands on to the floor of the loft when the rung gave way and the six hands let go. Cathal came to the bottom quickly, to find four of the eight prongs of a previously innocent-looking, ancient wooden hay rake sticking several inches into the right cheek of his arse. "Jasus! Are you all right, Cathal?"

the boys shouted in unison from above. "What the fuck do you think, you gormless bunch of prats!" hissed poor Cathal from below. "It's an everyday bloody occurrence in fucking Leeson Street to be attacked by an agricultural bloody dinner fork, isn't it, you stupid berks?"

"Do you want us to come down and help you, Cathal?" a voice said from above. "No! Definitely not. I'd prefer to fucking bleed to death down here alone. You bunch of useless cunts get on with the job and I'll find a wee cubby-hole down her to hide," answered a not very happy Cathal. "How's yer bum, Cathal?" asked another voice. "Just like my two fucking feet, you stupid twat, red-raw, bleeding and wearing the fucking Purple Heart. Now get on with the job, so that we can get the fuck out of here as soon as it's dark! And after slowly extracting the wooden rake from his posterior, Cathal, much the worse for wear crawled painfully to the far end of the barn and made himself unseen in a cobwebbed corner between some extinct pieces of early twentieth century horse-drawn agricultural machinery.

As he had crawled across the floor of the barn Cathal had raised a considerable maelstrom of dust, which was added to considerably by the movements of his three companions on the loft above, as they made themselves more comfortable for the day than Cathal had any slight hope of doing. As the dust billowed and swirled around poor Cathal, and his henchmen began to discern more clearly their targets across the open fields below, a partial semblance of tranquillity began at last to return to this picturesque and rustic scene. Cathal reached in his pocket for his half bottle and took what he justly considered to be a hefty and purely medicinal slug of best 'John Powers'. The effects of the undiluted liquor were soothing and soporific, and soon Cathal began to drowse. Just as he began to slip into his first good snore, he shook himself awake, and said to himself, "God, Cathal! You'd best be keeping your wits about you today, me boy. No sleeping now. Stay alert!" But the effects of the whiskey and the exertions of the night had been too much for his not-so-well-oiled physical system, and soon he caught himself dozing off yet again.

"God. Another bloody eighteen hours of this purgatory. I'll be like a bloody zombie if I ever make it back to the Falls. I'd better have a cigarette and move about a bit. And so Cathal rose most painfully to his mangled feet and began to shuffle up and down the barn floor, raising more and more billows of the fine dust in his tracks, until the whole vault-like space was like the inside of one of those ornaments that you get at the seaside and which snow over Santa's Cabin or the Eiffel Tower when you turn them upside down and shake them. Cathal got his Number 6 packet out and stuck his first cigarette of the day between his lips. He fumbled in his pockets for his matches and at last found them, a bit the worse for wear after the traumas of the night. He struck a match, and put it to his cigarette, and took a good long and soul-restoring drag - just as the red hot tip of his Number Six, added to the heat of the applied Swan Vestas match, caused the fine dust to ignite with the explosive force of several hundred sticks of gelignite.

Cathal exited across country, in one piece, and passed over a considerable part of the route that he and his companions had crossed only a very few hours previously. He eventually came down to twenty feet from a hard landing, where his fall was miraculously stopped by, firstly, the branches of a sycamore tree, and afterwards the top of an enormous clump of holly waiting for the silly season to bear its little berries. His three companions were less fortunate. They went in three different directions to Cathal and in many different pieces, most of the force of the explosion having directed itself upwards to their rather more comfortable position in the loft. But Cathal wasn't worrying, and wouldn't be for many hours. He was practising to be a late cuckoo, perched as he was on his nest of thorns.

A bleary-eyed, but somewhat refreshed, Colonel Mooney had boarded his refuelled Alouette exactly on 0400 hours, with the intent of making a quick sweep, at altitude, over the townland of Slaght, to ensure that his OPs were in position and that the situation was normal. The first radio-check from Delta 1 and Delta 2 would not be until 0600 hours, and until that time strict radio silence would be observed, unless the OPs were to come under attack or were 'blown' in any way, both of which possibilities the gallant Colonel knew to be highly unlikely. The sky was clearing rapidly of the last cloak of darkness and the sun was, from the height of the Alouette, at least, coming up in a golden semi-circle over the hills between Ballymena and Larne, and the mist was wafting upwards from the green pastures below. "It's a good morning to be a soldier," mused Mooney to himself, and for several brief minutes he reflected on other brave and brilliant dawns he had experienced across the breadth of the civilised and not-so-civilised world, during his two decades before the colours.

The Alouette had reached 500 feet and was fast approaching the North of the village of Slaght when the sky some 400 metres to the front took on a colour more comparable to the furnaces of hell than the dawn's early light. As an incredulous Mooney came back abruptly from his dreams of dawn ambush positions overlooking seemingly innocent, Communist-infiltrated, Malaysian kampongs to the reality of heading at one hundred and fifty miles an hour towards what appeared to be a much less innocent, wood and corrugated iron, rural Ulster barn, coming at five hundred miles an hour directly at him, the helicopter pilot, having been subconsciously attuned to fast reaction to danger by the presence of the searchlights at Hollywood, swung the Alouette over at an angle the manufacturer had never envisaged during wind tunnel tests and attempted frantically to outrun the fast-gaining agricultural structure.

Gravity, fortunately for Colonel Mooney and his panicky pilot, recalled the barn to earth in its now separating individual pieces just moments before the clock tower at Bradbury Lines in Hereford claimed another suitably poignant engraving. As the pilot fought for control over his mount, before it, too, joined the barn in pieces on the fields below, Mooney regurgitated his pork sausage sandwich and coffee breakfast over the Perspex in front of him, and broke out in a sweat so cold that his mighty manhood shrunk to less than normal human proportions within his now urine-stained crotch. Both men were so shaken by what had happened that they did not even notice the horrendous bang, which followed the explosion that had tried to chase them from the sky. At last, however, the pilot recovered control sufficiently to level out the helicopter's attitude and Mooney had got enough of a grip on himself and his bladder to begin to wipe his breakfast off the Perspex and see what the hell had nearly achieved what innumerable terrorist bands across the globe had never had the luxury of even coming close to achieving.

As a pale and still shaken Mooney surveyed the scene below, the good people of Slaght were emerging in confusion from their homes, some of which would need re-roofing before the next rains came in from inimical Catholic Donegal to the West. Within minutes hundreds of local farming folk were making their way cautiously along the roads and lanes that led towards where the Twelfth Field was soon going to be, in order to reach the epicentre of the scene of devastation now spread all around them. Above them the Alouette circled, as Mooney took in certain sinister aspects, which were not known to those on the ground. Firstly, to the due South of where the barn had so recently stood, there appeared to be a corpse nestled in a clump of holly, some fifteen feet or more above the ground. Secondly, on an iron gate some five hundred metres to the Southeast there was yet another apparent corpse. Indeed, this one seemed to have been crucified with barbed wire, if the Colonel's high-powered binoculars did not fail him. Then, in a field a further three hundred metres to the Southeast lay four hog-tied bodies, likewise apparently dead. And finally, a further two hundred metres due East, a group of four bodies were hanging from their toes from a chestnut tree, and a further two bodies likewise dangled head-down from a crab apple tree a few hundred feet away.

"Take her down into that field where the bodies are hanging!" ordered Mooney. He had to repeat the order a further two times and put his hand on his H&K MP5 before the reluctant pilot chose the lesser of two evils and swooped into a non-text book landing in the middle of what appeared to be a recently fertilised pasture, at least by the amount of manure that flew up in the downdraught and coated the slowly swinging bodies not too far away on the tree line. This decision by the Alouette pilot, to endanger his aircraft in a battle zone against all SOPs, was what saved, not him, but Colonel Mooney, from two certain and most definitely fiery deaths to come. But, in the meantime, while the pilot kept the engine running at high revs, Colonel Mooney walked cautiously, cocked MP5 in hand and at the ready, to the side of the field. There he quickly and professionally noted that the first four toe-tied bodies were not, in fact, dead, but were suffering from severe concussions which had been evidently induced by single blows to the back of the head.

"Hmm!" he thought to himself, as he walked across the field to the other two similarly strung bodies. One of these, to his surprise, he noted to be a 'man of the cloth', evidenced by the bloodstained dog collar that was vainly straining to hold a severely bruised and swollen neck onto a bloated head. This one, too, was still somehow alive. And so was the other one swinging nearby. "Bloody strange!" thought the Colonel. "All the hallmarks of my boys, that's for sure. But what the hell did they do this for? Jesus! Don't tell me they've cracked. No! Impossible, too well trained; too disciplined, those lads, to crack. But something must sure as hell have pissed them off fair and proper."

And, without further ado, Colonel Mooney carefully cut down the body of the good Reverend Mulholland and began pouring some life-restoring water from his belt canteen between Big Bertie's swollen lips. After loosening the Reverend's dog-collar and feeding him with as much water as he thought safe under the medical circumstances, the Colonel noticed the first flickerings of consciousness come to his patient's eyes. Big Bertie, in his dreams still wrestling with men from Mars, opened his eyes painfully and, though his sight was still blurred, espied what his brain informed him was a very fit and ferocious looking, murderous, rodent-eyed bastard in camouflaged uniform, brandishing a bloody great dagger in one hand and a bottle of some bitches brew in the other. He was about to pass out again, preferring the Martian invaders to this new monstrosity, when the camouflaged rat smiled and asked, "How do you feel, Reverend?" Now even more confused, Big Bertie was just about to reply, "How the fuck do you think I feel, you bloody eejit!" when the very thought of these words passed from his recollection by the furnace doors of hell opening yet again behind the ogre's head.

Both men were bowled over and over again down the field by a wind of hurricane force, coming to rest in the hedgerow and to lie there helplessly watching the sky grow white and then orange-red above them, before beginning to spiral upwards into an all-too-familiar mushrooming ball of flame. "Jesus! That old cunt MacTavish wasn't joking about the fucking nuke!" were Mooney's last words before the lack of oxygen beneath the fireball caused him to lose consciousness. Big Bertie was still trying to figure out these words and fit them into any sensible reference pattern, when he saw what appeared to be a helicopter come down to a smooth landing in the tree above him. Well! As smooth as helicopters normally land in trees, when they are upside down.

Now, in case you may be wondering what happened this time, let me take you back to the scorched patch of earth some seven hundred metres or so away, where once there had stood an ancient barn. The barn, which had appeared to have been unused for years by the inexpert townie eyes of the late deceased IRA team from Belfast, those same men who had taken such brief and yet comfortable shelter there from the light of day and the eyes of their enemies, had been *meant* to look derelict. The barn was, at least to several seconds ago, and indeed had previously been for some fifteen years, the secret storage facility of one of mid-Ulster's greatest non-Nobel Prize chemists, none other than Jock Allen, whose prowess in the arcane field of triple distillation of potato spirit (or 'poteen' as it is more customarily called in Ireland) was unequalled, at least within the Six Counties.

Prior to the celebration of the Glorious Twelfth of July each year, Jock would work eighteen hours a day, seven days a week (never mind the Sabbath, this is God's work!), to prepare a sufficient quantity of high quality moonshine to supply several thousand normally pleasant family men with an adequate degree of fiery rabidity to seal their commitment to Protestant hegemony for yet another twelve dreary months of rain and less potent alcohol. By a sufficient quantity was meant at least 1,500 gallons! This prodigious amount of poteen, enough to kill at least 150,000 teetotallers, render unconscious 25,000 twenty-five year olds, invigorate 20,000 alcoholics, and induce to murder 12,000 Orangemen, was lovingly distilled under cover of darkness in a number of clandestine operations scattered throughout the extensive peat bogs to the West of Kellswater and the Southwest of Slaght. Because of the vulnerability of the stills to capture by a thirsty and venal Constabulary, each triple-distilled batch of *usquebaugh* was transported to the ex-barn and stored in a large under ground cellar, access to which had been easily attained by a wooden trapdoor lying concealed beneath a carpet of highly explosive straw dust.

After the barn had gone airborne in the search for Colonel Mooney's helicopter at a few minutes after four o'clock that morning, a small

fire had remained to commemorate the site of the deaths of Cathal
Fahey and the three unknown soldiers of his valiant band. In the light
morning breeze the small fire had come across the wooden trapdoor
and began to feed hungrily on the latter, there being little else left at
the scene of culinary interest. After some fifteen minutes of palatable
but rather paltry rations the fire found its way, to its considerable
astonishment, but subsequently equally considerable excitement, into
a cavernous underground compartment, stacked high with hundreds
of Cantrell & Cochranes lemonade bottles, all full of a slightly viscous
and definitely non-carbonated liquid. Its curiosity aroused, our little fire
sent out a tongue of flame to see whether this intriguing liquid could be
of a thirst-quenching nature.

The tongue of flame first of all sampled the remains of several bottles
that had been broken in the blast of the barn above. "Nice!" remarked
the flame, and reported back to headquarters on the door above. And
so the fire decided to take a look for itself and went down into the
cellar. "Oh my! Oh my! Oh my!" fire exclaimed to no one in particular.
"What have we found here, my little beauty.?" And with that our little
fire sent other flames to lick around the 150 proof spirit, and since there
weren't enough dregs to go round everyone, fire started to crack open
an extra bottle or too. The cellar filled with the most delicious aroma
of pure alcohol fumes. And so fire fed on with ecstatic delight and grew
bigger and bigger, until the pressure in the cellar was just at that right
point for fire to explode to five thousand feet and fuck off over mid-
Antrim in a ball of cataclysmic flame. As fire ejaculated heavenwards,
his ecstasy became sublime, because as an unexpected main course he
was able to have Cajun-style, black roast Protestant, the vanguard of
the local farming folk having just at that time reached the site of the
newly relocated barn!

An awesome silence reigned over Slaght and its environs for some minutes,
broken only by the crackling of flames as the dry grass in the hedgerows
caught fire and - eventually - by the moans of those not yet dead and the
growing screams of those still very much alive. Shielded from the worst
of both recent blast-waves, and just regaining consciousness on account
of having been twice deprived of essential oxygen within the space of
thirty minutes, Lofty and his three companions, in their subterranean

fall-out shelter, surveyed the scene around them and inwardly cursed themselves for not having brought gas masks and NBC suits. All around them were bits of barn and a fine spray of broken glass. To their front, down by the road, were the dead and the dying, in suitably impressive numbers, even for people as accustomed to mass death as are the SAS. It was a charnel house.

Lofty drew a long breath and exhaled an equally long and tortured, "Well! Fuck me!" "What are we going to do, Lofty?" asked one of his companions. "Shouldn't we get out and help those poor people, for pity's sake?" "Yes, we should," replied Lofty, "but we are not going to do a bloody thing until we get the hold of the Rat and find out what the fuck he thinks is going on here, for I, as sure as hell, haven't got a bloody clue. Geordie! Try and raise him on the radio!" But no amount of calling was going to raise the Rat - at least not for the moment. "Try and get Delta 2, Geordie!" ordered an increasingly concerned Lofty. But Delta 2 had their own problems, and answering a fucking radio check was certainly not one of them!

Sticky and his boys had moved successfully into their hide on the hedgerow that overlooked the McKelvey farm and had just begun to get a good view of the dunghill in the growing light of dawn when an armless and legless corpse flew just over their hide and landed head down in the midden, to be followed directly afterwards by one of the missing legs and what looked like the working parts of a pre-war combine harvester. The bang that then ensued had done little to reduce their surprise! They were only half way through a torturous attempt to stop the ringing in their ears and figure out what the hell was going on when somebody obviously set off a 50 kiloton nuclear explosion in a neighbouring distillery, because for several minutes the sky rained glass and intact bottles on the roof of their hide and all over the field in front of them. This time, fortunately, there appeared to be no accompanying body parts, although Delta 1 would have soon corrected them on that point, had they not been at that very moment engaged in trying to find enough oxygen to live on for a wee while longer.

Delta 2 had been saved by their location from the horrors facing Delta 1. But their own special problem was sneaking up on them along the hedgerow, as 150 proof spirit Molotov cocktails ignited the grass and hawthorn bushes and a towering wall of flame began to encircle the hide. "What do we do now, Sticky?" said one of the troopers. "Well, we sure as hell can't stay here and be fried," said Sticky, no longer his usual taciturn self. "I don't know about you lot, but I think it's time we found another OP, and fucking quick!" And with that Sticky and the four of them scrabbled out of their hole in the ground and fought their way through the growing conflagration into the billowing white smoke that was now streaming downhill towards the McKelvey farm. At the bottom of the hill, and still under cover of the smoke, they dashed into an old thatched cottage, converted to a winter byre for animals, struggled under their mountain of gear into the loft and lay there, chests and minds heaving. All thoughts of stand-to had passed. It was survival now that counted, not what the fucking Army told you to do, because the 'fucking Army' had never trained you to expect to face *Apocalypse* bloody *Now* in Ireland all by yourself and without Mummy there to cuddle you!

As they lay there in that euphoric state beyond panic, they heard the faint sound of Geordie coming through on the headset of the radio. "Delta 2, over," said a shaky-voiced Sticky. "We can't seem to contact Sunray, Delta 2," said an equally shaky-voiced Geordie. "Maybe its the EMP effect," replied Sticky and added, "What the almighty fuck's going on here?" "We haven't a bloody clue, Delta 2. First that barn on Hill 301 took off into the air, and the next thing we know is fucking Hill 301 takes off after the fucking barn! There's at least twenty or thirty dead and dying civilians lying about three hundred metres in front of us. How the hell we lived I don't fucking know! Over."

"We had a stiff, minus a couple of bits, fly over us just before the first bang. Then we were petrol-bombed or something and had to get the hell out before we applied for a Kentucky Fried Chicken franchise. We're now in a building fifty metres Southwest of Red 1. We are in a position to set up HF and see if we can get through to the *real* outside world. Call you back in ten. Out." And Sticky and his men immediately set to work to rig their HF antenna along the rafters of the converted cottage and attempt to get through to Hollywood and/or Hereford. Fifteen minutes later, Sticky was on the radio again to Delta 1, informing them that

Mooney and his helicopter had gone mysteriously off both the air and the radar screen, ominously just about the time of the second explosion. Delta 1 and Delta 2 were to take no further action, other than routine observation, until either Colonel Mooney and the helicopter turned up, or they were ordered to exfiltrate after dark that night.

And where was the gallant Colonel? Just where we left him, of course. And there he will remain in unconscious peace until we need his input for a subsequent calamity!

CHAPTER EIGHT

When the shock of the first explosion hit Slaght, Mary McKelvey was in her kitchen, putting the finishing touches to the first part of her plan of revenge against Big Bertie Mulholland, and all that he and his kind represented to her devious but simplistic mind. Mary was hard at work at the old pine table, sewing black sergeant's stripes on to a cloth slide that would slip on to the shoulder tab of the British Army disrupted pattern camouflage jacket worn by the newly recruited, trained, and instantly promoted, Sergeant Ignatius Aloysius Moriarty of the 2nd Battalion The Parachute Regiment. Sergeant Moriarty, for his part, was busily engaged in what was for him a totally new experience, bulling a pair of second-hand DMS boots. Ignatius was in seventh heaven. Not only was Mrs. McKelvey grooming him in preparation for his acceptance by Ulster Protestantism as something other than an ambulatory and alcoholic freak show, she had also put him through a 72 hour condensed 'P Company', the quality of which would have rendered the staff of any military training department apoplectic with jealousy.

Mary had found that Ignatius was capable of a pain threshold that would have seen him through the very worst physical and mental tortures that the military mind considers 'character building'. This miraculous aptitude was undoubtedly due to a combination of centuries of inbreeding, as well as, it must be admitted, recent practical training at the hands of Sergeant Simpson, and anyone else who could get a thwack at the bastard, before Fate inevitably intervened on Moriarty's side. It certainly had little to do with the intellectual capability of the rough material that Mary had at her disposal! But then, a good soldier is better off without a brain. The British Army has always found that educated idiocy, defined by the dictionary as 'profound mental retardation', but recognised by the Ministry of Defence as 'officer material', is best left to those with plums in their mouths. 'Anal retentiveness', another requirement for those wishing to join the General Staff, was certainly not one of our Sergeant Moriarty's talents. His famed ability to shit himself at the drop of a fart would have immediately precluded him from passing any Regular Commissions Board!

For the past three days and nights, while not neglecting his studies in the complexities of Lambeg drum rhythms, Moriarty had undergone repeated instruction in drill, dressing (in uniform, that is, not what you may immediately have thought), fire and manoeuvre, weapon handling, explosive ordnance, ambush techniques, resistance to interrogation, garrotting, bayoneting, unarmed combat, vehicle maintenance, patrolling, sentry duties, and field cooking. About the only things in the military repertoire that he had not been introduced to were NBC warfare, combat survival in desert and jungle theatres, and battle inoculation. But Mary had every intention that Moriarty would be able to complete his military education in some, if not all, of these subjects before she no longer had any use for him. She had several times admitted to herself, however, that Moriarty was potentially the most efficient military machine that she had ever come across; and quite a few muscular military machines had come across her, and vice versa, in recent years, prior to her dyke-bashing session at Guildford and her subsequent flight to safe haven, pre-season training at Liverpool Football Club, and that fateful meeting with the short-term love of her life, Mike McKelvey, that passionate, perverted, big-dicked man, whose sudden roller coaster departure from comforting her loins she was now about to avenge. In the meantime, Mary revelled in the fury of the first explosion at Hill 301, and positively purred with satisfaction at the imagined destruction of its thermo-nuclear successor. It sounded as if someone else was in sympathy with her plans to reduce Bertie Mulholland's parish to ashes.

"But how", you may be asking yourselves, "does the bastard offspring of a tinker's daughter and a Roman Catholic Cardinal know so much of 'things military' to be able to produce a two-legged killing machine out of a beast-shagging mental dwarf from Celtic twilight zone Kellswater, in the space of time that it normally takes a Company Sergeant Major to teach a raw recruit how to tie his putties, salute with the right hand, and jack himself off by numbers?" Well, you had the clue long ago in Chapter 3, but then, being the dirty little wanker you are, you were probably too interested in the *positioning* of the evidence at that time, rather than in its significance for the future. To save time I had better spell it out for you. *"**Mea Culpa: Lourdes 1978**"*.

Shortly after the eventful night which culminated in Tinker Tom O'Flaherty expanding his arsehole by algebraic proportion, Mary had dressed herself in the most modest finery she could steal in Marks and Spencers, and had successfully secured a private interview with the aged Cardinal O'Shea, by dint of much pleading with a succession of Catholic bureaucrats, and assisted by a letter that promised to reveal all to the 'News of the World'. As a result of that interview, at which no other person was naturally present, Cardinal O'Shea made several frantic telephone calls to the Royal Army Chaplains Department and proceeded to use his own little 'black book' to secure the assistance, by downright blackmail, of the majority of the Catholic padres who had not yet been exposed as satyrs, poofs or pederasts by the gutter press.

Not many weeks later a smiling Mary was inducted into the Womens Royal Army Corps on a Special Regular Commission and began to pursue her childhood ambition of being able to drink and swear like a trooper without anyone looking askance at her for so doing. Of course, she also put her not inconsiderable talent to mastering all the other accepted skills of the WRAC, but she added to the latter many of a much more 'manly' type, that even the most moustachioed and gruff-voiced of the Corps' dykes had shunned, such as long distance running, sniping, free-fall parachuting, rock climbing, locksmithing, escaping from submerged submarines, and beating the shit out of lieutenants from line infantry regiments on dark nights outside the Roundabout Club in dreary Aldershot. Along the way she racked up a Queen's Gallantry Medal for saving the lives of a boat load of Royal Marines, who found that their ability to swim under the influence of two bottles of Navy rum apiece was as non-existent as their ability to steer their landing craft to a watery grave, in millpond seas, and on a bright moonlit night off Beachy Head, had proven second to none. Throw in a couple of first prizes at Bisley, a ready and regular acquiescence in giving the GOC Southeast District a 'bloody good blow-job, eh what!' and the captaincy of the WRAC tug-o-war team that humiliatingly thrashed the long-reigning Army champions, the Parachute Regiment, (and even more shamefully drank the useless bastards under the table in the 'boat race' afterwards), and, to say the least, it was not long before certain people in uncertain high places began to notice Lieutenant McKelvey.

It was thus that our Mary, just promoted Captain, and the youngest one ever in the history of the WRAC, found herself part of a highly classified unit of attractive young fillies, finely tuned to an impressive degree of perfection in a variety of skills that were hardly likely to enamour them to prospective husbands, were any such brave suitors ever to dare tread the sinister forbidden paths leading to the 'chocolate speedway', with malice aforethought in their eyes and the Vaseline on the bedside table. Mary and three other girls found themselves undergoing a special training course in an old Elizabethan hunting lodge, lost somewhere near Oxford. The course consisted of various methods of clandestine entry, most sophisticated instruction in silent and noisy assassination techniques, and hetero/non-heterosexual seduction methodologies which would have tickled the Marquis de Sade's flaccid penis bright pink. This latter subject included such wonders as 'rapid cardiac infarction through reverse inflationary fellatio', 'achieving ejaculation through the anal insertion of various foreign bodies', 'safe auto-eroticism and ending the problems of the impotent male', 'emergency digital extraction of super-greased, vaginally-inserted Japanese balls in threat situations', 'the non-lethal application of the Egyptian camel whip to the male gonadic hyper-erogenous zone without immediate loss of consciousness' and 'sodomy and buggery: their not-so-subtle differences explained in historical context, with reference to Royal Navy experience'.

As you may have guessed, Mary and her colleagues soon found themselves to be the expendable, front shafts of one of those magnificent deniable operations, planned by the drunken loonies of MI6, over Happy Hour behind the grime-encrusted windows of the bar on the top floor of their ivory tower South of the Thames. The Secret Intelligence Service, as it is correctly termed - although sometimes the secrets are very subtle paraphrases of interesting newspaper articles with a bit of what the trade calls 'padding'; the intelligence is not normally immediately obvious to anyone above Western Australian second form primary school education; and the service is always comparable to that of the world-renowned catering on any British Rail static or mobile salmonella-dispensing buffet - is famous for its conception of operations of a brilliance that never fails to awe its American and Russian counterparts and to confuse the hell out of the meek mandarins of Whitehall.

This one was code-named, '**LICKER**', and relied, for its success, on a degree of implausibility normally reserved for Walt Disney Productions – but why should those waspish, right wing, Yankee-fucking-doodling, American bastards think they have an exclusive right to the production of lurid fantasy? MI6 can conceive and execute works of genius and art far beyond the wildest dreams of virginal Snow White's sexless creators - and on a fraction of the budget, unless some other bloody Department like the Ministry of Ag. and Fishheads can be conned into forking out a budgetary fortune for gin and tonic for the boys; and without getting caught, if at all possible, although sometimes that has proven to be a teensy-weensy wee bit embarrassingly difficult; and behind the backs of those willy-watchers in the Effing CO, and those anaemic, self-appointed pseudo-vampires, and constipated pencil-up-the-arse-whingeing mathematicians in the bloody Treasury; and with brain-dead, non-working but most undeniably lower class, Labour Prime Ministers in blind and total ignorance of the truth, and lying unknowingly up to their teeth in the House of Commons; and without the need to preen and prance about the corridors of power and on the bloody telly every night, saying, 'look what a good boy am I', like all the fucking grey wasters in the murky ministries of public disasters, lack of bleeding culture, and 'it's always someone else's fault, not ours' non-accountability lurking in the cheap, cigar-smoke smog of so-called 'gentlemen's' club land North of the Thames!

No way, Sir! SIS would have had the bloody, simple-minded, virgin gang-banged by all seven dwarves in succession, and without the need of some silly old crone rendering the bitch unconscious with a Mickey-finned apple! For when MI6 gets its slack-jawed, halitosised teeth into a 'Code-named Operation', you can be bloody sure that the outcome will scare the pants off those idea-impoverished, rent-a-gay-a-day, same-old-same-old, dangly-dicked, chicken-littles in Disneyland. It's even rumoured that Leonard Bernstein had once formally requested the Queen herself for permission to put the 'Sixth Man' to music, but the Minister of State for the bloody Arts wouldn't allow it, on the grounds that, 'British moles were a protected species and, anyway, the KGB could be expected to sue, and to demand that they had prior copyright on the sorry affair!' And a good thing, too, otherwise a whole generation of British spies would have joined the brain drain and headed West to seek their fortunes in Hollywood; just as at least half of the previous generation had headed East to spend theirs.

OPERATION LICKER was one of a series of ingenious failures, designed to bring about the demise of as many members as possible of the Provisional Army Council of the IRA. Intelligence had been received from a usually unreliable MI6 source in Dundalk in the Republic of Ireland, that the PAC would be taking their 1978 annual vacation in Lourdes in Southern France, where the presence of hundreds of thousands of good Catholics on pilgrimage would enable them to have a good time without raising suspicion from either the intelligence services of the Western world, or from their wives, who would naturally not be accompanying them. Unfortunately for the 'boyos', the usually unreliable MI6 source in Dundalk was on this occasion unusually accurate, as much to his surprise as, subsequently, to theirs. To complicate matters even further, the top leadership of the other Catholic terrorist organisations in Europe, the Red Brigades from Italy, Action Directe from France and the Spanish Basque separatists of ETA, had likewise, and all too fortuitously, decided to holiday in Lourdes during the same fortnight.

So you can imagine the delight on all sides, when the Irish, Italians, Spaniards and the French all found themselves in town at the same time, in the same hotel and with exactly the same thing on their minds. Yes, you've guessed it! They were in Lourdes to make eye-boggling, knee-trembling love, not war. The **LICKER** girls had set themselves up in a rented house a couple of miles from the grotto, and were already getting in a lot of practice, servicing half the Catholic priesthood, by the time the word leaked to the assembled terrorists that a good time was to be had by all at the Villa de Plaisir. On the fateful night in question the walls of the Villa were shaking to the rhythm of bawdy singing, to the accompaniment of a combo of Mexican eunuchs, and the floors and foundations were moaning and groaning to the rhythm of the dreaded, two-arsed demi-devil, and all was building up to the point where the **LICKER** girls were about to introduce the assembled heads of Terror Inc. to the ultimate ecstasy, namely, 'death-throe peristalsis', when all went very, very wrong - as is the norm in well-planned MI6 operations throughout the centuries, since Queen Elizabeth first set up the service in order to find out whether Philip of Spain would be any good between the sheets. Well, as you are probably aware, the result of that first operation was the Spanish Armada, and **LICKER** was not in any way specifically intended to improve on that *piece de fuck-up*.

Unfortunately for all concerned, the usually unreliable MI6 source in Dundalk had had a massive and previously unwonted attack of conscience at 'shopping' his mates, and had rushed to confession in St. Mary's in Newry Street, where confessor of the day was Father Brendan O'Houlihan, probably the only priest in Ireland that summer's morning, who was not either bent as a clothes hanger, or working full time on perfecting the remote controlled bomb. Father O'Houlihan listened with considerable professional interest to the usually unreliable MI6 source before telling him to say twenty Hail Marys, and to get the fuck out of Ireland before any of the 'boyos' came back alive from pilgrimage and cut his bloody throat.

The good Father had taken a professional interest in what he had been told, because he, too, was not just what he seemed. Father O'Houlihan was a senior operative in the Vatican Thought Police, otherwise known as the 'Pope's Peepers". The very idea, that leading members of the community were using the sacred pilgrimage to Lourdes for an orgy of satyristic perversion, was anathema to O'Houlihan, and he lost no time in returning to his cell, flagellating himself with considerable and pleasurable vigour for half an hour, and composing a coded ham radio message to Monsignor Minelli, his feared and, some would say, fiendish superior in Rome. Monsignor Minelli had alerted his 'Vatican vice squad', borrowed the Pope's Canadair Challenger executive jet, with its pink upholstery and mirrored ceiling, and sped through the balmy summer air to the military airfield at the French *'Paras'* training depot and headquarters at Pau, not far from Lourdes, the latest French addition to a long history of nationally-approved, urban planned, modern-day Sodom and Gomorrahs. Minelli enlisted the support of the Commandant at Pau, who selected a platoon of his nastiest warriors, and the whole caboodle, red-bereted and black-breveted, armed to the teeth with Psalters, crucifixes, and sub-machine guns, raced into Lourdes and drew up in front of the Villa de Plaisir, in a cloud of dust and a screeching of unoiled Renault brakes, to all intents and purposes looking like the extras in the filming of 'Exorcist 7'. The *paras,* promised absolution by Minelli for anything-and I mean 'anything' - that they might have to do once inside the building, leapt from their vehicles with an enthusiasm rarely seen in active service, unless when attacking an enemy-held brewery.

The door to the house of wet dreams was blown open, unfortunately just as the MI6 'madam', an elderly senior officer who wore women's clothes, off-duty and, when required, on operations, and who walked in that funny mincing, hen-toed, ostrich-like way that only old Etonians or Conservative Party politicians do when wearing high heels, was unlocking it, in order to greet the next group of panting, one-horned, philanderers. Madame Blenkinsop, as he was known in the spy trade, was shredded like coleslaw in the blast, but died happy in the knowledge that, at long last, he had been involved in an operation that had not only stayed within budget, but, in fact, had realised a tidy profit already, and if allowed to continue for another month would enable the Chief to tell the Treasury and the Effing CO to 'stuff it up their jacksies' and declare UDI.

In the mayhem that followed the French *paras* slew the members of Action Directe to a man, just because they were French and had been enjoying themselves; castrated the Italians of the Red Brigades because the greasy wop bastards had had the downright effrontery, and the unforgivable lunatic audacity, even to think of fucking women on French soil; released the terrified ETA leaders, not only because they couldn't understand a damn thing the Basques were saying, but also because it was a matter of French Government policy and pride to assist ETA where possible, just to 'fuck up those castanet-clacking Dagos in Madrid', who were forever futilely trying to put a stop to a very lucrative smuggling operation along the Pyrenees, for which ETA's brand of terrorism was but a loose 'cover'. The Irish, who had been the original target, had the living daylights beaten out of them and were handed over to Monsignor Minelli and his inquisitors for what they were told would be 'special treatment'. When they saw Minelli's stern countenance and the flails in the hands of the Vatican vice squad, the Irish pleaded unsuccessfully with the *paras* that they wanted to be castrated like the Italians. But the *paras*, seeing the look in the Monsignor's eyes, and having yet another important and urgent task to fulfil, limited their compliance to the IRA's request by kicking all of them sharply in the balls. And as the sound of the descending flails and the shrill voice of the wrath of an Italian wop God began to fill the gaudy front parlour of the Villa de Plaisir, the *paras* raced upstairs to complete their part of the Monsignor's bargain.

The girls were rounded up and raped, as you might have expected, but the **LICKER** ladies had been fucking well prepared by their MI6 training, and they gave as good as they got, to their distinct personal pleasure and to the incredulous surprise of the *paras*, who hadn't been screwed like this since they believed Washington's promises that the United States Air Force would come to their aid at Dien Bien Phu. When the exhausted *paras* at last departed for Pau, and a well-deserved and much-needed R & R, Monsignor Minelli, his work of chastising the Provisional Army Council now complete, turned his attention to saving the souls of these poor unfortunates, who had obviously been forced into a life of prostitution by some evil procurer of the white slave trade.

Dismissing immediately the **LICKER** ladies' tale that they were undercover operatives for the British Secret Intelligence Service, which Minelli, in his privileged position as Chief Peeper to the Papacy, knew to be an organisation full of queers and incompetents, and therefore totally unfitted to conceptualising and successfully arranging a meeting of the leaders of Europe's principal terrorist organisations in a brothel in Lourdes during pilgrimage time, the good Monsignor told the girls to get sluiced out and dressed, in order that he could give them confession and put them on the way to the straight and narrow.

And so it came to pass that our Mary, still throbbing with the pleasures of the previous twenty-four hours, and thinking of taking a short break in Pau on her way back to debriefing in London, in order to check out the other three regiments of paras that she had not yet had the satisfaction of servicing, found herself in the confessional and receiving a stern dressing down by the good Monsignor, who proved to be the biggest and hardest prick that she had met so far in the upper echelons of the Catholic Church. But as the secrets of the confessional are sacrosanct, I leave it to you to figure out how Minelli led poor Mary up the straight and narrow garden path.

Monsignor Minelli, pulling up his sackcloth underpants, patted our Mary on the cheeks of her bare behind and said, "*Cara mia*, you are to imprint on your mind for all time the words '*Mea culpa*' and forever remember the sinful year of 1978 in Lourdes." And with that Minelli and the Vatican vice squad, beatifically smiling, left four satisfied young English maidens to divide their takings and report back to an MI6 headquarters, which would in no way be surprised at their failure to achieve the object of the Operation, but would be content in the thought that they had at last got rid of that 'bloody useless old faggot, Madame Blenkinsop'; that they had not gone over the budget misappropriated from an unsuspecting Ministry of Lack of Energy; and that the French and the Italians had got exactly what should always be coming to them. While sojourning for a short time in Pau, prior to returning to an old Elizabethan hunting lodge, lost somewhere near Oxford, Mary, who had admired the tattoos on the penis of a particularly fine specimen of French *para* senior NCO manhood, decided to follow the dictates of her recent well-endowed confessor. She wasn't daft, however, our Mary. There was no bloody way she was going to have her brain tattooed, that was for sure! She'd have it done at the scene of the crime, as it were, on the bumpy bit, just above where the *para* NCO's 'Chattanooga Choo Choo Tennessee' tattooed express had entered her Simplon Tunnel.

Now all would have been well, and those who had survived their hours of pleasure and pain in the Villa de Plaisir would have lived on in total anonymity until the next time they were caught, if only that useless limp-dick, Madame Blenkinsop, had done his job properly, and waited until after he had retrieved the tape recordings before getting his petticoats shredded to smithereens by a formerly solid, provincial French, oak door, ably assisted by four pounds of shaped-charge *plastique*. But then, even in death the incompetence of the average MI6 officer is straight out of 'Ripley's Believe it or Not'. Just before the arrival of the French emergency services (and, by God, you don't ever want to require assistance from that bunch of frog-eating ghouls!), the combo of Mexican eunuchs, finding themselves abandoned and unpaid in a town with more than its fair share of ball-less wonders for that time of year, decided it was only right that they should capitalise on their involvement in *'l'Affaire de Lourdes'*, as it was soon to be known, retrieved the incompetent shredded wheat Blenkinsop tapes, and immediately telephoned 'Paris Match' from the pay telephone in the nearest cafe.

When this scurrilous rag subsequently published a highly non-expurgated account of *'l'Affaire de Lourdes'*, complete with thirty colour photographs, the Chief of MI6 was not the first to realise that the *'chat'* was out of the fucking *'sac'*, and that the *'merde'* had yet again splattered into the old proverbial. Immediate damage assessment and control was carried out, at which the Service was truly incomparably expert after nearly five hundred years. The old Elizabethan hunting lodge, lost near Oxford, was shuttered and boarded up and put on the market before it could possibly be 'found', and the **LICKER** ladies were paid off from the slush fund (misappropriated from the Department of Health and Social Insecurity's budget for closing down public health before Maggie got in and did a better job of it) and returned to their units. And it was back in the showers at Guildford, where the dyke brigade had incautiously tried to get a closer look at what was written on Mary's shaven frontal nether regions and, perhaps, give **OP LICKER** a more physical connotation, that a fracas ensued and soon ended with the dyke brigade reduced in strength to a section-minus, and Mary forced through multiple justified homicide to flee the scene.

The 'Paris Match' article, repeated throughout the world, with the exception of the Republic of Ireland, the United Kingdom and the

Vatican, where sensible press censorship laws exist, caused some minor problems for the empty scrotumed gentlemen of the Red Brigades, who would never again be accused of fucking with anyone's sister. Rather more serious problems awaited the *senors* from ETA who were met by their wives as they infiltrated across a mountain pass in the Pyrenees into their Basque homeland, with yet another smuggled shipment of French engine coolant to tart up the year's vintage. Fortunately, however, they were saved from an immediate and very messy death by the arrival of the Spanish Army, who later on shot them all for 'attempting a mass escape from custody', while handcuffed, hog-tied, and swinging from plum trees by the neck. The real excitement happened at Scotland Yard, however, where a still disbelieving Commissioner of the Metropolitan Police took the formal surrender of the complete Provisional Army Council, who were accompanied by a UNHCR official to assist them in putting forward their case for political asylum. Thirty years apiece on Tristan Da Cunha was obviously what the 'boyos' considered eminently preferable to a return to the hearthside at Inishfree! Unfortunately, in a land like Ireland, where every man considers himself a leader, the shower of shite at Scotland Yard's surrender ceremony that morning was soon replaced by another bunch of loonies.

"And what about the other participants in *'l'Affaire de Lourdes'*?" you may well ask. The Commandant at Pau, as is the custom when sexual scandals occur in France, was appointed Minister of Defence, and went on to mastermind the destruction of his nation's greatest enemy, Greenpeace. At the new Minister of Defence's express order the platoon of *paras,* who had assisted the papal legate in *'l'Affaire de Lourdes'* was transferred overnight to Aubagne and the Foreign Legion, and the following morning to Mururoa Atoll, where they were to spend the remainder of the Minister's life sunning their bums and screwing the locals, with as much *vin ordinaire* and Kronenbourg as they could consume per day, and twice as much on *Camerone.*

Monsignor Minelli would have been transferred by the Pope to urgent pastoral duties in Teheran, but was saved at the last moment by a private showing of some home movies, which had such an electrifying effect on the His Holiness, that for while it seemed they would have to get the old smoke signals ready again in the Vatican. Cardinal Minelli, as he is now ranked, is a director of several banks, and continues to deny involvement in the 'P2 affair'. The intrepid members of the vice squad were last heard of attending a head-hunters' convention deep in the forests of Papua New Guinea. And last, but not least, the combo of Mexican eunuchs now have French citizenship and are appearing nightly at the Crazy Horse Saloon in Paris, wearing only guitars and maracas.

So now you know - -at last - why Big Bertie Mulholland's eyes lit up at the sight of Mary 'the fucking Fenian bitch' McKelvey's pudendum. And you also understand why our Mary was able to teach Ignatius all 'things military' with a professionalism that was commendable. "But what," you are still asking yourselves, no doubt, "is the bloody woman up to? Patience, dear friends, patience! All will shortly be revealed, but in the meantime we should find out what the others in this tale have been getting up to while we temporarily visited the corridors of British power by way of a British-staffed, French brothel and some latter-day hanky-panky in the Vatican.

CHAPTER NINE

We left the unconscious Colonel Mooney in the arms of a rodent-phobic Reverend Mulholland, under a tree of as yet unspecified species, in a hedgerow at the bottom of a shite-strewn pasture, at or round about five o'clock on a wonderful mid-Summer's morning in picturesque rural mid-Ulster. It is now five-thirty, or as the Rat would have put it, 0530 hours, and we must quickly hasten back to this bucolic scene. The tree, by the way, was a sycamore tree, but not the same one under which was a clump of holly embracing the insensate body of one Cathal Fahey, very soon to be 'late' of the Belfast Brigade, Provisional IRA.

On the dot, therefore, at 0530 hours, a few short but action-packed days before the Glorious Twelfth of July, a befuddled SAS Colonel came slowly to his senses with a strange ringing and whooping in his ears. (These bizarre sounds were produced rather less by his severe concussion and rather more by the vanguards of the Emergency Fire and Ambulance services arriving at the scene of *Apocalypse* bloody *Now*, just a few fields away to the North.) The Rat opened his eyes with painful slowness - and then shut them in horrified disbelief, having, to his confused and concussed brain, found himself in an obviously passionate embrace with a male (first time in his life since that unfortunate night he had got drunk on something that tasted like goat piss in Sharjah), and, worse, a gentleman of the cloth, who had apparently been a practitioner of 'golden showers' and an aficionado of 'Cadbury's limp-wristed 99s', at least going by the aroma and the evidence of at least two middens worth of excreta spread over the *corpus*, not yet, unfortunately, *delicti*, of the pseudo-religious sexual pervert!

Opening his eyes again the gallant Colonel, swearing with every fibre of his soul that he solemnly and sincerely promised not to tread forbidden paths again, drunk or sober, in the line of duty or without, espied a strange sight in the greenery above him. No, it was not a pterodactyl laying eggs in its aerie, although he could have been excused for thinking so; neither was it the Ancient Mariner's albatross perched in the rigging and taking a peaceful, but constipated, shit on the doomed and surly deckhands below. As his brain kicked into a virtually stripped first gear, the Rat realised that he was having the pleasure of a rather rare view of a sub-species of the genus 'helicopter', in other words, a fucking Alouette, hanging upside down in the branches of a bloody sycamore tree, with that useless prat of a sergeant-pilot of the Army Air Corps, dangling like a wet pair of distended long johns from his seat harness, half way in, and also half way out of where the pilot's side door had previously been.

While the Rat was trying to put this vision into a more logical geological context, without having to succumb to constant imagery from the Pleistocene or any other bloody era, Big Bertie Mulholland was struggling to become compost mentis, but was having some not inconsiderable difficulty in breathing through a mouthful of AVGAS, which was beginning to dilute his previous ingestion of half a gallon of poteen bomb and rotor-driven pig shit. Now the AVGAS, sustenance for latter-day pterodactyls, was dripping, drip, drip, drip, from a ruptured, reptilian, at present - and for a brief time only - non-airborne fuel tank above both befuddled figures, and if they didn't come to their senses or some form of realisation of the parlous reality of the situation quickly, the remainder of this tale must, through force of circumstances, be drastically fore-shortened.

"Where's my fucking radio?" swore the Rat at no-one immediately identified as consciously present, and staggered around the lower half of the field stamping his feet like a little boy in the throes of an almighty temper tantrum. "Where's my fucking radio?" he shouted again, thereby allowing the brain of the Reverend Mulholland to focus on something vaguely familiar, namely, the sexually explicit vernacular. "Where's my sodding, fucking, bloody radio?" went the third distress call, the one, in fact, that galvanised the good Reverend to the nearest to sanity he was to reach from now until the end of our tale. "Jesus Christ! Where's my fucking, hell and tarnation, bloody, sodding, fucking radio, you useless, over-ranked, turd-burgling bastard?" shouted the Rat yet again, but this time directing his venomous spleen at the poor sergeant-pilot, who was at the time still peacefully and totally obliviously a-dingle-dangling from above.

"Will ye stop that bloody blasphemin', ye hound of hell!" uttered Big Bertie in a voice that unfortunately was not as faint as his other senses. "What did you fucking say, you stupid git, you?" screamed the Rat, hoisting the Reverend Mulholland to his feet and nutting him between the eyes with the hardened scar tissue of his well-practised forehead. "What the fucking hell did you say, you shit-stabbing, piss-guzzling, pig-fornicating, fucking Irish excuse for a fucking pervert?" he added, slapping Big Bertie round the cheeks in quick time with a right hand that still, miraculously, held the water bottle that had earlier assisted in the attempt to bring the poor clergyman back from a suspended death.

"I said, 'Stop blasphemin', ye hound of hell!'" replied the Reverend, more than ever convinced that he was in a visibly one-sided death struggle with one of old Nick's bully boys, who was trying to push him towards the edge of the bottomless fiery chasm. Whereupon, Colonel Mooney, ex-Parachute Regiment, failed Staff College, and now - once again - of the SAS, kneed the poor padre with some fervent religious passion right in the balls, and commenced chasing the doubled-up, dog-collared, worse for wear, rural cleric uphill towards the higher end of the field, whence some thirty minutes previously the two of them had come a-tumbling down. Now this was most fortunate for both of them, though you may justly wonder why.

Aroused from confused dreams of being a well-hung and well-slung Icarus, and erectly thinking of getting a justly deserved hero's bit of Sicilian pussy at the far side of the old briny after a jolly good smooth flight from Crete, our Army Air Corps sergeant-pilot was a little bit unprepared for the semi-conscious upside-down reality in which he now found himself. Towards the latter end of a spiffing good solo he had distinctly heard a strict disciplinarian voice berating him, for some reason best known to the owner of the said voice. "Ah fuck!" he said to himself. "It's my bloody, know-it-all father, Daedalus, the old fraidy-cat. What the hell am I doing wrong this time?" And the naive young Icarus, just about to doom himself never to wear a sergeant-major's crown on his wrist, opened his eyes and saw a strange vision that jumbled itself downside-up into what seemed to be a raving mad SAS Colonel beating the shit out of a clerical hunchback, who was moving at impressive ball-clutching speed across the top end of a malignant green sky (streaked with mysterious and somewhat odoriferous brown clouds), and towards a line of upside down trees, where four bodies were wriggling right side up and balanced miraculously on Indian snake charmers' fall-back position ropes. Good though Army Air Corps training is, it does not prepare you for the impossible. A grounding in basic self-preservation, such as that provided by the Los Angeles Police Department, is probably more effective.

It just goes to show you! When you have had a bad shock and return self-pityingly to a semblance of consciousness, you should unfailingly do what the Doctor tells you. Don't panic, sit back, relax, undo your collar and tie, and the belt holding up the trousers that you have probably just recently, most inadvertently, and all too understandably, and totally excusably, soiled. Let some other silly bugger do the worrying for a change. Drink a cup of hot, revoltingly over-sweetened, strong Lipton's tea (or Earl Grey, if you are an officer), and don't try anything hasty. And, above all, think, you stupid bastard! Think!

But bold young Lochinvar had been in the Boys Brigade and not in the Boy Scouts, and, therefore, knew little of what it takes to distinguish the officers from the other ranks, namely, **self-preservation for Lieutenants and above first!** Like the good SNCO that he was, and pursuant to all the instruction he had received at Middle Wallop, our soaring Icarus followed the bloody SOPs, something that no sensible officer would ever have done, even if any sensible officer could have remembered them, let alone told you what SOP stands for in military jargon. As he baffled his brain into a higher state of quasi-consciousness, our darling sergeant-pilot struggled in a most un-drill-like manner, and with some pain to his compressed and compacted vertebrae, and bravely (Yes, poor stupid bugger, bravely!) struggled to reach his right hand to the send button of his radio. With a last (well, almost last) teeth-clenching, pain-wracked lurch, our future holder of a paltry Mention in Dispatches grappled at the send button and whispered hoarsely and heroically, "Mayday! Mayday! Mayday!"

On the third SOS, and immediately before he had commenced his intended broadcasting of the identification of his aircraft and its approximate last known position, the semi-severed wire from the radio battery terminal interacted with the fumes of the AVGAS, drip, drip, drip, and, with a most satisfying *thwump*, sent Icarus sunward to an unhappy ending that classical history had foretold, oh so many, many years before that fated day. The sergeant pilot, as his soul departed from his body, and his body departed from its original physiological structure, just had time to remember vaguely having heard that straggly-haired, gibbering, old fart, Patrick Moore, say on the telly one night, that Icarus was not only a non-hero in Greek mythology, but was also a haemorrhoid (or was it an asteroid - who cares?) following an eccentric orbit which reached within some nineteen million miles of the sun. "*Well, fuck it*!" thought the mind of the poor pilot as it flew from the disintegrating brain, "*I can get closer than that any fucking day. Just you watch me!*"

And a dumbfounded Colonel Mooney and a dumbstruck Bertie Mulholland were doing just that, having been interrupted in their uphill, meandering, cross country batterings by the fireball speeding sunward above their heads. "Jesus H. Christ! What the fuck was that?" said the Reverend gentleman. "What used to be my bloody helicopter, you stupid Irish berk!" replied the Colonel. But both men were too exhausted and lacking in emotion to continue their playful sparring of a few moments previously. They sat down sore, seared, and disconsolate at the top end of the field, right below the severed rope where just an hour before Big Bertie had been playing at conkers big time. When the Rat raised his eyes from the hands he had sunk his weary face into, he saw that the Reverend Mulholland was extending to him an olive branch, or, more precisely, the radio that had left the Colonel's possession rather precipitously, when the poteen driven fifty kiloton explosion had occurred earlier in the morning, and driven both of them rather rapidly and unprotestingly from the very spot in which they now once again found themselves. "Thanks, mate" said the Colonel. "Sorry about your balls and all that." he added, surprising himself at this slight hint of very unaccustomed regret.

Big Bertie, who was still tender on this particular subject - and many others, it must be admitted, decided that discretion was the better part of valour, and chose to restrain his reply to an expressive, "Hmmph!" which was actually all he really felt up to saying at the time. Within seconds afterwards, however, the morale, if not the erectile tissue, of both men underwent a major upsurge, as the radio crackled with Mooney's call-sign and a request for "Where the bleedin' hell is he, the bastard?" Now, that sort of poor radio security was exactly the right sort of medicine to restore vital systems in a Colonel's ravaged body! During the course of hearing a one-sided and most blasphemous, filthy and acrimonious conversation, the Reverend Mulholland gathered that a Scout helicopter was due to land before his very eyes any second now. It was a sight that he was not too sure that he was looking forward to, having watched the last infernal contraption make a less than textbook take-off.

But within the promised seconds two, not one, Scout helicopters landed in the field, and SAS troopers rushed to form a protective perimeter, while others, obviously patrol medics, stuck needles and drips into anywhere they could find a vein, it seemed, on the good Reverend, and placed a protective plastic encasement round his neck, which was beginning to look like that of a turkey on the run round the barnyard on the night before Christmas, after an unfortunate encounter with a pissed and none-too-skilful farmer. Not for the first time of late, Big Bertie passed into unconsciousness, the only difference this time being that it was the effect of SAS medical skill with the morphine syrette, and not the effect of SAS bloodlust with the karate chop and twenty feet of best para-cord. A stretcher took Mulholland to a waiting Scout, which would ferry him to yet another of his increasingly frequent visits to the Waveney Hospital in Ballymena.

But he would not get first class service there this time! Thirty dead, twenty dying and over fifty seriously injured were awaiting prior attention, the end of the queue being somewhere about five hundred yards from the hospital gates, at the end of a long line of commandeered meat wagons. The doctors in the Waveney were not unhappy, however, as they were able now to practice a hitherto unused medical art in mid-Antrim, namely, triage. Basically this means that if your legs, your balls, your torso, your arms, your neck, and your head are still attached to one another, and there are no major gaping holes immediately evident about your person, then some fucking unqualified student nurse may decide, after a wait of several hours in the teeming rain, the drifting snow, or 110 degrees in the shade, that they might have a 'go' at you after coffee break! On the other hand, if you do not meet the above criteria, you are well and truly fucked and had better accept it, because the first time they pay any attention to your moanings and groanings is when you try to rise out of the coffin at the end of the funeral service, only to find that you've bumped your nut on two inches of good mahogany, and can't make yourself heard, because the mother-in-law has deliberately sound-proofed the fucking box, and she's also paid the bloody organist to concentrate on foot pedals and high treble stops.

While the Reverend Bertie was airily half way to cloud cuckoo land, Colonel Mooney, bruised and battered, but now with a right 'dog-on', was attempting to ascertain what could possibly have happened during his temporary absence from the land of the living. He boarded the second Scout, accompanied by two troopers, while the remainder of the SAS team from both helicopters proceeded to restore life to the various strung up or struck down semi-corpses that Mooney had directed them to in the immediate vicinity. The older rustic, who had been skilfully crucified on the gate earlier that morning, was beyond saving, however, having drawn unfortunate attention to his trousers' right pocket by a large bag of unsucked aniseed balls, to which the local fox population had obviously been attracted, before going on to a more savoury diet of pink underdone chipolata, hairy meatballs, and best loin.

At five hundred feet and fuck the danger from snipers, Mooney ordered the pilot to sweep the area of the explosions in a tight circle. First thing he noticed was a total lack of co-ordination by the emergency services, but what was new! Next he spotted a dismembered corpse, arse over tit in the McKelvey's dunghill. Further round to the West were what appeared to be several interesting art-deco displays of eviscerated torsos, and around them a daintily arranged clockwork crimson of assorted limbs, innards, and footballs, some of the latter still wearing tweed caps. Moving further South the Scout passed over a tall sycamore tree, the sight of which caused a minor frisson to run down and back up the Colonel's spine. And he wasn't far wrong to shiver, either, because, as the helicopter swung round, a twitching body was to be seen, obviously not overly happy at its current location on top of the biggest clump of holly for miles around.

The helicopter then completed its circle and returned to the shit-strewn field, where local ambulance men had at last arrived to look for a sergeant-pilot, who was otherwise, and all over the place, disengaged, and to remove the Slaght Young Farmers and their erstwhile trainers - or those who were still alive - for medical, or, more likely, psychiatric treatment for their tortured bodies and souls. An RUC Scenes of Crime Officer was walking around the edge of the field, carrying his black box of tricks, and muttering to himself, "What the fuck! What the fuck!" But then, we can fully understand his predicament, can't we? Where the hell does one man, all on his tod, begin forensic investigation, when the scene of the crime resembles the morning after the First Battle of the Somme?

It was six o'clock. Time to talk to Delta 1 and Delta 2. A much relieved Lofty and Sticky gave succinct and disciplined reports of their version of the pre- and post-dawn events to an increasingly bemused superior, who was having difficulty figuring out whether what he was hearing was fact or fiction, and, therefore, was unable to distinguish the truth. Not that we can really blame him in the circumstances. The Rat gave a brief account of what he had seen from the air and experienced from the ground, leaving out - obviously - everything, which would in the slightest way reflect on anything other than his proven military experience and prowess. Nonetheless, he unwittingly and unintentionally got the distinct message across that, for once in his lifetime, he hadn't the slightest fucking clue what was going on. But Lofty, Sticky and the boys didn't hold that unspoken confession in any way against their Colonel. They had every sympathy with his struggle to comprehend the awful reality of the morning's events to date, and if they weren't convinced, Delta 1 would only have to give a more colourful description of the scene around them, and an olfactory military appreciation of the smell of deceased flesh wafting over them in the early summer's sun, for all concerned to be totally dumbfucked. No! It was certainly not one of those days where you have the free time and malicious intent to consider other people's lack of knowledge as a sign of professional or intellectual inferiority. No way!

The Rat gave orders to his OP commanders to stick with it, as planned, and informed them that, because of the morning's cataclysmic events, there was no doubt whatsoever that they were in the right place - and just at the right time. Lofty and the others in Delta 1 weren't one hundred percent sure that they were in the right place, for a hill a couple of thousand metres away would have caused a great deal less stress on whatever produces adrenaline. Apart from that, with the sun really out now, the stench was getting up your nose, and four men regurgitating last night's chicken a la king with three veg, including, naturally, fucking carrots, was not going to make living in a damned hole in the ground a lot of fun! To make matters worse, the scene in front of Delta 1's hide was now even more gruesome, as the smell of roast Protestant had attracted every bloody dog for six townlands around, and the bastards were now gorging themselves on all manner of titbits, most of which - fortunately for Lofty and the boys - no longer bore any resemblance to former human beings. Delta 2 were not much better off, although they had a much smaller visual selection to choose from. In the midden, not far from their vantage point in the old cottage, an upended IRA man was being gradually reduced to size by forty or so of the biggest, evilest, yellow-fanged, grey rats that Sticky had ever seen. "God! Why can't they eat a bit quieter?" he groaned, as three of the rats fought over some macabre morsel.

Grabbing a couple of patrol medics, released from their succouring of distressed Young Farmers by the arrival of a bewildered group of St. John's Ambulance Brigade volunteers, the Rat returned to his Scout and took off towards the West to find the dreaded sycamore tree, complete with nested holly bush, to see if the previously sighted twitching thing was still alive and could throw some light on the situation. As the Scout swooped down to land in the target field two minutes later, Colonel

Mooney noted that the body was no longer twitching. Neither was it nested in the holly bush! Instead it was swaying in the breeze some ten feet of baler twine beneath one of the biggest branches of the accursed sycamore. Standing around, some apparently admiring the distant view, others gawking like gormless idiots at the helicopter, was a small group of Neanderthals, who obviously were not as slow moving or as dumb as they were trying to look.

"What the fuck happened here?" screamed the Colonel, in a voice that had no trouble striking the correct chord of respect in the local yokels. "You, with the red hair and the pimples," shouted Mooney, pointing aggressively with his MP5 at one of the less unintelligent of the group. "Yes, you, dickhead! Do you see any other cunt here with red hair! Stand up straight, you stupid prick, when I'm talking to you. That's better. Now, what the fuck happened here?" "Well, your honour," began the red-haired peasant. "Don't you fucking give me any of that 'well, your honour' shit, you excuse for a brainless turd! I'm a fucking Colonel, not a layabout bloody judge! Now tell me what happened here, because if you don't, I'm going to ram the barrel of this gun up your clinkered arsehole, pull the trigger and give you the biggest dose of the shits you've ever had! Do you get my meaning, you useless cunt?"

"Yes, Colonel," replied the unhappy youth. "We were out looking for our mates. They didn't come back from training - I mean, Ah, mushroom gathering - with the Reverend Mulholland at four this morning, so we went to see what was wrong. And then Jock Allen's fucking old barn disappeared, and after that the top of the bloody hill disappeared, and we had to stop in the bushes so Sammy could have a shit, because he was sure that he saw a vampire flying this way, only it wasn't a vampire, because the sun was up. It was this fucking IRA man," stammered a shaking Pimples.

"What fucking IRA man. I don't see no fucking IRA man. All I see is a dead body swinging from a blasted sycamore tree, whereas ten fucking minutes ago he was complaining of a sore fucking arse and bouncing up and down on the top of that bastard holly bush. Now, I suppose, you are going to tell me that he found his own way, with two fucking broken legs and one broken arm, out of the bloody holly bush, then swung like fucking Tarzan into the first branches of the bloody tree, which, if you look carefully, are nearly twenty damned feet from the fucking ground. Whereupon he found, just by bloody luck, oh what a fortunate little man was he, ten feet of brand new baler twine, just exactly the same sort that is holding up the shit-stained trousers of that apelike fucking slant-eyed git over there. Yes, you, dickhead! Get over here, now, you chinless wonder!" And Squinty Hughes ambled across in the closest that he could achieve to a military 'on the double', considering that he had a clubfoot to add to his other physical attributes.

"What's your name, arsehole?" shouted the Rat, when Farmer Hughes had got as near to him as the poor fellow dared. "Squinty, Colonel," he replied. "Well, Squinty the fucking gimp! I suppose you are going to tell me that Tarzan over here committed bloody suicide!" "Yes, Colonel, that's exactly what happened," was Squinty's answer. "Well, how in the blazes do you know he's in the fucking IRA, then, shit for brains?" screamed a now totally apoplectic Mooney. "He told us so, before he died Colonel. Honest he did!" answered Squinty. "God give me strength!" sighed the Rat, suddenly losing the energy to be angry anymore. "And did Mr. fucking Gerry Adams here tell you anything else before he jumped off the branch with his multiple fractured legs?" "Yes, Colonel. He did," replied Squinty. And there was a long pause. "Well, out with it man, out with it! What else did he fucking say before he leapt into your loving outstretched arms below?"

And with that, and a furtive look at the others, Squinty took a deep breath and began. "He came to, just as we was pulling him out of the bush from the branch above. Well, the others was pulling, I were on top of the holly bush, seeing as the others told me they'd beat the shite out of me, if I didn't climb into the blasted thing and see who were up there. So I did, and put the baler twine under his arms, and I were giving him a leg up and he came to. God, he looked awful. And he'd shit himself, just like our Sammy over there when he saw the vampire." "Will you stop telling me your bloody life story, you cretin, and get on with it! What did he fucking say?" screamed the Rat, his energy for anger returning rapidly and his thumb twitching ominously on the safety of his MP5. "Yes, Colonel, sir. He asked me if I was Moriarty. I said I was Squinty, but I think he couldn't hear too well, him only having a bit of one ear hanging on. So he said that he was Cathal Fahey, and he was from the Belfast Brigade, and that somebody called the 'ferret' wanted to see me, quick like, and would I give him absolution. I told him, 'I'll gie ye more than fucking absolution, ye Fenian git', and dropped him on the holly again, just to emphasise me point. The boys on the branch shouts down to me to stop kicking the shite out of the bastard, and asking what he had said. So I told them. Well, Colonel, they says, 'Hang the fucker!' but when I turns round to do as they toul me, sure the fucker's got the noose from round his shoulders and sticking his head in it. I shouts to him, 'that's my job, you Fenian git!" But he just looks at me, funny like, and says "Up yours!" and rolls off the top of the bush! Honest to God, Colonel!"

"Jesus!" was all that the Rat could think of saying for the moment, not having come across an Irishman willing to commit suicide before, at least not while unassisted by drink. But as he thought more about it, there was a distinct logic in going off the deep end yourself, especially when you are sick and tired of your arse being sliced by holly bushes, and when to wait for a helping hand is only going to delay the inevitable. What the fuck! This bunch of loonies is maybe telling the truth after all, and, anyway, no Protestant judge in mid-Antrim is going to disbelieve their story, now, is he? "Have you searched the body?" asked the Colonel. "Not yet, sir," answered the one who must be Sammy, by the way he kept as many people as possible between himself and the swinging corpse, as well as continually pulling the seat of his trousers carefully from between the cheeks of his arse. "We was just about to do that, when the chopper came over."

A burst of 9 mm soon brought the body of Cathal Fahey to the ground, landing him on, and breaking, his remaining good limb in the process. But Cathal could no longer give a fuck. A quick but expert frisk of the remains clothes by one of the SAS corporals produced a half-empty packet of Number 6; a condom that had seen considerable use and would now never see better days; a Colt 9 mm pistol and two spare and full magazines therefor; an unopened packet of Polo mints; a brandy ball that had obviously had a couple of good suckings already, by the amount of lint and strands of tobacco adhering to it; a snot-caked handkerchief that had been cleaner when its manufacturer had embroidered 'Remember Bloody Sunday' on it in rather sinister feminine stitching in the Maze Prison; a letter from the 'boroo' referring to a good job opening in a butcher's shop on the Shankill Road; seven pounds sterling and a bit more in coins; and a wallet containing fifty twenty pound notes (which the SAS Corporal skilfully reduced to one, and pocketed the rest); photographs of one of the ugliest women that Belfast had ever seen, surrounded by seven apparent progeny, all evidently competing to be uglier; and a piece of relatively clean paper with writing on it. Apart from the money, all of this was quite an impressive collection for the pockets of a fifty year old Belfast unemployed carder and deceased terrorist.

"Give me the paper *and* the fucking money, Corporal Grieves!" growled the Rat, and the Corporal did so immediately, wondering at the same time how the old bastard could see through five paddys and his own back and detect the theft. The man was a bloody miracle, that was for sure. And the Rat, happy at being man pounds better off, released the body and the complement of local non-murderers into the sympathetic hands of a harassed RUC sergeant, who had just arrived red-faced and huffing and puffing on the scene, having been delayed in his arrival by a need to constantly touch other living beings and ask them if they knew his name, and was he really seeing all this carnage in poor wee, boring Slaght, where the biggest crimes were normally of a non-reported incestuous kind, and the most the police ever had to do was pretend to seize another batch of Jock Allen's wee still, in order to replace the Ballymena Barracks's depleted stocks. As the half-demented RUC sergeant ushered away his docile flock, all of whom were giving Sammy's bum a wide berth, the Rat went over to the Scout and sat on the floor with his legs dangling out, and began to open the piece of paper that had been found in Cathal's wallet.

Once he had the paper unfolded, Colonel Mooney was shocked by what he read. It started with a list of names, commencing with his own. It went as follows: 'The Rat, the Ferret, Pinky, Moriarty, MacTavish, Smythe-Gargle, Paddy, McCambridge, McKelvey, Mulholland' The good Colonel was struck by the fact that five of these names began with the letter 'M', or six, if you substituted 'Mooney' for 'Rat'. After the list of names was a hodgepodge of scribbling, but clear enough for Mooney to regard some of them as most ominous. 'Slaght, SAS, OPs, Simpson, Shit' ran the next decipherable list. Once again the Rat was struck by the fact that four out of the five on this part of the list began with the letter 'S'. At the same time he wondered to himself why Smythe-Gargle appeared on both lists, presuming, of course, that Smythe-Gargle was indeed the 'Shit' in question on the second part. "Good grief! The bastards are on to us!" thought the Rat.

Finally the page of uneducated scrawl ended with some Norse runes, which, with a bit of clever decoding, appeared to mean, '7th, 10am, McC-Ballymena, RUC, 2XASU, 106, followed, on the line below, by the words, 'fuck them over proper 8-11 and get the fuck out S on 12'. "Jesus!" said the Colonel, out loud, "if this is what I think it is, we've got a fucking turncoat in our midst." And calling to his lads, who were engaged at having a good chunter for not being as wealthy as the Rat now was, Mooney seated himself in the helicopter, put on his headset and told the pilot to head for the Ranger's Depot in Ballymena like a bat out of hell. He needed to talk to MacTavish quickly, as well as to that simpering superior bastard in Century House. And to do both effectively, the Rat needed to get to his secure communications equipment as soon as possible, if not several minutes before.

As the Scout was passing over the Braid Mill in downtown Ballymena, the Rat's tactical radio crackled. He looked at his watch. Good God! It was 0700 hours already. Delta 1, checking in first, had nothing of tremendous import to report, other than a punch up over territorial rights between two undertakers as to which legs belonged to which body, an altercation that had appeared to be about to add one further middle aged male Protestant to the body count, before the intervention of a platoon of UDR, newly arrived on the scene from their warm beds and cold wives, could do the only useful thing that they could possibly have done on that grim morning.

Delta 2's sitrep, though, was astounding, to say the least. According to the tinny voice of Sticky, a Captain in the WRAC, of stunning build and looks, had exited the McKelvey farmhouse, accompanied by a sergeant - yes, a bloody sergeant - in 2 PARA, and driven off in the direction of Ahoghill in an Army Land Rover. The Captain had been armed with a Sterling sub-machine gun, and a 9 mm Browning, while the Para had been armed with an SLR. Before driving the Land Rover out of the barn, where it had apparently been parked for the previous night, the WRAC Captain had turned to the Para sergeant and said, in a voice that was certainly used to command, "Sergeant Moriarty! Look at that mess over there on the dunghill. Make sure the area cleaning is a bit better when we get back. Right?" The Para sergeant had come immediately to attention and saluted smartly, saying, "Yes, Captain Thompson. I'll be right on it as soon as we get back!"

"Well, fuck me pink!" said Mooney to himself, just as the Scout was landing. "It is Moriarty after all. But what the hell is he up to in bloody Ulster? And who's this bloody dickwiper he's with. She sure as hell doesn't sound like that ugly horse, Lady MacTavish. God almighty! What the merry hell is going on here?" And with that he jumped from the helicopter, but, forgetting that his headset was still on his head, he was at once arrested and immediately floored, whereupon his skull struck the helicopter's port-side strut with an impressive-sounding thwack, thereby rendering the good Colonel unable to focus clearly enough to send the messages that should have been sent several minutes earlier, if he had been more careful. Just before the medics stretchered him away, the Colonel's prone form was rifled by none other than Corporal Grieves. The Corporal and his mates strolled off to a late breakfast in the canteen, content that Mooney might suspect them of having relieved him of Cathal's expense money, but he sure as hell couldn't prove it. Anyway, the bloody medical room staff at the Ranger's Depot would have had it away, wouldn't they! And chuckling amiably to themselves, they sat down to a well-earned greasy fry-up, while their superior was put on his first saline drip of this very 'special operation' - but not necessarily his last!

And, meanwhile, the hustle and bustle of the little mid-Antrim market town went on as if nothing horrific or horrendous had happened just down the road. It takes a lot to stop the gentle folk of Ballymena from earning an honest shilling. And anyway, a 'nice wee' tragedy like what had happened at Slaght, was bloody good for business, what with the undertakers needing to order more wood from the wholesalers, the number of granite blocks that would have to be cut and suitably inscribed for the headstones, the drink that would be sold to exhausted emergency services, police and military personnel, so that they could forget their trauma! Every ghoul in the town was awaiting eagerly the eight o'clock news to see whether the BBC had been able to piece together a more complete picture of the events of that morning than was available from the incoherent ramblings of those shocked members of the auxiliary fire brigade and the similarly wide eyed ambulance men, who had been the first outsiders on the scene at Slaght and, thus, the first harbingers of the tragic news that business would be booming that day, and merchants would perforce have to make do with a packed lunch.

Interestingly there was no sign of panic in Ballymena, no sensation of being at the leading edge of the terrorist war in Ulster, not the slightest fear that, at any moment, the Reverend Mulholland's 'Assyrian' armies of murderous Belfast unwashed were about to descend on the Borough. Perhaps this was complacency, an exaggerated trust in the presence of the beloved RUC, UDR and Royal Irish Rangers, who so far seemed to have protected the town from the horrors experienced by nearly every other conglomeration of more than fifty houses in the Province, or perhaps it was stupidity. Who knows? My own feeling is that Slaght, to the parochial mind of the citizens of the City of the Seven Towers, might as well be on the backside of the moon, as far as they were concerned. Since nothing had so far occurred to interfere with the decent Presbyterian occupation of making money - indeed, the contrary was true - and since the people of Ballymena viewed the people of Slaght in exactly the same way as those domiciled in Chelsea view the jungle bunnies of Brixton, perhaps the question should not be, 'Who knows?' but rather, 'Who the hell in Ballymena cares?'

CHAPTER TEN

A convoy of ten souped up 'Scrubbers Incorporated' laundry vans, containing 40 armed and eager Special Branch men, under the command of Inspector Simpson, was racing down the Antrim Line towards Ballymena at seven forty-five that morning, hell bent on increasing the prestige of Chief Inspector McCambridge, and cracking wide open the rotten egg of terrorism that was tainting his beloved Ulster. Just prior to leaving Castlereagh some thirty minutes earlier, the first confused reports had been passed to Simpson, indicating that 'something big had gone down' in the immediate post dawn period in the hamlet of Slaght. The Inspector's first thought, of course, had been of Moriarty, and as the convoy weaved its way, horns blaring, past the early morning traffic, Simpson could almost smell his prey. It was a mysteriously alien odour, a mixture of soap, freshly ironed starched denim, resin, and with a slight hint of gun oil. The Inspector had difficulty rationalising any and all of these scents with the stench of urine, stale sweat, and boked-up Guinness that he normally associated with Moriarty. "Weird! Bloody weird!" he mused, as the milestones clicked steadily by.

Past the crossroads at Carnaughts and over the brow of the hill the Scrubbers sped, heading at over ninety miles an hour towards the next crossroads at Cromkill. Coming up the road from Ballymena in the opposite direction, and also approaching the cross-roads at Cromkill was a slower moving convoy of ambulances, on their way back to the field at Slaght to pick up the next delivery for the Coroner, their fourth that morning already. Overhead swooped and swirled several Puma and Scout helicopters, concentrating on the transportation of the not-so-dead. Villagers huddled nervously in groups by the side of the road as the curious convoy of high-speed laundry vans crested the hill and met the incurious convoy of ambulances coming the other way. Just over the brow of the hill itself, parked on the left hand side of the road, and facing Ballymena, was a broken down, rusty grey, Massey Ferguson tractor, complete with a farmer, bum in the air, and head and shoulders half way into the engine, which he was skilfully attempting to repair with the assistance of a two pound hammer. Now. You are all going to say, "Come on! This is all getting a bit too surrealistic, surely?" Maybe you are right. But why spoil my fun? I'm enjoying this part!

The first and second Scrubber vans careered successfully round the tractor, and then lurched equally successfully back on to the left side of the road on two wheels, thereby avoiding what would have been a ghastly collision with the first of the convoy of ambulances. The next two laundry vans were less successful, slamming with the fervour of deliberate kamikaze conviction into the first three ambulances. The remaining six laundry vans were more fortunate, in that they did not collide with any ambulances. Indeed, they even managed to miss the tractor! The driver of the leading van of the remaining six in the convoy had had a lightning flash of premonition that danger lay ahead, just as he was beginning to crest the hill. It was probably something to do with the fact that he had that very second, espied an airborne ambulance. So, with the brilliant reflexes of abject panic, he had braked sharply and hauled his steering wheel to the left. The van bounced over the kerb, rushed across the sward, entered a newly mown hayfield by way of the hedge, and came to a sudden halt, with an enormous bang, when it struck a sleeping muck spreader. This enormous bang was not as impressive, however, as the next five bangs, as the succeeding Scrubber vans played 'follow the leader.'

Silence would have reigned for several seconds over this idyllic scene, if, of course, the sirens on the few remaining undamaged ambulances had not continued to wail. As the first two laundry vans drew to a halt and began to effect shaky nine point turns, Inspector Simpson caught his first view of the devastation. It was not a particularly pretty sight, and it would certainly take a cleverer man than himself to explain this one away to McCambridge, old school mate or not! When the surviving Scrubbers got back to the crash site, they were, however, pleasantly surprised to see that, while very little could be done for the occupants of laundry vans three and four, or, for that matter, for the occupants of ambulances one, two and three, the occupants of laundry vans five to ten were not seriously injured, just temporarily transport-less.

"It's a miracle," said Simpson, and the driver of his van was convinced that his superior was referring to the fact that only eight Scrubbers were dead or dying, and not thirty-two. But in this he was wrong, as Simpson was expressing his realisation that this reduced attrition rate would probably be acceptable to McCambridge, under the circumstances, and that his new Inspectorship would most likely remain intact. While some of the Scrubbers began to assist the surviving ambulance men to attend to the casualties, and others removed the weapons and spare magazines, radios and wallets of their dead or seriously injured colleagues, and still others started to direct the traffic that was beginning to build up on either side of the tangled mess, Inspector Simpson approached the gentleman farmer who had now withdrawn himself and his bum from their inspection of the mysterious wonders of the internal combustion engine, and was standing at the side of his ailing mount, hammer in hand and mouth agape.

The farmer's jaw dropped a damn sight lower when he recognised who was now purposefully striding towards him, Walther PPK drawn, and at that very moment being cocked and un-safetied. "Oh my God! It's that lunatic sergeant from Kells," our rustic was thinking to himself, with some understandable accuracy. Instinctively, but incredibly foolishly, he backed to the side of his tractor and raised his mighty two-pound hammer in self defence, whereupon Inspector Simpson had no hesitation in shooting him through the right hand, just like you see in the older cowboy movies. The bullet then hit the top of the TVO tank of the Massey Ferguson, which ignited quite nicely and sprayed napalm all over the old tweed jacket of the farmer, who then, deciding obviously that cremation was a greater evil than being shot by rent-a-loony of the RUC, took off surprisingly youthfully down the road, where two

ambulance men bundled him to the ground and bravely rolled on him
to put out the flames.

A slightly shop-soiled farmer opened his eyes again to see Simpson
standing menacingly over him, with the gun waving rhythmically
between himself and the two, no longer so brave, ambulance men. "Fuck
off!" shouted Simpson to the latter, who proceeded to do just that with
alacrity. "Where's Moriarty? He told you to do this, didn't he?" blared
the Inspector. The farmer, now more than ever convinced that he was
dealing with a madman, capable of absolutely anything, decided that he
had little chance of survival by telling the truth, and that the only way
to get out of this alive was to try to convince Simpson of whatever he
wanted to be convinced. "Moriarty stole me tractor last night. I've been
looking for it everywhere. I'd just found it when you lot came along."
the farmer blurted out, as convincingly as possible. "How do you know
it was Moriarty that stole it?" asked Simpson, for once acting like a
policeman and not as an alumnus of Purdysburn University. "He came
round to the farm with a bloody great gun and told me he was stealing
it." replied the farmer, beginning to sweat profusely, less from his first
degree burns than from having to think so unaccustomedly quickly.
"Where'd he go then?" asked Simpson, holstering his PPK to the great
relief of the farmer. "I don't know. He didn't tell me, but he headed in
the direction of Ballymena," lied the farmer appreciatively.

At that Inspector Simpson left the wounded peasant to fend for himself
and rounded up his more or less ambulatory Scrubbers, squeezed them
into the remaining two vans and headed off, at slightly slower speed
this time, in the direction of Ballymena, just over two miles away. He
had been surprisingly calmed by the farmer's lies. He knew in his heart
of hearts that he was getting closer every minute to his prey. He could
almost touch him, the sensation was so great. And as the two vans
entered the town and slowed in light traffic to cross the bridge and
head for the Barracks, the feeling of being close to Moriarty became so
intense that the veins on Simpson's head began to stand out and he had
some serious problems in breathing. Passing them in the traffic going
out of town over the bridge was an Army Land Rover, with a para in a
red beret behind the wheel. Inspector Simpson blinked in amazement
and shuddered deeply. He really had better see a psychiatrist, this time

voluntarily, because he had just seen Moriarty drive past dressed as a sergeant in the Parachute Regiment with a uniformed amazon sitting beside him, looking the spitting image of Mary McKelvey, the footballer's widow. "God! I could do with a cup of tea," he said to himself, and then out loud to the driver, "Thank Heavens we'll be able to get a bit of peace and quiet in the Barracks." But Ballymena's RUC Barracks was not at that moment a particularly peaceful or pleasant place to be. You see, the bloody British Army, in the shape of a female Captain in Intelligence and a sergeant driver/bodyguard in the Parachute Regiment, had just sprung Paddy McCallion, the mid-Antrim IRA leader, from his cell at gunpoint!

The eight o'clock news on the BBC that morning brought the disturbing news to the public of yet another major terrorist incident in Slaght, the little village whose name and hitherto peaceful rural existence had been blissfully unknown to ninety-nine per cent of the population until just a few weeks before. This time, according to the announcer, it looked as if another forty or so were dead, with a further fifty odd seriously injured, some of whom would be joining their friends on the big free magical mystery tour very shortly. It appeared, said the announcer, that two enormous bombs had been planted by an IRA team under a known PIRA terrorist, Cathal Fahey, and that this team and the aforementioned Fahey had joined their innocent victims by becoming practitioners of that favourite IRA sporting tactic, the 'own goal.' The Minister of State for Northern Ireland had been interviewed in London and had expressed 'outrage at yet another example of the most callous disregard for human life, etc., etc.,' as if he couldn't think up something new to say after all these years! The Democratic Unionist Party Member of Parliament for mid-Antrim, the Reverend Doctor Ian Paisley's remarks had been more to the point, as he made use of the free air waves to call on 'all God-fearing Ulster Protestants to be on their guard against the perfidious invasion of the Pope's pestilential armies into the very hinterland of loyalism' - and in his own bloody constituency, to boot!

The spokesman for the Army had come out with the usual twaddle about IRA ASU's lurking in every hedgerow, and had added his customary inane comment that the Security Forces were 'on top of the

situation'. If anyone in Slaght had had the life or energy to listen to the
eight o'clock news that morning, they would have politely suggested to
the Army spokesman that it was a pity that he and the rest of the bloody
Security Forces had not been sitting twiddling their thumbs on top of
a certain hill in their townland between four and half past that same
morning! From the usual bloody academic nerd of a so-called expert
on terrorism, pontificating a load of breakfast-time bullshit over the
telephone from the safety of his kitchen dinette in East Cheam, came
the totally astounding prediction that 'things do not augur very well
for the Twelfth.'

At twenty-five past eight, however, things got more interesting when
the announcer interrupted yet another moaning minnie from SDLP
appealing for 'calm and common-sense to prevail.' This particular eejit
must certainly have forgotten his last bloody good hiding at the hands
of his own fellow Republicans; otherwise he wouldn't be coming out
with a load of drivel like this. 'Calm and bloody common sense' - in
Ulster? Give us a break! The interruption was a news flash that the mid-
Antrim leader of the Provisional IRA had just been sprung at gunpoint
from detention awaiting trial in Ballymena RUC Barracks, and that a
Province-wide alert was out for him and his accomplices. Interestingly,
to any knowledgeable Ulster watcher (or in this case listener), there was
no mention of the number or description of the accomplices who had
assisted the breakout, obviously indicating that a typical 'double-speak'
cover-up by the Security Forces was grinding into operation. There must
have been some sort of cock-up in Ballymena.

Cock-up was a bit of an understatement, or at least Inspector Simpson
would have thought so, had he been listening to the news. He and his
bruised, but happy to be alive, laundrymen had parked at the back
of the Barracks and entered through the open rear door, somewhat
surprised at the lack of normal security, but putting this down to the
probable serious reduction in duty staff, because of whatever the hell was
going on in Slaght. Wandering around the downstairs of the barracks,
however, he found absolutely no one on duty, and it required some
further detailed search to find ten trussed up and gagged policemen,
varying from the rank of sergeant downwards, behind bars in one of the
cells in the basement. A search could not locate the keys, and it was with

difficulty that Inspector Simpson was persuaded by one of his Special Branch sergeants, that shooting at the lock would seriously endanger the lives of those incarcerated in the cell. To which ten sets of gagged heads nodded most enthusiastically.

Reluctantly Simpson sent off two of his men to locate the nearest garage, and get a mechanic down to the basement post haste with his oxy-acetylene torch. In the meantime, he would go to the canteen and have that cup of tea he had been thinking about before his waking nightmare on Harryville Bridge. Meanwhile, upstairs, one of his men made a quick telephone call to his mate on the BBC's news desk in Belfast, and after negotiating a suitable fee and insisting on the usual anonymity crap, informed him of what he had learned from the first policeman who had rolled across the floor of the cell in the basement, enabling him to remove his gag and bonds between the bars. The Special Branch man did not think of going to the canteen to tell his Inspector. "Oh no!" he thought, "Let that fucking lunatic find out for himself. If he can shoot a farmer in the hand for having his tractor stolen, what the hell will he do to me for telling him that his friend Moriarty's beaten him again?"

Twenty minutes later Inspector Simpson was joined in the canteen by a very unhappy, extremely angry and most embarrassed Duty Sergeant, just as he was buttering his second piece of toast. The Duty Sergeant proceeded to relate what had happened, and the language with which he related this was so foul that I am forced to summarise it for you. At approximately seven thirty that morning an Army Land Rover had drawn up to the car-park gate at the rear of the Barracks and a female officer and a sergeant in the paras, who was the driver, showed their ID cards. The policeman on guard had opened the barrier and let them in. The two visitors had then asked to see the Duty Sergeant, and informed him that they were here to interrogate the IRA prisoner, McCallion. No problem so far. They had been escorted to the cells and left alone, at their request. At this stage McCallion was still behind lock and key, and not looking very happy at the sight of the red beret in front of him. The Duty Sergeant had returned to his office and then, about two minutes later had decided that the three cups of coffee he had had during the last hour were at last taking effect, and that it was time to have a good morning constitutional.

He had exited his office, gone to the toilet, and successfully completed his business. He then opened the door to the cubicle, to come out and wash his hands, and found the barrel of an SLR pointing menacingly at his chest. While the Duty Sergeant was intoning a brief prayer of thanks for having just relieved himself, the Para sergeant had said, in a broad Ballymena accent, "Put yer hands on yer heed and head fer the cells." This he had agreed immediately to do, whereupon thirty seconds later he found himself incarcerated, gagged and bound along with all the other policemen in the Barracks, including the car park sentry and two others who had been on car bomb watch in the sangar at the front of the building. McCallion, the terrorist, was bouncing up and down and smiling like a bantam cock on heat, and had to be restrained by 'the big woman Captain' from taking an early revenge on himself and all the others present, everyone having regularly given the runt a bit of a 'good digging', when no one else was looking. Just as they were leaving the basement, the Duty Sergeant had heard the 'big woman' telling the wee Ballymena Para sergeant, in an accent from across the water, "Well done, Sergeant Moriarty! Phase One complete. Let's get on with Phase Two!"

Now, as you will no doubt have guessed for yourselves, the first mention of a Para sergeant and a woman officer had Inspector Simpson all a-tremble, with tea spilling from his cup into his saucer. The tale, as it continued, saw the trembling transform rapidly to something closer to 7.5 on the Richter Scale, and by the time the Duty Sergeant, who had wisely backed to the canteen doorway, and was ready to make a bolt for it, got to the final positive identification of Moriarty, he was beginning to understand that the San Andreas fault had just extended itself to run down the length of the Braid valley, and that any minute now Ballymena would be under the Irish Sea. The Beast of Beleek was roaring, ranting and raving, round the canteen, throwing whole cupboards of assorted dinnerware, cutlery and kitchen utensils in the air, and foaming vilely from a mouth that had twisted into a fearsome thing, resembling more Satan in the bog after a millennium of constipation than one of Ulster's plain-clothes finest. Thirty seconds of this, and discretion became by far the better of valour. Feeling as if he had just drunk two gallons of best Blue Mountain, the Duty Sergeant took to his heels and headed for the nearest public house to drown out the heebie-jeebies with as much whiskey as it would take to render him unconscious.

It took ten brave Scrubbers and four buckets of ice-cold water from the drinking fountain to bring Inspector Simpson back from total insanity to a less life-threatening, raving lunacy. Even so, aftershocks continued to rock the canteen for the following thirty minutes. But by the time he had calmed down sufficiently to stop foaming like a werewolf in season, the first contingents of RUC had arrived back from Slaght, having been told by an old pensioner the gist of the interruption on the eight o'clock news. Next came a company of UDR, looking for blood and not finding it, but getting into ambush positions nonetheless all up and down the street in front of the barracks. Just as the Inspector was beginning to understand the gravity of the morning's events at Slaght, and was getting ready to send every available man jack out on the warpath after Moriarty, McCallion, and that traitorous bitch, McKelvey, all hell broke out around and within the Barracks.

Liam O'Shaughnessy and Phelim the Ferret were late risers. It came with the job! And so they were as yet unaware of the explosions in Slaght, let alone the mysterious breakout of their poofter acolyte, Paddy McCallion. Even if they had been, it would have been impossible to prevent the three ASU's of able and determined young PIRA volunteers from the Falls from putting in their assault on the RUC Barracks at Ballymena, without the benefit of radio communications, which unfortunately had not been considered necessary in the planning. Twelve of Liam's finest storm troopers, armed to the teeth with Kalashnikovs and a 106 mm rocket launcher screeched to a halt outside the front of the Barracks and put a well-aimed anti-tank round through the armoured and rarely-used front door. This round, together with the two halves of the steel door and a lot of molten metal, whistled down the main entrance hall and exited through the back door into the car park.

The members of the three ASUs, never for one second suspecting that they had just been transformed into suicide squads, were running towards the hole where the front door used to be, when the constables in the sangar opened up with their sub-machine guns. A split second later a whole Company of UDR, hidden in their ambush positions up and down the street, also opened up with a rat-a-tat-tat, the like of which had never been heard before in Ballymena except when the massed pipes and drums of the Irish Guards had played to the assembled populace outside the nearby Memorial Gardens on Armistice Day, one peaceful year before this last lot of Troubles had begun. First to die in the hail of fire from a not-so-well aimed GPMG, from behind the protection of a scraggly privet hedge twenty yards across the road from the Barracks, were the two RUC men in the sangar. It wasn't the fault of the bomb-blast protection they were behind. That remained intact. But you can't be shooting sub-machine guns out of a firing port in a sangar without exposing yourself to incoming fire from an unintentionally accurate GPMG, now can you?

That, however, did little to deter the blood-lust of the stalwarts of the UDR, who continued to pump all they had got into the twitching but already well-deceased IRA bodies, now scattered like fallen autumn leaves over the Barracks's forecourt. Despite a frantic Company Commander, a rent collector out of uniform, screaming like a banshee for them to, "Cease Fire", the rain of lead continued until his men had run out of every last round of ammunition and the brick facade of the front of the Barracks had begun to crumble into dust and blow away on the wind. In the eerie silence that followed, a white bed sheet, tied to a broom handle, was stuck timidly out of a first floor window, and a weak voice croaked out, "We surrender! For Christ's sake, stop shooting, you stupid bastards! We bloody well surrender!"

It is unnecessary to go into detail concerning the quite bitter altercation, which then ensued between the RUC and the UDR in Ballymena. Let's say that what unfortunately was now to occur has been effectively hushed up by the relevant authorities. All that you need to know is that the RUC, with the exception of the two dead constables in the sangar, had not up to that point fired a single shot, a discrepancy which they now chose to rectify with a vengeance, as soon as they found out that the murdering bastards, who had demolished the front of their hallowed place of work, had ceased fire through lack of ammunition and not from any desire to take prisoners. Within minutes the more fortunate UDR soldiers were legging it wildly through the streets of the town, looking for a sanctuary that many of them were unlikely to receive in time. The less fortunate were being summarily executed, either by the time-honoured 9 mm bullet to the back of the head, or by becoming dangling ornaments on the lampposts stretching the whole way from the railway station right up to the Adair Arms Hotel, and on both sides of the road too! But now you will rather more fully understand why it was not until ten o'clock that a calmer Inspector Simpson, who had got four of the murdering UDR bastards himself before his PPK had jammed, had time to compose his thoughts and report to his superior, Chief Inspector McCambridge, cogitating in the safety of his office in Castlereagh.

When McCambridge at last put down the receiver, he looked thoughtfully at the ceiling for some minutes and then pressed the button on his intercom. "Mary, love. Hold all my calls. I don't want any interruptions for the next hour, even if it's the bloody Chief Constable himself. I've got a wee bit of thinking to do. Get me the Orbat of the Belfast Brigade. I think it's time to put the next phase into operation. Okay, love? Quick as you can, there's a dear!" And as Mary in the outer office got up to get the requisite file, McCambridge opened the whiskey drawer of his own filing cabinet and poured himself a really stiff one, which he began to sip with obvious pleasure, at least if the broad smile on his face was anything to go by.

After Mary had brought him the Belfast Brigade Orbat, McCambridge stared at it thoughtfully, doodled a few notes on the back of an old HMSO envelope, and picked up his direct line phone. Within seconds he was deeply into an interesting discussion with his opposite number in Dublin at the Headquarters of the Irish Special Branch, one Cecil O'Leary, as big a Machiavelli as McCambridge any day of the week and who, like his usual partner at golf, none other that Chief Inspector McCambridge himself, played off a handicap of seven and a bottle of whiskey a day. "Oh, God! I just love this job!" said McCambridge, after he had replaced the receiver some fifteen minutes later. And on the back of the same old HMSO envelope he began to strike out some of the names he had previously written down. "It may take another twelve to fifteen years, but we're gradually getting there, now aren't we?" he said to the wall in front of him. "Yes, me old fellow! Slowly, slowly, catchee monkey!"

In the Officer's Ward of the Military Wing of the Musgrave Park Hospital, whence he had been quickly transferred under cover of dark, and a blanket, by a terrified medical staff at the Catholic Mater Hospital, immediately on discovering his Army ID card in his inside jacket pocket, Pinky Jolly was responding very well to treatment for severe concussion caused by a shithouse door knob. He'd been having a dump in the bathroom of his suite when the front end and downstairs of the Europa Hotel had taken off in the direction of Cave Hill, and his life had been saved by the door blowing off its hinges and banging him on the head, thrusting him as far down the S-bend as Shanks design and a skinny arse would permit. It was thus that the main force of the explosion swept over the door and upwards, leaving Pinky unconscious, but not as deep in the shit as he would otherwise have been.

Pinky had only one problem, apart from the two black eyes, a constant low ringing in his ears, a gigantic goose egg on his bonce, apparent elephantiasis of the balls, severe bruising of the bum, and a lingering smell of Jeyes fluid. He had just learned that the staff of the Musgrave Park had automatically informed HQNI, MOD and his unit, in that order, that he was their patient, and that soon the SIB, General fucking Sir Hector MacTavish, the Military Secretary, and his Regimental Colonel would all be queuing up outside the door to ask him what the devil he thought he was up to, having a shit in civvies in a demolished suite in the Europa Hotel. This was not going to be very pleasant, and although responding to treatment, his brain still seemed too loose in his cranium to do any logical evasive thinking.

And so it was with some trepidation that he answered the telephone by his bedside, and heard the unmistakable voice of the Regimental Colonel on the other end. "Pinky, old boy. How's the old piles, what? Now don't deny it, Pinky. Word's all round the Mess about being caught with the old trousers down, eh what? Could have been worse, though, Pinky, could have been in bed with a fancy bit, eh? How are you anyway, old boy?" "Not too good, really Colonel ..." Pinky began to reply. "Excellent, man. Knew it would take more than the jolly old IRA to get you, what? Now, Pinky. I haven't any time to waffle on about you and those gorgeous nurses curled up beside you there, ha ha, what? Something's come up." "Oh God!" thought Pinky, "Here we go for the high jump!" But to his surprise - nay, his shock - the next words were not accusatory. Far from it!

"Pinky. Congrats, old fellow. Have to stop calling me 'Colonel' in the Mess now, what? Name's 'Reggie', by the way. I've persuaded the Military Secretary that you are just the right chappie for the job and he's scrubbed all those adverse Confidential Reports. No problem at all, him being a true Blue Jacket, eh what? Well, Pinky, must be off now. Oh! Do make sure you are at the docks in Larne at 0700 hours day after tomorrow to take charge of your Battalion, won't you now? Don't let me down, now will you? Took a lot of G & T to pull this off, me boy. Toodle Oo!" But before the Regimental Colonel was able to get the receiver back on its cradle, Pinky managed to intervene and asked if he could have the foregoing repeated once again, 'please, Reggie'. And with a painful sigh 'Reggie' spelled it out for Pinky Jolly in simple words that even his befuddled, loose, grey matter was at last able to understand.

Having been informed by MOD that the 3rd Battalion the Blue Jackets (known, to their annoyance, throughout the British Army, as the '3rd Blow Jobs') had been taken off seven day standby as an emergency reinforcement battalion for Northern Ireland, and was to be posted there forthwith, in view of the probability of heightened tension in mid-Antrim over the Twelfth, due to the mass murder of innocent farming folk in Slaght on the night of the drumming competition, all the senior officers of the 3rd Battalion, including the CO himself, had presented themselves at the Regimental Colonel's door. On admittance, they had said such things as, "What a beastly bore, Colonel, what?", "*Grice* season coming up in a month. Must get some practice in, what?" "Pater's expecting me to join him and the new wife at his *hice* on the Riviera for a spot of leave, what?", and a thousand other valid excuses why officers of calibre should be excused the tedium of getting shot at in Ireland, a business much better left to the NCOs and other ranks, and any other wallahs with rank on their shoulders, but insufficient centuries of in-breeding to be able to speak properly, what?

It was thus that passed-over Pinky Jolly became the proud owner of a lieutenant-colonelcy in one of Britain's oldest and least respected Regiments, the Commanding Officer of a Battalion of new recruits and the unfortunate criminal or alcoholic detritus of the other two regular battalions, and the leader of six companies of men whose immediate OCs and platoon commanders were made up mainly of regimental rejects, keen as mustard, funny speaking chappies from the TA, and a collection of Gunga Dins from the RAEC, the Pioneer Corps, other attached non-infantry units, and - last but not least - the bloody, brush-shafting, poofter Padre! Still, it was a start. Maybe now Pinky would get that medal he so well deserved, even if it was only for spending most of his military career doing jobs that real officers didn't have to do, like dying for one's country, or sending people on projectionist's courses!

Pinky lay back carefully on his pillow, having become agonisingly aware that his pain-wracked body had been stiffly at attention on the bed, ever since he had answered the telephone ten minutes earlier. But the pain was nothing. It didn't even matter that he knew he had been rubber-dicked yet again. This time, because of his seniority, he had been rubber-dicked into becoming a lieutenant colonel, and that was worth all the misery of the preceding ghastly years. He had forgotten to ask the Regimental Colonel if that fucker MacTavish knew, but he presumed that he didn't, otherwise he would still be plain old Major Pinky and, most likely, in the tender loving care of the bully-boys of the SIB, prior to a prolonged trip to the South coast at Netley, the home for mutters of the officer variety. It didn't even matter that the poofter padre was on the team. There were plenty of ways to ream out that disgusting bastard, if you were in Ireland, and you were a lieutenant colonel.

Pinky began to appreciate how Moses must have felt when he came down from the mountain with the tablets, after his lengthy chinwag with the Boss. It didn't matter what the fuckers did now. He had the bastards, just where he wanted them. Now that he was a battalion commander, he would be able to put into effect his loosely conceived plans for bringing down the plum-mouthed officer corps, and mid-Antrim was as good a place as any other to begin. And like all other battalion commanders, who have been promoted one rank above their level of competence (i.e., the majority, at least as far as the British experience would tell us), Pinky perked up and began to chuckle to himself, already believing that he had taken to his new superiority as to the manor born. Oh! Foolish pride and futile folly! But *we* don't care, do we? This is going to make things a bit more interesting from now on. That's for sure! I don't know about *you*, but *I* can't wait to see what happens.

CHAPTER ELEVEN

he MI room at the Royal Irish Rangers Depot in Ballymena had had worse patients that Colonel Mooney, but they had never had any as distinguished as a senior officer in the SAS. For that reason he was treated with the most professional care and attention possible, not only because of his rank and regiment, but also because of the common fear among the less lethally proficient soldiery of the British Army, that to do otherwise with a member of the SAS would give them an introduction into the higher levels of pain that most people, fortunately, are never given the privilege of experiencing. Thus, despite the seriousness of his helicopter strut-induced concussion, when he eventually came to, and demanded to be released immediately, the MO had no problem with saying, to himself, 'Fuck the Hippocratic oath, the bugger's on his own', and was totally acquiescent.

It was with a most fiendishly chronic headache, agreeably accompanied by the sort of hot flashes, which are normally the preserve of menopausal women, that Mooney struggled to the building which had been allocated to his team, and where his secure communications equipment had been installed. As he crossed the parade ground, still dressed in a hospital nightgown, that flapped in the light breeze and showed off his skinny bare bottom and finely muscled calves, he took a sloppy salute from a passing recruit platoon, and pondered his next moves. His concussion had caused him to forget about his loss of Cathal's expense money, but he still remembered that things were probably more serious in Slaght than either he or MacTavish had originally thought, and not only because of the increasing number of pine coffins at that moment being prepared in Ballymena by ecstatic undertakers, but also because he was up against a man whom he himself had trained. He had lied when he had last spoken to the GOC. Sergeant Moriarty of 2 PARA was one of the most deadly and accomplished killing machines that he had ever known, and the only reason why he had never been allowed to apply for selection to 22 SAS was because even the SAS are not supposed to *enjoy* mass murder. Sergeant Moriarty, as Mooney recalled, was the most single-minded, evil bastard that he had ever had the distinct privilege of meeting, and that says a lot for any honest man, who looks at himself in the mirror every morning.

At last, seated behind the obligatory, blanket-covered, six-foot table, and wondering why Corporal Grieves and his companions of the morning had been smirking 'knowingly', when they had briefed him on the information that had come in during his temporary absence from consciousness, the Rat made his call to HQNI and spoke to the despicable Smythe-Gargle, with a lack of civility that just reconfirmed the latter poor bastard's confusion at the strangeness of the downturn in his personal relations with senior officers during recent hours. At last Sir Hector came to the handset and listened intently to Mooney's concise, but necessarily lengthy, report. When the Rat had finished there was a long pause, but, just when he was beginning to think that the one hundred thousand pounds of communications equipment had been made in Luton and not in Kobe, and was therefore totally useless, the voice of the GOC came back on the air.

"Are you one hundred per cent sure, Mooney, that it was Moriarty?" asked the General. "I regret to say, General, that there can be no doubt. I interrogated the terrorist myself, just before he died," replied the Rat, lying, as he frequently did, through the large gap in his front teeth. "I want you to treat this with the greatest priority, Mooney. I'm relying on you. I don't mind what it takes in human lives, but you get that for fucker for me, won't you? And I repeat what I said before; make it slow and bloody painful when you do. Okay?" said an obviously very vengeful superior. And after agreeing to put the capture and slow torture to the death of one, Sergeant Moriarty, at the top of his agenda, Mooney signed off respectfully and allowed his thumping headache to slump forward on to the regulation blotter pad on his six-foot table. Discipline and training narrowly prevented his succumbing to the billows of nausea that swept over him.

Ten minutes and a welcome recuperative cup of sweet NATO-standard tea later, Colonel Mooney made his next secure call. Almost immediately he was put through to the very dingy Paul Haggard, Controller Special Operations of MI6, sitting behind his paper-strewn desk in the equally dingy headquarters of the 'slithy toves brigade', South of the even dingier poofter-packed toilets of Waterloo Station. Despite the introduction of a Kentucky Fried Chicken franchise outlet, and the partial sterilisation of the JU 88 shit-bombing pigeon squadrons, which occupied this Victorian mausoleum to the stink and filth of steam, Waterloo remained the home of diplomats and passed-over colonels of MOD, hell-bent on self-destruction through a little innocent two-a-side wanking before racing to catch the twenty-five past six to suburbia or Basingstoke, where Mildred the frigid Shrew would, of course, have purposely drunkenly burned another disastrous soup from her seemingly unending collection of recipes provided by rent-a-cobra, the dreaded practitioner of enthusiastic euthanasia, otherwise lovingly known as 'the fucking mother-in-law'.

Haggard was famed and feared throughout the not-so-intelligent intelligence world. As a man who had once been the best friend and drinking partner of the evil George Blake, Haggard had survived the latter's confession of working for the KGB and even his assistance in securing the bastard spy's escape from Wormwood Scrubs and his flight to good press coverage and the Order of Lenin in sunny downtown Moscow. But he still retained a close affinity to his old friend's greatest attribute, namely, causing the deaths of as many poor agents of MI6 as possible. Unlike Blake, Haggard did not limit himself to Europe. As Controller Special Operations, he could get agents killed worldwide, even in Antarctica, if given a bit of time and sufficient budget to get something suitable off the ground. Special Operations had been set up by 'C', Sir Maurice Goldfield, after he had watched the TV series, 'The Sandbaggers", which purported to be based on the Service's rather more lurid exploits. It seemed like a good idea, Sir Maurice had thought at the time. After all, if you are going to be suspected of and even damned for doing it on the bloody box, you might as well give the scriptwriters something really juicy to get their rotten teeth into.

Haggard and Mooney went a long, long way back. Despite the fact that the dingy prick from the 'slithy toves brigade' was as unmilitary a specimen of humanity as a wet paper bag full of curried rat shit, he had a talent for total megalomaniacal mayhem that the Rat appreciated, as a fellow professional. For some fifteen years the two of them had been drawn together, time and time again, in their pursuit of bringing down the 'evil empire', and any other bastards who happened to be queuing up for homicidal subjection, at the behest of the toadying mandarins of Whitehall or their Bermuda shorted masters in Washington. While Mooney was lean and mean and a true fighting machine, Haggard was short, dumpy, and incredibly incapable of the slightest physical exertion, unless you called the twenty-six hours a day manipulation of an IQ of 185 and membership of the governing board of MENSA to be modern-day mental aerobics. Haggard admired and respected Mooney for the totality and purism of his murderous talent. Mooney admired and respected Haggard for his unswerving ability to come up with regular, nay, copious, opportunities for him to exercise those talents - and all in the cause of freedom, and for good old Queenie, even if she would deny involvement, if ever put to the test!

"Haggy, old boy, I thought Moriarty was beachcombing in bloody Bali. He can't be. We've just had the Book of Revelations opened up over here, as you may be aware, and it looks as if someone's deciphered a few more chapters of the Dead Sea scrolls, because this is a nasty one, that's for bloody sure", were the first remarks of the Rat to his sinister partner in crimes never to be revealed by a sane British Government, Labour, Liberal or even Communist. "Are you buggers up to some doomsday bloody game that I've not been let into, or has the bastard gone off the rails at last?" he added. "I've had Jakarta Station check, and he is definitely, I mean definitely, still running a brothel in Bali. Head of Station even had a short time himself, and said it was 'Fucking A-one!'. Moriarty says he's happy there and doesn't want any other missions, or as he put it to H/Jakarta, 'Tell that loony Mooney and that dishrag Haggard that I'm out. I've got the King of Laos' fucking treasure and there is sweet fuck all they can do about it.' Honestly, Ratty, Moriarty is living in sin, sand, sun, and sex in Bali, and the only thing that's going to get him out of there is tertiary syphilis!"

"Christ! Well that means he's got a twin fucking brother over here. You ever hear of a Mary McKelvey, nee Thompson? According to my lads, and also some nincompoop of an SB Inspector who foams regularly at the mouth, that they've recently talked to, Moriarty is shacked up with her and the two of them have just this very morning broken out the local IRA leader from the police station. Jesus, the outcome of that little shenanigans was a body count of over fifty UDR men, apparently killed by their own bloody side. Now, that sure as hell, sounds like our Moriarty, doesn't it, Haggy? I hope you're not shitting me after all these years we've been keeping the world population growth rate under control. I could get a little bit pissed off, if that were the case, my old friend!"

The mention of the name Thompson, in a mutual context of female and large death toll, caused Haggard to commence to hyperventilate and clutch for his worry beads. "You said Thompson, Mary Thompson?" he asked breathlessly. "Yes!" replied an increasingly exasperated Ratty. "Good God!" replied Haggard, and proceeded to relate to Mooney all the important details of '*l'affaire de Lourdes*', and the subsequent mass and fatal dyke-bashing '*affaire de Guildford*'. "Ratty! That bloody woman's lethal. Jesus, if she gets caught and comes up in court, me and the bloody Government are down the sewers, and not through a flush toilet, either. God, Ratty! You have to get rid of her. She's gone over to the other side obviously. She's an unguided bloody missile. If you don't stop her, she'll be ricocheting round the corridors of power like a wet fart before we know it, and all we've worked for will be covered in faeces."

"Shit!" said Mooney. "Haggy, I'll take your word for it about Moriarty, but this is big here. All hell's broken out and I've got the feeling that the devil has only sent out a platoon of imps so far, and that there are whole fucking battalions and brigades of bloody warlocks standing ready to follow any minute now. Don't forget our compact, will you?" And the Rat was delighted to hear Haggard respond quickly and firmly, "Don't worry, Ratty, I might stab the others in the back with regularity and pleasure, but you and I are in this together for the duration. Too much blood has flowed under the proverbial bridge, and too much money is in the joint Swiss account, for you and me to begin suspecting each other of not being honest at this late stage, old friend." "Okay! Don't worry, Haggy. It's just that I've been blown up twice today, apart from being chased by a fucking barn and struck by the left foot of a bleeding helicopter," said Mooney. "You sure you're all right?" asked Haggard, slightly confused by the last remarks. "Oh yes! I'm all right. I'm also fucking hopping mad. Look, Haggy, check on Moriarty in Bali just one more time, please. Meanwhile I am going to get to the bottom of what is cess-pooling around here, if it is the last thing I do." And with that, the Rat cut the connection, shouted for another cup of tea, and regretted that he had done so, because the noise caused his headache to swell back, like a tsunami hitting Honshu after the arse had dropped out of the Pacific Trench. Four codeine and his cup of tea later, the Rat summoned his NCOs and began to plan for every eventuality, including the mass murder of the citizens of Ballymena, if this was to prove necessary to get to the bottom of the mess he now found himself in.

Into the bar of the Republican Club in the Ardoyne at ten minutes to twelve that day came a well-refreshed Liam O'Shaughnessy, followed a minute later by his Chief of Intelligence, Phelim 'the Ferret' O'Malley. First Liam, and quickly thereafter, Phelim, sensed that something was wrong. The other good Provos present were ill at ease and did not wish to look them straight in the eyes. "God!" thought the Ferret instinctively, "The buggers have sold us out, and any minute now the fucking paras are going to burst in the door and shoot shit out of the OC and me, while the rest of them stand round the bar, scratching their bollocks and eating fucking smoky bacon potato crisps." Equally instinctively Phelim put his hand into the pocket of his donkey jacket and felt the reassuring grip of his Smith & Wesson. The very action of doing this had an electrifying effect on the rest of the bar's scrotum-scratching, lunchtime clientele, who now proceeded to compete with one another in the old Belfast game of how many paddies can squeeze through a door at gunpoint at the one time.

"What the fuck are ye doing?" hissed Liam, going for his gun in his jacket pocket, and thereby causing the log jam in the bar doorway to burst, as if the Spring melt floodwaters had just turned the bend in

the river. Liam was also nervous at the reaction of those around him
to his own entrance and the slightly later entrance of Phelim, and was
beginning to suspect that he was for the chop, particularly now that
Phelim had his hand in his right pocket. "Something's up here, Liam,
and I don't like it. No! I don't like it one bit!" replied the Ferret, now
believing that Liam was in on the conspiracy with the other traitorous
bastards. But at that moment the gunfight in the Ardoyne Republican
Club corral was temporarily postponed by the twelve o'clock news
coming on the TV that nestled in the corner above the left end of the
bar, protected by a mass of iron bars and chains from being stolen, as
if any good Republican would even dream of committing suicide by
doing such a thing!

Alone, and still without a drink in their hands, Liam and Phelim
watched the TV camera's portrayal of the mass murder at Slaght earlier
that morning. They also registered, without undue sense of loss that
their loyal and not so bright retainer, Cathal Fahey, and his three
comrades without arms and legs, had shrugged off their mortal coil in
airborne pursuit of the aims of the Cause. Still dumbstruck by the sheer
size and scope of the successful slaughter of Protestants in Slaght, they
then saw, with disbelief, the results of the IRA raid on the Barracks at
Ballymena. Another twelve of their own good men dead, but over fifty
peelers and UDR bastards now playing harps at the back entrance to
hell. God! It was bloody unbelievable. Just then the screen blinked and
the photographs of a smiling and ecstatically sensual Mary McKelvey,
followed by a less than flattering shot of obviously hung-over and rather
agricultural Ignatius Moriarty, were seen, and some dunderhead in
RUC uniform was being interviewed about these two terrorists who
were wanted for the break-out of the 'vicious and highly dangerous'
Paddy McCallion, 'famed and feared' mid-Antrim IRA commander,
from Ballymena earlier that morning. "Jasus!" said Liam out loud.
"Vicious and highly dangerous, famed and bloody feared'. The only way
you could possibly call McCallion 'dangerous' was if you bent over to tie
your shoe lace and forgot the bugger was behind you undoing his zip!"

"Holy Mary! I can see now why those yellow bastards were looking
at us a bit funny and in a hell of a hurry to get out of the bar," said
Phelim. "You're right", said Liam, "They think we are responsible for

all that, and they are shitting themselves in fright." "Begod, Liam, if I thought that you and I had arranged all of that, I'd be fucking afraid of us myself, that's for bloody sure! This Moriarty's a fucking genius! We must get someone to him quickly. We don't want him going and getting himself killed in some bloody backwater like Ballymena, when the bugger looks as if he could die a martyr's death in the Houses of Parliament in London, and taking the whole load of the bastards there with him. I'll get another team down to Slaght and see if we can locate him as a matter of priority."

"Good on you, Phelim", said Liam, "You do that. But I am beginning to think that there is a lot more that we can make out of this situation. If we play our cards right, we're going to do more for the Cause in the next few days than even blowing up the Houses of bloody Parliament would achieve. Just think, lad. Over a hundred and forty of their side gone already and probably a lot more about to peg it in hospital, and only sixteen down on our side, and plenty more eejits willing to join them if I crack my fingers twice. If this goes on right up to and over the Twelfth, we'll have the biggest Protestant backlash there's been since the strikes in '74. There'll be barricades all over Belfast and the Prods will be giving the RUC and the Army stick, and the soldier boys will take it for twenty-four hours before they get pissed off and send in the paras, and then the UVF and the UDA can have their own Bloody Sunday! The Peace Movement and the bloody women's organisations wont have a hen-toed, knock-kneed leg to stand on, and the priests are going to be locking themselves bollock-naked in the vestry closet with the altar boys and the communion wine. All hell will break loose, and we, Phelim, we are going to be right back where we want to be, two roosters in a hen house full of plump layers!"

"Good God, Liam! Do you not think we might be biting off a bit more than we can chew? I mean, its no secret to you and me that, if the Prods really wanted, they'd push the Army up a dark entry and sweep through the New Lodge and the Ardoyne like cod liver oil through a baby's bum. The Falls would last a bit longer, but they'd soon burn us out nonetheless." said a sober Phelim, and suddenly remembering that he had been in the bar for thirty minutes without a drink, he felt understandably faint, and shouted to the cowering barman for "two pints of Bass and two wee doubles". "Don't you worry, Phelim," said Liam, warming to his new plan. "If we play our cards right all the shite will be going on in Slaght and in the Protestant areas of the city only. Okay, there might be a bit of a problem along the Peace Line, but nothing we can't handle with a bit of planning beforehand. What I'm talking about, Phelim, is getting the Prods to go against the police and the Army. If we give the situation in Slaght a bit of a helping hand in the right way, we'll have them at each other's throats before they know it. Then the Prods will get the soldiers removed from Ulster, and we'll be able to get on with sorting them and the RUC out at our own pace and our own time. What do you think, Phelim?"

"I think it's bloody dangerous if we get it wrong, Liam, but I see what you mean. Let's give it a go, as long as we think we can get out of it alive ourselves." replied Phelim, now beginning to mull over the possibilities. "Liam. I think what we need to do is to send a few good teams to mid-Antrim to help stir up the shit. At the same time we get all the rest of the boys here in Belfast ready to man the barricades, for if it goes the wrong way, it'll be like when the German bombers came over and missed the shipyards - there wont be a lot left to sing songs about, that's for sure!" "I know what you mean, Phelim. I'll leave the planning to you. Just make it good, and as fail-safe as you can."

"Where do you think McCallion and Moriarty and that big lass are now, Phelim? We need to get in contact with them. Don't want them going off at half-cock and screwing it all up, do we?" "I'll keep trying to find the bugger, Liam. It shouldn't be too difficult. He's sure to make contact with some of his lads soon. Then I want to talk to Moriarty himself. We need to know where he's coming from and where the hell he thinks he's going. He's got a lot of talent, but if he's going to blow up half of Antrim without our permission, we might have to dispose of him. We can't afford some amateur fucking around and messing up our plans, even if he is the best thing we've seen since sliced bread." "I agree with you there," said Liam, "Rules is rules, after all, though it would be a pity if we had to put him through a kangaroo court all the same. Still, as long as we get the maximum use out of him in the meantime, that's what counts. Right, Phelim. Let's drink up and get out of here. There's a lot to be done."

And when they had gone the barman handed his apron and dishcloth over to one of his colleagues and said that he was off to visit his dying granny at the Mater Hospital. But he didn't go anywhere near the poor old bitch, her not being in the Mater Hospital, but in Milltown Cemetery, and this was his first and last mistake as a stoolie for the Branch. Instead he went to the City Centre and, twenty minutes after he had made a phone call, he met up with his handler in the back room of a butcher's shop. The barman passed on everything that he had overheard, received a couple of fivers, and waited - as he had been trained - for ten minutes after the SB man had departed, before starting his own way back to the Ardoyne Republican Club. He had just come out of the security fence protecting the City Centre when a passing green Cortina, heading, with two of the Belfast Brigade boyos from the Short Strand, to blow up North Queen Street RUC Station, went prematurely into non-geostationary orbit. (Another perfectly executed 'own goal'!) As the barman rocketed over the nearby rooftops he could see, in the smoke hazed distance, the green fields of Antrim stretching away to the North and looking unsuspectingly peaceful for the time of year.

Meanwhile, just as our former barman was coming down to land on the spiked railings of a Presbyterian Church, there was evil afoot, miles and miles away from Belfast. Now, in your naiveté you may have thought that only the Irish are eejits and that only the good Protestants and Catholics of Ulster are involved in self-immolation in our tale. Wrong! Very wrong! There is one place where the murderous tendencies of the local population far outdo in professionalism and dedication the lunacy of the Irish, and it is not Beirut, either! It is Glasgow, or more specifically, the less salubrious parts of that fair city of unemployment and intellectually short people. If you think that Billy Connolly is 'stage-Glaswegian', and is just putting on an act for your benefit, you are far wrong. He is as big an eejit as he makes out to be. The only difference between Billy Connolly and the rest of the people of Glasgow is that he can afford to pay for the drink that he consumes, and he wears bananas on his feet.

Most of you uneducated morons who have got this far will be wondering why a load of drunken Scotsmen would want to get themselves involved with the Ulster situation, when there are plenty of other ways to pass the time North of the border, like, for instance, sticking your cold hand up somebody's kilt and seeing his reaction when you grab his unwrapped goolies, or attempting to complete the 'whisky trail' in one day without missing out a single distillery, or trying to calculate how many sunny days they've had in Elgin this year and seeing if you've got more than one left after you've divided the number by two. But then, most of you will be English, and know bugger all about history, other than that some perruqued ponce by the name of Clive of India opened the Empire, and that Harold got a third eye at the Battle of Hastings. The sum total of your knowledge of Scottish history will probably have been gleaned from watching repeats of Treasure Island on the TV, and that'll not get you very far, that's for sure. You see, to have a full understanding of the nature of the lack of Scottish culture, you have to appreciate that the thrifty buggers came from Northern Ireland originally, although for what reason nobody other than the Scots themselves can ever fathom. It's a bit like leaving Spitsbergen to go and set up house on Novaya Zemlya, and not too many have done that, I would think. Scotland's a great place, if you like rain, more rain and a good blizzard in season. It's the sort of place where mothers-in-law get their training - cold, miserable, mean and mousy.

Glasgow prides itself on having more Orange Lodges than Ulster. (That's an exaggeration, of course, but then it's not just the Texans or the Australians who think that they are bigger and better than the rest of us!) Most of these Orange Lodges are simply fronts for Glasgow Rangers Football Supporters Club, or, rather, the more violent majority of the Rangers supporters. They were established to kick shite out of all Glasgow Catholics in the unlikely event that Rangers ever lose a game against their Fenian rivals, Glasgow Celtic. As such, the Orangemen of Glasgow are not only tried and proven poor sportsmen, they are at the same time even more rabid than their counterparts in Ulster, especially when it comes to putting the boot in the nether regions of someone who hadn't up till then realised that it was a crime to have received a third class education at a school called St. Mary's, or that having an 'O' and an apostrophe in front of your surname could get you killed on a Saturday night.

Your average Ulster Orangeman is usually in the Lodge for the drink and the pretty sash, with a bit of a lark shouting 'Fuck the Pope' in a loud voice and with the safety of numbers, while walking four miles away from the easiest and straightest route home, under the armed protection of the RUC and the British Army, in order to pass through a suitably small and vulnerable Catholic ghetto on the Twelfth of July. Your average Glasgow Orangeman is an entirely different kettle of smelly fish! He's big enough of an eejit to get totally blootered in the pub on a Saturday night and then single-handedly take on the whole of Glasgow Celtic Supporters Club, on their own turf, at two o'clock in the morning - and win! No normal Ulster Orangeman would be that daft, but then maybe Glasgow hasn't got its own Purdysburn, and needs to release its tensions outside of a padded cell. You should be required to get a visa and your head examined before venturing into the wrong parts of Glasgow, at any time of the day or night, unless you are the proud owner of a squadron of Chieftain tanks.

There are two things in particular that distinguish the Glaswegian, Catholic or Protestant, from the higher species of the ape, namely, his ability to vomit on demand, and the use of his favourite weapon, the 'Glasgow kiss.' The former is a phenomenal attribute, and years of painstaking dedication appear to go into being able to perform at any venue, and in a myriad of Technicolors that are truly Impressionist. Only two non-Glaswegians have ever come close to the high standards of Sauchiehall Street, Brendan Behan and his folk-singing brother, Dominic. The former is famed for having two pictures of his fine self on the front page of a Toronto newspaper at the one time; the one on the left showing him receiving the Freedom of the City, and the one on the right being a more atmospheric portrayal of the great author lying in the gutter later the same evening. Young Dominic was not to be out-done, however, as he gave a brilliant performance at the Oxford Union, when he was speaking against a motion concerning the existence of such a thing as a 'stage Irishman'. In order to re-inforce his position in defence of Irish culture at the vital moment of the debate, he threw up the twelve pints of excellent Guinness he had earlier consumed in the Union bar. He lost the debate, but he sure as hell impressed the intellectuals with the vehemence of his arguments and the breadth of his vision.

But 'the Glasgow kiss'! Now, that is a true art form. It consists, in short, of finding a perfect stranger in a public place, either unaccompanied or with several hundred bodyguards. Either way makes no odds. You then proceed to pick an argument about why this stranger is 'looking at you like that' or 'who does he think he is, to be thinking at all.' There are several customary variations in the preamble, but they all are just a brief interlude of courtship or foreplay, before the real kissing starts. The perfect stranger, accosted by the mating Glaswegian, is approached by the latter and then nutted with some force, right on the bridge of the nose, by the opposing forehead. It is a matter worth some scientific research, because the Glaswegian, in making his lightning move, never damages his own nose or head. Far from it. If his chosen playmate of the evening is not already on the ground and yelling for Mammy, the nut may go in two or three more times. An aficionado of this art can even succeed in driving the nose of his mate right through the brain, and can thereafter continue to practise his skill in the canteen of Barlinnie Prison, where the Glaswegian Kiss Olympics are held nightly. But back to the subject of Glasgow's Loyal Orange Lodges and their part in our unfolding saga.

In the wasteland of Maryhill in Glasgow there stood, in the year that we are visiting, a dog-shit grey brick Victorian building, the home of "Loyal Sons of Maryhill, L.O.L. 666". At five o'clock on the afternoon after the morning massacres in Slaght and Ballymena, as soon as the Unemployment Exchange and the bookies were shut for the day, the brethren of L.O.L. 666 assembled in the main hall to be briefed by the Reverend John McCartney in connection with their forthcoming trip to Ulster for the Twelfth celebrations. The previous year they had gone to the Field at Finaghy outside Belfast, but that had been a disappointment, as the Reverend Dr. Ian Paisley had not been on his usual demagogic form, and had not whipped them into that fervour necessary for the successful hijacking of a jumbo to Rome to have afternoon tea with the Pope. Neither had their Ulster comrades joined them, when they turned off the direct route back from the field and tried to invade a Catholic enclave being protected by the gentlemen of the Parachute Regiment. This was particularly disappointing, as most of the brethren of L.O.L. 666 were part-timers in 15 PARA TA, also headquartered in a bleak building in Maryhill, and were looking for a chance to show off their prowess to their 'Regular' mates. As a result the visitors from Maryhill had a prolonged tour of the ICU facilities at the Royal Victoria Hospital. This year, however, they would be visiting the Field in mid-Antrim; and this time they would be going prepared, with all their handguns and a few recently acquired sub-machine guns concealed in the instrument cases of their accompanying flute band.

The Reverend John McCartney was a fine example of a true Scottish Presbyterian. His Protestantism was of a purity of which John Knox himself would have been proud. There was only one straight path to Heaven, and that was over as many Fenian corpses as it took to pave the road. Fire and brimstone were not to be future pleasures of the flesh in Hell; they were to be meted out in generous measure during this short and painful spell of life on earth. Even the coldest and rainiest day in Glasgow could not dampen the enthusiasm of the Reverend McCartney for his chosen calling, the purification of humanity from the stench of Rome. It was thus, in terms of, 'No Surrender', that he, as Master of the Lodge, addressed his brethren that afternoon. He informed those present, some of whom had been too hung-over to have seen the news from Ulster on the TV earlier in the day, of the tragic events in Slaght, and reminded them that this was the very site of the Twelfth Field that they would be going to defend in several days' time. By six o'clock the good Minister had them eating out of his hand. This year, whether the locals in Antrim had the balls for it or not, L.O.L. 666 was going to do more than a wee bit of 'religious cleansing'. Fuck the fact that there wasn't a Catholic for miles around Slaght. If needs must, they'd march to Belfast and invade the Falls Road!

The meeting of the Lodge over, the Brethren split up and went to their favourite pubs, where they would reconfirm their faith yet again by drinking themselves into a murderous rage. This rage was only heightened when the nine o'clock news on the TV gave a detailed and full colour description of the events at Slaght, and the steadily mounting death toll of the UDR in the attack by the IRA on Ballymena. A senior RUC spokesman referred to this latter debacle as a 'slaughter of innocents', and in a way he wasn't too far wrong. As chucking out time came - and, in Glasgow, that time varies, depending on how big and brave the landlord thinks he is - groups of Maryhill Orangemen headed out across the city, armed with half bottles in their pockets and forgoing their normal visit to the corner chippie for cod, curry, and chips, and began to hunt down any Catholics daft enough to be walking the streets at that hour of the night. Finding no volunteers available only increased their anger, and so they vented their spleen by burning the odd car and giving patrolling policemen the fear of their lives. There is nothing more vile or despicable, nothing more murderous or marauding, than a Glaswegian with a skinful and no one to fight. In the end there was nothing else for it, and they had to fall back on the old Glasgow standby. They began to batter the shite out of each other, thereby reducing by twenty-five per cent the number who would be risking their lives (and everybody else's) by visiting Slaght for the Twelfth.

The Reverend McCartney did not take part in such nocturnal diversions, but neither did he condemn them. He was the first to appreciate that they were good training for the 'big day', and as a student of the psychology of the Glaswegian mind, he knew that there was nothing more likely to get one of the Brethren into the right frame of homicidal frenzy than having the daylights beaten out of him by two or three of his best friends. Yes! They would do all right, his flock, not like Paisley's bloody, weak-kneed pansies. He was a bit more impressed by what he had learned about the high moral values, as practised by the Reverend Bertie Mulholland. The Reverend McCartney considered that any man of the cloth, whom the worthy Dr. Paisley himself had tried to exorcise from the Free Reformed Presbyterian Church, on no less that eight occasions, had to be his sort of preacher, a man who could wield the sword in his right hand, and didn't need to consult the Bible in his left, as he already new all the bloodier bits off by heart. Yes! McCartney was ecstatic that there had been a mini-Armageddon in mid-Antrim. He just hoped that the Fenians wouldn't scurry off South before he arrived in his role as Fifth Horseman of the Apocalypse!

CHAPTER TWELVE

The new day arrived without any major incidents occurring in mid-Antrim, although there had been a worrying flurry of individual raids on the homes of UDR and RUC men overnight, and a significant number of both legally and illegally held weapons had been stolen. Of course, none of this was officially reported, and the Army was, therefore, unaware, but 'those in the know' in the upper echelons of the RUC and the UDR were beginning to get a little concerned, with the exception of Chief Inspector McCambridge, who, as always, remained calm, cool and collected in the face of forthcoming adversity, particularly from the security of his well-guarded office in Castlereagh. But then, McCambridge knew more about what was going on than most. A particularly interesting report from one of his men had passed across his table early that morning, concerning a conversation overheard between the OC Belfast Brigade PIRA and his Chief of Intelligence. The Chief Inspector had been delighted at the aggressive intentions of O'Shaughnessy, but a little concerned at the Ferret's caution. This latter sensitivity would have to be noted down for the future. It just wouldn't do to have anyone back-sliding at this stage of the game. In McCambridge's opinion 'cold feet' were the sole preserve of the wife, and should not be an attribute of leading members of sectarian terrorist organisations. That sort of thing was most definitely not good for business!

During the course of the morning he passed the intelligence to Smythe-Gargle at HQNI, making sure that he exaggerated the role and importance of the man, Moriarty, although it wasn't difficult to exaggerate the abilities of that particularly intriguing character. He must get to know him before he died, McCambridge thought to himself, and he meant Moriarty's death, not his own! In the meantime Smythe-Gargle rushed from his office to the nets at the edge of the cricket pitch at Lisburn, where General Sir Hector MacTavish was getting in some batting practice as a way of calming the tension that was racking his nervous system. A young subaltern was bowling up another fast ball when Smythe-Gargle, wisely standing behind the nets, brought the General up to date and reached the exaggerated part concerning Moriarty and a big-busted Englishwoman, and what they were going to do to the future of the British Army. This had such a dynamic effect on Sir Hector that he thwacked the ball with a force, speed, and style more typically seen on a baseball diamond. Off like a guided missile it went, fortunately over the head of the young bowler, and one hundred feet away, at the edge of the pitch, it struck a rose-pruning Paddy McGonigle right in the knackers. Now Paddy may not have had the occasion or the interest to use these particular organs for a considerable number of years, but that didn't cause any reduction to the severity of the pain he felt when he came out of the lightning flash of shock that bolted through every nerve fibre in his body.

By the time he had managed to get his first gasping breath, Paddy was surrounded by several concerned officers in cricket whites, and a pimply Smythe-Gargle, all at a loss as to how to resuscitate a man after an eighty mile an hour blow in the unprotected goolies by a well-hit cricket ball. Not knowing what else to do, they confined their assistance to inane comments, such as, "Does it hurt, old chap?" "Bloody well caught, Paddy!", and "Maybe we should get somebody to rub them for him." At the back of the group stood a fuming MacTavish, who had no sympathy for poor Paddy's family jewels, and appeared, by the way he was wielding his bat, to be about ready to use the gardener's head as a new ball. But it wasn't Paddy's head that was in danger, it was pimply Perry's, and as Smythe-Gargle, once again having forgotten the ancient penalty meted out to the bearer of bad news, looked round, this realisation came rather quickly to him. Fortunately, however, he ducked just in time, whereupon Paddy, who had just been assisted to a standing position by two of the officers, a position he had absolutely no desire to be in for at least another year, took the full force of a cricket bat across the side of his face, knocking his false teeth over two rose bushes and into the wheelbarrow of best horse manure, that he had only five minutes earlier been happily pushing.

"Drat it! Bloody missed!" growled the General and stomped off, purple-faced, in the direction of the clubhouse. The other officers stared at Smythe-Gargle as if he was pariah, it having impressively quickly dawned on their otherwise slow-thinking grey matter, that the ADC was no longer in the Old Man's favour, and, therefore, of no bloody use to anyone. With a collective and snooty 'Hmmph!' and their toffee noses in the air, they turned their backs and moved quickly after the GOC, in order to be in position, should Sir Hector require confirmation of what an idiot his despicable ADC was. Smythe-Gargle was left standing over the semi-conscious body of Paddy McGonigle. He was torn between an almost overwhelming need to break down in tears and a desire to shoot himself with his 9 mm Browning High Power. Perry did neither. Instead he looked intently at the bloodied and moaning McGonigle, and slowly, ever so slowly, a look of infinite nastiness came over his acned face. It was a look the like of which his face had only once before projected, when he had tied a knot in his wet towel and covered it with Algipan, the sportsman's horse liniment, just before giving that little faggot, Thorpe Minor, a good thrashing on the bollocks for touching his bottom as he was entering the cold plunge in the school changing rooms after a game of rugger. (Needless to say, the little faggot, Thorpe Minor, had been held down by four of Perry's mutually acned friends in the Sixth Form, as this painful punishment was being executed.) "No!" said Perry to himself, "No bloody General's going to make a fool of me in front of my inferiors. The Smythe-Gargle motto isn't, '*Shaft Behind The Arras*', for nothing! Just you wait and see!"

And with that Perry went over to the wheelbarrow and retrieved Paddy's false teeth, washed them none-too-well under the garden hose and put them in his pocket. He then tipped the horse manure among the roses and lifted a protesting McGonigle into his new official transport, and slotted himself behind the shafts. Off this most incongruous pair then wobbled in the direction of the gardener's hut, where, after making a cup of hot sweet, non-NATO-standard tea for Paddy, and helping the old man to insert his dung-stained teeth the right way up in his swollen gums, Perry began to prepare some hypothetical questions to the first Irishman with whom he had found any affinity since his arrival in this accursed isle.

Perry deliberated to himself for some time, allowing the incapacitated McGonigle the opportunity to decide what, in retrospect, was the more painful, the cricket ball or the cricket bat. Eventually Paddy reached the conclusion that it was a 'tie' for first place. He had never understood the English passion for the bloody game, what with its 'silly man out' and its 'googlies', or whatever the hell they were, but he believed that he had had a minor enlightenment about what the latter term meant, and he sure as hell now understood the former! As the hot tea began to have a restorative effect on his morale, if not on his savaged body, Paddy began to take in his surroundings for the first time in fifteen minutes. All his pots and tools were, comfortingly, in their right place. The only thing odd was that that male tampon, Pimples Smith-Gobble, or whatever his vixen of a mother had called him, was sitting on his bench, merrily pulling the leaves from a prize begonia that Paddy had hoped would win a prize in the Ulster Show. He lurched to his feet in righteous horticultural anger, felt the sudden rush of blood from his head to where his balls had once been, thought better of it, and sat down for a further good throbbing. Eventually he plucked up enough wind in his lungs to say in a croak of a voice that sounded more like his eighty-nine year old Uncle Sean than it did himself, "What do you want with me, Captain. Haven't you and your kind done enough to me and poor Ireland for the last eight hundred years? And would you stop desecrating me bloody begonias. They're the only friends I've got left, as far as I can see."

"Paddy, old boy. I'm frightfully sorry about what happened. How are the old dingle-dangles anyway?" asked Perry. "They might be bloody 'dingle-dangles' where you come from, Captain, but they used to be the finest set of hydraulic action meat injectors in the whole of Ulster, let me tell you. And now, thanks to your bloody leader, all I've got left to take to the grave are two polythene bags of prime mince!" was Paddy's heated reply. "Understand, old boy. Fully sympathise with you, what?" said Perry. "What do you mean, 'What'?" asked a disgruntled McGonigle, recovering more and more by the minute, and feeling that he would be able to walk unassisted by at least the year 2000 AD. "What do you mean 'what do you mean, what?', what?" replied a confused Smythe-Gargle. "Ah! Fucking forget it! I'm too bloody knackered to even care!" replied McGonigle, which set Perry off laughing like a hee-hawing donkey with a head cold. "Bloody good, Paddy. Knew you wouldn't take it lying down, what? Super joke, eh, 'too bloody knackered' what? You've got spunk, Paddy - well, maybe not for a couple of weeks, but you know what I mean, eh what?"

By this time Paddy was edging his right hand towards where a newly sharpened pruning knife was lying on the bench on which Perry was sitting, intent on castrating the pimply little bastard and burying him in the compost heap, where eventually he could repay the damage he was doing to the begonia population of Lisburn. But Perry Smythe-Gargle had come of age in the last twenty minutes and was showing the first signs of following in the footsteps of his inglorious ancestors, who were infamous in English history for having changed sides during the Civil War no less than seventeen times, and three times, as far as is known, within the first fifteen minutes of the Battle of Edgehill alone! His 9 mm was up Paddy's left nostril an inch past the foresight before the gardener had even seen it leave its holster, something, which seemed to surprise Smythe-Gargle himself. Clearly our Perry had not just been idly playing pocket billiards during weapon training at RMAS.

"Now, now, Paddy. None of that, old boy. Just a friendly chat, that's all I want. I need a bit of advice, and I hope that you will be able to give it to me. I don't want to beat around the bush. I'm sure you have got better things to do, like putting a bread poultice on your willy, or some such. But don't fuck me around, Paddy! I've decided to be very nice to you, and I want to be very nasty to someone else, and I think you are the key, okay?" By this time Paddy was adding a lacerated nostril to his other woes, but the prospect of a 9 mm bullet clearing out his sinuses put even an eighty miles an hour cricket ball and a piece of best Suffolk willow into true perspective. He withdrew his hand from the bench and positioned it with the other one, delicately cuddling and comforting his groin. "Okay, Captain, you win. What do you want me to do for you, poison fucking MacTavish's lettuces?" sighed McGonigle, with that lassitude of the soul which always comes when you realise that, even at your own advanced years, a crunch in the groin by a speeding cricket ball, and a blatter round the jaw with the bat associated with the same, all have a price which must be paid sooner or later.

"Hmm! Not a bad idea, Paddy. Not bad at all. Tell you what. We'll keep that one in reserve, shall we? But I was thinking about something a little more spectacular, what? More public. A blistering good humiliation followed by a slow and painful death, preferably on the nine o'clock TV news. Yes! That's more the sort of thing. What do you think?" asked Perry. "Captain, if I had the slightest fucking clue what you are bloody talking about, then I might be able to have the luxury of an opinion. But since I don't have anything other than a sore face, and set of balls that are going to gyp like buggery when they eventually drop down out of the wrong hole, I'm afraid I'm totally in the bloody dark! We can carry on here till dark while you gibber away like the eejit you are, but could you at least gibber less like a fucking baboon. Would you have the decency to stop speaking like Harry Secombe on the Goon Show, and tell me in simple, plain English, what the hell it is you want of me?

EH WHAT!"

"Oh! I see. Sorry about that, old boy. Getting a bit ahead of you, what? Training you know. Sandhurst and all that. Quickens the old brain waves. Officer corps, what! Have to train the bloody men to understand. NCOs usually do the interpreting. Super fellows! Backbone of the British Army, what?" said Perry, but realised by the glazed look passing over Paddy's eyes, that the old gardener was either having instant recall of his brief fielding career, or that he hadn't understood a word that he had been saying. "Oh, dear! Not too good at talking to the ORs, you see, Paddy. Tell you what! I'll try the old BBC la-di-dah, okay, what?" "I don't care if you chant it in fucking Latin, but for Christ's sake get on with it, or put me out of my misery with your great big gun. I just want to go home, kick shit out of the greyhound, ring the necks of me racing pigeons, and tell the missus she'd better find a fancy man, for I'm in the spare room from now on, God spare me!" And Paddy McGonigle got the closest he had been to tears, other than picking the onions in his allotment every year, since he had pulled his zip up rather too quickly at the age of eighteen, on the first night his Da had taken him out drinking, the Ulster equivalent of telling your son about the 'birds and the bees'.

"Well, Paddy, it's like this. For some reason the General has decided to take a distinct dislike to me, just over the last two days. I think he's gone batty, or something, but he's not so rational, now is he? He meant to hit me with that bat, and if it hadn't been for my keen survival instincts, it would have been my teeth in the horse manure, and I haven't the advantage of false ones, like you, you lucky devil. Now, if he carries on like this, either he's going to kill me or he's going to destroy my career. Same thing, either way, old chap. But then you paddies wouldn't understand 'honour', and 'the Regiment', and that all sort of thing, would you? I suppose not. Well, I'm not going to stand for it, Paddy. I'm going to put my foot down before it gets worse. See what I mean?" And Paddy answered, "Yes! I do!" which was an out and out lie, for he didn't have a fucking clue. But it was easier on the nerves and the ears than having the simpering prick go through it in bloody Papua New Guinea pidgin the next time round.

"Excellent, my dear chap! Well, I think, Paddy, that you could do me a very big favour. I'd be *awfully grateful*, you know. Will you help me, Paddy?" Paddy was torn between total incomprehension at what the slithering skid-mark was talking about and the magic words, albeit rather Public School English, '*awfully grateful*.' 'Grateful' was the same in any language that Paddy knew, and he only spoke one, and that with a nauseatingly broad Belfast accent. "You tell me what it is you want me to do, for God's sake, and then I'll tell you how '*awfully grateful*' you'd have to be," answered Paddy, switching the less contused part of his brain into horse-trading mode. "Bit embarrassing in a way, really, Paddy. Don't really know how to put it. Wouldn't like you to take it the wrong way. Terrible scandal, if it got out, that is, you know, what?" "I don't know what the fuck you are talking about, you plum-sucking cretin. Now fucking tell it the way it is in four letter words, or fuck off and play cricket with your own nuts, you stupid English pillock!" screamed a frustrated Paddy, who now couldn't care a damn if Smythe-Gargle shot him through the snot-hole or danced naked on the hut bench with his kidney wiper in his mouth. He'd had about enough. Any more and either he was going to slit his own throat or blow Shit-Bubble and the rest of the smarmy gits from here to Tipperary - and without a choir of flabby, uniformed, concert hall non-combatants to keep the bastards in tune!

"Yes. Well, ahem. Yes. Take your point, old chap. No need to get all uppity now. There's a good fellow. Not too easy, you see, what?" said Perry, and was stopped in the continuation of his ramblings by Paddy making a lightning swipe for the pruning knife and commencing to cut his own throat. "Good God, man! Stop! Please, stop! I'm doing my best." Whereupon Paddy sighed again and put the knife down on the bench again, and, in a churlish and begrudging fashion, accepted Smythe-Gargle's offer of his fresh, up the left-hand shirt sleeve, snuff handkerchief, in order to stem the new flow of blood from the latest wound of the day.

"Paddy. Are you all right? Good. Well, here goes! Paddy, I want you to put me in touch with the IRA. Not just anyone. One of the important chappies. Must be someone at the top, who can make decisions. You know?" "Jesus, Mary, and Joseph!" whistled Paddy. "Have you taken leave of your senses, man? How in under God do you think I would know anybody in the IRA, me working for the Army and all? And how in the hell do you'd think they'd even listen to me? They'd think me head was cut! Next thing is I'd have a damn sight more than sore balls! I'd be swinging from a lamppost, dead, with bullet holes in me elbows and knees, shot through both ways, and covered in tar and the guts of a best eider-down mattress! You know what your problem is, don't you. Your fucking head's on the wrong way round and all you can see is the hairs growing out of the sheugh of your arse, ye lunatic. I've never heard as much utter balderdash in all me life!"

"Wow, Paddy! That was quite a speech. Must be feeling a bit better now that you've got all that of your chest, what?" said Perry. "Patrick McGonigle, I'm deadly serious. I want to talk to someone very senior in the Belfast Brigade Provisional IRA Staff about solving a small mutual problem to our joint satisfaction, namely, the assassination in most humiliating circumstances of one, General Sir Hector MacTavish, K.B.E., D.S.O., M.C. and two bars. Simple, isn't it. "Good Lord, Captain, you'll get us both killed!" said a frantic Paddy, rushing over to the door of the hut and opening it to check for MI5. "Don't worry, Paddy. Sandhurst, old boy. The Six 'Ps", what!" "What the fuck are ye gibbering about now, ye demented arsehole?" asked Paddy in a breathless voice, having rushed to the far end of the hut to check out the window at that end for any lurking SAS assault teams ready to storm the building. "The Six 'Ps', Paddy. Oh, that's another good joke, eh what? Paddy makes a seventh 'P', hah, hah!" laughed Perry. "Bloody Paddy's going to shit himself in a minute, if you don't shut the fuck up", said McGonigle lurching ball-less to the side window, to spot for Japanese snipers in the elms across the lawn. "Six 'Ps'. Prior Planning and Preparation Prevents Piss Poor Performance. Oh, dear! That makes seven. 'Fraid you'll have to be the eighth 'P', Paddy. All right with you, old boy?" said a smirking Perry, preening himself like a cock pheasant at having come up with such a spiffing witticism.

"You're not serious, ye eejit. Tell me you're not, pray to God!" pleaded McGonigle. "Never more so, Patrick, me old fruit. Never more so. Now, you run off, well, toddle off might be easier, and I'll pop in to see you here at eight tomorrow morning for the instructions on timings, RV and the rest of the jolly old show, what? Knew you'd turn out to be a brick, Paddy. Always had an eye for the old retainers, you know. Sterling yeoman stock. Pater says not too many left now. Puts it down to the fact that they went over the top with too much enthusiasm at the Somme, what! Mind, you, not too many good yeomen where Pater is at present. Mostly bloody dagos, as far as I could see. Well, tatty bye, Paddy. See you at eight on the dot tomorrow morning. Toodle-oo." And with that Perry Smythe-Gargle, latest traitorous turncoat in the long history of shafting behind the arras Smythe-Gargles, exited the gardener's hut and marched off confidently in the direction of the GOC's residence, where he would pretend to act as if nothing untoward was happening. At the same time he would sleep with his pistol under his teddy from now on, and he would keep a beady eye out for that old fucker MacTavish doing a pre-emptive strike on him, before he was able to get the wellie in first.

Paddy McGonigle sat with his head in his hands for half an hour before deciding what to do. He had forgotten most of the pain in his groin and head, although the pain had certainly not yet forgotten Paddy. At last, with a deep sigh of reluctance, he stood up and put on his old jacket, hanging on the back of the door. He would have to tell the Ferret, even if it meant his death. There was no other way for it, now. That blithering poncing eejit, Snot-Goblin, was likely to spill the beans at a moment's notice. Better to see what the Ferret said first, before he made a run for it to the caravan at Ramsay on the Isle of Man and assume the identity of an itinerant nobody. Why, oh why, all those long years ago, had he volunteered? Yes! Bloody volunteered his services to the Cause. What had he got out of it? Not a fucking penny, a lot of mental grief, and a set of sore balls. But as he was shutting and locking the door behind him, Paddy paused and looked up at the magnificent mansion on the hill. "*Awfully* fucking *grateful*. Well, Captain Peregrine Shite-Stubble. I'm going to see just how grateful you can be. And I'm sure as hell not going to say a fuck about that aspect of our new relationship to that weasel, O'Malley!" Without further ado, Paddy McGonigle, the spy just in from the cold, headed limpingly towards the bus stop and his journey to meet with Karla in the back streets of a small ghetto in Ulster. There was a smile on his face - part grimace at having to walk like John Wayne, just off work after six days in the saddle, and part sheer, unadulterated Belfast greed.

Despite the sunny weather and the total lack of breeze, the ship was experiencing swells normally attributed to gale force winds in Finistere in February; but they were not near the 'frog hatchery', these particular storms, they were in St. George's Channel, between England and Ireland. H.M.S. Intrepid was living up to her name, both as 'intrepid' and as an 'assault ship'. That is, she was being incredibly fucking daring to be at sea in strange weather like this, and she was being 'gang-banged' by the briny in a way that made 'Grievous Bodily Harm' look like a euphemism for tinea pedis. For twelve hours now, ever since they had boarded in balmy conditions of eighty degrees Fahrenheit and faulty air-conditioning at Devonport, the 3rd Battalion The Blue Jackets had literally been on the high seas, and there wasn't hardly a man jack of the sorry bastards literally or figuratively within one hundred miles of the land of the living. The Royal Navy personnel would have been taking advantage of the situation, bringing buckets of rancid pork fat down to the troop decks, for the breakfast predilection of the vomiting soldiery, as is their humorous wont, if they themselves had not been otherwise very much engaged in the ultra-serious survival business. No-one on the crew, not even the Captain himself, an old salt with a slight suspicion of tar-brush in him, called Mickey Greston, had ever seen seas like this in home waters in early July - and with no winds to play the Ride of the Valkyries over them. It was really like something out of the tales told about the Bermuda Triangle. A steely blue sea under a cloudless and windless sky, and waves as big as skyscrapers passing underneath and by on both sides, and all seeming as if they were coming out of a Coleridge nightmare.

On the bridge the Captain turned to his Number One and said, "Jesus, Jimmy, I've never seen anything like this in my life, except on the Sea of Japan when an earthquake had happened. Are you sure there haven't been any plate movements recorded? "Nary the one, Skipper," Jimmy replied, loving every minute of the excitement. This was what he had joined the Senior Service for in the first place, the lone challenge against all that nature could throw at you, 'rum, bum and baccy', to paraphrase how Winston Churchill had put it, and all bolstered by a firm and oft-quoted belief that he was a direct descendant of the fictional Horatio Hornblower, which, while it gave his peers much ideal amusement, had certainly not enamoured him with the Admiralty nor accelerated his promotion prospects.

"Jimmy, get them all in life-jackets, before they're too fucking sick to put the bloody straps on. I don't like this one bit, I can tell you," said the Captain. "With respect, Sir, is that not being just a little bit jumpy. Teach the bloody green jobs of the Ramblers Association a bit of a decent lesson, weather like this will, wont it? Anyway, we've been through worse, haven't we, Sir", said the Number One. "Look Jimmy, I know we've been through worse, but that was in the Iceland fucking Gap in the middle of bloody January, and not with a caboodle of vomiting juveniles aboard, all armed to the teeth with first line ammunition. It's too chancy, Jimmy. Just do as I say!" And having clamped his authority right down the throat of his Number One, the Captain raised his binoculars to peer out across the eerie emerald caverns opening on the starboard side of the ship. "Jesus, Skipper, Jesus!" was all the respectful reply that Captain Greston got from his second-in-command, and that reply he considered not only insubordinate, but downright bloody blasphemous. With the blue electric fire in his eyes that had got him the nickname of 'Gripper' Greston, he turned round to grab his Number One and escort him by the ear to the chart room for a little *tete a tete*. But still having his binos to his eyes, he saw not Jimmy, but what Jimmy had seen. "Jesus H. fucking Christ", he whispered, in an awesome voice that caused the Petty Officer on the wheel to do the unthinkable and look left instead of forward, fortunately without taking the wheel in the same direction as his now transfixed eyes had gone. The PO, a man of few words, limited his awed reaction to what he saw to a simple, "Jeeeeeeezzzzzuuuussss!"

We will leave the bridge to sort out in their minds how a VLCC tanker of 500,000 tons could be upside down and moving majestically southwards, stern first, on the crest of a wave that was a good hundred feet high and growing. Suffice it to say that it was a strange and somehow magnificent sight, the 'Shell Glory' travelling south in such an unwonted manner, while the rest of the seas were running fiercely in a Northwesterly direction. But they are competent people, the Royal Navy and I'm sure that they will come up with a good reason, both for this and the alleged loss of a large quantity of 3rd Blow Jobs' stores over the side of the Intrepid at or about this point, when they had been supposedly safely consigned to the vehicle deck many feet below. The sinisterly smiling, slant-eyed Quartermaster of the 3rd BJs would, naturally, assist in the Board of Enquiry, and, like most QMs, get away with bloody daylight robbery while the innocent went to military prison or had their careers blighted.

Despite the prevailing aroma of bilious and sphincteral eructation that issued from the mal-functioning air-conditioning, and the slippery meat and three veg goo on the decks, walls and ceilings, that would take the blue jobs a good trip to the Caribbean for exercise with the First World War Lease Lend harbour patrol boat of the Trinidadian Navy (and as much ace of spades as your pay-packet could cover in a month), to clean up, there were still several able bodied quasi-seamen and one non-seaman (but interested in having some seamen), who were oblivious to the traumas, personal and naval, which were taking place around them. The former consisted of the complement of Chinese cooks and mess stewards, most of whom had shipped on Intrepid some ten years before in Hong Kong, passport-less and future-less, as an alternative to being pushed back through the fence in the New Territories and making their profuse apologies to the unsympathetic gentlemen of the Red Guard. The latter consisted of the poofter Padre of the 3rd BJs, one of the more eccentric products of the Royal Army Chaplains Department, and a former altar boy and, subsequently, an almost defrocked Private Secretary to a recently deceased Cardinal O'Shea of Liverpool. Padre Appleblossom was a fine figure of a man.

Six foot three and a one-time Junior ABA Heavyweight Champion, our Falstaffian Padre was not your ordinary bum bandit. He was a total glutton. Still, he was a man of the cloth, and he, therefore, always gave as good as he got. He was both bender and thruster, a rare combination in the Swiss chocolate confederation, and he had a particular penchant for the utilisation of mass orifices, preferably with himself in the middle. There being, as you will appreciate, not much in the way of catering required on this little voyage from Devonport to Larne, Appleblossom was in his element, and the Chinese coolies were many months' salary the richer, even if they were glad that it was a short trip this time, for to satisfy this particular 'roundeye' would necessitate the on-call presence and skills of a good Navy micro-surgeon for anything more extended than a two day voyage, and certainly a round the world trip would be physically out of the question. For bums are bums, you normal persons must remember. They are not made of elastic, nor are they for prolonged bungee jumping, at least not within the recognised international safety regulations.

There is something, which I should mention at this stage, something that is rather important, really. The British Army regards all Chaplains as padres, and, therefore as Men of God. The Army, with the exception of certain narrow-minded Scottish Regiments, does not pay much attention to non-military stupidities such as denomination or sect, nor does it really give a damn about whether its padres believe in the virgin birth or transubstantiation or sacrificing virgins with a bread knife under an upside down cross. The unit Chaplain is there for the troops' morale, plain and simple, for you need a padre to talk to the lads about 'death before dishonour' and all that sort of stuff, before they go over the top! Now Padre Appleblossom was such a Man of God. He was the nearest that many, indeed most, of the Blow Jobs would ever get to a Man of God, until they had the pleasure of meeting the Creator Himself, which, by the military nature of things, especially in the Blue Jackets, some would do a lot sooner than others. But there was a little tiny wee conceptual problem in this current context of military operations. The 3rd Battalion The Blue Jackets was about to emerge on to the world stage in sunny and distinctly Protestant mid-Antrim, with a Catholic Padre carrying the Banner of Freedom in their vanguard. This sort of unintentional fuck-up is the responsibility of a special section of the Ministry of Defence, of that I have always been sure. It must be called the 'Square Pegs in Round Holes Department", at least as far as this little sortie into the ulu goes. There was no doubt to anyone in the Battalion's mind, that Padre Appleblossom came from the 'Round Hole Department', whereas most of the post-pubescent bluebeards in the 3rd BJ's were usually looking for slant-eyed entries, and not Chinese male ones either! But we will leave the Chinese to tot up their windfall earnings on their abaci, and Appleblossom to complete his variation of the Royal Army Chaplains Department's annual Battle Efficiency Test. We, dear reader, must go back and briefly see an old friend, before beginning the vinegar strokes of this sad tale!

Ballymena has certainly not been the same since the arrival of Inspector Simpson and the 'depleted' Scrubbers Inc. But you could hardly accuse *them* of being at fault - well, apart from their disposal of those few useless fat twats in the UDR who had the audacious temerity to surrender to superior force on running out of ammo! While we have once again been visiting seedy non-persons South of the Thames, gaining insights into the tactical genius of the IRA, witnessing the corruption of a pimpled prick and his comrade in arms, an elderly shit-spreader, and, finally, joining the Navy and the boking BJs on the jolly old 'Love Boat', life has been going on in its usual abnormal fashion, as it has an unfortunate habit of doing, wherever the Beast of Beleek is to be found. For over thirty-six hours now the remaining laundry vans of Scrubbers Inc. have scoured the townland of Slaght and its immediate environs, but not a pubic hair of big Mary or a faecal sniff of Moriarty are to be found. Touts have had the shite beaten out of them - and then been offered incredible out-of budget sums of money, but the enemy have gone to ground. The search has been extended, and wholeheartedly joined by the biggest conglomeration of lynch mobs known in the history

of Ireland since the Civil War, and ably and willingly funded by the
newly established Funeral Directors Association of Mid-Antrim, who
formalised themselves to beat down the wood yards on pricing, and
certainly not to pass on the discounts to the delightfully increasing
number of out-of season customers. God! It is fun! But while the
slaughter of the innocents is expanding to hitherto unscathed and
most verdantly promising parishes, let us pretend to be flies on the wall
and spend a few moments in silent contemplation of how the Special
Branch mind works in situations such as these. You will not be bored,
I guarantee!

Since his arrival in the City of the Seven Towers Inspector Simpson had
been doing a lot of deep thinking. While the uniformed members of the
RUC and the remaining four companies of the UDR swept through
the countryside, in search of anyone who vaguely resembled a terrorist,
and using the time-honoured Ulster tactic of kill the bastard first and
ask questions later, Simpson was a much more subtle person. He knew
that it was a waste of time and energy searching haystacks, when all
you had to do was wait for the needle to come to you. Thus, he put his
experience into gear and began to plan.

First of all, there was absolutely no doubt that, with the Twelfth coming
up and being - locally at least - centred on the backwater of Slaght,
Moriarty and Co. would be attracted back to the scene of some of their
crimes. It was irresistible, just like flies round a cow's bum! Secondly,
there was going to be a considerable security presence in Slaght on
the Twelfth, so it was important not only to ensure that the targets
were caught *entering* the area, but also - just in case they were already
holed up there, that they were prevented from leaving it, otherwise
some other organisation might get Moriarty first, and that would be
totally unacceptable. Simpson's thinking on this important point was
not complicated by senseless considerations such as the protection of
innocent human lives. As far as he was concerned, the citizens of Slaght
could go and get fucked! He had the same opinion about the superior
bastards in Ballymena, too. No, the good Inspector was motivated in
all of this by his upbringing in 'God's own little dry closet', the village
of Cullybackey, where self-preservation was imbued into children at
an early age, and, indeed, had to be in a place where other members

of your family, let alone the dirty old man next door, began to take a serious interest in your body by the time you could walk. What the Inspector needed, he decided, was a foolproof plan. And, idiot that he was, he decided on the spot that he was just the man who could draw up such a fallacy.

A careful perusal of an Ordnance Survey map brought Simpson to the brilliant deduction that there were only four roads running into Slaght, and that these met slap bang in the middle of the hamlet at a cross roads, where speeding cars full of pissed parishioners of the Reverend Mulholland also frequently met, with a 'slap bang', on Friday and Saturday nights after the pubs had shut. He presumed that the Army and the UDR would be 'controlling' the fields and the woods as usual, since they seemed to consider, for some inexplicable military reason, that terrorists liked to get covered in cow-shit and scratched to shreds by brambles just as much as they did. In fact, as far as Simpson's lengthy experience went, the Army seemed incapable of understanding what roads were for, except as a means for them to get from one impenetrable bog-crossing or mountain-climbing expedition to the other. They had a funny idea, the Army, that is, of what the normal Irish terrorist was like. In Simpson's experience the only way you could get a terrorist to go into a field willingly by day or by night, was either because he was bursting for a quick shit, or because he had scored at the local hop and was going to give big Lizzie, the butcher's daughter and chief regional slut, a good stabbing with the mutton dagger.

And so, very logically for an Irishman, Simpson deduced that Moriarty and Co. would need transport in and out, and that they would, therefore, have to use one of four roads. All he had to do was to cover those four roads. He was already aware that Scrubbers Inc. had gained a certain notoriety in the area, due to the massive accident in nearby Cromkill on the day of their arrival, and also because they had been refusing adamantly to stop, when waved down by local women wanting their husbands' dirty 'smalls' hoovered or incinerated. Four sets of two outstretched fingers waving out of the windows of passing laundry vans in non-Churchillian fashion had certainly not endeared the Scrubbers to the blowsy peasantry! It was necessary, he had concluded, to have a change of cover, and he had informed Chief Inspector McCambridge of this and had given an estimate of the outrageous budget required to effect the transformation. To his surprise, for the second time, McCambridge could not have been more helpful and had readily acquiesced, even to the extent of sending a motor-cycle courier down to Ballymena with ten thousand pounds in readies, unsequenced, too, and which, rather interestingly, he had not had to sign for. In fact, he was specifically ordered not to mention the matter in any paper work whatsoever!

The original two undamaged Scrubbers Inc. vans, and a further two that had been salvageable from their meeting with the Cromkill-based sleeping muck spreader, had been joined by six other vehicles from the seemingly endless Castlereagh pool, and were now undergoing conversion in Kennedy's Garage on the Cullybackey Road in Ballymena. Kennedy's had been commandeered, lock, stock and barrel, and the employees had been inveigled into long overtime by large sums of untaxable money, and without the use of force, which made a pleasant change from normal relations between the Special Branch and the public. The conversions would be ready on time and would be deployed as follows. Four telephone line repair vans would be positioned on the four roads leading in and out of Slaght, all some one thousand yards from the entrance to the village. In the Twelfth Field itself there would be strategically placed: one Calor Gas-fuelled fish and chip vending outlet; one van selling ice cream, salmonella, and candy floss; one pick-up truck stocked with dulse and yellow man, and a variety of other sweet coloured things that had certainly not passed any checks by the Ministry of Health, but were all that Simpson could locate on time; and last, but by no means least, a furniture van fitted out like the inside of McKendry's pub, and loaded up with a variety of ales and a vast quantity of poteen from the Ballymena RUC Barracks's own personal stocks. The latter had been hard to obtain without recourse to violence, but the Duty Sergeant had at last been quite reasonable, particularly after Simpson had reminded him about the promotion he would probably be getting for having a good two-coffee dump on the morning of the McCallion break-out, and for having been blind drunk and cowering in the safety of a neighbouring public house during the subsequent attack on the Barracks and the massacre of the UDR. Apart from all of these, there would be four unmarked patrol cars designated as a quick reaction force and dedicated to the Inspector himself, and his personal selection of the most accomplished murderers in his team. He had not been idling his time on the morning of the Ballymena massacre. He had been alert to others' activities while giving the *coup de grace* to his own selected victims, and he had spotted some men who showed special talents and abilities!

Apart from these static or mobile vehicle teams, Simpson had secured some forty re-inforcements from Castlereagh, all of whom would be dressed appropriately on the Twelfth, and would ostensibly join in the festivities. He had at first considered forming his own SB Orange Lodge, but could not think how he was going to find a banner and a band, together with all the other important regalia, at the last moment, particularly as the Master of the RUC's own Lodge, whom he had approached for help, had told him in no uncertain terms to 'bugger off' as no 'bloody ill-conceived Special Branch operation' was going to keep him, his brethren and their Lodge appurtenances away from their rightful place at the Field in Finaghy. Next best thing, he decided, was to have one SB man join in with each of the thirty individual lodges expected on the day and thereby keep an eye out for any infiltrators who may be having the same clever ideas as himself. The ten extra re-inforcements would mingle with the crowd of spectators at the Field. Everyone would be armed and equipped with pocket radios. The vehicles would also be well stocked with sufficient ammunition to take on the whole of the IRA, if they came out of their holes South of the border, or the UDR, if those bastards were after revenge.

Having briefed his men on the brilliance of his plan, and having informed them of the new 'shoot to kill as many as possible' policy, that McCambridge had told him about earlier, Inspector Simpson gave them the night off to get pissed and told them to relax on the following day. They would not have to report for work until six PM, but after that it would be non-stop for the duration, probably right through until the early hours of the thirteenth of July. He gave each man a generous ten quid from the money left over from Castlereagh's unaccountable slush fund and bade them a fond and fatherly farewell, which scared some of those who knew Simpson of old, and made all of them check the genuineness of their new wealth by holding the notes up to the evening sun as soon as they got out of the Barracks gate. As SB men, the last thing they needed was to be arrested by the unsympathetic idiots of the uniformed branch for passing dud fivers!

There would be no relaxation for Simpson, however, because he still had a lot of thinking to do. He felt quite confident, however, even if his sense of smell for Moriarty had temporarily seemed to have failed him. But this did not give him any cause for alarm. He instinctively knew that it would come back as soon as the little bastard came within five miles of him, and he wouldn't even have to be downwind to detect him. He went into the canteen and poured himself a cup of tea, munched at a couple of ginger nut biscuits, and slowly made his way back to his office. Once seated behind his desk again, he called Castlereagh to make his final report of the day to Chief Inspector McCambridge. The latter was most complimentary about his plans, and expressed his confidence in 'my friend Jimmy's' ability to achieve the expected results, the latter being unspecified, but obviously, under the new 'shoot to kill as many of the bastards as possible' policy, these did not need to be spelled out.

One final remark made Simpson sit up in his chair and growl with that passionate vindictiveness that only Ulster Protestants possess. McCambridge informed him that the British Army battalion due to arrive on the following day to protect the innocent (if they could find any) of mid-Antrim, was the 3rd Battalion The Blue Jackets, under the command of a Lieutenant-Colonel Jolly. Colonel Jolly, McCambridge confided, was suspected of having been a high-level source of the Provisional IRA during all of his previous nine tours in Ulster. If something was to happen to Jolly, McCambridge had not so subtly hinted, justice would be done. And, he had added, if a few Blow Jobs were to go the same way on the big day, only their mothers would mourn, and then most likely just because of the loss of an extra pay packet.

While Inspector Simpson was mulling over this new and disturbing intelligence, McCambridge was on his fourth large glass of whiskey and beginning to enjoy himself. It would not be long now. The day he had planned for was at last just around the corner and the sweet smell of success was already in the summer evening air. It was an added bonus that he had just found out that Liam O'Shaugnessy's old friend

Pinky was going to be at the party, too. God works his little miracles in mysterious ways, that's for sure. And in order to ensure that all concerned would be in the picture, McCambridge picked up his phone and called his friend at the Belfast Telegraph, and told him as much as he needed to know about the build-up around Ballymena. As a final aside he mentioned the 3rd BJ's and emphasised the lengthy Ulster experience of its CO, Colonel Jolly, and his close relationship to the GOC. The reporter read between the lines, and after the conversation was over he decided that this time he would not only tell Phelim what he had heard, but that he would slip the word to a few of his other media friends and earn himself a few favours for the future. Wild horses and the mother-in-law weren't going to keep him away from Slaght on the Twelfth. There were journalism awards at stake here, and maybe even a position on one of the big London dailies, or, just think about it, a war correspondent's job with CNN!

It was almost midnight when Paddy McGonigle was at last ushered into the snug at the rear of O'Hanlon's pub off Demerara Street on the Falls. Phelim rose immediately to his feet and helped the old man to a seat. "Jesus, Mary and Joseph, Paddy. What the hell happened you? Did you fall off the bus?" After pouring a couple of stiff whiskeys into Paddy, Phelim heard a full account of the events at Lisburn that day. It was incredible, not unbelievable, just pure bloody incredible! He would have to think about this for a time, before deciding what was the best thing to do. Just then the publican opened the sliding hatch near Phelim's head and said, "Phelim. There's some eejit on the phone for you. Won't take 'No' for an answer. Says it's urgent, very urgent. None too fucking polite either, I can tell you." Looking annoyed at the interruption, Phelim stood and leaned over Paddy. "You take it easy for a wee minute Paddy. I'll be right back as soon as I've chewed the ear off whatever ignorant cunt is on the phone. Then we'll decide what to do about our young Perry the Prick. Okay?" And with that he went out into the main public bar.

When he came back five minutes later, however, it was with a smile on his face. He had begun to berate the reporter, who had been calling every pub in Belfast for the last two hours looking for him, but as soon as he had heard the gist of what was so urgent, his annoyance had quickly dissipated. "Paddy. You have made me a happy man this day, believe you me. Have another wee drink. Now here's what we are going to do. And the two of them huddled over the table for the next hour. It was well into the 11th of July morning when two volunteers escorted Paddy and Phelim in a black taxi to a safe house in Norglen Parade, by which time Paddy was smiling as if he had just won the pools, and Phelim was not far behind him. Paddy, though, was pissed. Phelim, however, had never been so stone cold sober in his life. Eight o'clock that morning was going to require every nerve in his being and all his years in the intelligence and survival businesses to pull his plan off successfully.

CHAPTER THIRTEEN

I t is now the morning of the 11th Night. How can a morning be a Night, you ask? Well, in Ireland, of course, that should be no problem. But when you think about it, if you can have the morning after the night before, or a hair of the dog that bit you, why can't you have something as simple as the morning of a Night? The 11th Night, in any case, is really a compound noun, used in Ulster to convey the partying that goes on at that time, in order to ensure that all the Orangemen get up on the Twelfth morning too hung-over to drink until they've had a good walk in the countryside, ideally in the pouring rain, and have reached the Field itself. To not have an 11th Night would mean whole lodges being absent through taking the wrong road, and the hedgerows of the safer parts of Ulster littered with early morning vomiting loonies - not a pleasant sight, and one normally left for the Twelfth afternoon.

Colonel Mooney sat at his desk poring through the transcripts of the OP reports of the past few days. It was all very strange. No sign of life whatsoever at the McKelvey farm, and, indeed, Delta 2's reports contained little of value other than that the rats had lately vacated the midden, now that the upside-down body had been reduced to a gnawed skeleton. Delta 1 seemed to be fixated on reporting vast numbers of laundry vans racing up and down past the Orange Hall, with the occupants giving the glad finger to all and sundry. Airborne reconnaissance had come up with even less, other than confirming the presence of at least two laundry vans constantly to-ing and fro-ing in the immediate vicinity, and the Rat's attempts to get anything out of that Special Branch bastard, Inspector Simpson, had been totally to no avail. At last, in frustration, he had had to call Castlereagh and talk to that slimy piece of turd, McCambridge, but there he had surprisingly been lucky. McCambridge had been able to provide him with a lot of information, most of it disturbing.

Firstly, he had learned that the RUC and the UDR, very typically, were keeping under tight wraps the important information that a large number of thefts of UDR and RUC weapons had been taking place during the past few days, and that these were attributed to the IRA terrorist leader, McCallion, and his men, some of the latter having been recognised by their victims. Secondly, the 3rd Battalion The Blue Jackets was due to arrive, and a sorrier shower of shit you could hardly imagine, in Mooney's opinion. An opinion apparently shared by McCambridge, who had had considerable prior experience of them in Belfast over the years. While the cannon fodder of the 3rd BJs was likely to be an embarrassment and get in the way of his SAS operation, Mooney was more disturbed by the information that one of the Blow Job's senior officers was suspected of being a traitor, although McCambridge had been either unable or unwilling to pinpoint which one. "Maybe have to shoot the whole bloody lot of them," thought the Rat.

The Colonel had mentioned, in passing, the mysterious fleet of laundry vans, which had been scouring the area, and that they had equally mysteriously disappeared in the past twenty-four hours. McCambridge conjectured that these may be IRA teams from Belfast, getting to know the lay of the land before the Twelfth, and postulated that all vans from now on should be regarded as highly suspect. Mooney certainly agreed with that. McCambridge had also informed him that he expected large numbers of the Orangemen on the Twelfth to be armed, in view of the recent mass murders, and that a major confrontation could be expected. He said that he was concerned about whose side the UDR would be on, in the event of such a confrontation, and both men had agreed that there was really little doubt. Scratch them on the arm and the orange blood would run freely. With best wishes for the following day, McCambridge said, "Goodbye Colonel", but then had added one further obscure afterthought. "And don't forget it's the 11th Night tonight, now, will you, Colonel?"

"Impertinent bugger!" said Mooney to the wall. "Of course I know it's the bloody 11th of July, and like any other day it has a morning, an afternoon and a fucking good night! Cheeky sod!" But the Rat had a lot of planning to do, and didn't have time to waste on further consideration of inane remarks by fatuous policemen, and so he turned his mind back to working on his plan for the morrow. He was going to have to keep Delta 1 and Delta 2 in their OP positions for another thirty-six hours or more, but that was no problem. His men were tough and had done this sort of thing in worse conditions than these. The remainder of his squadron he was going to use as a flexible strike force, with his two Scouts, two Pumas, and a replacement Alouette, squeezed out of a very reluctant Army Air Corps Colonel under threat of violence to his person, either in the air at times of peak danger, or stationed on the playing fields of Carnaughts Primary School, which he had commandeered for the Twelfth as his forward base. Despite the fact that the School was closed for the holidays, the Headmaster had proven to be a right obstructive sod, and only a case of whiskey had made him consider his public duty and become slightly more amenable. And him wearing a British Legion pin in his lapel, too! What is the world coming to?

His Land Rover patrols would be engaged in mobiles around the target area throughout the period from now until the temporary arrival of sanity in the Ballymena area, hopefully sometime on the 13th. He had briefed his men carefully on what he intended to do, and they had listened to him with very obvious satisfaction. They were never happier than when a usually reluctant British Government, albeit non-democratically, by word of mouth, from the only person in Whitehall who knew, Maggie herself, said that the kid gloves were off and that they could shoot to kill. It didn't matter to them that Maggie would deny her involvement, if and when the usual brown dobbin hit the fan. They were used to that. All in all, thought the Rat, things are shaping up fine. There was only the 'X-factor' to be considered now, the little spanner that proverbially always got in the works. But that, too, was nothing new for the SAS. Like the Boy Scouts, they would be prepared for any eventuality when the time came. Or, at least, that's how it usually went. But maybe not this time. Mooney had forgotten that 'the little spanner' is called 'Murphy's Law', and the inventor, Patrick Joseph Murphy, was never in the British Army in his life, but had been well and truly executed by the bastards!

Breakfast time at the GOC's mansion had been a miserable affair. Neither Sir Hector nor poor Perry had got much sleep during the preceding night. Perry had lain awake listening to the General pace up and down the corridor outside, muttering to himself, and cocking and re-cocking his pistol. The sounds of 9 mm bullets pattering on to the floor, and then being reloaded into their magazine again and again, was almost as terrifying as the one shot that was fired, which was hopefully a negligent discharge by one of the Monkey's patrolling outside, and not further intimidation of the ADC by his increasingly lunatic boss. Normally Smythe-Gargle would have reported such an ND immediately, and had the offender humiliated, fined, reduced to the ranks and everything else that officers, who normally are not allowed near ammunition, and are, therefore, never in the position to negligently discharge, except at night on the sheets, love to do to the unfortunate common soldiery to prove their own superiority. But not tonight. Either the General would get him as he entered the corridor, or the Monkeys would shoot him for exiting the mansion! But eventually Perry had fallen asleep just before dawn, pistol gripped firmly under his teddy, left thumb in his mouth, and lulled to bye-bye land by the incessant muttering of the name 'Moriarty' by the pacing General outside.

While a bleary-eyed MacTavish stirred the congealed yoke of a fried egg round his plate with a fork-full of pork sausage, Perry had briefed him on the day's programme. The major highlight was to be a press conference at 1100 hours at the HQNI mess, after which the invited press corps members would partake of a sumptuous lunch and too much alcohol at a grateful and generous British Army's expense, before driving drunkenly back to their offices to file reports, which would be a million miles from anything on which they had been briefed. But then, the gentlemen of the Fourth Estate have never allowed the truth to get in the way of a good story, now, have they? As Perry read from the briefing notes he had compiled for the General, he at last came to the reference to the reinforcement battalion, which was designated to provide security for that unfortunate village with the unpronounceable name in mid-Antrim.

For the first time that morning the GOC seemed to perk up, and his eyes showed signs of their previous steel. "3rd Battalion, eh, Perry?" said Sir Hector. "Old Pinemartin is still CO, isn't he?" "Yes sir," replied Perry, and, as you are aware, he was in error. "Excellent! Excellent! I'll be going to Ballymena tomorrow, me boy. You and I are going to review the troops and take in the Twelfth at Slaght. And, with any luck, Pinemartin and his boys are going to bring me a couple of heads on a plate. No! I must make sure that they capture those two alive. Any decapitating going to be done, I, General Sir Hector MacTavish, am going to be the one wielding the sabre, what? Excellent idea. What do you think, me boy?" Perry wasn't really in the mood to commit suicide by telling the General what he thought, so he limited his reply to the safety of, 'Absolutely, sir!' "Okay, then. You can go off to the office now, Perry. I need to be alone for a while. Didn't sleep a wink last night. See you at the press conference." And without further ado the General headed off upstairs for a welcome sleep, and Perry Smythe-Gargle exited the French windows, and headed over the lawn and through the Scots pines in the direction of a gardener's shed, and a meeting with fate.

On opening the door of the shed Perry saw the back of old Paddy bent over his bench, composting some flowerpots. Closing the door behind him, Perry said, "Got you, Paddy! You should never turn your back to a door in situations like this, now should you?" "No, you shouldn't, Captain Smythe-Gargle. Nor should you believe what your eyes tell you when you enter a potting shed, either!" said a voice, that sounded just as broad Belfast, but a lot younger than old McGonigle's. And the man, who had turned round and was now facing Perry, with a nasty looking 357 magnum in his hand, was certainly not McGonigle, even if he was wearing the old man's clothes and his cloth cap. "Who the hell are you?" asked the ADC, beginning to regret having had baked beans with his two kippers that morning. "Sit down, Captain. Sit down and listen, otherwise I've wasted my time and risked my life coming here, and I wouldn't like that. Indeed, that would annoy me so much,

I would have to go for second best. And second best, captain, would be to blow your brains all over Lisburn. Do you understand?" Perry sat down. In a funny way he felt quite proud of himself. He had had no problem whatsoever in understanding!

'Now, Captain, a little bird tells me that you want to talk to someone very senior in the Provisionals. Well, that's me. I'm Phelim O'Malley, Chief of Intelligence of the Belfast Brigade, as no doubt you are fully aware, and I'm very interested to know why the ADC to General Sir Hector MacTavish would want to meet privately with someone like me. Don't tell me that old fool of a prancing carthorse, your boss, wants to pass on the message that he wishes to formally surrender and hand me his sword, because I'm not likely to accept either his word or his sword, unless to use the latter to cut his throat."

"Well, Mr. O'Malley, the General doesn't know anything about this, only you me and the old gardener chappie, I hope! And anyway, the General will be needing his sword for the next forty-eight hours, because he intends to use it to cut off the heads of that fellow Moriarty and the General's wife." "Now why the hell would he be personally interested in a mid-Antrim terrorist, and what the fuck's Sir Hector's bloody wife got to do with it?" asked O'Malley with that confusion which always overwhelms those who are in conversation with Smythe-Gargle for the first time. And, to cut a long story short, Perry proceeded, for the next forty minutes, and with frequent requests by Phelim to retrace his steps and explain things in 'fucking English, will you', to inform the Ferret of the background to Moriarty, Lady MacTavish, the Blue Jackets, particularly the 3rd Battalion thereof, his fear of the General's sanity and his own life, and a host of classified details of which hitherto O'Malley had only had an inkling. To Phelim it was as if Pandora's Box had opened. There was so much to assimilate and try to comprehend, and so little time available, at least on this present occasion, to do it.

"Fascinating!" was all that O'Malley could really think appropriate to say in the circumstances, when Perry had come to an end. "Fascinating. So you want us to help you get rid of the old General, and in order to do that you are ready - no, you've just done it - to shop the whole of the British fucking war effort in Ulster. Well, well, well! I wish I had met you a long time ago, my boy. Don't mind if I call you Perry, do you, now that we are going to be partners, as it were?" "Not at all, Mr. O'Malley," replied Perry. "And you must call me Phelim, my lad, because you and me are going to get to know each other very well, I think. But enough of the niceties for the time being. Let's you and me do some planning for tomorrow."

And with that we will leave the potting shed and the conspirators, and make our way across to the HQNI Officers Mess, where selected members of the Belfast press corps are arriving for a binge at the British Government's expense. With booze on the menu most of them were in position in the large bar by 1030, and getting enough down them to enable them to stomach one of MacTavish's famed lengthy, boring, and meaningless press conferences. Fortunately, these were few and far between, as the press corps and the General shared a totally virulent mutual disrespect. As the General's favourite pre-prandial tipple was a 'jolly good G & T, make it a double, why not, you talked me into it, with not too much of the old T, my boy, ha! ha!' as he was wont to say with monotonous regularity every time he was in the mess, the gentlemen of the press were downing gin as if it was an endangered species and about to go out of fashion. They did this, not out of a wish to curry favour with the GOC, but out of a desire to drink the Mess dry of the foul bloody stuff, and then really piss the old boy right off. Unfortunately, this was a sheer impossibility, as the sergeant-major in charge of the Mess bar had previous experience of being gin-less on a MacTavish grand entrance, and was bloody sure that he wasn't going to subject himself to that kind of a public dressing-down ever again - especially not in front of these civvy subhumans from what he considered to be very well termed, the 'gutter press'.

At ten minutes to eleven a rather red faced, evidently sweaty under the armpits, Captain Smythe-Gargle arrived, having run the whole way to the Mess from the potting shed. Having seen that the assembled rumour writers were well on their way to an alcoholic Second Coming, he smiled cunningly, and went to the porched entrance to await the arrival of the GOC. Dead on the dot of 1100 hours the door to the Mess bar opened and in marched the elegant figure of Her Majesty's most senior officer in all Ireland. With Perry like a lap-dog traipsing dutifully along behind his heels, he swung to the rostrum placed conveniently at the end of the bar, thwacked his swagger stick down with a crack on the counter, and bellowed, "Sergeant-Major, make mine a G & T, a double, and go easy on the bloody tonic this time, there's a good fellow, ha! ha!". Having got his G & T in less than a second, the sergeant major being one of the Army's great survivors, MacTavish took a long draught and said, "Gentlemen. Good morning. I will begin with a brief on the current situation, then give you some idea of what we expect for tomorrow, and how we intend to deal with it, and finally, before a good stiff noggin or two and a few of bottles of the old froggie wine, I'll take questions from the floor." But in the course of the next forty minutes Sir Hector hemmed and hahed and said sweet fuck all that would be printable, let alone readable. Ten minutes in, the members of the press corps were succumbing to their over-indulgence of free gin between 1030 and 1100 hours, and most were fast asleep and snoring. Thirty minutes in, virtually everyone, including the bar staff, was in cloud cuckoo land, and the General had to thwack his swagger stick very hard several times on the stroke of minute forty to get the press conference back into a semblance of sobriety and order. "Questions, anyone?" he bawled.

While the others were looking mournfully at their watches, with the less than happy realisation that there were another twenty minutes of excruciating hell to get through before they could get down to the real business, one member of the Fourth Estate, the only one to have been wide awake throughout the whole briefing, and to have limited his normally prodigious alcoholic intake to a small Britvic orange with no ice, rose to place his question to the GOC. It was none other than our seedy, until now anonymous friend, the gentleman who acted as the unknowing go-between from Chief Inspector McCambridge to Phelim the Ferret O'Malley. What would he have given to know that O'Malley was just that minute slouching, with a most convincing McGonigle-esque limp, past the Mess entrance, on his way to the main gate and a hopefully easy departure from what had been so unbelievably and ridiculously easy to get into in the first place?

"Stevenson, Sir Hector, Belfast Telegraph. I have several questions, General." At this the reporter's comrades in arms looked at him as if his head was cut. "Firstly, sir. You said that the 3rd Battalion The Blue

Jackets, part of your proud old Regiment, as you took such great pains to emphasise, is commanded by a Lieutenant-Colonel Pinemartin, and that it is one of the finest battalions in the British Army. What I would like to know, sir, is why my very reliable senior military informants tell me that the 3rd Battalion is now, as of thirty-six hours ago, under the command of a Lieutenant-Colonel Pinkerton Jolly, and also why these same informants tell me that this 3rd Battalion, that you so admire, General, is called by the rest of the British Army, 'the worst of three bad Blow Jobs', and also why the Ministry of Defence has obviously sent such third rate soldiers to the defence of poor Ulster at such a dangerous and difficult time?" And with that Stevenson of the Belfast Telegraph sat down smartly, with a smirk a mile long across his eleven o'clock shadow, to a resounding roar of applause from a much refreshed press corps. Even the Mess staff had begun to applaud, but had rapidly thought better of it.

While Perry instinctively moved back out of swagger stick range, and also to see if the General was wearing his pistol, which fortunately he was not, Sir Hector MacTavish grew about two inches in height and about four around the chest, and his faced puffed out in a divergence of frighteningly garish colours, the sort that normally signify the initiation of a massive and fatal heart attack. "You, sir, are one of the most impertinent persons it has ever been my displeasure to meet. You are a typical product of the sewers that form the normal domain of your profession." (That certainly got the attention of the buggers in the press corps, I can tell you that for nothing!) "How dare a petty-fogging, pusillanimous, priggish, little, blunt pencil pusher for a scurrilous wet rag like your sectarian, filth-mongering excuse for a newspaper, cast such ridiculous and filthy aspersions about the honour of the Blue Jackets. If I were not restrained by my privileged position, I, sir, would have you publicly horse-whipped. And to add to your insolence, you dare to correct me and tell me that I don't even know who my own Regiment's battalion commanders are! Pinemartin is, I say, *is* the CO of 3rd Blue Jackets, and Jolly is a passed over, worthless toad of a man who should have been cashiered for having the audacity of even breathing, years ago!" There was a short pause at this stage, while pencils scraped over notebook pages, in a frantic attempt to get everything down verbatim.

The man from the BBC News was even better, however, for he had signalled to his cameraman and got the whole thing on tape.

Stevenson stood up again, at which his comrades gazed in total awe. "A further question, General, if I may?" "You may not, you useless prick. Sit down before I call the guards," bellowed MacTavish. But Stevenson had that terrier quality found in all good muckraking investigative journalists, when they find to their surprise, that they are on to the truth and wont have to invent a load of plausible lies. "I refuse to sit down, General, or is it that you have something to hide? My next question, sir, is as follows: What is the nature of the relationship between the alleged IRA terrorist who was involved in the armed attack on Ballymena RUC Barracks, that ended in the death of two constables and over sixty, at the last count, honest volunteers of the UDR - what is the relationship between this man, Moriarty, and your estranged wife, Lady MacTavish, and is Lady MacTavish the woman masquerading as a Captain in the WRAC at the break-out of the mid-Antrim IRA leader, McCallion, or is she not?" At which Stevenson sat down triumphantly to a growing swell of applause from the members of the press. This time the Mess staff, including the sergeant major, joined in happily, although doing their level best to keep their clapping hands below the counter of the bar.

Perry was moving towards the door before the imminent detonation of the GOC took place, but was stopped by a half-empty G & T striking him on the temple, and Sir Hector screaming at him, "And as for you, you useless little bent prick, stop squeezing your bloody blackheads and get me the guard immediately!" But the guard, in the form of the monkey patrol were already bursting into the room and rolling all over the place trying to find firing positions and locate the terrorists, having been totally convinced by the screams of their beloved ticket to fame and fortune, that the Provisional Army Council, Black September, the Baader-Meinhof and Uncle Tom Cobbeley and all were squeezing the boss's balls between the white hot jaws of a carpenter's vice just out of the foundry furnace. When they found no obvious target, they shot up the ceiling and the bottles behind the bar, just to relieve the tension. All of this was captured live on the BBC News camera for the general public's predilection, and to enable the Military Secretary to make suitable recommendations to the Chief of the Defence Staff and the

Prime Minister in due course. As the firing slowed, the massed phalanx of press men, delighted at the sheer brilliance of their joint scoop, grabbed as many undamaged bottles from the bar as they each could hold - with the ready assistance of a beaming sergeant-major - and, hoisting Stevenson of the Belfast Telegraph onto their shoulders, chaired their new-found hero out of the mess and to the nearby car park. Fuck staying for lunch and a few bottles of sour froggy wine, when you're not welcome! They'd be able to have fifty lunches on the value of this morning's performance, and champagne, too, once their editors got a load of this. God! There is nothing better in this life than being able to view other people's dirty linen, hanging unwashed on the clothesline of so-called public morality!

Eventually the MO arrived with four of his burliest medics and succeeded in calming down the GOC sufficiently to stick a needle in his bum and take him off to the big mansion on the hill for a good rest, before the quick trip back by RAF Andover to UK and an Enquiry, which all of them knew very well was the only possible and logical conclusion to this day's events. But, then, they were all very wrong. Our Hector hadn't got where he was by being sent back to Blighty before he was fine and ready. The court martial would bloody well have to wait. General Sir Hector MacTavish, K.B.E., D.S.O., M.C. (and two bars) was from this minute forward working on his own and very personal agenda, and woe betide anyone who got in the way! Years of bitterness had welled up inside him. He knew, deep down in his heart of hearts, that the BJs were truly a load of shit. He knew, too, that Lady MacTavish had not been loved or well cared for by himself, and that it was his own fault that a big-dicked Para could so easily cuckold him. The problem was, he had not wanted anyone else ever to find out that he appreciated these truths. The lie that he had lived for years was about to be exposed to public view. There was only one thing to do, and Sir Hector was about to do it. You, of course, will have to wait to find out, because I, for one, am not a pseudo-gentleman of the press, and, therefore, I will not reveal to all and unwashed sundry the personal confidences of a hero of the Nation. No, sir! Well, at least not yet, sir!

Perry sat down on a bar stool and had two or three enjoyable and well-merited stiff ones with the sergeant major. They didn't talk much, but they sure as hell had a lot in common to smile about. Eventually, at one o'clock, after sharing a cold buffet lunch on the counter with his newfound friends on the ecstatically happy and, by then, three-quarters pissed Mess staff, Perry strolled back in the direction of the mansion. He hadn't felt this way since his little bitch of a sister's little bitch of a dog had got run over by Pater in the shooting brake one fine Spring morning some fifteen years earlier. "Yes, Perry, my boy. You're old enough now to realise that the Army is not for you. You are going to make a much easier and better career for yourself, just purely and simply by being the right nasty bastard that you've always been, but that you've always been taught to suppress. Are we going to have fun? Yes, we are!"

And with that we must leave Lisburn and hasten back to the high seas, where the swells have abated somewhat, and two groups of day-trippers are about to join our little party. We are going back to Larne, that little port where the ferries from Scotland arrive and depart, and where the next part of our tale is about to unfold. Don't worry about the poor GOC and his monkey troop. I'll take care of them in the meantime, and soon we'll all see how well they are taken care of in Slaght, on the morrow. It's getting close, you know, the finish. The tension is building up. The only problem is, we know more than the others involved, don't we? Well, maybe, except for the excrescently evil McCambridge, that is. And that's not really fair, is it? But no matter. Fuck him, and them!

H.M.S. Intrepid having been delayed by the strange and ominous seas, Lieutenant-Colonel Pinky Jolly had had a very long wait at Larne for the arrival of his new Battalion. Thus it was, as he was strolling up and down the dockside yet again, trying his best to act like he thought a Colonel should act, albeit covered in nasty bruises and in civilian clothes, and, God knows, he'd certainly known enough of the arseholes (colonels, that is), that he had the pleasure of seeing the Antrim Princess arrive, the ferry from dear old Stranraer across the water in Scotland. It was a pretty sight, and Pinky felt some of the pleasure that the trippers must have been feeling, watching them disembark, until he saw them forming up on the dockside into a series of quasi-military groups, complete with accompanying bands, unfurling grotesque orange banners and marching off to a long line of waiting hired Ulsterbuses. "Bloody Scottish Orangemen," he thought, "coming over just to add to the troubles. Why don't they fuck off back to Scotland and invade Newcastle. Then they'd soon get what was coming to them." Pinky hated extremism in any form, but religious extremism never failed to disgust him. That's why he liked the IRA and the chaps in Whitehall so much. They weren't extreme about anything, except graft and the chance to screw as many secretaries, British Railway porters, or other people's wives, as possible.

While Pinky was strolling up and down and bemoaning the State of the Nation, the Reverend McCartney was drilling the drunken brethren of the 'Loyal Sons of Maryhill, L.O.L. 666', into the best semblance of order that he could manage at short notice, after a six hour slow and difficult sailing on rather tempestuous seas, and the assistance of as much alcohol as they could down. He was proud of them, however, as not a single one had thrown up through seasickness, although this did worry him somewhat, as that meant they would probably make up for it on the buses to Ballymena, by throwing up through an excess of drink. But no matter. Buses can be hosed down, and it was all in a good cause anyway. He couldn't wait to get to the Adair Arms Hotel in Ballymena. He had booked the rooms almost a year ago, under the name of the 'Evangelical Mission to the Outer Hebrides'. Just you wait to see the faces on the receptionist and the bellboys, when Glasgow's premier and most feared militant Orange Lodge walked in the door and demanded their rooms! The lily-livered arseholes of Ballymena would be shitting themselves all over the foyer. They deserved it, these effete people of Ballymena, in McCartney's opinion. They had made money out of other people's troubles for too long. Now it was time for them to partake of the spice of life themselves!

The Ulsterbus organisation was at its usual brilliant best, and the Scottish lodges that were heading for Belfast and the Field at Finaghy on the morrow, sped off first in a haze of black diesel smoke, leaving only one bus to fit on thirty pissed Maryhellions and a twelve piece, equally pissed, flute band, let alone all their accumulated baggage, instruments, and numerous cases of booze. We will leave the good Reverend McCartney to berate the beleaguered communications systems of backward Ulster and await the arrival of the second dedicated Ulsterbus, at that moment just outside the town limits of Larne and delayed by the need to change

a blown tyre. We will move back to the immediate dockside, where
H.M.S. Intrepid, with its complement of none too military able, and
certainly none too physically competent, BJs was just arriving. Both ship
and crew looked the worst the wear for their short voyage, and that said
volumes for the state of the Ramblers Association, as a recently much
chastened Jimmy the One, would have put it. As the ramp was being
lowered, Pinky saw a sole, and immaculately dressed, military figure
standing before him. His eyes lit up with joy and with recognition.
It was old 'Scrapper McIlhenny', a sergeant major as long suffering
and as long serving in the BJs as himself, and he was now wearing the
distinctive badge of a Regimental Sergeant Major. All at once Pinky's
nervousness vanished. With a fellow unfortunate like Scrapper on side,
the 3rd BJs could take on the world - given time, a complete change of
personnel, and a hell of a lot of sheer bloody lucky hope or hopeful luck!

Pinky strode proudly up the gangplank and veritably blossomed when
he received a magnificent salute from the RSM. "Good to see you,
Colonel," said Scrapper. "And bloody good to see you, Mr. McIlhenny!
God, you really are a sight for sore eyes! Sorry I can't return your most
welcoming salute, what with being in these silly civvies. Don't suppose
you have any spare kit with you?" "All taken care of, sir. As soon as I
got the word that you and I had been promoted, I realised that we were
both on our own against the rest of the holidaying bastards and I raided
your room in the mess. Picked up all your kit, checked out your personal
weapon, and stole as many of old Colonel Pinemartin's rank slides as I
could get my hands on. Come down to the cabin, sir, and get changed.
I'll look after the unloading. It'll probably take a while, though, because
the trip has been the worst I've ever experienced. Even the blue jobs
have had enough. And the effect it has had on the shower of shit that
supposedly, in Blue Jacket RHQ terms, constitutes a battalion, has been
downright diabolical. Can't blame these young lads too much, though,
sir. They don't know any better, most of them. We'll soon whip them
into shape, given a chance." "'Fraid we might not get too much of a
chance, Mr. McIlhenny. But you and I are going to do the very best
we can with what God has bountifully given us. Right?" "Right, sir!"
responded the proud RSM, for the first time in his career feeling that
he was serving under an officer who was more concerned with the job
in hand than he was with the next promotion or medal in line.

While Colonel Jolly was escorted below to introduce himself formally to his new rank, the RSM began the delicate task to trying to remove a battalion of men and its equipment, and - more importantly in military terms - its first line ammunition, from a ship of Her Majesty's Royal Navy, without the lot, including the men, going missing. He wasn't helped a lot in this by the fact that most of his CSMs and NCOs were also very much the worse for wear after the voyage. But difficult times have a way of bringing the best out in the strangest people, and RSM McIlhenny worked wonders by a mixture of gentleness and that unadulterated ability to put the fear of God in Satan himself, which comes only with the exalted rank of a Regimental Sergeant Major of a Regular Army battalion in the British Army. So it was, therefore, that the 3rd Blue Jackets were lined up, and the Battalion's vehicles as well, along the side of the quay, by the time Pinky Jolly came on deck again and descended the gangplank. Only a few remaining stores had yet to be unloaded, with the exception, of course, of those that had spuriously gone missing overboard from three decks below, in the midst of the worst weather Captain Greston had ever seen, and under the paper-transferring direction of the Quartermaster of the Blow Jobs. It was one of those minor miracles that you see frequently when the military machine is working at its best, namely, when the man at the top knows what he is doing, and the ORs below follow blindly behind with their thumbs up their bums and their brains in neutral. By the time that Pinky was shore-side again, the 3rd Battalion looked the part, as long as you didn't go too close or smelled their fetid breath. It was one of those days, the Colonel thought to himself, when you just knew that God was in his Heaven and having a nice quiet cup of tea!

"Orders are we are to wait for transport. Ulsterbuses, I believe. Right, Mr. McIlhenny?" said a proud Pinky. "Yes, sir! And an escort of Saladins from the Royal Hussars. Very adamant they were on that, sir. No moving under any circumstances without the Royal Hussars." And both men looked across the dockside to where the Maryhellions were boarding their second bus, tyre now repaired, and moving off in their two-vehicle convoy to Ballymena. "Bastards!" said Pinky. "Quite agree, sir'" said the RSM. "You're from around these parts, aren't you, Mr. McIlhenny?" asked Pinky. "Yes sir, from this very town of Larne itself. Never thought I'd be coming back in these conditions though. Can't stand what's happened to this lovely country myself. Full of madmen, if you ask me, begging your pardon, sir." "No problem, RSM. I fully agree with you. Bloody tragedy. Why people can't live together in peace and harmony beats me. Not helped one bit by the death and glory boys in the Army, either, is it? Nor the religious and politically biased bastards in every other bloody organisation that has anything to do with Ireland. Bloody tragedy, that's what it is." And just as Pinky and the RSM were beginning to feel depressed, the highly distinctive and totally unforgettable whine of souped up Saladin engines could be heard above the screeching of the seagulls, which were diving into the harbour waters to pick up a plethora of disgusting titbits which were in the process of being hosed overboard, now that the Navy had got a chance to swill out the amassed two days puking of the green, slithering, and not so fucking mean machine that had just so recently disembarked.

Two Saladins of the Royal Hussars skidded round the side of the nearest warehouse to where the 3rd Battalion was vainly trying to lose its sea legs, and came to a halt in a horrendous screeching of brakes. The first Saladin had obviously better brakes than the second, however, or maybe the driver of this armoured car was not as quick in his reactions, because the second fifteen-ton vehicle rammed impressively into the rear end of the first. Being armoured, of course, there was little damage to either. The first Saladin, however, shot forward with a dramatic leap, its driver having presumably just released the pressure on his brakes, and banged much more impressively into the front of the parked personal Land Rover FFR of the Commanding Officer of the 3rd Battalion The Blue Jackets, in which was seated, to attention, the large and immaculate personage of the CO's personal driver, one Corporal Whittaker. It wouldn't have mattered a damn whether Corporal Whittaker had applied his brakes or not. Both he and the Land Rover left the side of the CO, to whom both had just that minute been introduced, and entered, in a double pike dive, the murky waters of Larne Harbour. After a short pause a bedraggled and very pissed off Corporal Whittaker emerged on the oily surface, minus his Land Rover and his personal kit. He was not best fucking pleased! Fortunately the crew of H.M.S. Intrepid, to whom such incidents are quite normal, especially when dealing with the Royal Marines, their customary passengers, were alert and equipped to rescue Whittaker before he, too, joined his transport and kit at the bottom of the harbour.

The turret hatch of the first Saladin opened and a jovial and rakish face peered out. Seeing that his own vehicle was not in immediate danger of following the CO's Land Rover into the sea, a broad smile beamed out, and a very upper class voice spoke into a radio handset. "Murray, drinks are on you tonight. Now, don't let us make a silly booboo. Put her in reverse, gently, and move back a little bit, okay?" And when this essential manoeuvre had been completed, the rakish figure doffed his headset, stuck on a beret that had seen better days and sprung out of the hatch and swooped in one skilled movement right to the ground before Pinky and the RSM. There it gave the slackest salute imaginable, even if one was in the Ugandan Special Forces, which fortunately one isn't, and said, "Afternoon, Colonel. Sorry we were a bit late. Little fracas with a funeral procession on the way here. Silly billies thought they had right of way. Now they'll have to get themselves a new box. Sorry, keep forgetting. Nigel's the name, Nigel Dewar, like the whiskey, ha! ha!" At which he stuck out his right hand, and Pinky, unable to think of anything appropriately succinct and military to sum up the situation, stuck out his, and received a firm and brisk handshake. "Bit of a pity about the old Rover, Colonel. Your chappie all right?" asked Captain Dewar, and waved across to Corporal Whittaker who was in the process of being hoisted in some breeches buoy contraption to the deck of Intrepid. Whittaker gave him a passionate middle forefinger right back, which had Dewar chortling away merrily for a moment, before he shouted out to the Corporal, "Well done, man! You're a good sport!" Whittaker's reply was fortunately drowned by the horn of the Antrim Princess, now making here way back to sunny Stranraer.

There being, as both Pinky and Mr. McIlhenny knew only too well, absolutely no way in which anyone can chastise a cavalry officer, without losing face oneself, everyone tacitly agreed to carry on as if the whole incident had been a dream, and got down to some quick convoy planning for the drive to Ross's Factory, a derelict mill near the crossroads at Kellswater on the Antrim Line and the operational base, for the next few days at least, of the 3rd Battalion The Blue Jackets and their attached troop of Royal Hussars. Now it is normally only half an hour's drive from Larne to Kellswater, but a full battalion convoy is a strange and sinister beast. If the vehicles at the front are doing twenty miles an hour, the vehicles at the rear will be doing between sixty and eighty to keep up. If you don't believe me, try it with some friends sometime, but make sure you get your brakes checked beforehand. The journey, therefore, would take at least one and a half hours as long as nothing untoward happened.

The fleet of Ulsterbuses drove on to the quay and the 3rd Battalion embussed without too much confusion, despite the fact that each man was carrying around eighty pounds of kit. First line ammunition is impressive in its bulk, and is the reason why we rarely go to war, as only one man in fifty has the stamina and the build to carry the stuff on the run for more than 500 yards! The MTO having commandeered a fresh FFR for the CO from the Signals Platoon, and the four tonners now packed and ready to roll, the convoy moved like an anaconda through the streets of the little port of Larne, that were bedecked with colourful bunting, which hopefully had been washed since the last time it had been used to give our Moriarty a dry enema. Gradually the town dropped behind and the convoy began the long climb up Shane's Hill, the bleak and mountainous moor land that had to be crossed before descending to the more fertile valleys of mid-Antrim. Just over the top of the hill the convoy had to overtake a VCP which appeared to be searching two Ulsterbuses, the very ones in which the Maryhellions had recently left Larne. A smart-looking Para sergeant was frisking down a line of Jocks drawn up along a dry-stone wall. He was kicking their legs apart with a controlled professional ferocity, which both Pinky and the RSM admired as they passed by. Some of the other paras, however, went leaping over the dry-stone wall on seeing the Saladins and the Army vehicles approaching, but this too was done with such obvious fitness, and their subsequent abilities at camouflage and concealment were of such a high standard, that no one in the vanguard of the convoy thought to question why their reaction had been so bizarre. The late afternoon sun shone weakly towards the West, as the convoy neared the turn-off on the left to Kells and Connor and the last part of its journey. It was getting unseasonably cool and the paleness of the sun did not foretell a good day on the morrow. No shepherd would be delighted, put it that way.

Back near the top of Shane's Hill the OC mid-Antrim Battalion (a fancy name for thirty men!) Provisional IRA, Paddy McCallion, and his not so merry men, had by now clambered out from behind the dry-stone wall, and had returned to assisting Moriarty and big Mary in the pleasant task of being unpleasant to Glaswegian Protestants. When everyone had been frisked and found to be weaponless, they were all herded back on to the buses, now driven by two of McCallion's men, the original drivers having joined the prisoners of war in being tied at the wrists but not yet the ankles. With two seemingly Army Land Rovers in front, and a similarly apparent RCT four tonner in the rear, this smaller convoy headed off down the Ballymena Line, but turned left in the direction of the extensive pine forest at the pimple of a hill called Tardree. Just where the winding country road entered the gloom of the forest, the vehicles turned right up a long unused lane, passed over the top of a low hill and, lost to view from the road, stopped outside a long, low, stone building. Over the front entrance to this strange structure was a peeling, painted sign, 'County Antrim Venture Scouts Headquarters.' Over the past few days it had been the Rear HQ of 'Task Force McKelvey'!

Five minutes later and the brethren of 'Loyal Sons of Maryhill, L.O.L. 666' were lined up in a large dank and dusty stone-flagged room and looking none too happy. Facing them were half a dozen of McCallion's more able men, the OC himself, and, of course, Mary McKelvey and her able second-in-command, Ignatius Moriarty. The Reverend McCartney was just recovering his aplomb somewhat, having missed most of the latter part of the mystery tour through the scenic Antrim countryside, due to an SLR butt in the solar plexus for opening his mouth once too often. It was high time, he considered, to assert his authority. "Now look here, your Commanding Officer is going to hear about this. I'm going to complain to the Scottish Office, the Northern Ireland Office, the Cabinet Office, the Ministry of Defence and the General Assembly of the Reformed Church of Scotland about this unprovoked assault by the Security Forces on our innocent persons. How dare you kidnap us and, most particularly, how dare you strike me, a Minister of Religion? Don't you know who I am?"

"You're that fucking blethering eejit, McCartney, from Glasgow, aren't you?" answered McCallion, beginning to enjoy his new role as spokesman for the Revolution. "And who are you, and what is your name and unit?" shouted McCartney, getting into the stride that made even God tremble when he mounted his pulpit on a Sunday morning. "I'm your worst fucking nightmare, McCartney. I'm Paddy McCallion of the Provisional IRA, and I've been waiting for years to get my hands on one of you shit-stirring, dog-collared bastards, especially one from over the safety of the water." At this news the Maryhellions shrunk into themselves and back against the wall. Several wet patches began to appear on the fronts of trousers, but whether these were caused by abject terror or the present inability to go to the bathroom, no one knows for sure. There is surely no worse news for a Glaswegian Protestant, with the beginnings of a well-deserved hangover coming on, than to find that he is in the hands of a bunch of murdering Fenians who are definitely not famed for giving quarter to their captive enemies.

Out in front, and all alone, McCartney stood defiant, and began to rant and rave about Judgement Day, and retribution, and the massacre of the innocents, and a load of other fearful bullshit. It was a proud and stirring sight, but the Orangemen huddled together behind him did not seem to share either his assurance of hellfire and brimstone descending on the assembled members of the IRA on time, or his confidence that God was on their side. They were all shaking their heads, as if to say, 'He's not with us. Honest to God!' Mary, though, had better things to do than stand around and listen to McCartney and McCallion exchange views on who would have the better chance of going to Heaven. She'd had enough of religion in her life, of whatever variety or colour. So she stepped forward and made her sole contribution to the debate, by nutting the good Reverend right between the eyes with such a sickening crack that half of those present had to make a conscious effort to hold down the contents of their stomachs, while the other half, mainly the Glaswegians, were looking on in spellbound admiration. McCartney, apart from his newly broken nose, was likewise dumbfounded. That was the last straw for him, a bloody Fenian harridan having the gross audacity to give *him* the Glasgow Kiss, and in front of the leading members of his congregation. He lurched forward and with his wrist-tied hands tried to deliver a haymaker of a sidswiping blow to Mary's face, but before he could get a good connection, he found himself on the floor, searching in the gap between his legs for his unmentionables. He would have been better spending his time looking for them in the roof of his mouth, for when Mary had seen him coming, she saw not McCartney, but Mulholland, before her, and the kick she had put into the reverend gentleman had started about fifteen miles Northwest of Tardree, and was accelerating past Mach 2 when it struck.

Now that the Reverend McCartney was no longer interested in having any further conversation, and that she had got the undivided attention of the Glaswegians, Mary gave orders to McCallion, and he and his men started to strip the Orangemen to their underwear (not a pretty sight, I can assure you, so we'll forget about describing it) and to hog-tie all their visitors, including the two Ulsterbus drivers and the dozen sixteen to eighteen year olds of the flute band. The latter, to man and boy, had already decided to give up a musical career, and to remain celibate on the Isle of Skye for the rest of their lives. That completed, she directed her men to begin going through the suitcases of their captives, and for everyone to get dressed in whatever dark suits and bowler hats fitted them. Having ensured that each one of her team was dressed as well as possible, and that each man had an Orangeman's sash, he handed out the other Orange Lodge appurtenances to McCallion's chief subordinates, and gave Paddy himself the Master's gavel. For the next two hours the captive Scotsmen were entertained to a spectacle never before seen in Ireland.

Thirty members of the Provisional IRA, led by Ignatius Moriarty on a fifer-less Lambeg Drum, and complete with the Loyal Sons of Maryhill banner, marched in full Orange Lodge regalia up and down the dank hall until both Moriarty and Mary were satisfied that every man jack could pass himself off as an Orangeman. Once drill was over, there was a further period of practising shouting, 'Kick the Pope', 'Fuck the Pope', 'Up the Pope', 'Burn the Fenian Bastards', and many other colourful Ulster Protestant expressions designed to make RUC community relations programmes rather more difficult to implement. Assured that none of her men would make an incautious slip and reveal himself to be a Catholic, Mary nodded to Moriarty, and Ignatius began to teach

McCallion and his men the three verses of the National Anthem of Protestant Ulster, 'The Sash My Father Wore'.

As it drew on towards eleven o'clock and darkness had deepened, Mary and her new Orange Lodge joined in one final and resounding chorus to the 'Sash', and marched out the door to their militarised transport. The Reverend McCartney and his brethren lay listening or sobbing in the stygian gloom to the last line, as it reverberated into the eerie pine-clad hills. "Its terror to them Papish boys, the sash me father wore." McCartney groaned audibly, because for the first time he had grasped the full significance of the lyrics of the 'Sash'. All three verses were about a visit by Ulster Orangemen to Glasgow, wearing the sashes their fathers had worn before. "Oh God!" he moaned aloud, "They're on their way to Maryhill! They're going to kill our women and children and burn down all the Presbyterian Churches in Glasgow. Oh my God!" The assembled brethren didn't themselves fathom how their respected minister had reached this strange conclusion, but the sincerity with which he had moaned it struck deep into their hearts and minds. To a man they were all in immediate and instinctive agreement. If they could get out of this thing alive, some Irish bastards were going to pay for it, and if they couldn't find any Fenians, any other colour of Christian would do. And God help any Chinese restaurateurs or Paki brush salesmen that they might come across on the way! Without further ado, everyone began to try to find out how you can extricate yourself from being hog-tied in the darkness of an abandoned Scout Hall, without strangling yourself in the process. It was to take until ten o'clock on the 12th before the first person was able to slip his bonds and begin to release the others. Much was to happen in the meantime, before we have Mr. McCartney and his unhappy band of merrymakers rejoin the party.

CHAPTER FOURTEEN

—•✠•—

At six o'clock on the evening of the Eleventh Big Bertie Mulholland had discharged himself from the ICU of the Waveney Hospital in Ballymena. The nursing staff had strongly opposed his decision to do so, informing him that he was risking his life by leaving before the specialists found some reliable way to ensure that his head did not fall off his recently elongated neck. Big Bertie had at first tried persuasion, calling on the loyalty of the nurses to the Protestant cause. Being informed, however, that most of the nurses were either from Cork, Galway, or Botswana, and that two thirds were thus Catholic, and the other third was so far undecided, he became even more convinced that his place on this momentous day was with his poor parishioners, and, most decidedly, not in the medical care of the enemy. He had, therefore, finally secured the whole-hearted agreement of the hospital duty staff that he was fit to leave, by the convincing presence of two hastily purloined scalpels grasped in his trembling hands.

Mulholland lurched through the car park and, still in his night-gown, staggered barefooted on to the Broughshane Road where he managed to get a lift to Slaght, by the simple expedient of walking out in front of a passing hearse, and removing the driver from his seat and ownership, before he had got over the shock of his thirty yard skid and the crash into the back of a parked butcher's delivery van. And so it was, then, that the Reverend Mulholland arrived in his parish in a hearse with an occupied coffin in the back, and a dented bonnet festooned with rather obscenely pink strings of pork sausages. Delta 1, who observed the arrival, and who witnessed the half-naked apparition struggle out of the vehicle and into the Orange Hall, were, to say the least, nonplussed.

Big Bertie, having sent one of his men to dispose of the hearse and another to get him some clothes from the manse, assembled his senior officers and began planning the security of the Twelfth Field for the following day. After all that had happened, he quite correctly had come to the conclusion that the remainder of the population of Slaght was under threat, and that drastic measures would be required to ensure that he still had a congregation and a stipend on the thirteenth. Nothing was going to be left to chance this time. No reliance was to be placed on the British Army, the UDR, or the RUC. This was out and out war, and it was every man for himself. All the weapons caches, lovingly cared for over the past ten years, were to be opened and their antiquated, but by no means obsolete, contents issued. Slaght's Orange Lodge, named the 'Defenders of the One True Faith', would be ready for the Devil to open the Gates of Hell and, come what may on the morrow, the Gates had better be wide open, because legions of Fenians would be making their grand entrance to the tune of 'Derry's Walls'.

At exactly 1937 hours, according to Delta 1's meticulously kept log, Lofty and the boys observed the arrival of seventeen tractors, pulling trailers heaped high with old scrap wood and rubber tyres. These tractors turned into the field, at the top of which their OP was sited, under its large clump of gorse, and then proceeded to climb the hill in procession. By the time they had all come to a halt, engines still chugging noisily over, a phalanx of Slaght's youth, male and female, aged everywhere from four to eighteen years, marched into the field and also climbed to the top. Once the Pied Piper's army had reached the convoy of tractors, they began unloading the contents of the trailers and piling everything into a tall mound, right on top of Delta 1's position. Within five minutes of this operation commencing, Lofty and his three companions were in pitch darkness, and could detect nothing but the smell of seasoned pinewood and old lumber. Needless to say, this caused them some small consternation.

When they radioed their next report to Colonel Mooney at 2000 hours, they expressed, with impressive calmness, as one would expect from such modern-day heroes, their apprehension that the inhabitants of Slaght were up to something. What that something was, neither Mooney nor his staff could as yet figure out. Mooney was not a happy man by this stage. He had personally selected the two OP positions himself; only to have lost Delta 2's even before first light on the initial morning of the operation. Now, while Delta 2 was apparently confined to skeleton monitoring, Delta 1, his eyes and ears on what was happening in the Orange Hall, was totally blind. He waited until the next radio report from Delta 1 at 2100 hours and told them to bug out of the OP thirty minutes after last light, which should be around 2315 that night. Delta 1 should then attempt to find a new OP position, possibly in the loft of the Orange Hall itself. He appreciated that this would be tricky, but it was the best that he could think off in the meantime.

At 2115, after attempting in vain to see if there was any possibility of finding an escape route from the current entrance to the hide and out through the pile of wood and rubber tyres, Lofty came to the decision that there was only one thing for it. They would have to dig at ninety degrees to the line of their hide and break through some estimated thirty feet on the downhill side of the woodpile, facing the Orange Lodge itself. In their very cramped conditions, such a feat was not going to be easy - which, as they found, was the understatement of the SAS year to date! But they went to it with a will, and by 2245 their digging, scraping and scratching had got them some twenty feet towards their ultimate objective. By this time, however, all four men were exhausted. Lofty decided to call a halt and rest up for fifteen minutes. He sent one of his men back down the underground trench to bring forward their bergens, the radio, and their personal weapons.

This was not an easy task and took the trooper three trips for the weapons and the radio. He had just entered the original hide at the top of the hill to retrieve the first of the bergens, when he detected a hint of smoke wafting in through the observation slit. He thought nothing more of it, and struggled and cursed back down the tunnel with the first of the bergens. It took a full two minutes to where Lofty and the other two troopers were farting and cursing in the darkness. A short rest, and then he started out again in the direction of the original hide. He was not a happy camper, our trooper. He had been cooped up underground for days now, crapping in tin foil, pissing in plastic bags, and scratching all the time at the vermin, which had been attracted to the unaccustomed diet that semi-fresh underground Englishman had provided.

When he entered the hide on the fifth trip, to manhandle a second bergen full of kit back down the tunnel, the trooper began to cough and his eyes began to water. The smell of wood smoke was much stronger this time, and there was a first hint of the nauseating stench of burning rubber. "What the hell is going on?" he thought to himself, and clambered to the observation slit and pushed it upwards as far as it would go. The sight that confronted him was stunning. Whereas earlier it had been black as pitch under the pile of jumble, it was now pleasantly bright - that is, if you consider looking at the inside of a twenty foot tall and sixty feet in diameter bonfire, from its exact base centre, a pleasant sight! The trooper slammed the observation slit shut and sat whimpering for a few long seconds in the dark. He re-opened it again, just to check that he really had gone completely mad, and a small stream of burning pitch from the pine wood above trickled down the back of his neck. His actions from that second onwards were impressively dramatic. No longer motivated by fear, but galvanised by pure, stark raving mad terror, he shot off back down the new tunnel like a rabbit with a ferret on its arse, rocketed over the one bergen and the radio and weapons and, reaching the tunnel face, grabbed one of the entrenching tools and began to dig like a crazy man, all the time whimpering, "Oh my God! Oh my God!"

It took several seconds for Lofty and the others to get over the shock of being rammed in a body width tunnel by a human torpedo. When Lofty had recovered, however, he pulled the trooper back from the tunnel face and slapped him hard several times, which eventually succeeded in getting his attention. "What the fuck do you think you're doing, you stupid cunt?" asked Lofty. "You could have fucking killed us. Can't take the claustrophobia, eh? In that case it's RTU for you, me old mate. No doubts about it!" "Get fucking off me you stupid lummox," shouted the trooper, the noise deafening in the confined space. "Fucking get off me and dig for your bloody life. The wood they piled on top of the hide was for a fucking bonfire, and the bastard's in full flame and just about ready to follow us up here!" And sure enough, just at that moment the smell of smoke began to become obvious, and a small flickering candle flame could be seen in the distance, where the tunnel had started.

"Jesus!" said Lofty. And like four moles with half a pound of chillies up their back passage, the SAS shovelling machine went from a squatting start to somewhat past warp speed. Muck and dirt were flying everywhere and the tunnel was going nowhere near quickly enough forward in the desired direction, when the candle flame twenty feet to the rear began to flow towards them. "Dig upwards! Dig upwards! It's our only chance. And without further ado, four entrenching tools dug into the roof of the tunnel and quickly broke through into two feet of glowing embers on the edge of the bonfire. With their balaclavas and their webbing seemingly on fire, Lofty and his men, professional to the end, grabbed their personal weapons, the radio, and the one remaining bergen, and shot forth into the night, with a marked resemblance to Roman candles on Halloween.

As soon as they had rocketed out of the hole, Lofty and his boys became rather pre-occupied by the necessity of dancing up and down with violent jerky motions, in a futile attempt to get rid of all the red hot ash and white hot embers that were burning through their clothes. After thirty seconds of this activity, however, the immediate danger of being self-barbecued was over, and for the first time they were in a position to take in their surroundings. Immediately their attention was drawn to the bonfire, where the flames had begun to reach the apex. To their horror they saw two bodies tied by barbed wire to two stakes. One of these was dressed in what looked like a white wedding gown, and was wearing a funny white hat. The other was dressed in a green frock coat, and wearing a tricorn hat over a flowing black wig. Both looked to have been dead for some time and would not, therefore, be complaining too much about the flames, which were already licking around their lower limbs.

As if that was not a bad enough sight for four men, who were convinced that they had just narrowly avoided a similar, but underground, fate, Lofty and his lads became aware of a growing, growling sound coming from all round them. When their eyes adjusted to the light they found that they were surrounded by several hundred men, women and children, none of whom seemed too pleased at having their Walpurgisnacht public burning disturbed by the sudden emergence of subterranean exfiltrators. A closer examination of the circle of presumed members of Witchhunters Anonymous revealed that some of the men were armed, and were rapidly beginning to get over their surprise at having been so rudely interrupted in their hideous labours of the night. "Bug out right!" shouted Lofty, and all four released their safety catches and, firing into the air just above the heads of the human cordon in front of them, they broke through the perimeter, and raced off into the night in the direction of Cromkill. Neither hawthorn hedge nor barbed wire fence prevented their escape, for fear can make you fly!

After some desultory firing at the black figures disappearing into the murk, the circle regrouped around the Eleventh Night Bonfire, a tradition throughout Orange Ulster, and Big Bertie's finest huddled together at the edge of the light, to ask one another what it was that they had seen emerging from the flames, and what new threat was now upon them. Meanwhile, the tailor's dummies tied to the stakes, and dressed up to represent the Pope in all his finery, and King James II in his wig and tricorn hat, began to burn merrily and drip molten plastic on to the pyre beneath. Some of this molten plastic made its way into the grave-like hide beneath the centre of the fire, so recently vacated by Delta 1, and it was thus that our old friend flame came upon the three abandoned bergens, and their more interesting contents. Ignoring the plastic piss-bags and the dainty foil wrapped turds, and shunning the ration packs and smelly socks, flame found something it had never come across before - at least not in a hole under a bonfire in Slaght. In each of the three bergens there were Schermuly flares, ammunition, detonators, and lots and lots of lovely C4 to play with. And immediately to play our little flame verily did go!

Fortunately for most, but not all, of the gentlefolk attending the late night festivities before the Twelfth, the explosion was channelled upwards by the hole in which it ignited. With an enormous 'Crummmpph', the bonfire took off into the sky, chased by six Schermulys, and followed microseconds afterwards by the enthusiastic 'Bang, bang, bangs' of spare ammunition. His Holiness and King James led the parade, and reached an altitude of one hundred and fifty feet before the rest caught up with them. But, as we know, what goes up must come down. And down it certainly came; only this time the base diameter of the erstwhile bonfire had expanded considerably. With a congregational, "Aw! Shit!" the circle of spectators copied the bonfire's spreading example, and took to their heels in a 360-degree bomb burst. This was no case of women and children first! This was every man for himself.

Delta 2 had been morosely contemplating yet another night of excruciating boredom when the explosion occurred, and in the light of the Schermuly flares over Delta 1's hill, they could see the burning bodies of a man and a women dropping to earth, followed by what appeared to be several severely charred houses and a garage. Sticky, realising that the explosion had occurred in the approximate area of Delta 2's position, immediately tried to contact Lofty on the radio, but to no avail. The sound of shooting was dying down by the time Sticky gave up, with the gnawing fear in his stomach that four of his comrades had failed to beat the clock. After a hurried discussion with his three companions, he decided that he and one other would leave their OP position, and go and see if anything could be done for their comrades. They climbed down from the loft, and were just about to leave the building, when a hundred or so men, women and children screamed down the hill and through the farmyard, as if Lucifer himself was after them with a scythe. Sticky had just time to note that several of the men were armed, before the mad rush exited the McKelvey's front gate and headed off into the night.

By the time they had crawled along the hedgerows, to where they could get a view of where Delta 1's OP position should have been, Sticky's worst fears were confirmed. All that remained, with the exception of a field full of burning kindling, was a very large hole in the ground. Two bodies, one seemingly female, and one with long black hair, were lying at the edge of the hole, obviously dead, because their lower limbs were charred and twisted. One of them had had its head twisted round to look backwards, and was staring sightlessly in rigor mortis, directly at Sticky. Just at that moment it burst into flame, and began to melt before his eyes. It was the most disgustingly gruesome thing he had ever seen in his life, and he turned away from it in horror. "They're goners! No doubt about it. But where did those houses and that garage come from, and who *are* those two people burning over there, and who were all those others who rushed through the yard, and what the fuck's going on, that's what I'd like to know?" rushed Sticky, closer to panic than he had ever been in either of his poaching or Army careers. "Let's get the hell back to the OP. Fuck radio silence! The Rat's going to go galactic when he hears about all of this.

The sound of the emergency vehicles racing from Ballymena to Slaght could be heard in the distance, when Sticky and the trooper neared the farmyard once more. Just as they had reached the entrance to their hideout, several Army Land Rovers and four tonners swept into the yard, and drew up outside the McKelvey home. A platoon, of what appeared to be a most unlikely mixture of Paras and UDR, got out and entered the house, lugging weapons and a rather incongruous collection of civilian suitcases and holdalls. A long pole like object in a cloth bag and an enormous drum were also carried carefully in through the front door. Two men carrying SLRs stayed outside, obviously on guard. Their faces were blackened with camouflage cream, and they looked as if they meant business. By the time that Sticky was ensconced in the loft once again, he was more than a little confused, and was beginning to seriously contemplate premature voluntary early retirement, and a return to the safety of civilian crime.

Delta 1's headlong flight Eastwards began to slow in pace and urgency halfway between Slaght and Cromkill, and at length the four exhausted and nerve-wracked men slumped down together in a rather non-tactical heap in a ditch beside the road, about fifty metres from a gate, that had apparently commenced its manufactured existence as the top and bottom ends of a brass bedstead. Just as Lofty was debating whether to breach an SAS lifetime's discipline and let the lads have a smoke, and to see whether there were still the makings of a good brew in the one remaining bergen, the four men were brought back to alertness by the sound of vehicles approaching and slowing to a halt by the gate. The next thing they noticed was the entrance into the field of some twelve armed men, and not in uniform either. "Strewth!" said Lofty inwardly, "What the fuck now?"

Four of the Belfast Brigade's best ASU's had been brought together by Phelim the Ferret, on Liam O'Shaughnessy orders, and they were now making their way, rather unwillingly, into enemy territory, for the sole purpose of 'creating a bit of a noise and then getting the hell out', as the Ferret had put it. They had intended to open up on the Orange Hall from the safety of the hill opposite. The hill they assumed would be unoccupied, and if they had arrived earlier they would have been seriously wrong in the assumption. They were right, however, in assuming that they would be 'creating a bit of a noise', although, as it turned out, they were totally in error in thinking that they would then be 'getting the hell out'. Indeed, they were going to see hell from the inside very shortly.

"Bugger!" said the first in the long Indian file. "I've just stepped in a big cow clap!" "Shut yer mouth, ye eejit! Do you want the bloody Army or the fucking Prods to know we're here?" hissed a more authoritative voice. "It's all right for you," said the first voice. "These are my best brothel creepers." "Will ye fucking well shut yer gub!" said the second voice, angrily. "Didn't the Ferret tell us the bloody SAS has got OPs here? Do you want to end up like Cathal and the boys, ye eejit?" "Fuck the SAS!" said the first voice. "Them bastards don't scare me. And who do you think you are, to be ordering me around, you Ballymurphy git? You wouldn't last a day with us in the Ardoyne against the Paras. Them's real enemy, not that load of green bereted puke, you've got to play with!" "Listen to the big man talking. If he talks like that boys, he must be another of them Ardoyne touts!" said voice number two. "You'll fucking regret you ever said that, you bastard!" spat voice number one with venom. "Aw! For fuck's sake! Will ye both give over, ye gormless shites?" pleaded a third voice. "Who the fuck said that?" said voices one and two in unison. "Me!" said the third voice, unhelpfully. "Who's you?" said voice number two. "Denny Cahill from the Short Strand! And if you two don't fucking put a sock in it, I'll bang yer heads together so hard, yer teeth will rattle for a week. Now fuck off and get a move on!" said voice number three menacingly, and whoever Denny from the Short Strand was, he must have been a bit nastier than Anonymous from Ballymurphy and Unknown from the Ardoyne, for they both immediately went very quiet, and recontinued their trudge across the field. There were more oaths, as the gallant band encountered

further little mounds of sweet-smelling fertiliser, but they were muttered
between teeth not normally accustomed to grinning and bearing it.

Now none of this had gone unheard, for Lofty and his boys were in
the ditch not twenty feet away. Quickly he came to a decision, and
motioned with his right hand for his three companions to spread out
along the ditch. Lofty had had enough of Slaght. He had been party to
two and a half explosions. He had almost joined a wedding couple in
being burned at the stake. Several hundred Protestants had shot at him
from their broken circle. A bloody barn had fallen on him. He had been
pelted by glass, poteen-fuelled Molotov cocktails, and body parts. And
now some bunch of Provisional IRA goons had the sheer audacity to
arrive on the scene from which Delta 1 had intended a fast departure.
This was the final straw. On the other hand, it was a consolation prize,
of sorts! Twelve paddys in a row, all armed and aimless in the dark. Too
good to miss, and at that range it would be nigh on impossible to miss.

"Evening all!" called Lofty in his Dixon of Dock Green voice. "Now
what's going on 'ere? Were do you lot think you're going?" "Aw! Shit!"
said voice number one. "Fuck!" said voice number two. "Bugger!" said
number three, and then added a quick, "Run like fuck, lads!" But before
they could move more than their trembling knees, Delta 1 opened up
on automatic, and did not stop until they emptied their magazines.
Then, pausing just long enough to change magazines and pick up an
interesting haul of brand new AK-47's, Lofty and the boys legged it
through the gate and across the road into the opposite field, and then
moved quickly but tactically in a wide arc that would bring them round
to the rear of their new position, Slaght Orange Hall. Fatigue was
forgotten. New reserves of adrenaline had been found. It was now well
past midnight, and high time they got into position for their grandstand
view of the Twelfth.

Lofty and the boys found the Orange Hall wide open, well lit, and
totally deserted. They helped themselves quickly to some sandwiches,
which were conveniently plated on a trestle table, and found a way into
the roof space above the rafters. They were just in time, because, no
sooner had they got securely into their new position, than Big Bertie
Mulholland and his chief henchman arrived back from their tour of the

bombsite, that had earlier been the scene of the Eleventh Night bonfire, but which now looked more like the Houses of Parliament would have, if Guy Fawkes hadn't got drunk, and pissed on the fuse. Sounds of fierce automatic fire to the East, some fifteen minutes after the explosion, had further delayed the good Reverend, but he was in no physical condition to check this out himself. As he hobbled back into the Orange Hall, two of his best men were making their way carefully across the fields to see what they could find. They would get a pleasant surprise.

The armed Orangemen, now fully in a siege mentality, went at the sandwiches as if this might be their last meal. Big Bertie, however, was not hungry. He just sat at the table and glowered into his cup of tea. As the last crumbs were being wiped off the plates, Big Bertie's two men came back from their search for the scene of the recent automatic fire, and what a tale they had to tell! Twelve dead men, all very obviously of the Fenian variety, according to the contents of their pockets, and all unarmed, although there were quite a number of full spare magazines of ammunition in their pockets. "Who could have killed them?" thought Bertie aloud. "Billy," he shouted to one of his men. "Go and get on the phone to the 'Telegraph' news desk, and to the BBC, too. Tell them the loyal Protestants of Slaght have ambushed and killed a dozen IRA men on their way to kill innocent women and children. Tell them to send the camera boys quickly, before anyone else gets the bodies. Yes, lads! I know it is not strictly true that we killed these sons of Satan, but whoever did it was on the side of the Lord, and the Lord is on our side. So we might as well take the credit, mightn't we? Maybe it'll stop any other murdering so-and-sos from daring to enter our homes and assault our loved ones." And his loyal acolytes agreed with everything Big Bertie said. Why shouldn't they take the credit, particularly after what they had been through? Some of the braver ones even began to swell out their chests with pride, at their prowess in the defence of their territorial and religious integrity. "Aye! Yer right, Reverend!" said Billy. "I'll make sure the 'Telegraph' and the TV know who's who and what's what in our townland."

The Reverend Bertie Mulholland, latter day battered baby that he was, summoned up his remaining reserves of strength, and proceeded to outline his defensive plans for the Twelfth to his closest henchmen.

Above, in the roof-space, Lofty and his men listened avidly. For the first time in almost a week they had an inkling of what was going on, or, rather, what one side considered might be going on, *if* that one side had the opportunity, later that day, to influence the events that Fate was so generously bequeathing to the loyal citizenry of Slaght. More and more details, concerning weapons, manpower, defensive positions, fall-back positions, get the hell out and run like fuck positions, and a lot more besides, filtered through the rafters, ably assisted by the booming voice of Big Bertie, and his continual need to repeat everything twice, so that the thicker of his parishioners could understand. It was a veritable gold mine of information! "Wait until the Rat hears this lot," thought Lofty. But then a horrible crawling sensation came over him. "How is the Rat going to hear this lot?" Lofty moaned inwardly. As long as the armed might of the 'Defenders of the One True Faith' were encamped below, as was their right, of course, it being their Orange Hall and not the canteen at Bradbury Lines, there was no way that Lofty would be able to get a radio message to the Rat, unless he had a serious desire to be peppered from below by the massed guns of the mid-Antrim Protestant Arousal! "Fuck!" said Lofty to himself, and then emphasised his frustration by saying, "Fuck!" several more inward times in succession. There was nothing for it, but to await the departure of the assembled Orangemen to their welcome beds.

But when you have just arrived at the Day of Reckoning; and you have seen a fair number of your relatives unexpectedly, and, most definitely, unintentionally, shrug of this mortal coil during the previous few weeks; and you have borne witness to three major bomb attacks on your beloved homeland; and you are preparing to host the assembled ravening masses of mid-Antrim Protestantism within the next few hours; and you are expecting, at any moment now, the 'Assyrians' to come down like the wolf on the fold; and the wife's a frigid oul bitch, anyway; it is not bed that you are thinking of at a time like this. No way! There was too much adrenaline flowing in Slaght Orange Hall on that Twelfth morning, to allow sleep to push bloodlust on to the back burner.

And, apart from that, there would have been little sleep for our good Orangemen from Slaght, even if they had gone home to the unpleasant prospect of the old cold feet and shoulder, for at that very hour, the last before dawn, an old Irish lady was making an exceedingly large number of house calls, and was getting right pissed off at finding none of her customers in their beds, where they should have normally have been on the eve of their deaths. The old biddy has various names and forms; the 'Caller of Doom', the 'Lady of Death', 'Babd', 'Morrigan', the 'Bean-Nighe', the Bean Si', the 'Banshee'. Our Banshee was present in her form as 'Babd', the Goddess of Battles, who appears just prior to a person's death and announces the fact by wailing and crying outside the ancestral home in the wee small hours. Well, Babd was not in a good mood. She was getting fair pissed off with having to visit God-forsaken Slaght every second night for the past month, and she was up to her scrawny neck in wailings and moanings. They were a bloody uncooperative lot, these Protestants. Not at all like the good Catholics of the Falls Road, who were prepared to take her seriously, and die on time, and as ordained by herself and the gentlemen of the 1st Battalion The Parachute Regiment, fortuitously just coming up the street at the same time. No, these bloody Protestants showed no respect for the old Celtic Gods. Just five minutes ago she had wailed and moaned bloodcurdlingly outside the McKelvey farm, and two darkies had told her to, "Fuck off, ye oul bitch!" What was the world coming to, when simple country folk couldn't take a plain hint. And, more's to the point, what were two darkies doing alive in Slaght on a summer's night? Well, she'd teach these bastards a thing or three, and put the fear of God back into them. And, giving the McKelvey farm an airborne and most unfeminine two fingers, she headed for her last rendezvous of the evening, before returning to her daylight haunt of Shane's Castle, on the shores of Lough Neagh. Soaring into the night air, with her white tresses and her long linen shroud floating sensually in the wind, Babd headed for the Orange Hall. She still had a substantial number of calling cards to hand out to the local peasantry before dawn.

> ''Twas the banshee's lonely wailing
> Well I knew the voice of death,
> On the night wind slowly sailing
> O'er the bleak and gloomy heath.'

But despite all her wailing and moaning and groaning and keening, she didn't have much luck attracting the attention of any of the Protestants

drawing up their battle plans in the Orange Hall. She was very aware
of the four men hiding in the loft, and knew fine well that they were
paying her a great deal of attention. Indeed, one of them was in such
paroxysms of fear, that he might just become a premature candidate for
her professional skills. But no! It was the others in the Orange Hall that
she had come for, and if the bastards weren't going to show any respect,
she'd have to use other tactics. And so it was that Babd, changing her
form once again, this time into the nightmare figure of Morrigan,
reluctantly dropped to the ground and gave the main door of the Hall
a vigorous hammering with her gnarled fist. After five minutes and
grazed knuckles she at last succeeded in drawing someone's attention
to her knocking, and the door opened. A bilious red Protestant face
peered out, then disappeared again. "Reverend Mulholland. Yer wife's
at the door," a voice called out from within. A minute later the door
was pulled roughly open and Bertie's angry face thrust itself into the
night. Morrigan began to wail. "Fuck off, you stupid bitch. I've told
you never to bother me when I've got the work of the Lord to do. Go
home at once and knit yourself a chastity belt, or you'll get my leather
belt around your arse when I get back." And, without further ado, the
door slammed in Morrigan's face. She stood there, fuming. But what
could she do? Mulholland was not on her list, was he? No, more's the
pity! "Aw! Fuck it!" she said, and flew, raging into the air. As she passed
over the roof, she said "Boo!" to the frightened English face peeping
through a gap in the slates, and sped off home to Shane's Castle, while
a fearless SAS trooper passed out in terror below her.

I know what you are thinking. Banshees? Poppycock! Stuff and nonsense!
Nobody believes in ghosts nowadays! Well, dear reader, you are free to
think that way, if that is your desire. But, when your time comes, I hope
you will be more prepared to face reality than the Orangemen of Slaght
that July morning, and that you will rush downstairs for a last cup of tea
and a kick at the dog, before it is too late. And anyway, if four fearless
men of the SAS now believe in Banshees, you would be rather foolish
not to do likewise. And as you will find out shortly, Slaght was full of
fools, just like you, that night. Except that, by nightfall, most of the
fools in Slaght, unlike you, I hope, will be dead, as ordained.

It is almost four in the morning, but there is still no sign of dawn's rays on the Eastern horizon. Dark clouds are sinisterly scudding from the dereliction of Donegal and bringing with them a fine mizzle, the lightest form of Irish rain, soon to turn to a drizzle, with which those of you, who are English, will be more familiar. And soon the drizzle will become a shower, and - if all goes according to plan - the shower will become a summer thunderstorm, as Donegal sends her wonted depression Protestantwards to the East. There is nothing like a good Fenian rain to help the Twelfth off to its accustomed cheerful start. The mid-Antrim God may be a Presbyterian, but he sure as hell knows bugger all about meteorology, otherwise he would ensure better weather when he sends his impis out on their post-Reformation rites of passage.

And it is now time for you to sleep, so that you will be fresh for the Endepunkt of our tale. I hope that you do not dream of Morrigan or Babd, and that you are spared the sudden urge to rush downstairs for the last cuppa. May your dreams be more pleasant than those of the majority of our latter-day heroes, now almost ready to meet their Maker. But before you disappear briefly to Elysium, spare a thought for the innocent. I needn't advise you to make the thought a brief one, need I?

CHAPTER FIFTEEN

—•⚜•—

y six o'clock in the morning of the Twelfth, Slaght and its environs were lying under a glowering black cloud, streaked from time to time by sheet lightning, and soaked wet through. It was as if the very weather itself was in mourning for the dead, until you sat down and thought about it in more detail. Then you realised that the weather had no bloody sympathy for Slaght at all, otherwise it would have bucketed down over a reservoir or fifty miles out to sea. No, the sub-tropical rains which were pouring down on Slaght had arrived earlier that morning from Fenian Donegal, and had obviously little intention of leaving, at least until they had had a bit of their own back, and a good view of the retribution to come. Everywhere else in Ulster on this important morning, even, most surprisingly, over the Field at Finaghy outside Belfast, the sun was beaming forth in a cloudless sky, and temperatures had already reached a comfortable seventy degrees Fahrenheit. But not in Slaght! With cumulo-nimbus clouds bunched fist-like over the parish, starting at five hundred feet above sea level and stretching upwards into the stratosphere, there was no bloody way the sun was going to waste his time throwing any light on an already doomed situation. And, to make matters worse, the ambient temperature in Slaght was a miserable fifty degrees! It was all grossly fair, when you think of it. Why die on a sunny day, when normal Nova Scotian weather is more suitable for the occasion?

But the weather, inclement or idyllic, means little to the gentlemen of the SAS, and Colonel Mooney had had little problem in marshalling his troops at the Rangers Depot at 0530. Well, to be quite frank, he had had a bit of a problem with the Army Air Corps and RAF helicopter pilots, one of whom had had the audacity of telling him, in a downright insubordinate manner, that "only a fucking lunatic would fly a helicopter in this weather", but the usual promise of an extended paid holiday researching the toxicity of the bite of the *fer de lance* and other venomous serpents of Central America, had eventually got the craphats to see some sense. And, thus it was that Colonel Mooney and his QRF flew off Southwestwards in the direction of Carnaughts Primary School, on time and according to schedule, while the remainder of his Squadron set off by road to patrol the routes in and around the village of Slaght.

As the flight of helicopters approached the scene of so much recent violence, the sky grew darker and darker, and the cloud level forced the pilots to drop almost to the rooftops. The Rat was just beginning to realise that maybe the yellow bastards of the bat brigades might have had a point after all, when the tower of Bertie Mulholland's parish church suddenly appeared out of the murk, and disappeared equally suddenly behind, albeit minus a rather ornate brass weather vane and one hundred feet of trailing copper lightning conductor, the latter having been, most fortunately, not too well connected to either the tower or the earth. Automatically, with a rending scream of horror, the Alouette pilot, an experienced sergeant-major, pulled the flimsy helicopter up into the blackness of the clouds, determined not to hit any more religious edifices until he got to his destination. Now, you don't really want to make a habit of flying any form of airborne transport into the midst of a raging storm cloud, especially if you have one hundred feet of lightning conductor and a weather vane wrapped round your undercarriage. Normally the aviation experts would call this a 'no-no'. But, when you have no alternative, and you are acting through panic and not through common-sense, for otherwise you would still be in bed on such a morning, there is little else you can do, other than have fun watching nature stage a fireworks display that would have done justice to Queenie's Jubilee. At least the other helicopters in the flight had no problem in seeing where their leader was going, although their pursuit of Mooney was a bit strobiscopically tiring on the old eyes.

Somehow or other the Alouette and its passengers managed to get to one hundred feet above Carnaughts Primary School without a mid-air explosion, but one hundred thousand volts earthing down from the clouds, via the helicopter and one hundred feet of lightning conductor, and striking the roof of the school, wrote off Mooney's idea of using the building as his HQ for the rest of the day, although the conflagration would be a useful beacon for subsequent airborne expeditions into the gloom surrounding the area. "That bloody Headmaster will be looking for more than just a case of Scotch," thought the Rat, as he reached *terra firma* and took in the view. And, sure enough, through the sheets of rain, squelched an irate figure, brandishing a cane that was obviously intended to hammer some sense into an SAS Colonel's brain - or at least where the worthy schoolmaster obviously considered this particular SAS Colonel's brain to be located. "God!" thought Mooney, "As if I didn't have enough to contend with. Now I've got the bloody education authorities on my back, too!" And to pre-empt his imminent assault, and to delay his reckoning with the Treasury, Mooney shouted to two of his men, "Handcuff that fucker before I have to shoot him. If he gives the slightest trouble, throw him in the fucking fire with the schoolbooks. With all the whiskey I've given him, he'll burn well enough, and with any luck there'll be no evidence of his existence within the hour!"

Having removed the immediate danger of having a sore bum, or of committing justifiable homicide, the Rat commandeered the row of dry closets at the edge of the school football field as his operational HQ. There, where generations of grain and potato fed minor bottoms had constipatedly strained and groaned, or shit in their knickers, rather than place their bare cheeks on the wooden seats at ten degrees below zero on a February morning, Colonel Mooney awaited the 0600 hours OP reports from Delta 1 and Delta 2. The SAS Ops room at the Rangers Depot in Ballymena had heard nothing from Delta 1, since the bonfire of the vanities had gone skyward the previous night. And, from what Delta 2 had reported, there was some scepticism about whether Lofty and the lads were still alive, or whether they were currently fertilising a large area of mid-Antrim farmland. Mooney, however, had no doubt in the survivability of his men, and had refused the others permission to loot the personal kit of the team members of Delta 1 - at least not until he had first shout. After all, he was the boss, and if the man at the top has got no perks, why bother accepting all that silly subordination to the military system for all those years.

Just like clockwork, exactly on the dot of 0600 hours, the Reverend Mulholland and his men having at last gone home, not to bed, but to get dressed in their best suits and regalia for the big day, Delta 1 came on the air, and the Rat breathed a secret sigh of relief - not so much at his men being still alive, but more at his continued ability to get it right. When he listened to Lofty's terse account of their escape from the very fires of Hell, the Rat's chest swelled with pride at the courage and resourcefulness of his lads. When he heard of the public burning of the wedding couple, his face paled with distaste at man's cruelty to his fellow man (and woman), and especially before the poor couple had probably had the chance of enjoying a touch of post wedding night lumbago. The ambush on the twelve man IRA team, after the escape from the mob of mad Prots around the bonfire, was pure poetry, and if the Rat had known that the 'Defenders of the One True Faith' Orange Lodge in Slaght were, just that very minute, being accredited the kill on the BBC Northern Ireland six o'clock news, he would not have been best pleased. The infiltration of the roof-space of the Orange Hall had been yet another example of military skill at its finest, and the intelligence gained, from Big Bertie's overheard briefing of his henchmen, was going to be of considerable use during the course of the day to come.

Lofty finished his report rather hesitantly, with a colourless description of Mrs Mulholland's arrival by air, without the benefit of parachute, plane, or independently supporting wings, at the door of the Orange Hall, and her subsequent rude treatment at the hands of her husband. Mrs Mulholland's final action of saying 'Boo' to Trooper Scott, and giving him the old military two fingers, before flying off into the sky Southwards, was inexplicable, nay, fucking out and out incredible! But the others in Delta 1 confirmed Scotty's story, unbelievable though it sounded in the cold wet light of dawn. Finally, under the section, 'Admin & Log', Lofty put in the request for Scotty to see the MO and the Padre, and not necessarily in that order, as soon as they got back to civilisation - and by 'civilisation', Lofty emphasised, neither Scotty nor the others meant anywhere within five hundred miles of Slaght.

After congratulating his men, and telling them not to worry - he'd seen stranger things himself over Slaght than an airborne Mrs Mulholland - Colonel Mooney took the OP report from Delta 2. Sticky was his usual taciturn best, evidently having got a good grip on himself since his earlier, and most lurid, reporting on the burning bodies where Delta 1's OP had once been. He related that activity at the McKelvey farm was following a strict and impressive military procedure, with the two sentries on guard outside being replaced every hour. Obviously the house had been commandeered as a forward operations base by the Paras and some liaison personnel from the UDR. It made sense, although the lack of interest shown by the occupants at the time of the bonfire explosion was a bit funny, to say the least. "Must be strictly following orders not to get involved until later in the day," mused Mooney. And once again he decided to check with Lisburn, to see whether they knew what task the McKelvey farm occupants had been given.

But once again the Rat put the decision off until later, there being more urgent matters to attend to, such as getting out of the way of the newly-arrived, frying pan-wielding, schoolmaster's wife, who was at that very moment battering the living daylights out of two of his best and toughest men, and moving towards him with a speed that her bulk most certainly belied. "Oh! Fuck! Here we go again!" said the Rat, as he dodged the first swing of the cast iron skillet. And lucky he did dodge it, too, because not to have done so, with such alacrity, would have resulted in his removal, most permanently, from the remaining events of the day. Locking himself in one of the cubicles of the dry closet, Mooney waited until the harridan had been subdued by a mixture of tear gas, PVC rounds, and a good poking with an electric cattle prod. When it was safe to come out, the Rat, tears streaming from his eyes and smudging his camouflage cream, shouted at one of the Puma pilots to 'take that fucking hog-tied bitch off into the air and drop her into Lough Neagh, or the biggest bog hole you can find!" Fortunately for the schoolmaster's wife, a radio message from one of the SAS mobile patrols distracted Mooney's attention, long enough for four of the troopers to bundle the woman into a Land Rover, and drop her in a ditch at the side of the road a couple of miles away.

Meanwhile, two miles to the South, at Ross's Factory, Pinky and Mr McIlhenny had just returned from their first recce of the village of Slaght and its surrounding hills and fields. The orders that Pinky had received from HQNI were that 3 BJ was to occupy the high ground in an approximate circle round the area of the Twelfth Field, to stop any attempt by IRA units at infiltrating cross-country. He was also to put four major VCP's on the four roads into the village, to prevent armed mobile units of blood-crazed Republicans from shooting up the assembled Protestant masses on the move. He was to hold one Company in reserve at the Factory, ready to move in support of the remainder of the Battalion, or to block any attempts by attackers escaping North along the Antrim line.

It had looked simple on the map; and it looked equally simple on the ground. But the intelligence briefing on the events that had recently taken place in Slaght, including an up-to-date account of those of the previous night, told both Pinky and his RSM, that this was not going to be as simple as it looked. They had viewed the twelve IRA bodies in the field between Slaght and Cromkill, and if the Protestants could shoot like that, this particular Twelfth was going to be quite something! Given the untrained and rag, tag and bobtail nature of the forces at his command, Pinky, after consulting Mr McIlhenny, decided to put his most reliable sub-units on the four VCPs, and maintain a platoon of the remaining soldiers of any quality under his personal command. If anything difficult needed doing this day, he and Mr. McIlhenny would most probably have to do it themselves.

Just as he was about to summon his company commanders to give them their orders, one of his mobile reconnaissance patrols radioed in to say that a flight of helicopters had landed at Carnaughts Primary School, some thirty SAS officers and men had alighted, and had immediately proceeded to set the main school building on fire. A group of them had subsequently beaten up a middle aged man, who had been remonstrating at them with a cane in his hand, and, after subduing the aforementioned male, they were now in the process of battering fuck out of a rather large middle aged lady, who was giving as good as she got, ably assisted by a frying pan. "Good God, Mr. McIlhenny! I bet you that's old Mooney and his merry men, up to their usual 'hearts and minds' programme." "Sure sounds like the devil himself, or his twin brother," replied the RSM, smiling. "Well, if it is the Rat, we're really going to have fun today! Bad bastard though he is, he's one hell of a soldier, and it will make me feel a lot better knowing that he and his men are around. That's for sure." said Pinky, and returned to his task in hand.

HQNI was in utter turmoil. At the order of the Military Secretary, who had been less than polite on the phone, Sir Hector MacTavish, K.B.E. and so on, was to board a special RAF flight at Aldergrove at ten o'clock that morning, and return forthwith to London, and to an early and ignominious conclusion to a previously distinguished career. After an attempt to appeal to the old BJ boys network, Sir Hector found that even this, usually sacrosanct nepotistic institution, didn't work, and that Maggie herself was in on the act to drum him out of his beloved Army. The Military Secretary, whom Sir Hector himself had assisted to that powerful position, had had the gall to question the General's sanity over the telephone! He had even threatened a Court Martial, if Sir Hector didn't stop calling him a 'fucking wet turd' and other less than military terms of disrespect!

So, without further ado, Sir Hector MacTavish, complete with acned ADC and bodyguard team, went AWOL in three Land Rovers, but not before deliberately running down the ex-chunkie Corporal on guard at the main gate, and then reversing back over him again, as if to emphasise some point of military discipline. Needless to say, Perry Smythe-Gargle was both delighted at the way things had turned out to the gross humiliation of his now hated superior, and in terror for his life, being surrounded by this group of murdering pawns under the control of a megalomaniacal old fart - but a megalomaniac with a gun! Forty minutes later, along the road from Belfast to Antrim, the small convoy drove into the entrance to the 'Pig and Chicken' bar and restaurant, concealed the vehicles round the back, and proceeded to order breakfast from a cowering manager and staff, whose attempt to inform the military that they were closed, had been met by a succession of rifle butts to the softer parts of the lower abdomen.

In the vast beer and puke smelling bar, Sir Hector and his men began to plan their assault on Slaght, the 3rd Battalion the Blue Jackets, and anyone else who got in the way, and all with the principal objective of securing the slowest and nastiest possible death for a former Sergeant Moriarty, an extant Lady MacTee, and a snivelling, back-stabbing, little shit of a Colonel, none other than our Pinky Jolly. The brain-dead drongoes in the RMP bodyguard team, not being privy to the orders of the Military Secretary in London, and Perry Smythe-Gargle not likely to pass these on to them, what with Sir Hector brandishing a variety of weapons in both hands (except when shovelling fried eggs and boiled tomatoes into his gaping mouth), were listening intently to their boss and his murderous plans. This was what they had been waiting for. At last, a chance to put their training at Pontrilas into practice, and against enemies of the State, traitors and philanderers, to boot! God! It was good, on that 12th of July morning, to be thick as pig shit and a bodyguard in the RMPs! Just goes to show you, if you wait long enough for what you want, you'll most likely get exactly what you deserve, and a damned sight more than you desired.

At breakfast in his home off the Malone Road, Chief Inspector McCambridge of Special Branch was watching the latest BBC Northern Ireland news programme at seven o'clock. The first newsreel film of the ongoing slaughter at Slaght was being shown, and McCambridge was delighted to see the hole in the ground, under where the 11th Night bonfire had been, and which had obviously previously contained one of Mad Mooney's two OPs. "I wonder whether the bastard's boys were in the hide when it went up?" he thought to himself. "No word of any military casualties, but then, the SAS never reveals those sort of things, if they can help it. Bad for publicity, hee, hee" Just then the telephone rang in the hall, and McCambridge went off to answer it. Five minutes later he was back, his face positively aglow with good humour. "Excellent! Bloody great! So Sir Hector has flown the coop in the direction of Ballymena, pursued by the merciless might of the SIB and half the bloody Province Reserve Battalion from Palace Barracks. Fucking marvellous! I would have *hated* it, if that old cunt hadn't been able to make it for the finale. Well, nothing much to do now but stir up the last bucket of shit." And, after downing the remains of his bowl of porridge, Chief Inspector McCambridge went to his telephone again, and made a call to the RUC Barracks in Ballymena, where he asked to speak to Inspector Simpson immediately.

Inspector Simpson put the phone down on its cradle, and stared through the bomb-blast curtains at the back car park of Ballymena Barracks, where his men were in the process of peeling a ton and a half of potatoes, battering cod and plaice, and trying to unstick themselves from two hundred cubic metres of candy floss that had encircled the area, due to some stupid berk having left the flossing machine on all bloody night. But he had temporarily forgotten what he had been about to do to whomsoever it had been with sticky fingers and a sweet nocturnal tooth, and concentrated on what his good friend and superior had just told him. 'Sir Hector MacTavish, a traitor to the Queen, on the run, and protected by a small Army of SAS-trained pseudo-policemen, and coming his way. Arrest or kill on sight! Preferably not the former, if you want to stay alive yourself!' "Well, fuck me!" he said to the world in general. "This is getting a wee bit bloody much! AWOL bloody mad generals, fucking chinless military policemen, all coming to fuck up my day! Well, I'm not having it! Moriarty's all mine. Nobody else can have him. I don't care if they are future inmates of the Tower of London, or King Billy himself. I'll kill any bastard that lays a finger on Ignatius Aloysius Moriarty, until I can crucify the fucker myself!" And, stamping his feet pettishly, he grasped for his SMG and his Walther, and headed out to the car park, and the road to ultimate destruction.

In the Orange Hall at Slaght, the Reverend Bertie Mulholland, resplendent in his neck-brace and his finery, and wearing a black bowler hat, as all good Orangemen must do, surveyed his Lodge before exiting in formation into the teeming rain for the March to the forming-up point at the cross-roads in the middle of the village. There they would meet up with all the other Lodges, at that very moment themselves marching through the deepening puddles, hung-over and pissed wet though, towards Slaght; fifteen along the road from Ahoghill; ten from the direction of Portglenone; seven from neighbouring Cromkill; and a massive thirty-five from Ballymena, the last bastion of the True Faith in Ulster, and, indeed, in the whole Universe, should today go drastically wrong. Sixty-eight Orange Lodges, including Bertie's own. This was going to be a wonderful sight, and guaranteed to put the fear of God into any Fenians daft enough to risk double pneumonia by showing their pockmarked, vice-ridden faces in the townland of Slaght on the day of the Deluge!

In the McKelvey farmhouse, behind drawn curtains, the sixty-ninth lodge was at its final preparations. McCallion and his men, all dressed in dark suits, and all wearing long overcoats, not just to keep off the massed cats and dogs, which were streaming from the black clouds

billowing phantasmagorically over the rolling fields of Slaght, but also
to hide the SLRs (modified by now to have folding stocks, by a buxom
armourer, Mary nee Mata Hari McKelvey), the SMGs, the AK-47s,
and all the other panoply of war, which the mid-Antrim Battalion of
the Provisional IRA had either had in stock, or had purloined from
the gentlemen of the UDR and the RUC during recent days. The new
Master of 'True Sons of Maryhill, L.O.L. 666', Paddy McCallion, was
immaculate in his brand new, black, three piece, his long Burberry, his
Thompson sub-machine gun (I kid you not!), and his sash, gauntlets,
and gavel. He was 100% the true-blue Orangeman, and nobody other
than an expert in DNA could have told the difference between Paddy
and the real thing.

Mary was still in her battle fatigues, her work now almost done. When
her 'boys' went out that door, all that was left for her to do, was to
change her clothes into something more feminine, gather up her few
prized possessions and the substantial sum of money left to her by the
death of her dear Mikey, put everything in a suitcase, put the latter in
the car in the barn, have a last cup of tea and a tinkle, and then exit the
same door herself, in order to take a grandstand view of Armageddon,
before leaving for Aldergrove, the first available flight, and a new name
and life, somewhere far from Prods and Fenians, and all the other
bastards who had made her life a misery, since the day that Cardinal
O'Shea had diddled her mother in the Cathedral vestry in Liverpool,
after plying poor Moira with six bottles of communion wine and the
promise of absolution and a five pound note.

In the corner, near the Wellstood cooker, stood Ignatius Aloysius
Moriarty, a changed man since he had come under the tutelage of big
Mary. Now he was a Lambeg Drummer, just about to exit through
the front door as the vanguard of a 'real' Orange Lodge, and take his
rightful place in the annals of Protestantism in mid-Ulster. He was also
a highly trained killing machine, for apart from a stolen Walther 9mm
taped to his right ankle, he had ten pounds of Semtex explosive strapped
round his waist. At a suitable time the Semtex and a detonator would
come together, be secreted inside the drum, and the Lambeg positioned
to very best effect, slap-bang in the middle of the floor of Slaght Orange
Hall, at which point Ignatius, and the good Orangemen of Maryhill

and McCallion, would then fuck off smartish, to get out of Slaght and, if possible, mid-Antrim, before Big Bertie and the rest of his crew went skyward in search of Nirvana.

For part of the change that had come across Ignatius was his desire to no longer be a Protestant! It had been nothing but beatings and thumpings ever since he had done his first crap on the midwife's lap at the tender age of five minutes out of the womb. There were other things, better things, in this life than being a Presbyterian and going to the boring hell of a Free Reformed Heaven. That, he had found out, was for sure. He'd learned a lot in the last ten days, much more than he had in all his previous years put together. And he'd certainly had fun, even more fun than a gallon of whiskey and two barrels of Guinness falling off a lorry on the Antrim line could have ever given him. And the people who had given him this fun, Mrs McKelvey, Paddy McCallion, and all the others present in the farmhouse kitchen that morning - they were all Catholic! And, what's more to the point, they treated someone called Ignatius Aloysius as one of *them*!

"No! Fuck being a Protestant anymore. Catholics don't have to protest about their religion," thought Ignatius. "I'm me, and I'm proud of it. And what's more, at last I can get away from all of these depressing eejits, who think that the sun shines out of Slemish Mountain's back passage, and that the Braid River is as mighty as the fucking Mississippi. I'm off out of here, and I'm never coming back!" And without a further Protestant thought in his excuse for a brain, Ignatius Aloysius Moriarty, late of religious no-man's land, late of the Parachute Regiment, and soon to be late of the Mary nee O'Shea-O'Flaherty McKelvey School of Bomb Making and Lambeg Drumming, turned towards the big table, lovingly stroked the instrument that had brought about his transformation into a human being, placed the strap round his neck, and became a Roman Catholic.

Just then the sound of martial music began to filter up from the direction of Slaght crossroads. The time had almost come. And *this* time, Moriarty's mother really would have ensured that the little bastard was still-born, that is, if she had had any inkling, whatsoever, what his exit from that farm door was about to do to her beloved Ulster. But before we join Ignatius in the most demonstrably passionate glorification of his religious conversion, we once again must make a brief interlude, and return to the edge of the forest at Tardree, and to the County Antrim Venture Scouts Headquarters, where events are beginning to take place, which will have a more than considerable bearing on the satisfactory outcome of our little tale.

During the hours of darkness, and the subsequent passage of dawn towards mid morning, the assembled Brethren of L.O.L. 666 from Maryhill had been struggling to grasp the reality of their situation, and, more's to the point, struggling to get out of it. While commencing in their labours with a deep and thankful appreciation of the fact that they were still alive, and that no one was the worse for wear, other than those who had pissed or shit themselves earlier, and, of course, the good Reverend McCartney, who was a bit more nasal in his consonants than previously, the desire for revenge among the Maryhellions had fertilised and taken deep root. But, since none of them was Houdini, it nonetheless took a long time before anyone could make progress in the unravelling of his bonds.

It was one of the young bandsmen, a future acolyte of celibacy on the Isle of Skye, who was the first to break loose, although his rush of freedom was accompanied by a parallel rush of blood to those joints, which had previously been tightly bound. Thus it was that our young bandsman lost brain control over his half paralysed legs, fell forward, and cracked his head on what remained of the nose of the Reverend McCartney, who had rolled closer to the youth, in order to be the first person to be released. The remnants of the McCartney schnozzle, which had been, at one time in the distant past, or two days before, of a proud, non-pimpled, and noble Roman prominence, and totally suited to a self-appointed leader of the 'wee free' Kirk, were now more applicable in a comparison with Mohammed Ali's sparring partner, or a Waterloo Station tramp, in the final throes of tertiary syphilis and sclerosis of the liver. Moreover, the internal parts of the McCartney nasal bone structure were now driven even closer, by the bandsman's excusable but regrettable fall, to an entrance into the not-inconsiderable McCartney brain structure, and the outcome of that would be something to write home to Granny about!

But, after thirty minutes every one of the Maryhellions, the junior flautists, the side drummers, the trumpeters and trombone players, and the two Ulsterbus drivers, had been released from their cordage, and all and sundry were out for blood. They had to wait a further fifteen minutes, however, until several buckets of water brought the Reverend back from his very, very near-death experience. His immediate action, on regaining a semblance of his senses, was to order the assembly to take to the roads. It was soon drawn to his attention, however, that those who normally wore underpants, and who hadn't shit in them too much, were still wearing them, whereas those who didn't, or who had, were totally bollock-naked. Hardly the gear to be dressed in for an excursion on the public highway! A search of the former prison premises found an extensive cupboard full of Scout uniforms, most of which seem to have dated from the pre-War period, judging from the knee length shorts. But, *faute de mieux*, as they say. And so it was that the Loyal Sons of Maryhill emerged into the mid morning light at the edge of a forest, fucking miles from where they wanted to be, and without a clue of where they were, or wanted to go, anyway, and began a painful march back along part of the route that they, correctly, suspected they had come the previous evening.

But, good planning was on their side. 3M, otherwise known as Moriarty, McKelvey and McCallion, had made a drastic mistake. They had not searched or seized the instrument cases of the band. These were opened, and the weapons they concealed were now grasped in the hands of a vengeful band, who had every intention of putting the marauding of Gustavus Adolphus's mercenary troops through Germany during the Thirty Years War into very true perspective. After a walk of twenty minutes the first vehicle was hijacked - a tractor and trailer. After a further ten minutes a cement lorry and a busload of Darby and Joan Club members from Rathfriland had been added to the former. In their new found transport the Maryhellions hit the staunchly Protestant village of Kells and Connor, and when the locals asked for quarter, they fucking got it - and hanged and bloody drawn! Leaving the smoking pyre behind them, the phalanx moved boldly off in the direction of the hamlet of Cromkill, where the fervent descendants of Cromwell would exact similar vengeance within twenty minutes, prior to crossing the

Antrim line and heading down the last one mile of tar macadam to Slaght and their fated end.

And, as the comedian Dave Allen used to say, 'may their God go with them', for sure as hell, no one else in his right mind would be seen in the company of a bunch of knee-shorted, shitty-kecked Glaswegians on their way to the Sauchiehall Street equivalent of Valhalla. But maybe even a Scottish Presbyterian God would be a wee bit nervous about being seen anywhere near where the Maryhellions are going on this, their last day.

CHAPTER SIXTEEN

I f the good Lord had not still been in Beirut, and if the sun had been shining, the scene at the crossroads in Slaght would have been enough to stir the heart of anyone, Protestant, Catholic, or downright Agnostic, who loves a good parade. But marshalling the sixty-eight attendant lodges and their accompanying bands was not an easy task, and not only because the driving rain made it difficult to see more than ten yards with any accuracy. It was more because the crossroads was the lowest-lying spot in the whole townland, and getting all sixty-eight soaked lodges into any semblance of order, while hung-over, and wading knee-deep in the swirling waters of the newly-formed River Slaght, was not the easiest of responsibilities, even for a Household Brigade RSM to shoulder. By dint of his booming voice and the judicious use of a blackthorn walking stick, the Reverend Bertie Mulholland was at last able to give the order to "MARCH!" and off the phalanx moved, slowed only by the need to carry some of the fifers at shoulder height, to prevent them being swept away by the vicious undertow.

With sixty-eight bands playing, at any one time, fifty or more different tunes, and the noise being enclosed by the low-slung black clouds above, the cacophony could only be compared to a Chinese funeral, or one hundred orchestra brass sections attempting to play the 1812 Overture in different keys and tempos at the same time. As the parade rose Moses-like from the Red Sea of Slaght and on to the firmer and higher ground of the Protestant Promised Land, the squelching of trench-footed hobnailed boots was added to the din. Along the route, on both sides of the road uphill to the Orange Hall and the Field opposite, mothers and children, and any fool who chose the wettest day of the century to come and gape loose-jawed and drooling at Ulster Protestantism in its fullest flight of fantasy, were lined up, sheltering under sheets of plastic, old fertiliser bags, lorry tarpaulins, and - in one bizarre case - a cellophane wrapped copy of the 'Catholic Herald'. The latter gentleman, just recently released from institutional care, was savaged to death by a pack of wild two-legged dogs from one of the Ballymena lodges towards the front of the procession, and, thereby, became the first, but by no means the last, innocent casualty of the day.

As the procession passed the gate of the McKelvey farm, Bertie Mulholland rabble-roused his lodge into a paroxysm of 'Fuck the Pope', and other choice ecumenical phrases. Inside the farmhouse, Mary nee 'Heavy Metal Jacket' McKelvey flushed with passionate rage, but controlled her boiling emotions by her knowledge that sweet vengeance was yet to come. When the end of the procession eventually reached the gate, she opened the front door, and the well-drilled Brethren of 'Loyal Sons of Maryhill L.O.L. 666' emerged, unfurled and raised their banner, and, with a triumphant and swaggeringly sober Ignatius Aloysius Moriarty, and his Lambeg Drum, in the lead, joined the parade, hidden from curious view by the ever stronger squalls of cold rain sweeping sideways from the West. The sixty-ninth lodge, the 'visitors from across the water', had arrived at last, and its members were ready and willing to show solidarity with their mid-Ulster Brethren in the ongoing struggle against the Antichrist and his fallen archangels, the Pope, the Taioseach, U2, the Clancy Brothers, Senator Edward Kennedy, and the Malone Bakery.

The sixty-ninth lodge had no trouble in entering the Twelfth Field and taking a position on high ground over-looking the scene. They assembled in the lee of yet another sycamore tree, and while they awaited the beginning of the morning's speeches, and calls to arms from Big Bertie and other prominent promoters of the social and economic benefits of sectarianism, Paddy McCallion and some of his boys wandered over to a van, which was dispensing hot tea, and fish and chips. It was there, after reaching the front of the queue at the counter, that Paddy McCallion came face to face with Inspector Simpson, under deep cover and up to his elbows in batter. But, protected as he was by his bowler hat, sash, gauntlets and other Orange appurtenances, Paddy was not immediately recognised by the Beast of Beleek, although the latter was sure that he had seen the face somewhere before. "Probably in the Unionist Club, or the Protestant Gun Club, or the Annual General Meeting of the B-Specials Benevolent Society, or the like," Simpson thought to himself, and was then distracted by an order for forty plaice and chips, accompanied by a rather rude, "and make it fucking snappy!"

For the next thirty minutes, despite the typhoon raging around them, the assembled masses tucked into whatever provender Inspector Simpson and his men, and the other, more innocent, traders, were purveying. In particular, but not totally gender-exclusively, the men folk began their normal pagan ritual of wetting their insides with vast amounts of alcohol, in order to stop themselves from being washed away on the rising tide. It was only when the speechifying began, that Inspector Simpson was in any position to relax, count the considerable profits that he was making for Bob McCambridge's private slush fund, and have the energy to reflect on the events so far. Something was troubling him, something his sixth sense of survival was telling him he had better not bloody well ignore. But try as he did, his brain was still befuddled by VAT calculations, and wondering how much of the profits he could surreptitiously pocket, without Chief Inspector McCambridge ever being any the wiser.

At last, at 1130 on that momentous morning, the time had come for the Reverend Mulholland to climb on to the back of the builder's lorry that was the speaker's dais, and address (or, in his case, harangue) the crowd. All at once the silence was palpable, and even the floodwaters and the rain seemed muted in respect - or fear. With or without his pink neck-brace, he was an imposing figure, and one who would have struck fear into the owner of Paradise, Himself, if he ever had the unlikely ending of entering there! Bertie stood silent, and glowered, for effect, at the assembled masses, and when he had the attention of even the biggest eejits or most slavering drunks among them, he swelled out his chest, until his waistcoat buttons were in danger of popping, grabbed the microphone in his hand, and boomed out, "Brethren! We are gathered here together in the name of the Lord God, and the Lord God is not your weak-kneed Anglican God, nor is he that excuse for a

Being that the full-bladdered Methodists call a God, and he is certainly not, in any shape or form, that corruption, that pestilential contagion, that abomination, that after-birth of a Dublin whore, that the Pope and his pagan minions dare call a God, that Antichrist, that fornicator, that slithering homunculus, that odorific slime that aborted from the bowels of the Enemy of the True Religion. No, Brethren! We are here in the name of the God of Orangeism, the God of Ulster, the God that will this day wreak his vengeance a-plenty on any Fenian infiltrators into our Protestant parish of Slaght, and will dash the skulls of those infiltrators on the Rock on which the Orange Order was built, just as Cromwell, the Lord Protector, would himself be doing throughout Ireland, this very day, had he not been so sadly taken from us by old age, and the need to defend the Faith against the High Church Anglican Papists of Whitehall and the Northern Ireland Office!"

There was, of course, much more of the same to come. But we must pause briefly, in order to go back a few seconds to that part which went, 'any Fenian infiltrators into our Protestant parish of Slaght', and take a close look at the strange facial twistings and turnings of Inspector Simpson, as the full might of twenty years or more of Special Branch experience, as well as a very large frisson of fear, toy with the Reverend Mulholland's dire warning. "Oh shit! McCallion's here! Oh fuck! Oh shit-fuck, fuck-shit, we're in the middle of a fucking free-fire zone!" And he shouted to his subordinates to get their guns out, and, "Get the bastards!" But, in the heat of the moment, he failed to elucidate to his men, who the 'bastards' actually were, and further explanations of, "they're dressed up like Orangemen, you stupid cunts!" did little to improve their comprehension.

Now, you can just imagine it, can't you? Simpson and his men emerging from a variety of mobile retail outlets, brandishing a not-inconsiderable array of small arms, and into the middle of a crowd of several thousand wet Protestants, congregated for the sole purpose of swearing another year's fidelity to the tenet of murdering Fenians in large numbers. The effect was electrifying, and you know very well what electricity does to you when you are standing in water up to your knees and are soaked wet through? To say that panic ensued would be the understatement of the year! At least twenty women and children, and a further four

drunk and incapables, were trampled to death in the first mad rush
to get out of the immediate vicinity of the fish and chip van, only to
meet similar casualty-causing surges coming from the direction of the
candy-floss outlet, the beer and whiskey dispensary, and a variety of
other SB-run stalls.

But Big Bertie Mulholland and his men had been prepared for any
eventuality, and, at the first screams of panic, the Brethren of 'Defenders
of the One True Faith' drew out their weapons from their places of
concealment, and rushed round in circles looking for Fenians to kill.
But it was not easy to distinguish any obvious Catholics, so the selection
process was more random than it ought perhaps to have been, and
several visiting and unvouched-for strangers went to meet their Maker
down below, before the Orangemen of Slaght could force their way
through the circling crowds and find their true enemies, the armed
men of the former 'Scrubbers Incorporated', who seeing other armed
men approaching them, immediately identified the latter as the IRA,
and began to open fire. It was a little bit like the 'Gunfight at OK
Corral', only with the casualties more evenly apportioned between both
sides. After five minutes, however, all ammunition immediately to hand
having been expended on both sides, and, apart from a couple or three
lynchings, just for the fun of the thing, the battle temporarily subsided.

Inspector Simpson, having seen the way the tides were turning in ever
increasing circles before and against him, had taken refuge behind a
group of stout peasant ladies, holstered his pistol, and waited for the
first chance to flee the area. The Brethren of Slaght had rounded up
the surviving members of the SB at the Field, and were listening in
total disbelief to their protestations of being members of the RUC.
With such disbelief, in fact, that another half dozen were lynched
before the Reverend Mulholland had identified one of the bodies as
definitely 'one of ours', and had called a belated end to the bloodletting.
While he and the other leading Masters assembled on the back of the
rain-swept builder's lorry, in order to work out a good story to protect
themselves from any subsequent legal action, Moriarty and McCallion
surveyed the scene from beneath their protective sycamore tree, now
gaily festooned with the slowly swinging bodies of half a dozen former
members of Ulster's finest. The IRA had come out of the whole affair

totally unscathed, having been pre-empted in their own assault on the masses, by a fortunate combination of good military discipline and by having been taken unawares by 'first-strike' Simpson. Just then, to the surprise of everyone in the Field, including Ignatius and Paddy, the sound of a fierce gun battle was heard from the direction of Cromkill.

The convoy of tractor and trailer, ready-mix cement lorry, and former Rathfriland Darby & Joan Club transport, bearing the new County Antrim Venture Scout Troop, after a not-so-silent massacre of the citizens of Cromkill, had arrived at a road block set up by one of Inspector Simpson's sub-units, at the bottom of a hill some thousand metres from the Orange Hall. Behind this road block, and well dug in, and not enjoying lying in trenches full of rainwater very much, either, was one of the four major VCPs of 3BJ. When the SB sergeant in command had stopped the Reverend McCartney's convoy and asked, "Who the fuck do you think you are, a Sunday outing for fucking fairies?" he had been gunned down on the spot, as were the other three surprised plain-clothes constables in his team. All of this was observed by the VCP, a further two hundred metres back in the direction of Slaght. With surprising discipline the Blow Jobs waited for their officer's command to open fire, which was given when the Maryhellion convoy had progressed a further one hundred metres up the hill. The GPMG in the SF role at the VCP swept with fearsome accuracy the leading tractor and trailer, which disappeared in a fireball. The third vehicle, the bus, suffered a similar fate, although a fair proportion of the Venture Scouts were able to get out and flee through the hedgerows for the comparative safety of the tree line.

The middle vehicle, from which the Reverend McCartney was pretending to control his side of the battle, swung right, mounted the hedge, and took off with an impressive burst of speed in the direction of the top of the hill and Slaght Orange Hall. The VCP's fire seemed to have little effect on the slowly turning ready-mix drum on the back, and soon the cement lorry was out of effective range and picking up speed on the flat ridge, which led directly to its original destination. Across the small valley, in the Twelfth Field, the assembled Brethren watched with horror this latest apparent threat to their very being. "Open Fire!" shouted Big Bertie, and every available gun was trained in the direction of the cement lorry and its vulnerable cab, and let rip. Now the distance was obviously too great for accurate fire, or for even the bullets from the hand guns to reach the truck, but the massive power of the attack was enough to scare the remaining shit out of the driver of the lorry, and he decided not to stop out front, but to park inside the Orange Hall itself. With a tremendous wrench of the steering wheel, the lorry and its four flat tyres spun round in an impressive skid and ended up three quarters of the way into the building. A final bullet from the Field pinged into the levers at the rear of the truck, and the spinning of the ready-mix drum reversed. Fifteen tons of best Portland cement, sand, and gravel mix began to fill the gap caused by the lorry's entrance.

Above, where the roof space had once been, Lofty and the lads from Delta 1 found themselves rotating uncomfortably between the ready-mix drum and the slates. They had missed most of the attack, but they would, despite this, have quite a lot to tell the Rat, and they weren't going to wait another five minutes until 1200 hours to do so. Fuck both him and fucking radio silence! This was all getting a bit beyond a joke! Colonel Mooney, at that moment in his Alouette one hundred feet above the Field, was surveying the scene below him with what can be only described as total amazement. There were at least twenty bodies swaying from assorted species of deciduous trees. A further forty or so bodies were either prone, or writhing miserably, all over the top of the hill. Squads of Mulholland's goons were dumping selected civilian dead unceremoniously in the hole, which had once been the residence of Delta 1. And now, fucking armed Boy Scouts were spreading out across the surrounding fields, engaged in a fight to the death by the troops of 3 BJ, from their positions controlling the high ground, where they had been sited to stop the IRA getting in, but were now, with surprising accuracy, stopping the great-grandsons of Baden-Powell getting out. "It is all a bit of an existentialist nightmare, this bloody Irish situation", said Mooney to the pilot, who knew fuck all about existentialism, but wholeheartedly agreed with the Colonel.

And as the Alouette swooped across the valley and towards the Orange Hall, Mooney could see a bloody great cement lorry bursting through the BJ's cordon and headed in the same direction. Just then the Alouette began to take some of the inaccurate incoming fire from the Orangemen in the Twelfth Field, and the pilot, most wisely, headed up into the clouds, as the cement lorry raped and pillaged the front door of the Hall. While in the clouds, the Rat's radio blared into life, and he listened with some sympathy to Lofty, who seemed rather out of breath, presumably because of his counter-rotational attempts to prevent himself being deposited on the floor of the Orange Hall, which was now apparently occupied by fucking middle-aged Glaswegian Boy Scouts, promising the Second Coming over Slaght, any minute now!

The Rat told a protesting Lofty to remain where he was for the time being, an order that obviously did not enamour the Colonel in the slightest to the lads in Delta 1. With some reluctance the pilot was persuaded to come down out of the clouds, and make a quick run over the roof of the Orange Hall, to see what the situation was in more detail. As they swooped over the Hall, the Rat was able to verify that what Lofty had described was totally accurate. He was also able to get a finer appreciation of how Lofty and the others in Delta 1 were loyally following his order to remain in their less than comfortable position, because four MP5s poked out from between the slates on the sagging roof, opened fire at a ridiculously easy range of fifty feet, and crippled the hydraulics of the Alouette. Despite the best efforts of the pilot to get to safety and Carnaughts, the helicopter lurched violently, and headed aimlessly towards the Twelfth Field, where it landed upside down in the very same Special Branch decorated sycamore tree, beneath which a bemused Ignatius was standing fearless and alone - McCallion and the other IRA men having decided that braving the rain in the open field was better than awaiting the arrival of some upside-down airborne dignitary.

The Rat peered down into the face of Ignatius peering up through the branches and bodies below. "Who are you?" said Moriarty. "Colonel Mooney, 22 SAS, and who are you?" was the reply. "I'm Moriarty, former Protestant. Pleased to meet you, Colonel Mooney." said Ignatius. "Are you any relation to a Sergeant Moriarty, formerly of 2 PARA, and now running a short time brothel in Bali, Indonesia, by any chance of the imagination?" asked the Rat. "No, Sir, though I was a sergeant in the Paras for a wee while, but only because Mrs McKelvey wanted me to be," answered Ignatius. "Well, well! Mary McKelvey! I'm a friend of her old boss, Paul Haggard, you know. But maybe she would recognise him under another name," said Mooney. "Any friend of a friend of Mrs

McKelvey's is a friend of a friend of mine," said Ignatius, and began to climb into the tree, where at last, perched on a branch, he was able to cut the Rat free from his safety harness, get him right side upwards, and assist him to a soggy, *terra* not so *firma*.

But when they got to the ground they found themselves surrounded by a bloodthirsty group of Big Bertie's gauleiters. Motioning to Ignatius, one of the latter asked menacingly, "Who the fuck's that on a wet day?" "His name is Mooney, and he's a Colonel in the SAS," replied Moriarty, with that terrifying honesty about names that had so often got himself in trouble, but this time was going to get someone else deep in the mergatroid. "Mooney's a fucking Fenian name. I bet you know MacTavish, that Fenian turncoat cunt at Lisburn, don't you Mr. fucking Mooney?" growled the chief gauleiter. "As a matter of fact, I am well acquainted with the General Officer Commanding Northern Ireland, and may I draw your attention to another fact, that only lieutenants are addressed as Mister. I am not, Sir, a Lieutenant, but a Colonel," was the Rat's defiant response. "*Well*, you've got a fucking Fenian name, *and* you know that bastard MacTavish, *and* you haven't got an invitation to this particular party, *Mister* fucking Colonel. Get him lads! String the bastard to the highest branch you can reach," was the gauleiter's unsympathetic answer to the Rat's insistence on being called by his proper rank.

And all would have not fared well for Colonel Mooney, if the sergeant-major pilot of the Alouette, who had been listening attentively to the foregoing, had not remembered that his name was O'Toole, that he was from Galway, that he had been a good Catholic for at least one day in his life, and decided, therefore, that a quick 'Mayday!' was very much in order. Yes! You've got it right. Well done! The little wire to the battery was half severed, drip, drip, drip, etc. Now, the Rat, having been through this once before, but then at half a field's length, decided that a closer proximity was injurious to health, and, thus, he grabbed furiously at Moriarty, who grabbed equally furiously at his Lambeg drum, and the two of them burst through the astonished cordon of threatening Orangemen. The latter had only just time to hear the voice calling "Mayday!" for the third time in the greenery above, when they, six sylvan swingers from Castlereagh, and another member of the Army Air Corps' fast depleting ranks, sped upwards into the welcoming clouds. The sun was beaming over Donegal to the West, especially at having spawned yet another delightful little baby sun in the storm clouds pondering over Slaght to the East.

We will leave the evil Inspector Simpson cowering behind his corseted bodyguards; Mooney and Moriarty, cementing their new-found friendship by legging it across the Field out of the way of the descending mechanical and biological debris; Mulholland and his peers sorting out a cast-iron alibi; and McCartney, Delta 1, and the concrete-depositing ready-mix lorry with their uncomfortably close proximity; and we will pay a brief return visit to Ross's Factory, some few miles away, where Task Force MacTavish is about to join up with the British Army's third worst collection of Blow Jobs. There had been a slight bit of a problem on the other side of Antrim, where a UDR road-block had foolishly attempted to halt the fast moving convoy, commanded, out front, like no other General in his right mind would ever do, by Sir Hector himself, and had met the full might of a senior officer's wrath, and a couple of hundred rounds of extremely well placed automatic fire. Free now to assault Slaght in the search of the three true enemies of the Crown, Sir Hector, a seemingly limp-wristed Smythe-Gargle, and the monkey troop, arrived with yet another screech of brakes at the main gate of Ross's factory, and demanded to see the CO. On finding that the "Colonel is out on the ground, Sir", Sir Hector was not best pleased, and took pains to get across his displeasure by demoting all the officers present to the ranks, something never before accomplished by a General in the field, but ably and efficiently done on this occasion, at gun-point. A summary execution of some of the poorer examples of the Officer Corps was just about to take place, when Sir Hector, almost too belatedly, suddenly realised that he had been about to order the deaths of some of his own beloved BJs in a most illegal manner, and relented, commanding instead that they be hand-cuffed and locked up until such time as he could form a rather more 'legal' drum-head Court Martial, and then execute the bastards! Just as this was being done, the door of a mill room, which had been temporarily converted to a mess hall, flew open, and a burly and most military-like Padre Appleblossom shot forth, brandishing a junior member of the Army Catering Corps on the splintered and ungreased end of a broom-handle. It was a shock to all concerned, although the ACC private was himself far past caring!

"And who, Sir, the fuck are you?" screamed the General at the Padre. Appleblossom immediately dropped his handling charge, drew himself up to his full height and stature as a gentleman of the cloth, a former ABA junior champion, and Chaplain to a battalion in one of the finest Regiments in the British Army, saluted smartly, and said with impressive *sang-froid*, "492397 Captain Appleblossom, General, Padre of this wonderful Battalion in the best regiment in the Army, God Bless Them All!" Somewhat mollified by the response, but still wondering why an ACC private had been impaled anally on an Army-issue broom-handle, Sir Hector demanded an immediate clarification of what bestial religious rite the good Padre had been in the process of inducting the unconscious private into. "Caught the bastard drinking the Mess port, General. As Mess President I have warned the little alcoholic snitch about such behaviour on several occasions, but as he is one of Colonel Jolly's fornicating bum-boys, I've not been able to give the blighter the shafting he deserves until today, General." replied a quick-witted Appleblossom, knowing only too well the two pet hates of MacTavish's military career, Pinky Jolly and rampant queers. By putting both together, plus the heinous crime of sacrilegiously daring to importune the Mess port, Padre Appleblossom had once again saved his career, and, this time, had undoubtedly saved himself from summary execution.

"Hmmph! I should bloody well think so too! That bastard Jolly in command for forty-eight hours, and look what the Regiment's come to!" said Sir Hector, brandishing his SMG in the direction of the genuine BJ officers and the attached stand-ins, who were at that very moment being hand-cuffed and led away to some subterranean mill-race, where they would await the outcome of the General's future, to discover whether they would add to the statistics of today's activities, or be saved at the last moment by some avenging angel, which seemed rather unlikely under the present circumstances. "Captain Appleblossom, are you a man of God or are you first and foremost an officer in the Blue Jackets?" asked the General, with that pomposity that only senior officers in the Army can bring off, without too much sniggering in the ranks. "A true Blue Jacket, first and foremost General!" was Appleblossom's shouted and inevitable reply, survival of the fittest being the motto of the Royal Army Chaplain's Department.

"Right then. You are now the Commanding Officer of the 3rd Battalion, and I hereby promote you in the field. Your orders are to take the remainder of the troops at your disposal, and go to this village of Slaght, and arrest the following three persons, as enemies of the Crown, namely, one Sergeant Moriarty, formerly of 2 PARA, Lady MacTavish, formerly of, er, er, formerly of Bidston Hall, Birkenhead, and the pseudo-Lieutenant-Colonel Pinkerton Jolly, traitor to his Nation, pettifogging prick, and, now I find, a member of the chocolate ASLEF. Arrest them alive, bring them to me, and make sure that you leave their arses alone. Any subsequent tricks with military property up the incorrect orifices, and I will supervise operations myself, understood?" "Yes, General. A pleasure, if I may say so," said Appleblossom. "I don't mind if you say the Lord's Prayer backwards in seventeen different oriental languages. Just bring me their persons alive, and preferably still very much kicking, and there's a medal in it for you, my boy!"

Having condemned the common soldiery to the tender care of the biggest buggerer in the British Army, Sir Hector got back into the front of his Land Rover, and ordered his small convoy to head back to the main road and make haste to Slaght. As his vehicle, driven by a military policeman with obvious tunnel vision, edged blindly out on to the Ballymena line, it met with a sickening crunch with the rapidly decelerating lead van in a convoy of the Belfast press corps, on its way belatedly to witness the ongoing slaughter of the innocents. Stevenson of the 'Telegraph', who was in the front van, had hosted a bacchanalian orgy the previous evening, at his editor's expense, which explained their late departure from an overnight stay in the cells at North Queen Street RUC Station, and an early morning meeting with a Justice of the Peace, in connection with false accusations of assaulting police officers in the course of their duty. A severely bruised and hung-over Stevenson emerged from the tangled mess of Land Rover and van, to come face to face with an irate Sir Hector MacTavish, now wearing a windscreen, halo-like, on the back of his head where his gold-braided hat had previously been rakishly perched.

"You! You bastard! Now I've got you!" screamed the General. "Oh, shit!" said Stevenson, accurately summing up exactly what he was standing in, and up to his neck. "I don't suppose you're insured, Sir

Hector?" was the only other thing Stevenson could think of saying under the circumstances, just before the General opened fire with his SMG. Twenty dead journalists and a BBC Northern Ireland camera team later, the Land Rover convoy continued its interrupted journey to Slaght, with the monkeys firing randomly at anything which took their fancy, including an SAS mobile patrol, which had just turned off the main road and was heading for Carnaughts Primary School. It was probably this last action which brought the sinecure of the RMP bodyguard team to an earlier conclusion than might otherwise have been the case, because the SAS mobile patrol, as soon as they had extricated their two stripped down 'pink panthers' from the privet hedge at the front of Mrs Carson's house near the cross-roads, set off in hot pursuit. It was going to be a bit of an unequal contest!

Turning left at high speed at Cromkill crossroads, Sir Hector and his merry men tally-hoed over the hill and made towards the battlefield. As they swerved past a burned-out bus and the charred remains of a tractor and trailer, a group of soldiers could be seen laying something on the road ahead. "What's that they've got, General?" asked the driver. "What's what whose got?" was the immediate response. "That there, across the road, Sir," said the driver. "Oh! That! Those are caltrops," replied the General. "Oh!" said the driver. "Fuck!" said the General. "Brake!" screamed Smythe-Gargle. "Too late!" groaned the driver. And all four tyres of the lead Land Rover were slashed to ribbons as they raced across the caltrops at sixty miles an hour. The caltrops then made a quick decision to entwine themselves round both front and rear axles, which had the interesting result of ripping both from the chassis of the vehicle at the same time. A wheel-less Land Rover containing the former GOCNI, his ADC and two very frightened RMPs commenced a short flight into the air, over the hedge, past the 3 BJ GPMG SF pit, and landed upright beside Lieutenant-Colonel Pinkerton Jolly and RSM McIlhenny, spattering both with low-octane petrol and a considerable quantity of mud and stones.

"You, you bastard!" shouted an apoplectic MacTavish, groping around in the wreckage for the first available weapon he could find, but only managing to tightly grab the balls of the driver, who up until then had been attempting forlornly to extricate his head from between the spokes of the steering wheel. Ignoring the unearthly keening sound coming from the driver's shredded lips, the General, having at last found a bigger and better gun than anything the driver had on special offer, stepped out of the demolition derby and strutted purposefully forward towards Pinky, his remaining monkeys rushing from their vehicles to form two lines on either side. "You are forthwith relieved of command, you perverted poor excuse for an officer! Shoot him men!" ordered the General. And there were two immediate and lengthy bursts of fire. But it wasn't coming from the monkey troop, as they were in the unfortunate position of being the targets. Just as old Paddy McGonigle had said, it wouldn't take much to dispose of the General's bodyguards, which was exactly what the gentlemen of the ambushed SAS mobile patrol were now in the process of proving. Two long bursts of automatic fire into the backs of the two rear monkeys soon had both rows of deadbeats falling like skittles on the grass. "Thanks, lads!" called Pinky. "Bloody good timing - and shooting!" "Don't mention it, Colonel. Piece of piss with shits like those!" called back the SAS sergeant. "We'll leave you to arrest the General."

"What do you mean, 'arrest' him?" shouted Mr. McIlhenny. "Haven't you heard, Sir? He's no longer GOC. He's 'arrest on sight'. Orders from on high in Downing Street, and from what the grapevine tells us from Hereford, our Maggie would be quite happy if some unfortunate accident was to remove her of the embarrassment of court-martialling the old fart!" answered the SAS sergeant. "Jesus! Tell me you're not joking!" called Pinky. "Word of honour, Colonel. He's all yours." And with a vague semblance of a salute, the SAS sergeant returned to his vehicle, and set off on his way back to Carnaughts. "Well, well, well! What a wonderful world this is," breathed a dumbfounded Pinky at a smiling McIlhenny. But just then the RSM caught sight of Sir Hector and the raised muzzle of an SMG pointing at both himself and Pinky, and, rugby-tackling the latter from a standing start, both men rolled out of the line of fire of the first burst of SMG on automatic, which splattered the ground where they had stood a micro-second earlier.

When they had slithered to a halt in the mud and had time to look up, Pinky and Mr. McIlhenny found themselves staring right into the barrel of the General's SMG, in which was now inserted a new and full magazine. "Got you, you horrible little creep! Now I'm going to get my own back for my poor horse that you had the temerity to shoot from under me, and in public, too! What do you say to that, eh?" sneered the Sir Hector. "Not a lot really, MacTavish, although I was sorry that I killed a poor dumb animal, and not the pompous bastard astride it. Talking about getting astride dumb animals, how's Lady MacTee these days, by the way? Still doing professional rumpy-pumpy for the Parachute Brigade?" answered Pinky in defiance. "You, you, you baaastaaard!" shrieked the General and pressed the trigger. As Pinky and Mr McIlhenny prepared themselves, in the very short time available, to meet their Maker, a small red hole appeared on Sir Hector's forehead, followed by a loud bang to the rear. Looking round Pinky and the RSM saw a much bedraggled Peregrine Osbert Smythe-Gargle rise out of the wheel-less ruins of the demised General's Land Rover and holstering his pistol. He walked slowly over to the prone body, kicked it a couple of times nonchalantly, and said to no one in particular, "That wasn't too difficult, was it now, Perry me old fruit, what?"

"Jesus! Smythe-Gargle! Thank God you were there. You saved our lives," said a grateful Colonel Jolly. "Think nothing of it, Sir. You don't know how much I enjoyed it. Glad to be of service. Oh! By the way, Colonel, don't suppose you would do me a small favour, eh what?" said Perry. "Certainly. Whatever I can do," replied Pinky. "Well, it's like this, Sir. I'm leaving the old BJs, and the bloody Army, and I'm leaving as of this minute. Be terrible decent of you, if you would put the old resignation in for me. Don't want to leave any unnecessary loose ends. At least, not where I'm going." "You're leaving the Army, just when you are beginning to shape up into a fine officer?" questioned Pinky, years of loathing of the Smythe-Gargles of this world having disappeared in the foregoing two minutes. "What are you going to do in civvy street, Perry?" "Well, Sir, I've got a very good job lined up. Pays well, too!" answered Smythe-Gargle. "What sort of job?" asked Pinky. "Can't say, really, Sir. Top Secret. Security, that sort of thing. You know?" replied Perry. "Too bloody well, that's for sure. No Matter! Anything else we can do for you, Perry?" said Pinky. "Don't suppose anyone will miss one of these Land Rovers from Lisburn, will they?" answered the former ADC. "Don't suppose they will. Feel free to take what you want. And best of luck, me boy, whatever you get up to in your new job," called Pinky, as Smythe-Gargle gave the last salute of his military career, hopped into one of the Land Rovers, switched the ignition on, and accelerated off down the road in the direction of a right turn at Cromkill, the open road to Belfast, and a rather interesting project on which to sharpen his newly-acquired business acumen.

As Perry sped past Ross's Factory the first vehicles belonging to the reserve Company of the 3rd Battalion the Blue Jackets, under the command of the new Colonel Appleblossom, late of the Royal Army Chaplains Department, were emerging for their quick trip to Slaght, and the search for the three targets given to them by a very recently deceased former GOCNI. Their departure had been somewhat delayed due to the fact that Appleblossom wanted to pick the best looking young men in the Factory, and this had necessitated searching every nook and cranny in the place, for the prettier young things had no intention of receiving either a bed locker inspection or a dressing down from their new CO, if at all bloody possible! But when the last sphincter-twitching little sweetie had been routed out of his hidey-hole by the judicious use of the old threat, "Come out now you little fuckers, or it will be all the worse for you later!", the show had at last got on the road. Ten minutes later it left the brilliant sunshine over Cromkill and entered the storm zone under Slaght.

Colonel Father Appleblossom made straight for the Twelfth Field, considering that his first priority was the capture of Lady MacTavish and the infamous Sergeant Moriarty. Pinky Jolly would be easy to catch later on. Jolly was the bastard who had made his previous twelve months very miserable and very celibate, by putting two regimental police corporals, both well-known throughout the Blue Jackets as being semi-professional queer bashers in their spare time, on twenty-four hours a day physical guard duty on his every move outside the Officers Mess; and both thugs armed with pick helves, which they had used on several occasions, when he had only been fawning, or simpering, or just licking his lips at the very thought of a little innocent speleology. No wonder he had almost gone over the top on HMS Intrepid, when seasickness had reduced his 'minders' to a full-time occupancy of the Royal Navy's largest vomitorium. He'd enjoyed his Chinky meals, but tonight, after bagging, or maybe de-bagging, Moriarty, Lady MacTee, and the unsympathetic Jolly, he intended to have a whole row full of little plump and muscular Yorkshire puddings. There was just nothing like home cooking! He almost shivered in anticipation. Just think, he now had over five hundred of the four-cheeked darlings under his command, and, before the night was out, a few of the choicer morsels would be under his control.

As Appleblossom and his pretty boys drove through the gate into the field, and cruised to a slow halt beside the builder's lorry dais, the Reverend Mulholland was just getting into full swing once again, and was haranguing the crowd about loyalty to the Queen, and, in the same breath, about how the English had always done the poor Protestants of Ulster down. He had considered calling for the signing of a Covenant in blood, but there was plenty of extra gore still puddling around the Field, and signing a Covenant only really worked if the blood was your very own. Instead he concentrated on condemning the RUC and the British Army for not only failing to protect Protestantism in general, but also Slaght and its populace in particular, and was vowing a renewed declaration of UDI and the creation of a 'No-Go Zone" for the Security Forces in his beloved townland. You can see, therefore, that he was hardly in the mood to be civil to a poofter English colonel who was also a card-carrying priest of the Church of Rome.

Hidden in the back of the former SB fish and chip wagon were Colonel Mooney and Ignatius Moriarty. They had been having a most interesting conversation during the last half-hour. Mooney had questioned Moriarty in detail about his background, Mary nee the avenging angel McKelvey, Paddy McCallion and his boys, and, in particular, his intentions for the rest of the day, and, if he was to survive that, his ambitions for the future. The answers were fascinating, to say the least. The McKelvey woman was every bit as good, and every bit as bloody dangerous, as old Haggy had said. What she had managed to achieve in such a short time was quite remarkable, and if her loyal subordinate, Moriarty, was able to complete his own special task, Mooney's verbal orders from Queen Maggie the First would be carried out almost to the letter. Fantastic! All they needed now was a good diversion, so that both could unstick themselves from the congealed fat and batter on the floor of the chippy van, and get about their allotted tasks. But first the Rat had a few private words in Ignatius's ear, and then he wrote an address and telephone number on a page torn from his message pad, and slipped it into Moriarty's breast pocket.

"Now don't forget what I told you, Sergeant Moriarty, will you?" said the Colonel, as he peered carefully over the lip of the counter. "No, Colonel. I won't," was the reply. "Excellent! Now get ready. If what I think is going to happen, does happen, we will be out of here in the next couple of minutes. Keep your head down now, won't you? No sense in wasting all that talent by being careless on the vinegar stroke," advised the Rat. And then the sound of loud shouting could be heard outside, followed by growing swell of obviously violent public discontent. With a last friendly pat on the shoulder, Mooney sent Moriarty and his drum out the door and over the top. A few seconds later, urged on by a row of holes that had appeared suddenly in the side of the van, the Rat exited the door like a whippet after a hare.

When Appleblossom's Land Rover had rudely pushed its way through the seething crowd of humourless Orangemen, splattering the nearest with mud from their knees to their bowler hats, and thus endearing the British Army even more to the Ulster masses, Mulholland had just got to the part, where, at a momentary loss for words, he decided that a few rousing choruses of 'Fuck the Pope', and other important policy statements, were in order. As the last ring of bystanders broke to make way for the new Colonel Appleblossom, Big Bertie boomed out, "Fuck the Pope! Fuck the Whore of Rome! Fuck the RUC! Fuck the Toads of Whitehall! Fuck the Bloody Army!" In one leap, just as if he was entering the boxing ring again, to batter the living daylights out of some new pretender to his well-earned ABA belt, Appleblossom was on the back of the lorry, and had Mulholland by the throat. Now this was not a nice thing to do, because the neck brace was having a difficult enough job as it was, keeping the bastard's neck on his shoulders. "How dare you, Sir!" shouted the ex-heavyweight. "How dare you blaspheme, curse His Holiness, attack the Security Forces and the British Government, and you a man of religion?"

"And who the hell are you?" croaked Mulholland into the microphone, which was in imminent danger of entering his right nostril. "I, Sir, am

Colonel Appleblossom of the 3rd Battalion the Blue Jackets." "Well, Colonel fucking Appleblossom of the 3rd Battalion the Blue Jackets," cried a voice from the back of the crowd. "Why are you wearing captain's pips, and what are those little crosses on your lapels?" shouted Pinky Jolly, shouldering his way through the throng at the front of an all-too-familiar group of tough looking BJ regimental policemen, and accompanied by a glowering Mr. McIlhenny, who looked ready to bugger the Padre himself. At the mention of 'crosses', the crowd had sucked in its breath. "I was promoted in the field by Sir Hector MacTavish, General Officer Commanding HQNI, himself." At the mention of MacTavish, the Fenian who headed the military out of Lisburn, the crowd breathed out, with a low and menacing hiss. "MacTavish is in the field across the road, with a bullet in his head, orders from Maggie Thatcher!" the RSM shouted to Appleblossom. This news was greeted by a drawn out "Ooooooh!", as the Orangemen greeted the welcome news of MacTavish's demise, and in their own very townland of Slaght. And at the same time quite a number of those present decided that having a woman Prime Minister, even with one of her Da's prize plums in her mouth, was maybe not so bad after all. At this news Appleblossom paled visibly, and unconsciously released his one-handed stranglehold on the Reverend Mulholland's savaged larynx. "Promoted in the fucking field, were you, you Fenian git? Well, you're going to be buried in *this* fucking Field. Get the bastard lads!" screamed Big Bertie, his voice several octaves higher than its norm. "We'll have a real priest to burn tonight. Get the fucker!"

Seeing that the world was fast crumbling around him, and that the fires of Hell would be more than figuratively flickering round his nether regions in a very short while, Padre Appleblossom crossed himself, which really got the crowd going, and commenced giving himself the Last Rites. But maybe God has got a bit of a temporary soft spot for poofter padres after all, or maybe it was because Babd had forgotten to put Appleblossom on top of her long list, but death by burning was not on the cards for our ex-boxer. Fate intervened at just the wrong moment, in the form of Paddy McCallion and his boys, who had at last spotted the missing Moriarty, and his drum, exiting the Field and about to cross the road in the direction of the Orange Hall. It was time for the diversion to begin. Having positioned themselves once again on the high ground, near where the lynch mob's sycamore tree had once stood, while the massed drunks of the other sixty-eight lodges stood around the builder's lorry, McCallion's boys were well placed and raring to go. On the nod from Paddy, and just as the leading members of the crowd were reaching to grab Appleblossom from his penultimate resting place, the Brethren of 'Loyal Sons of Maryhill' opened fire.

Down by the lorry it was like being at, but not in, the butts at Bisley. Those, who had nothing else important to do on that day, died in large numbers. Those assigned to carry weapons and protect the Field briefly did the former, but totally failed in the latter duty. Those who were lucky, just because there were the unluckier ones between them and the incoming fire, fell back in a mass panic, and raced for the only available sanctuary, the Orange Hall on the hill across the road. Behind the lorry, in the safety provided by metal, rubber and a hundred dead and dying bodies, lay Big Bertie Mulholland, unfortunately under Padre Appleblossom, whose writhings were not of a sexual nature, but, nonetheless, were just beginning to provide the good Reverend with some rather unwholesome food for thought. Also safe in the scrimmage, but not in any of the positions of the Kama Sutra, were Pinky and the RSM, both of them taking aimed shots at the IRA men on top of the hill, and beginning to enjoy the falling plate competition.

Just then the GPMG from the VCP down the road succeeded in a most impressively rapid change of arc, and began putting down heavy fire on the line of boyos, who up until then had been thinking it was a walkover. Those who could see the reality of the situation and who possessed a good set of legs, upped and ran for it, disappearing over the top of the hill and into the waiting arcs of fire of the outer cordon of 3 BJ. It was all over in a matter of minutes. One man had seen the danger of legging it for the open countryside, and that was Paddy McCallion. He crawled to where a pile of Special Branch dead from earlier in the day had been heaped, wormed his way among them, shuddered to himself, and awaited the chance to slip away from his first and last battlefield. Fuck the IRA! He was out of it for good. If he survived the next twenty-four hours, he was for over the water, and some good consenting adults, maybe even a Scots Guardsman or two.

As the last echoes of gunfire died over the surrounding hills Ignatius rounded the rear of the Orange Hall and entered through the open back door. Quickly he put down his drum, loosened the goatskin on one side, took off his coat and the Semtex blocks strapped to his body, placed the latter inside the drum, affixed an electric detonator attached to a battery and a timing device made out of a Mickey Mouse watch, and retightened the skin. With a last loving stroke across the surface of the drum, Moriarty said his final farewell to Protestantism, slinked back out the door, and headed for the distant tree line in the direction of Ballymena. He was just over the brow of the first hill when the vanguard of the fleeing Orangemen reached the Orange Hall and entered exhaustedly. Shortly afterwards the Reverend Mulholland and the other dignitaries arrived, still annoyed at having lost their opportunity of burning a real live priest, Pinky and the RSM having taken Appleblossom into military custody at very persuasive gunpoint.

While the others broke out the 'Defenders of the One True Faith' lodge's secret stock of whiskey, and commenced to calm their unravelled nerves, Mulholland went to the centre of the Hall and clambered laboriously up to the cab door of the cement lorry, whose drum was still relentlessly turning. He pulled out the dead driver, switched off the lorry's engine, and reached across to drag out the body of the passenger. "Dead Boy Scouts attacking his beloved Orange Hall. What could possibly happen next?" he thought, and got the fright of his life when the passenger opened a blackened eye, and a weak voice said, "Bertie Mulholland, is it really you. Thank the Lord. I'm not in hell after all." "Jesus! Is that you McCartney? What the fuck are you doing knocking down my bloody Hall, and you one of us?" And five minutes and half a bottle of whiskey later, the poor Reverend McCartney, now sole member, Protestant or Catholic, with the exception of his *alter ego*, Paddy McCallion, that is, of 'Loyal Sons of Maryhill L.O.L. 666', had told his painful tale of woe to Mulholland and the others. Just then the engine of the cement lorry burst into life again.

Having said 'God speed' to Moriarty, Colonel Mooney had spent some time wondering how to extricate Delta 1 from their former roof-space OP position. He had been in two minds about leaving the bastards there, particularly because he just hated flying into sycamore trees upside down in Alouettes, and *especially* if it was the accurate fire of his own men, that had caused his most recent experience of powerless flight. But he had at last relented, mainly because things had gone rather better, strangely, than he could have expected, and partly because even he did not relish the thought of leaving his own men, attempted murderers though they might be, to the mercy either of Mulholland's vengeance or the efficiency of Moriarty's explosive device.

Having alerted Delta 1 to his plan, and, to their considerable shock and even more considerable concern, his continued existence as a living entity with no fucking sense of humour, the Rat had summoned two of his mobile patrols to the area to provide support, and had clambered over the mound of quick-setting concrete, through a gap in the wall near the top of the drum, and had settled himself behind the wheel. Unable to reverse because of the concrete tank trap at the rear of the lorry, he did the only other thing possible. Switching on the ignition, he drove slowly forward through the assembled Orangemen, swerved carefully round a Lambeg Drum sitting innocently on the floor, and exited through the back wall. While those who had not fallen under the wheels of the juggernaut were looking at the rear of the lorry fast disappearing across the fields, the bedraggled members of Delta 1 dropped to the floor. "Aw, fuck it! This is to good to miss!" said Lofty, and he and his three comrades put a magazine apiece of MP5 ammunition into the backs of the assembled Orangemen, and then hobbled as fast as their stiff legs could carry them, and jumped into the Land Rovers waiting on the main road by the gate to the Hall.

Inspector Simpson was having increasing difficulty in retaining a firm grip on the last vestiges of his sanity. To make matters worse, cowering in the rain behind his big-bosomed escorts, and in his shirt sleeves, because it had been uncomfortably hot deep-frying all those fish suppers in the chippy van, he was not just shivering with cold, and a terrible ache had begun at the bottom, front and back, of his lungs. "Bloody double pneumonia!" he accurately self-diagnosed. When the IRA had opened up, the large ladies had fled the scene at quite remarkable speed, and Simpson had lurched after them through the rain. "God, I'm cold! It can't get much worse than this, can it?" he asked himself. But it certainly could, because at that point, just as he was climbing over a gate, the top bar gave way, and he bounced on his goolies rather sharpish on the next bar down, leaving his unmentionables not only swollen, but covered with deeply embedded splinters. "Oh shit!" he moaned, over and over again, and when he next felt well enough to attempt to proceed, he crawled off downhill in the direction of the McKelvey Farm. He was weaving in and out of consciousness when he came to the nearest shelter, the derelict building that housed Delta 2, who were following the events at the Field on their radios, and feeling a bit pissed off at being left out of the action.

Inspector Simpson fell through the doorway, inched across to an inviting pile of hay, and lay there in agony, breathing laboriously for the next ten minutes. When his head had stopped swimming in circles round the bare room, he gathered his remaining strength, struggled to a kneeling position, pulled down his trousers and underpants, and peered between his legs at his poor balls, and their recently acquired crown of thorns. He was just about to pick the first splinter delicately out, when he saw an upside down face appear in the open doorway. It was not a friendly face, even if it had been the right way up. Indeed, it was the most frightening thing that he had ever seen in his life. And to make matters worse, the bulky body that was on top of the face had developed two enormous fists, which were now fumbling frantically with its fly-buttons. "Aw, shit!" groaned Inspector Simpson again, and he was absolutely right!

When Mooney and the cement lorry had exited the rear of the Orange Hall and taken off across the fields into the gloom, and the resultant release of Lofty and the boys self-imposed and uncomfortably rotating captivity had occasioned another brief and one-sided fire-fight, Pinky Jolly and the RSM were just about to send Captain Appleblossom off to the guardroom at the Rangers Depot in Ballymena. But, understandably, they had been distracted by the new events taking place across the road from where they were standing by their parked Land Rover. Appleblossom seized the moment, and gave Corporal Whittaker, the CO's driver, an almighty haymaker on the chin, turfed him unceremoniously out of his seat and into the mud, and revved off in the direction of Ahoghill. As he went round the first bend, the Padre saw the second major 3 BJ VCP in the distance, and decided, unwisely, as events will shortly show, not to try and outrun radio communications.

So he leapt from the speeding vehicle into the ditch, and thereafter made his way into a nearby farmyard. It was then that he espied the crawling Simpson on his less than triumphant entrance to the derelict building. He would have ignored the Inspector altogether, if he hadn't taken a quick look through the unglazed window, to make sure that the recent arrival posed no threat to his further attempt at escape. It was then that he saw that most beautiful of sights, the male bottom, and just in the right position, too. "Well," he thought to himself, "Buggers can't be choosers. I'm sure that I can spare a few minutes, if this poor fellow can." Now, we wont go into the more lurid details of what then occurred, other than to say that the screaming from Inspector Simpson would have put old Morrigan right out of a job. No! There may be innocent heterosexuals reading this, and I wouldn't want to be responsible for setting another load of benders and thrusters off on a career in the Home Civil Service or Conservative politics. Not me!

Suffice it to say that Appleblossom was reaming the skin off the inside of Simpson's rectum for the third time in close succession, and the screaming had now lowered to a gagging whisper, when a little voice said behind the Padre's bare bottom, "Two's up?" Now, a lesser buggerer than Appleblossom would have immediately shot his load and subsequently shot off into the dark bloody quickly, at such an unexpectedly phrased interruption to his satyrical pursuits. But not our Padre. He just replied, "Feel free, old boy. By the way, I'm Father Appleblossom, Chaplain to the 3rd Blow Jobs. Who are you?" "Name's McCallion, Father, and bless me, for I am about to sin!" And without further ado, Paddy McCallion, OC mid-Antrim Battalion of the Provisional IRA, slotted neatly into third place on the starting line, and the race was on. Simpson, who was still in pole position, passed out at this stage, but that did not effect his active participation.

All was going remarkably smoothly, and Appleblossom was beginning to revise his plans, and was considering settling in for the night, when Sticky and the boys in the loft above, who had heard and seen all, could contain their disgust no longer. With a fury that was increased by their failure to kill anything, other than a few rats, since their arrival in this benighted place, they stealthily descended from their hiding place, and added their commando daggers to the two mutton ones which were well into the sixth verse of 'Do the hokey-cokey'. It was over in a matter of seconds. There was not much that could be done for the unfortunate Simpson, however, other than extract the Padre's dick from his rectum, before *rigor mortis* set in. When this had been accomplished, first by neatly slicing the offending member off at the root, and then by deftly skewering it out on the tip of a knife blade, Simpson curled up in a whimpering ball, and gazed ravingly at horrible pink shish-kebab and the bodies of his recent despoilers. He was away with the birds, and eventually the SAS lads gave up trying to do anything for him, and trussed him up with para-cord, to prevent him from doing damage to himself - not that it was likely, in his condition. Just then another explosion boomed over the nearby hill, and a further interesting collection of airborne detritus descended on the farmyard.

The Orange Hall was the scene of chaos for several minutes after Delta 1 had taken unpleasant vengeance on the back rows of the Brethren trying to wave farewell to the Rat and his cement lorry. It was a charnel house to say the least. People were shouting and screaming, some in pain, others in anger, most in fear. Bertie Mulholland, noble until the end, shouted at the assembly to "Fucking calm down, you bunch of yellow-bellied eejits, and get the weapons out. We're back in business again." But the more he shouted at them, and the more he raved about 'guns, and shooting, and taking on the fucking British Army, as well as the rest of the human race', the more panicked they all became. Finally, in complete desperation, Mulholland grabbed the Lambeg Drum, and climbed on to the table. "Fucking shut up, ye eejits!" he shouted one last time, and his right arm swung down and struck the drum. 'Blam!' it went, and successfully caught the attention of those reeling in crazed circles closest to him. 'Blam!' he went again, and a further group calmed to the familiar tone of the drum, the battle call of Protestant Ulster. And, to ensure that even the outer circles of terrorised Brethren had at last got the message, Big Bertie swung his fist at the drum, one more time. As live human and dead goatskin came into contact on the third blow, a '**BLAM!**', the like of which no earthly Lambeg Drum had ever made, echoed across mid-Antrim, as the Reverend Mulholland, his visitor from Glasgow, the Reverend McCartney, and the remaining Orangemen of Slaght (and quite a few from neighbouring lodges, too, thank the Lord!), at last answered the call of the Banshee, and flew

Heavenward in search of Saint Peter, only to find out that the big church in Rome really had been called after him, and that there was no way that a Fenian Doorkeeper was going to let this particular fine mist of body parts in through the Gate to mess up Paradise. No! There was a sign on the Door saying, 'No vacancies. Apply below.' And so, instead of harps, it looks as if it is panpipes the boys from Slaght will be playing from now on.

From her vantage point on the far hill, under a spreading chestnut tree and a good golf umbrella, Mary McKelvey smiled happily, sighed with satisfaction, that 'all's well that ends well', turned on her heel, and descended the gory slope to pick up her car and head for the airport. As she was passing the door of the old cottage, four men in balaclavas jumped out on her and pinioned her to the wall. "It's her, the one that was dressed up as a WRAC captain, that bitch McKelvey, the bloody terrorist," hissed Sticky. And all four SAS men drew back and trained their weapons on the buxom figure standing against the wet basalt slabs. Just as they were about to put the 'bitch' out of everyone's misery, a cement lorry careened into the farmyard, and before it had stopped itself six feet into the gable end of the house, Colonel Mooney jumped down, raced across, and said, "Don't, for Christ's sake, shoot her lads! She's one of ours."

"Mary McKelvey, you are a star! You've done everything you set out to do, and you can now go on your way to the airport, and get out of this hellhole of Ireland. Get yourself a new life, love, somewhere in the sun. And keep out of this sort of business, otherwise we might have to come looking for you one day. Now, have you got everything you need?" asked Mooney. "Yes, Colonel. Thank you! I'll be on my way." And our Mary opened the door of the barn, got into her car, and was just about to drive off, when she stopped and wound the window down. "Colonel?" she called. "How did the others fare?" "Don't you worry, my dear. They all did well, and their deaths were gloriously effective." "I'm sorry about Moriarty," she said, hesitatingly, "He was so brilliantly innocent." "Yes. But I'm sure he'll be happy in the place where he has gone," said the Rat, in a curiously semi-religious undertone. With that, Mary rolled up the window, took one last look around her, and drove

out on to the main road, and joined the long queue of emergency
vehicles, transporting the dead to the overworked coroner in Ballymena.

Late that night, in a dirty back street just off the Ardoyne, a car,
with its headlights off, drew to the entrance of an alleyway. A figure
emerged from the gloom and quickly got into the car. "Good evening,
Perry," said the Ferret. "It went even better than expected, didn't it?" "It
certainly did that, Phelim. Now, to business. I agree to the terms. What
is the first thing that you want me to do?" answered a new civilianised
Smythe-Gargle, or should I rather say, plain 'Mr. Smith.' "Well, I think
it is about time there was a wee leadership change around here. What do
you think? Or is it too early for you to start work?" answered the Ferret.
"No problem, old boy. Nothing like getting right down to it from Day
One, eh what?" said Perry. "Excellent! Now, here's what you need to do,
and then I'll give you the wherewithal to do it?" and Phelim whispered
softly in Perry's ear.

At four o'clock in the morning a stealthy figure climbed in the back
window of a safe-house in Leeson Street on the Falls, garrotted the
sleeping guards, and crept upstairs to the front bedroom. A man lay
snoring and farting alcoholically in the dark. The stealthy figure nudged
the man into wakefulness. "What the fuck's the matter now?" said a
disgruntled voice. "Mr. O'Shaugnessy. It's your early morning wake-up
call," said the figure through the gloom. "Oh! Jesus, Mary and Joseph!
You're the fucking SAS, aren't you?" moaned Liam. "Not quite old
boy! Bit closer to home than that. Couple of minutes from now and
I'm the new IO of the Belfast Brigade." "Yer head's cut, ye eejit! Phelim
O'Malley's the fucking IO of the Belfast Brigade," replied a confused
O'Shaughnessy. "Well, not for much longer, old boy. In a couple of
minutes Phelim is going to be the OC.," said the voice, in a rather
smirking tone. "But I'm the fucking OC, you blethering eejit!" shouted
Liam. "Sorry, old boy. You're just a teensy-weensy little bit out of touch,
eh what?" And Perry then shot Liam O'Shaughnessy, right between
the eyes, three times with a silenced Browning. A few seconds later, the
stealthy Mr. Smith was out in the street again, and well on his way to
a new and very lucrative career.

CHAPTER SEVENTEEN

he year 1995 saw an end, at least temporarily, to this particular period of the long-standing, and, in the future no doubt, on-going Troubles in poor old Ulster. But mid-Antrim, apart from the little flare-up that we have been avidly following, has been remarkably calm during the past fifteen years. Of course, Maggie's plans to remove the top boys on both sides only worked, like everything else to do with Ireland, 'after a fashion'. It could have been better, but, then, it could have been much, much worse. Ballymena continued to prosper and to look with disdain on its tiny neighbour, Slaght. In Slaght, however, much had changed. The Presbyterian Church, Free, Reformed, or otherwise unaligned, suffered a tremendous recession in popularity, and only the odd eejit with an IQ of below fifty still keeps to the 'one true Faith'. Now Slaght boasts a Hindu Ashram, on the hill where the Orange Hall once proudly stood; a Buddhist wat, right at the very spot where Delta 1 almost met with a fiery end; and Big Bertie's old parish church, still minus a weather vane and a lightning conductor, is the venue for dances and the other less innocent pastoral frolics of modern rural youth. Apart from the odd incursion by the Holy Rollers and similar religious freak shows, God, in Slaght, is no longer malignant. Indeed, he is most successfully and endearingly benign.

And what about those who survived that brief but traumatic period. Well, poor Sergeant Simpson is still in the care of the State, although he is as happy, I suppose, as any raving loony with a horror of pork sausages and a fearsome constipation can be. Sticky is now retired from

the Army and is running a survival school for rich businessmen in the
Black Mountains, and reportedly 'creaming it in'. Lofty was last heard
of in Afghanistan in the mid-eighties. It is not known whether he is still
alive, but it is thought unlikely, as his last Satcom transmission, picked
up by a National Reconnaissance Office American satellite, was garbled,
but seemed to be referring to the imminent arrival of an entire Soviet
Airborne Division right over the village from which he was directing
training for the mujahideen.

Mr. McIlhenny, after a successful conclusion to his Army career, is
now Manager of the vast estate owned by the Smythe-Gargles in the
North of England, a change in the latter family's fortunes having taken
place during the commodities boom of the mid-eighties. For a while,
Paddy McGonigle, late of a potting shed at HQNI in Lisburn, was the
Chief Grounds man at Castle Arras, the Smythe-Gargle family seat
in Yorkshire, but he is now very comfortably retired and living with a
succession of nubile young oriental girls in a simple, flower-bedecked
cottage on the grounds of the estate. Mary nee O'Flaherty has never
been heard of or seen since, but rumours about her surface from time
to time in intelligence circles. She must be being a good girl, however,
for there has been no need for the SAS or anyone else to track her down.

"And," I can hear you asking, "what about Mooney, Moriarty, Pinky,
Perry, and the others who came out of it alive? Where are they, and fare
they well?" That's an interesting question. But first, before I tell you,
you must promise to keep what I am about to reveal completely and
utterly secret. Don't you even think of breathing a word of it, otherwise
you, too, may be getting a nocturnal visit from a stealthy figure!

It is a balmy summer's afternoon on the Mediterranean coast of France,
not half an hour from Nice. Four figures are walking slowly towards
the ninth hole of a splendid links course, followed by a golf cart, being
driven by a wizened but smiling old man, probably a millionaire, by
the look of him. They are a rum lot to find together in such relaxed
and open circumstances. The old man in the golf cart, admiring the
flower beds dotted over the greens, and caring little for the intricacies
of the silly game being played by the others, is none other than Paddy
McGonigle, taking a brief break from shagging himself into senility in

Yorkshire. One set of partners in this interesting golf match is composed of General Sir Pinkerton Jolly, recently retired as Chief of the Defence Staff, and the former RSM McIlhenny, shortly also about to retire from his second career as custodian of the Smythe-Gargle family fortunes. The other twosome is made up of Percy Smith, for many years Europe's most wanted terrorist, former Chief of the Provisional Army Council, but now a 'respectable' leading Sinn Fein politician, and the man who brought about the breakthrough in the peace talks between the Provisional IRA and the British Government - and made himself and his close associates one hundred million secret US dollars, for his pains in so doing. His partner is the most sinister figure of the modern TOP SECRET world, none other than the infamous Brigadier Mooney, the very mention of whose name strikes fear into the hearts of Prime Ministers throughout the Commonwealth, and, indeed, is known to cause the odd trembling in less civilised places, like Paris and Brussels. He is currently the Security Advisor to the Prime Minister, and is rumoured to be quite efficient in areas where the Republican Party Watergate burglars were sadly lacking, both in undeniability and finesse.

All five men have been close friends and business associates since the early eighties. There is a sixth, even more TOP SECRET member of the team, the 'slithy tove', Haggard, but he is indisposed this day, being a sufferer from chronic gout, and is back in the Jacuzzi in the Presidential Suite at the Hotel Miramar in Nice. Yes, they are a strange collection of people. All either openly, or secretly, multi-millionaires. All equally responsible for the prolongation of terrorism in Ireland and the British mainland for the past fifteen years, and just as responsible for its recent ending, and much back-slapping in the corridors of power in Washington, Dublin and London. And all, likewise, very much involved in the removal of successive heads of terror in Belfast and the Irish Republic over the years, especially the evil Phelim O'Malley, ostensibly killed by the Official IRA on a dark night and in a safe house off Leeson Street on the Falls, in the late Autumn of 1983. The method of assassination used by the Officials was, according to the coroner's report, the garrotte!

Our four golfers and their sedentary but mobile companion have arrived at the ninth hole, standing right on the edge of the dunes stretching down to the shore. They pause, while McGonigle reaches one of them, Brigadier (Retd.) Mooney, a pair of high-powered binoculars. He looks out to sea. There in the bay, two beautiful yachts have just dropped anchor, and a small motorboat is ferrying a passenger from one of the yachts to the other. It is an idyllic scene.

On board the MV 'Fair Play', one of Ireland's two wealthiest men, Bob McCambridge, retired servant of the Crown, steps forward with two glasses of champagne to greet his guest, the other richest man in Ireland, by the name of McCleary, and a former very senior official of the Dublin Government, and who is the owner of the other yacht, the MV 'Fair Dos'. They seat themselves on comfortable sun lounges and exchange the usual relaxed comments of the *nouveaux riches*, such as, "This is the fucking life, McCambridge!" and "You couldn't beat it with a big stick, McCleary, could you?" Both these men have made their vast fortunes from the terror business, not by being in it, by any means, but by surreptitiously and most cleverly running it for their own profit from the outside. These are the true *eminences grises* of the reign of fear that has shaken Western Europe for so long. They and their pan-European colleagues, all of whom are unfortunately not on board the 'Fair Play' on this balmy afternoon.

As McCambridge is leaning over to refresh McCleary's glass from the Bollinger chilling in the ice bucket, a rubber-suited figure rises over the side-rail of the yacht, and steps on to the spotless deck, darkening the golden teakwood with seawater droplets. The figure removes its diving mask with one hand, the other being occupied in holding a silenced MP5. "Good afternoon, gentlemen. So glad you could come," said a voice with more than a trace of a Ballymena accent. "Who the fuck are you?" whispered McCambridge, as his suntan paled to a jaundiced yellow. "To paraphrase Dirty Harry, 'I'm your worst fucking nightmare', a Paddy with a gun; and a timetable to keep, unfortunately, otherwise we could all do this much more satisfactorily and, oooh so much more painfully!" said the figure in the wet suit. "Who the devil are you, you bastard?" hissed McCleary between his clenched teeth, and began to rise out of his chair, whereupon a burst of fire ripped his chest open. "Nobody you would know," said the figure to the dying face. "But *you* know who I am, don't you, Mr. McCambridge?" The latter shook his head until it looked as if it would auto-rotate right off his neck. "No. I've never seen you in my life. Who are you?" asked the terrified former SB chief. "I'm your old friend Simpson's wet dream, or at least I was until he found out that Ulster being buggered by the Catholic Church was meant to be taken literally and not figuratively," answered the figure calmly. "Oh my God! It's *you*, isn't it? Moriarty! Fucking Moriarty!" wept McCambridge, as he sank to his trembling knees on the deck. "Well! Now that we've been properly introduced, Bye Bye!" laughed Ignatius, and pulled the trigger one last time.

Major Moriarty, just about to retire from 22 SAS, hero of the Falklands, hero of the Gulf War, and unsung hero of countless clandestine operations over the previous fourteen years, walked over the two bodies to the railing nearest the shore, and waved towards the distant group of golfers at the ninth hole, before diving overboard into the sea.

Ten minutes later two explosions were heard, as the 'Fair Play' and the 'Fair Dos' went down to look for the submarine from which our hero had earlier emerged. He's come a long way from Kellswater, where we first met him, has our Moriarty. And I'm sure he still has a long way to go.

GLOSSARY

A.

ABA   -   Amateur Boxing Association

Adams   -   Gerry Adams, former Head of the Provisonal Army Council, Leader of Provisional Sin Fein, and currently Chief Minister Of the Northern Ireland Government

ADC   -   Aide de Camp, a young officer who is personal assistant to a General

Apprentice Boys   -   A Protestant fraternal society for young men

Ardoyne   -   A Republican stronghold in Northwest Belfast

ASLEF   -   UK train drivers and operators labour union

ASU   -   Active Service Unit of PIRA

AVGAS   -   Aviation fuel

AWOL   -   Absent without authorized leave, ie., a deserter

B.

Bake   -   Mid-Ulster dialect for "head"

Ballymurphy   -   Republican stronghold in West Belfast

Beat the clock   -   SAS expression meaning "to survive". Dead SAS personnel have their names inscribed on the Clocktower in their Headquarters

Black Bush	-	Old Bushmills Black whiskey
Blootered	-	completely drunk
Blue jobs	-	Royal Navy personnel
Boke	-	Vomit
Boortry	-	Blackthorn, sloe bush or tree
Boroo	-	Unemployment bureau
Boss	-	How SAS soldiers address an SAS officer
B Specials	-	Part-time RUC

C.

C4	-	Military plastic explosive
Caltrops	-	Sharp spikes on a chain or strip of material, designed to be thrown in front of a vehicle to blow its tyres
Crack	-	The Irish word "craic", meaning conversation, usually of a jovial nature
Cratur	-	Mid-Ulster dialect for "creature", meaning "whiskey"
CSM	-	Company Sergeant Major

D.

| DMS boots | - | Directly moulded sole boots, British Army issue |
| Dulse | - | A type of dried edible seaweed, popular in Ulster |

E.

| Eejit | - | "idiot" in Scots-Irish slang |
| Effing CO | - | FCO, Foreign and Commonwealth Office |

F.

Falls Road	-	Most prominent Republican stronghold in West-Central Belfast
Fenian	-	Any Catholic or Republican, to a Pretestant
FFR	-	Fitted for radio
Finnerty	-	A prominent Republican gang of Down and Armagh
Free State	-	Eire, the Republic of Ireland

G.

Git	-	A despicable person
GPMG	-	General Purpose Machine Gun
Gub	-	"mouth" in Scots-Irish slang
Gyp	-	"hurt" or "hurting" in mid-Ulster slang

H.

H-Block	-	Republican wing of the Maze (Long Kesh) prison
Hide	-	An underground dug-out OP of the SAS
Hopkirk	-	Paddy Hopkirk, famous Ulster rally driver

I.

INLA	-	Irish National Liberation Army
IRA	-	Irish Republican Army

J.

Jobbies	-	Faeces, turds

K.

Karla	-	KGB mater spy in Le Carre's trilogy *"Tinker, Tailor, Soldier, Spy"*
Knox	-	John Knox, Scottish Covenanter

L.

L.O.L.	-	Loyal Orange Lodge

M.

MI room	-	Army Medical Corps surgery
MO	-	Medical Officer
Monkeys	-	Army slang for the Royal Military Police
MP5	-	Heckler & Koch sub-machine gun
MTO	-	Motor Transport Officer

N.

NAAFI	-	Navy, Army, Air Force Institute, military café/shop
NIO	-	Northern Ireland Office
NORAID	-	Northern Aid, a US non-profit raising money for Catholics adversely affected by the Troubles (but Also for PIRA)

O.

OC	-	Officer Commanding
OG	-	Olive green

OIRA	-	Official Irish Republican Army
OP	-	Observation post
ORs	-	Other ranks
Oul', ould	-	Scots-Irish for "old"

P.

PAC	-	Provisional Army Council
Paisley	-	Rev. Ian Paisley, leading Loyalist demagogue
PARA	-	Parachute Regiment
Paras	-	Parachute-trained soldiers
P Company	-	Severe selection unit for parachute soldiers
PIRA	-	Provisional Irish Republican Army
Poteen	-	Illegally distilled whiskey
Prod	-	Catholic slang for Protestant (also Proddy)
Prot	-	Army slang for Protestant

Q.

| QRF | - | Military Quick Reaction Force |

R.

RCT	-	Royal Corps of Transport
Republican Club	-	Illegal, unlicensed pub in Catholic Belfast
RMAS	-	Royal Military Academy Sandhurst
RMP	-	Royal Military Police
RTU	-	returned to unit, kicked out of the SAS
RUC	-	Royal Ulster Constabulary
Rupert	-	Other ranks slang for an "officer"

S.

SAS	-	Special Air Service
Sash	-	Orange sash worn over the shoulder by Orangemen
Scout	-	A type of British Army helicopter
SDLP	-	Social Democratic Labour Party
SF	-	Special Forces
SF role	-	A machine gun in the "sustained fire" role
Sheugh	-	A muddy area
Shite	-	Scots-Irish for "shit"
SIB	-	Special Investigations Branch of the RMP
SLR	-	7.62 mm FN Self-loading Rifle
SMG	-	Sub-machine gun
SOP	-	Standard Operating Procedure
Spacer	-	Another word for "eejit"
Snug	-	A private room off the main pub bar
Stickies	-	Members of the OIRA
Still	-	Where poteen is distilled
Stormont	-	Site of Northern Ireland government offices

T.

TA	-	Territorial Army
Taig	-	Protestant slang for a "Catholic"
Tout	-	An informer
Troubles	-	The Ulster problem of the sixties to nineties

U.

UDA	-	Ulster Defence Association, a Protestant para-military organization
UDI	-	Unilateral declaration of independence

UDR	-	Ulster Defence Regiment, local part-timers
Ulu	-	Military jargon for remote jungle or terrain
UVF	-	Ulster Volunteer Force, an extreme Protestant para-military organization

V.

| VCP | - | Vehicle Check Point |

W.

| Wellie | - | A kick, or "to kick" |

Y.

| Yellow man | - | A sticky, yellow Ulster candy/sweet |

Lightning Source UK Ltd.
Milton Keynes UK
UKOW02f0340071016

284654UK00002B/72/P